SHATTERED

JOAN JOHNSTON

New York Times *bestselling author of*

OUTCAST

the Bitter Creek novels, which include

THE COWBOY
THE TEXAN
THE LONER
THE PRICE
THE RIVALS
THE NEXT MRS. BLACKTHORNE
A STRANGER'S GAME

and the Hawk's Way series

Please visit her Web site at
www.JoanJohnston.com
*for a complete listing
of her titles and series.*

JOAN JOHNSTON

SHATTERED

A BITTER CREEK NOVEL

MIRA®

ISBN-13: 978-1-61523-971-9

SHATTERED

Printed in U.S.A.

Great editors are a precious gift.
This book is dedicated to my editor,
Linda McFall.

Prologue

"What else have you lied about?"

Kate Grayhawk Pendleton wished she could simply walk away from the imposing older woman dressed in a black St. John knit suit and Chanel tuxedo heels standing across from her. Unfortunately, she was still bedridden after waking a week before from a four-month-long coma.

She readjusted the pillows behind her on the hospital bed, then tugged awkwardly at her cotton hospital gown. She needed time to decide how she was going to answer the angry question posed by her mother-in-law, Texas governor and presidential hopeful Ann Wade Pendleton.

"I don't know what you're talking about," Kate said warily.

"I'm asking who you bedded down with after **you** married my son. I'm asking who got you pregnant, because it sure as hell wasn't J.D."

"What makes you say such a thing?" Kate replied. "Lucky and Chance—"

"Are somebody else's brats. Don't bother lying. While you were in that coma, Lucky injured himself on a broken window and needed a transfusion. The twins' blood type proves they aren't my son's children."

Kate blanched. She'd kept her secret for nine long years. She hadn't told a single soul that her eight-year-old twin sons, Lucky and Chance, had been conceived with a man who was not her husband.

"If I'm going to get myself chosen by the party as the next Republican presidential nominee, I need to know what bats might come flying out of the belfry," Ann Wade said, her voice as sharp and cold as ice. "I can't afford to have some cretin come forward in the middle of my campaign and name himself as the father of my grandsons."

Kate realized that Ann Wade wasn't upset that she'd cheated on her husband. Wasn't even upset that her grandsons possessed none of her blood. What had made Ann Wade so furious was the fear that Kate's misstep might interfere with her political career.

Kate felt sick to her stomach.

She'd allied herself with the Pendleton family as a nineteen-year-old, still wincing from the stunning rejection she'd received from the man she really loved, Texas Ranger Jack McKinley. When Jack had married his high school sweetheart, J.D.'s admiration had been a balm for her wounded soul.

She'd looked at J.D. Pendleton with stars in her eyes. What she'd seen was a University of Texas football hero with wavy blond hair and striking blue eyes.

She hadn't known J.D. was a man without honor, a spoiled child of privilege, who would cheat on her within a month of their wedding. Hadn't known she was marrying a man who would fake his own death, desert his military post and flee to South America after blackmailing his own mother.

Kate pictured the twins' biological father in her mind's eye, a tall, rangy man with silver-streaked black hair and steel-gray eyes. Remembered exactly how and why she'd gone to bed with him.

She felt her face flush anew with the hurt and humiliation she'd felt on that long-ago night when she'd caught her husband in their hotel room with another woman *in flagrante delicto* and he'd told her, "Get the fuck out! Can't you see I'm busy?"

In a daze, her chest aching, she'd taken the elevator downstairs to the bar at the Austin, Texas, Four Seasons. She'd walked up to a perfect stranger, taken his large hand in hers and said, "Come with me." She'd led him to the registration desk and said, "We need a room."

He'd supplied his black American Express card and took the key card the pretty desk clerk handed him. As they'd walked away he'd asked, "Are you sure you want to do this?"

"I've never been more sure of anything in my life."

He'd been gentle and tender, more so than J.D. ever had. She'd been embittered and impassioned. The sex had been excoriating. She'd cried for half an hour in his arms afterward as he smoothed her long black hair behind her ears and kissed her forehead.

She'd had to live the past nine years with the consequences of her rash act of defiance. She'd never told her lover that he'd become a father that night. It wasn't until she'd seen him on Channel 12 News that she'd realized who he was. And the horror that might haunt them all if the truth were ever known.

Kate felt her insides go cold. What if Ann Wade hired a private detective? The stranger had used a credit card to pay for the hotel room they'd used. Could it still be traced after all these years? The twins' father might be exposed. The scandal would be enormous and devastating to her children, to her mother-in-law and to Jack McKinley, the man she had never stopped loving.

Finding the stranger she'd slept with wouldn't be easy. Predicting his response to the knowledge he had two sons was even more difficult. And terrifying. Kate took the safe course, the only course she knew would keep her sons safe from harm. She looked her mother-in-law right in the eye and lied.

"I have no idea who the twins' father is. He was someone I met in a bar. I can't even remember what he looked like. You'd be wasting your time looking, because I doubt he can be found."

Ann Wade arched a perfect brow. "I guess we'll see about that."

1

"Why are you here?"

Private Investigator Harry Dickenson felt a shiver roll down his spine at the sound of Wyatt Shaw's quiet, raspy voice. Shaw stared at him from ruthless gray eyes, his lean, powerful body coiled behind a stone-and-glass desk, like a silent predator stalking unsuspecting prey.

Harry wondered if the rumors he'd heard were true. Was he alone with a brutal killer? Someone who'd, literally, gotten away with murder?

Harry's blood felt like ice in his veins, despite the heat of the April sun streaming through a wall of windows. He was standing on the top floor of the newest, and by far grandest, Shaw Tower, a combination hotel, condominium and office building in downtown Houston, Texas. From his vertigo-inducing perch, Harry could see the far-reaching geographic boundaries of the city, nearly forty miles away.

It was hard to believe how much of that real estate was controlled by the indecently wealthy man sitting before him. Was it so wrong to want a little piece of that pie for himself? This was Harry's first venture into extortion, and he was a little nervous. But he was certain Shaw would pay—and pay well—to learn the tantalizing secret he'd come here to sell.

Harry tried to meet Shaw's piercing gaze as he made his demand for cash, but he couldn't quite raise his eyes that last six inches. He focused instead on the crisp collar of Shaw's white shirt, the smooth knot of his patterned blue silk tie and the lapels of his dark blue blended wool suit, as he said, "I have information of vital interest to you."

"I'm listening," Shaw said.

Harry saw a flicker of movement over his shoulder and realized they were no longer alone in Shaw's office on the Tower's 80th floor. He started as a man two or three inches taller than Wyatt's reputed 6'4", and maybe fifty pounds heavier, stepped into his line of sight.

"You wanted me, Boss?" the man said, speaking to Shaw as though Harry wasn't there.

Harry wondered how the gargantuan man in a cheap brown suit—who reminded him of the enforcers he'd seen in Mafia movies—had been summoned and realized Shaw must have hit some button on his desk. He thought back to the female secretary in the outer office. The older, benign-looking lady in a skirt that fell two inches below her knees and sensible pumps had made him feel perfectly safe coming into what he could now see was a cage of steel and glass from which there was no escape.

Harry licked at the sweat above his lip, recognized it for the anxious gesture it was and stiffened his spine. He was the best at what he did precisely because he didn't allow himself to be intimidated.

Nevertheless, he felt his bowels shift in an instinctive animal response to mortal danger.

"I'll be with you in a minute," Shaw said to the big

man he'd summoned. Then he fixed his steely gaze on Harry. "You were saying?"

Harry watched as the big man guarding the door, who had an ugly scar on his cheek and a crooked, many-times-broken nose, took a pose that reminded him of a military man "at ease," his meaty hands behind his back, his tree-trunk legs spread wide. The enforcer's dark eyes, under heavy black brows, stayed focused on Harry as though he were some lower form of life, a bug this big man would like to squash.

Harry mentally shook his head. He was anticipating trouble where there might be none. Shaw had done nothing overtly threatening. It was the information Harry had dug up on the man sitting across from him that was scaring him shitless.

Harry fought the urge to turn tail and run. He chided himself again for letting his imagination run wild. Surely Shaw would be grateful to hear what Harry had discovered, even if he was also shocked by the revelation.

"I want your agreement to pay before I tell you what I know."

Harry waited for Shaw to ask what it was or how much he wanted or refuse to pay or say *something* that would give him an idea where to go from there. He'd never suspected, when Governor Pendleton had hired him to hunt down the biological father of her daughter-in-law's twin sons, that his search would lead him to this enigmatic man.

He'd brought a picture of Lucky and Chance, in case Shaw asked to see them. The boys had blue eyes and black hair like their mother, Kate Pendleton. And were long and lanky, with square chins, strong noses and high cheekbones like their father, Wyatt Shaw.

Harry hadn't believed his luck when he'd finally stumbled on the truth. The governor had mentioned a reunion her son and Kate had attended in Austin at the Four Seasons. The trip would have been around the time of the twins' conception, nine years ago. Shaw hadn't been as well-known then, but the brand-new receptionist at the hotel, who'd taken his American Express card at the Austin, Texas, Four Seasons that fateful night, had become the current manager of the hotel.

The incident had remained fixed in her mind because it was the first of the new Centurion Cards—a black AMEX card with supposedly unlimited credit—she'd ever seen, and it had been handed to her by an extraordinarily good-looking young man with silver wings in his black hair.

The manager told him that when she'd recognized Wyatt Shaw with his infamous father on TV less than a year later, she'd marveled at how close she'd come to flirting with a dangerous criminal. She'd admitted to being jealous, that long-ago evening, of the strikingly beautiful woman holding the handsome man's hand.

And yes, she'd confirmed, the lady in the photo Harry had shown her was the same woman Wyatt Shaw had taken with him on the elevator to the penthouse suite he'd booked.

Harry had quickly realized he'd stumbled onto a gold mine. He could get paid again and again to keep his mouth shut about the information he'd discovered: Mob Boss Dante D'Amato's bastard son, Wyatt Shaw, was the father of Texas Governor Ann Wade Pendleton's grandsons.

Governor Pendleton, who'd hired him, would pay, of course. He could also sell his willing silence to the twins' very wealthy great-grandfathers, who'd probably fork over a hunk of money to keep the world from knowing who their granddaughter had screwed while she'd been married to another man.

Jackson Blackthorne, Kate Pendleton's paternal grandfather, owned a ranch the size of Vermont in South Texas called Bitter Creek. Kate's maternal grandfather, King Grayhawk, owned an equally impressive ranch called Kingdom Come in Wyoming, where he served as that state's governor. The two men were lifelong enemies, a fact Harry was sure he could use to his advantage.

The mind boggled at what the tabloids might pay for such juicy gossip.

In the end, Harry had decided that the man who stood to gain the most—the knowledge that he had eight-year-old twin sons—was the man who'd be willing to pay the most. So even before he told Governor Pendleton what he knew, or approached either of Kate's influential grandfathers, or phoned the first tabloid magazine, he'd come here to confront Shaw.

Considering the menacing man standing just inside the door, and the even more dangerous one sitting behind the desk, Harry knew he was walking a tightrope over an abyss.

Greed gave him the courage to take the next step.

Harry glanced at the hulking figure by the door, and said, "I want half a million."

The demand was met by silence.

Harry struggled not to fidget while he waited for

Shaw to speak. He'd thought long and hard about how much he could ask Shaw to pay. He'd dreamed of a million, but realized if he got half of that, with what he'd already saved, he could buy a small fishing boat and a condo on the gulf near Corpus Christi and be set for the rest of his life. With a net worth over half a billion, half a million was a drop in the bucket for Shaw.

"I'm sure whatever it is you think you know isn't worth that kind of money," Shaw replied at last.

"This information has nothing to do with your... uh...business activities." Harry had nearly said *illegal* business activities. The U.S. Justice Department had been unable to prove Shaw had ill-gotten gains under the Racketeer Influenced and Corrupt Organizations (RICO) Act, although they'd taken him to court at least once to try. And the Houston cops hadn't yet found enough evidence—despite the woman found strangled in Shaw's bed six weeks ago—to charge him with murder.

Wyatt Shaw seemed to walk between raindrops.

But Harry knew the rich man's life hadn't always been so blessed.

His mother had been Dante D'Amato's mistress until her death, under suspicious circumstances, when Shaw was twelve. The child born on the wrong side of the blanket, so to speak, had succeeded so spectacularly that the government—read FBI—refused to believe he'd done it without help from the mob.

Harry was pretty sure the Feds monitored every dollar in and out of Shaw's many business activities, looking for enough evidence to bring down his empire. Which only convinced Harry that Shaw would know how to pay him the half mil without raising any red flags for the IRS.

"Has to be a woman," Shaw said in disgust. "What is she claiming?"

Harry had expected the dismissive look on Shaw's face. The man had never been married and didn't have a steady girlfriend, though there was no shortage of women in his life. Harry had discovered from a lady lawyer Shaw briefly dated that he always took precautions to ensure there was no unwanted child.

Which made Harry wonder if the dead woman found in Shaw's penthouse suite might have been pregnant. And trying to extort money from Shaw. As he was.

Harry shuddered. The medical examiner's report on the murder victim hadn't been released to the public yet, and Harry's usual connection in the M.E.'s office had been too spooked to leak it to him. Which meant anything was possible.

Harry's investigation also revealed that Shaw usually bedded his dates in his—now infamous—penthouse at the Shaw Tower, or an equivalent locale. Not one of them had been to his personal retreat, a ranch compound north of Houston.

Ancient live oaks, which never completely shed their leaves, kept the structures within Shaw's compound hidden from Google Earth. But from county records, Harry knew Shaw had built a modest, four-bedroom home, stables large enough to hold a dozen sleek quarter horses and on-site housing, a sort of bunkhouse, for his security team. To guarantee his privacy, Shaw had surrounded the compound with eight-foot-high river-rock walls.

His isolated compound—and his isolated lifestyle—made a powerful statement: Shaw lived a life without strings, a life without human connections. So Harry expected him to resist the idea that he had twin sons, maybe even to dismiss Harry's suggestion as ridiculous.

Luckily, Harry had proof. DNA results made it 99.9 percent certain that Shaw was the twins' father.

"Who sent you here?" Shaw asked.

"I want your promise to pay before I say anything more."

"You'd take my word?" Shaw said cynically, lifting a brow.

Harry shrugged. "You have a reputation for sticking by it in business deals." Which this was. Sort of.

"Bruce, escort this man from the premises."

"Wait!" Harry reached into his jacket and found his wrist handcuffed by Bruce's gigantic hand. How had the big man moved so fast? "I don't have a weapon," Harry babbled, afraid the monster was going to crush his bones. "There are papers in my jacket. And a photo."

"Let him go," Shaw said.

With a shaking hand, Harry pulled out the papers he'd been reaching for, which had been folded in his suit coat pocket. They rustled as he unfolded them and took the few steps forward to lay them on Shaw's desk.

Shaw spread the papers apart and stared at them, his brow furrowed. "This looks like—"

"It's the results of a DNA test," Harry interrupted. "You can see that the first chart matches the second two almost exactly."

"The second *two?*"

"You have twin eight-year-old sons," Harry blurted. Shaw's brows arrowed down and his lips pressed flat.

Harry was afraid to breathe, waiting for Shaw to deny paternity despite the DNA results. He expected the businessman to ask how Harry had gotten his DNA. It had been easy, since the man ate most of his meals in restaurants. A fork he'd eaten from, a glass he'd drunk from, was all Harry had needed.

Instead, Shaw said, "Who's the mother?"

Harry licked his lips. "Half a million."

Shaw nodded curtly.

"Her name is Kate Grayhawk Pendleton. She's the governor's daughter-in-law. She lives in San Antonio." He laid a 4"x6" photograph beside the DNA results on the table. It showed the smiling mother standing between her identical grinning sons, one slender arm resting on each boy's narrow shoulder.

Harry watched several emotions flicker in Wyatt Shaw's narrowed gaze, none of which were pleasant. The expected shock. Anger. Disgust. And then, a great deal more anger.

"Her husband?" Shaw asked.

"She was widowed eighteen months ago. Her husband died serving in Afghanistan."

Harry was glad for the husband's sake that he was dead. And he wouldn't have wanted to be in the woman's shoes when Shaw caught up to her. For half a million, he figured he owed Shaw a heads-up on the woman's current situation. After all, the businessman had been back and forth to China a dozen times over the past six months and might not have kept up with the local news.

"Mrs. Pendleton was shot last October by that assassin trying to kill the governor. She was in a coma for four months and spent about six weeks in a rehab

facility. She seems to have come out of it just fine. She
went home ten days ago."

"Tell my secretary where you want the money
wired," Shaw said through tight jaws.

Harry couldn't believe it had been that easy.
Couldn't believe Shaw was actually going to pay.

Then he saw Shaw's glance slide to Bruce, watched
his chin drop the littlest bit, sending some kind of
message to the big man. Harry felt the sudden urge to
run. For a moment he was frozen, like a frightened
rabbit, panting for breath.

Then he made his move.

His eyes darted from Shaw to the big man as he hurriedly backed his way out of the office, leaving the test
results and the photograph on the glass in front of Shaw,
letting the heavy wooden door slide silently closed
behind him. He glanced over his shoulder, alarmed to see
Bruce pass through the same door a few seconds later.

Harry paused at the secretary's desk long enough
to say, "I'll give you a call and let you know where to
wire the money."

She didn't ask "What money?" She must be used
to business deals made on a handshake. Or in this
case, a chin nod.

Harry hustled to the elevator, pushed the button and
was relieved when the doors opened as though the
elevator always waited on the 80th floor for Shaw. He
stepped inside and pushed the button for the ground floor.

He felt his breath catch when he realized Bruce
was headed for the same elevator. He stabbed the
"Door Close" button several times. And breathed a
sigh of relief when it began to close.

Several thick-knuckled fingers appeared between the nearly closed doors and they opened again. Bruce got on the elevator with Harry and stood facing the door, his hefty arms crossed over his substantial girth.

Harry felt his heartbeat ratchet up, felt the blood pound in his temples, and realized he hadn't taken his blood pressure meds that morning. Hell, hadn't taken them for a couple of days. He tried to calm himself, afraid he was going to have a heart attack. Or stroke out.

The elevator didn't stop once on the way down, even though Harry prayed that it would pick up another passenger. It raced past thirty floors of offices, twenty-four floors of condominiums, twenty-one floors of hotel rooms (no thirteenth floor), the third floor hotel lobby, and the second floor boutiques, never once stopping.

He should have known Shaw would have a private express elevator. He managed not to pant, but he was having trouble catching his breath. He told himself he was being stupid. Big Bruce here hadn't made a move toward him. In a few moments the elevator doors would open and he'd be safe.

Maybe he'd buy that beachfront property somewhere out of the country. He was just realizing how much fallout there might be once the governor realized what he'd done. Not to mention the girl's two grandfathers.

Harry was out of the elevator the instant it stopped on the ground floor. The two-story-high glass-walled space was empty except for a black-suited guard behind a black granite desk who kept out the riffraff. Harry hurried past him.

Behind him, he heard the guard tell Bruce, "The

Boss told me to remind you to take care of that business quietly."

Harry felt a spurt of terror so great he nearly fainted. He should have known better than to try and extort money from a man like Shaw. He pushed his way through the revolving door, squinting against the glare of the sun off the mirrored building across the street. If he could just get outside onto the sidewalk, he'd be okay. He could see it was crowded with people.

As he left Shaw Tower, a gust of hot wind blew grit from the street into his eyes. He swiped at his stinging eyes and realized his face was dripping with sweat. He looked down and saw he'd sweated all the way through his suit jacket under his armpits. What the hell? He squirmed as a bead of sweat slid down between his shoulder blades. Oh, shit. That was a symptom of heart attack, wasn't it? Profuse sweat?

Harry nearly giggled with hysteria. He was scaring himself to death. He had to control his panic or he was going to do Big Bruce's job for him. He forced himself to walk more slowly. He glanced over his shoulder long enough to see that Bruce was still following him.

Harry was determined to put the width of the street between himself and Shaw's enforcer. He weaved his way across tacky, sun-heated asphalt, in between honking downtown traffic, almost running by the time he got to the other side of the street. He realized Bruce was no longer behind him. The big man was still walking along the opposite sidewalk.

Harry heaved a quiet sigh of relief. He was done with his brief life of crime. It was too damned stressful. He put a hand to his heart, which was finally slowing down. He glanced once more at Big Bruce. Now he was talking on a cell phone.

Harry reached the corner and stepped off the curb, his gaze riveted on Bruce.

He heard a scream from the sidewalk catty-corner from him. His head jerked toward the sound. Harry saw a young woman, her eyes wide with horror, her hand urgently pointing to his right—in the opposite direction from where he'd last seen Big Bruce. Harry yanked his head back around to see what had frightened her. Adrenaline pumped into his veins, making his heart hurt so bad he put a hand to his chest.

As close as the truck was, Harry could see the rust on the metal grille, which rose as high as his shoulder. The driver had obviously run the red. Harry calculated the time it would take to get out of the way. And realized he was fucked.

In the final seconds before disaster struck, Harry's gaze shot over his shoulder to Bruce. The big man was pocketing his phone. Harry's head whipped back around as he heard the screech of brakes. Then the garbage truck hit him and he went flying.

2

Kate was expecting Jack McKinley, so she answered the knock at her door with a smile on her face. Her heart skipped a frightened beat when she saw who was standing there.

"You look surprised to see me."

Kate felt a visceral response deep in her womb as she stared into Wyatt Shaw's steel-gray eyes. Without wanting to, she remembered Shaw as she'd left him in the middle of the night, asleep amid tangled sheets, dark lashes lying soft on sharp cheekbones, rough beard shading the rugged planes and hollows of his face.

"May I come in?"

His raspy voice raised gooseflesh on her arms. He'd used that mesmerizing voice to murmur his approval as she caressed his powerful body, measuring the breadth of his shoulders with her palms and teasing the whorls of black hair on his chest with her fingertips.

He stood quietly at her front door, patiently awaiting her invitation to come inside. All his attention was focused on her, as it had been that long-ago night.

She tried to speak, to send him away, but her heart was caught in her throat. He'd been patient that night, too, coaxing her compliance. She'd been heartsick, feeling unloved and unlovely, a rejected woman seeking revenge against her husband.

Kate closed her eyes to shut out the too-vivid memories, but in her mind's eye she saw the soft play of light and shadow on his face above her and the fierce look of desire in his eyes. She had never felt more cherished. She had never felt more loved.

"Are you all right?"

She opened her eyes, but it didn't help. She'd kept the memories at bay for long years, but now that the flesh-and-blood man stood before her, they rushed back with frightening clarity.

She remembered most the urgency of his need. And how it had healed the hurt. The heady feeling as she realized this man craved her body as a dying man craves water in the desert. The soothing balm of his raspy voice as he extolled the pleasure he found in the petal softness of her skin. The laughter that tumbled from her lips as she reveled in the power of knowing he couldn't get his fill of her. That he could never get enough. That he would always want to touch her, taste her, love her.

She would never forget the satisfied masculine sound in his throat as he'd felt how wet and ready she was for him. At his urging, she'd wrapped her long legs around his whipcord lean hips as he moved inside her. In the throes of passion, she'd gripped handfuls of his thick black hair, running her fingers through the silver wings at his temples that had made her guess his age as much older than he was.

He'd been only twenty-nine.

Which made him thirty-eight.

Her glance skipped to his mouth. She remembered bowed lips that had been soft to the touch, his first kiss so tender it had made her throat ache with unshed tears. There were no signs of softness in him now. His lips were pressed flat and bracketed by deep grooves. His eyes, deep-set and gray, reminded her of thunderous storm clouds.

Shaw hadn't moved a muscle, hadn't moved a hair, but she felt the threat of his presence, the threat of... his desire for her.

He was wearing a Savile Row suit that should have made him look civilized. Instead, she saw the tension beneath the masterfully tailored cloth, the power in corded sinew and bone. She felt her nipples peak as his nostrils flared, inhaling the scent of her like a stag in rut. Felt the blood fill her nether lips as she stared into heavy-lidded eyes that told her how much he wanted—needed—to be inside her.

She had to remind herself who he was. Yes, this was the stranger with whom she'd spent the most passionate night of her life. But Wyatt Shaw was also the son of mob boss Dante D'Amato. And a suspected murderer.

Her gaze skipped down to his long-fingered hands. Those hands had caressed her with infinite tenderness. Had they also strangled the woman found naked in his bed? It had only been six weeks since the sensational story had hit the tabloids. Billionaire businessman Wyatt Shaw was accused of murdering a call girl in his suite on the top floor of Shaw Tower.

A call girl?

That gave their night together an entirely new complexion. Had Shaw thought she was a call girl, too?

Had she left before he'd put his money on the bedside table? Was the magical night she remembered merely one more sexual encounter with a call girl for him? Had she been lucky that long-ago night to escape with her life?

Kate was afraid to look back up into Shaw's eyes, afraid the question—the accusation—would be there in her own.

Her knees felt rubbery, and she stiffened them. She glanced beyond Wyatt's shoulder, searching the street for Jack's SUV, hoping he would stay away until she could get rid of this apparition from her past, this stranger who'd ruined her sleep for far too many nights over the past nine years.

Kate shuddered at the thought of Texas Ranger Jack McKinley confronting Wyatt Shaw with his gun drawn. She didn't want Jack killing the father of her sons. Or Wyatt killing the man she loved.

"We need to talk," Shaw said.

"I don't have anything to say to you."

He lifted an arrogant brow that accused her of the terrible wrong she'd done him. But said nothing.

"You can't have them." Kate knew the instant the words came out of her mouth that she shouldn't have spoken them.

"By *them* do you mean *my sons?*" he said, the sudden menace in his voice raising the hairs on her nape.

She tried to slam the door, but he was too fast for her. He simply caught the frame with his palm, waited until she let go, waited another moment until she stepped back, then strode inside and closed the wooden door with a quiet *snick* behind him.

She turned to face him in her tiny living room like a lioness defending her cubs, even though the twins were at school and wouldn't be home for another hour. "You can't have them. They're mine."

"And mine," he said inexorably.

She could see that denial was futile. Somehow he'd found out the truth. "Who told you?"

"A private investigator hired by your mother-in-law."

Kate groaned and lowered her face into her hands. She suddenly lifted her head and asked, "Does Ann Wade know?"

"I have no idea. The P.I. who contacted me was killed shortly after he left my office."

Did you kill him? The words stuck in Kate's throat. There was no sense asking, since he was unlikely to tell her if he had.

"When did you know the twins were mine?" he asked.

Kate felt a frisson of fear skitter down her spine. She had never been a good liar. The telltale pink blotches on her creamy skin always gave her away. But she was terrified of what the man standing in her living room might do if she told him she'd known within weeks of that fateful night that she'd gotten pregnant during their liaison.

The same day she'd gotten a positive result on a home pregnancy test, she'd seduced J.D., who'd gloated at how brief her sex boycott had been after she'd caught him in bed with another woman.

"You were a stranger I met in a bar," she said to Shaw. "I didn't know your name. I didn't know how to contact you."

"You didn't answer the question," he said, anger simmering in his eyes. "When did you know?"

"I couldn't be sure my husband wasn't the father," she lied. And felt the sudden heat on her throat and cheeks.

His eyes narrowed. "It's a simple question."

Whenever she'd felt guilty over the years that she hadn't sought out the stranger from the bar to tell him the truth, she'd reminded herself of the circumstances of their encounter. It was a night out of time.

She'd felt vindicated when she'd discovered who he was.

"What did you expect me to do when I found out I'd gotten pregnant while having sex with a perfect stranger?" *A stranger accused of graft and corruption, of extortion and murder. And that was before a woman was found strangled to death in your bed.*

His brows arrowed down at her admission that she'd known from the start what he'd just learned.

"You could have gone back to the hotel," he said. "There were people there who knew me. You could have found me."

"To what purpose?" she demanded. "I was married. For all I knew, you could have been married, too."

"I wasn't."

"I didn't know that. Besides, there was always the chance that my husband—"

"You've cheated me out of knowing my sons for eight years."

Kate's blue eyes flashed up at him. "I notice you never came looking for me!"

"I couldn't find you. And not for want of trying."

Kate was startled. He'd searched for her? Why? "Just because the sex was good—"

"The sex was fantastic. But that wasn't why I came looking for you."

Kate knew she'd regret asking, but she couldn't stop herself. "Why, then?"

He shrugged. "It doesn't matter now."

Irritated by his reticence, she snapped, "So why are you here? What do you want?"

He met her gaze with annoying calm and said, "I want to meet my sons."

"No." Kate's throat was tight with dread, but she forced herself to add, "They believe J.D.—my husband, who was killed serving in Afghanistan—was their father."

"I don't want my sons growing up without a father."

As he had, Kate realized. The first time she'd seen Shaw on TV was the day he consoled Dante D'Amato on the steps of the federal courthouse in Houston after his two grown, legitimate sons had been killed by a car bomb. The mob boss was on trial for RICO-related offenses, and the reporter suggested that D'Amato's sons had been murdered in an effort by underlings to wrench control of the mob from D'Amato's powerful hands, in expectation that he would be convicted and go to prison.

When a roving TV reporter asked a grieving D'Amato who would take the roles in his business left vacant by his sons' deaths, D'Amato slid his arm around Wyatt Shaw's broad shoulders and said, "I have all the help I need right here."

The news anchor at the station had explained that Shaw's mother had been supported by D'Amato, who'd bought her a home in Houston, but they'd never been married. Thereby suggesting, without actually saying, that Wyatt Shaw was Dante D'Amato's illegitimate son, and that he might be expected to take over the mob if his father was convicted.

The film clip that followed showed a grim-faced man with silver-winged black hair shoving his way through a crowd of reporters as he left the federal courthouse.

It was the man she'd picked up in the bar of the Four Seasons, a man passionate beyond her dreams and tender beyond belief.

Kate had blanched with horror at the discovery that she'd lain with a man who'd been accused, along with his mob boss father, of having business competitors maimed and murdered. She'd followed the trial on TV. Neither Shaw nor his father had been convicted. The witnesses had all recanted or disappeared.

The pictures Kate had seen in the tabloid newspapers of that poor strangled woman had put an end to her romantic fantasies about the stranger with whom she'd spent a precious night of lovemaking.

She'd viciously squelched the memories that arose whenever she compared that single night of passion to sex with J.D. She'd comforted herself with the knowledge that her husband might be a selfish lover and a womanizer, but at least he wasn't a criminal.

Or so she'd thought.

"You don't have to worry about Lucky and Chance growing up without a father," she told Shaw. "I'm involved with someone. I love him very much, and we're going to be married." She was certain Jack wouldn't mind if she stretched the truth in a good cause. They hadn't discussed marriage yet, but she was sure it was only a matter of time before they did.

Jack's divorce would be final within the next month. And J.D. was...no longer in the picture.

"Since I'm going to be married," Kate began, "I—" Shaw was already shaking his head. "No, you're not."

"You can't stop me!"

"We both know your first husband isn't dead. Which precludes your marriage to another man."

Kate's face blanched. "How could you possibly...? Why would you think...?"

"I've done some investigating of my own in the week since I discovered I'm a father. You can't marry another man, because you're still married to J.D. Pendleton, who isn't buried in Arlington Cemetery after all. He's alive and well and left the country for Brazil the day after you were shot."

"J.D.'s in Brazil?" Her husband had threatened to kidnap her sons and take them to South America if she didn't pay him a quarter of a million dollars to get out of her life, but she'd been shot before she could ask one of her grandfathers for the money. Although Kate was the daughter and granddaughter of wealthy men and women, J.D. had gambled away her personal trust fund within a few years after she'd gotten control of it when she turned twenty-five.

However, J.D.'s mother had given him $250,000 in "hush money" which he'd presumably used to disappear. The governor didn't want the world to know her son was a live deserter, rather than a dead war hero.

Kate's greatest fear, before Wyatt Shaw had shown up on her doorstep, was that J.D. would return, once again threatening to steal Lucky and Chance, and demanding money that she didn't have to disappear. "Do you know where J.D. is now?" she asked.

"No. But there are dangerous men out there looking for him."

"*Dangerous* men?" Kate asked, confused. *Your* men? she wondered.

"Your husband was trading military weapons for heroin in Afghanistan."

Kate gasped. She'd known J.D. was in trouble. He'd hinted as much to her when he'd shown up in her kitchen last fall looking gaunt and ragged a year after she'd supposedly buried his remains. But she'd never suspected him of doing anything so awful. "How do you know that?"

Shaw ignored the question and continued, "Your husband blew up that ammo dump in Afghanistan—and faked his death—to avoid paying the consequences for skimming profits on the arms-for-heroin deals he was negotiating between parties here in the States and the Taliban. He absconded with twenty million dollars worth of heroin that didn't belong to him.

"There are people who intend to find him, get back their product—or the cash he got for selling it—and make an object lesson of your husband."

"What does that have to do with me?"

"The bad guys are closing in on J.D."

"How do you know all this?"

He lifted a dark brow as though the answer should be obvious, although it wasn't to Kate. Did he know about J.D.'s situation because he, personally, was chasing him? Or was it some other criminal element with whom Shaw had close ties, like his father, Dante D'Amato?

"Suffice it to say, you and your—our—sons aren't safe with your husband on the loose."

Kate lifted her chin. "The man I've been seeing is a Texas Ranger. He'll be happy to protect me."

"Who's that?"

Kate debated whether to tell him, then decided it was better not to bring Jack into this. "None of your business."

Kate didn't like the look in Shaw's eyes. He had no right to be jealous. Or possessive. But she didn't want to exacerbate the situation, so she said, "Nevertheless, this man is willing, and able, to keep an eye on me and my sons. His divorce will be final any day now and—"

"He's planning to move in?"

Kate heard the challenge in Shaw's gravelly voice, watched as his eyes narrowed and his hands formed into powerful fists. It seemed safest to say, "We haven't planned that far ahead."

She was still looking forward to making love to Jack for the first time. They'd been on the verge of consummating their relationship last fall—kissing in the hall, on the way to her bedroom—when Jack had been called away to confront a killer. Shortly thereafter, Kate had been shot. She'd only recently come home.

So, despite the fact she'd first attempted to seduce Jack ten years ago, when she was nineteen, she still had no idea what kind of lover he was. Which was surprising, when Kate thought about it, because she'd gone to bed with Wyatt Shaw within thirty minutes of meeting him.

Kate felt her breasts peak at the memory of his mouth on her naked flesh. She quickly lowered her gaze, mortified at where her thoughts had led her. Again.

She made herself picture Jack's beloved face instead. She imagined his dark brown eyes looking down at her, imagined her fingers threading through his sun-streaked chestnut hair. Jack was tall, like Shaw, but his skin was burnished by wind and sun. She ached to have Jack kiss her, touch her, in places where... Where Wyatt Shaw already had.

"You can't marry anyone so long as J.D. is still alive," Shaw said, interrupting her disconcerting thoughts. "The way I see it, right now—and for the foreseeable future—my sons don't have adequate protection."

"*My* sons," Kate automatically corrected, her chin lifting pugnaciously, "are my responsibility." When Shaw continued to stare at her, she grudgingly corrected, "All right. *Our* sons are my responsibility. I don't want or need your help."

"The danger is real."

He sounded concerned. But the fact was, they were strangers who, a long time ago, had found solace—and physical pleasure—in each other's arms. An image of herself trembling as she watched Shaw's callused fingertips stroke downward across her flat belly flashed in Kate's mind. She made a growling sound in her throat, angry that memories of herself in bed with Shaw were so unforgettable.

"You'd all be safer if you came to live with me in Houston until J.D. is found," Shaw said.

"That's out of the question."

"My compound is surrounded by high stone walls.

I have twenty-four-hour security cameras and guards with dogs that patrol the perimeter."

"That sounds more like a prison than a home," Kate snapped.

"Lucky and Chance..."

When he paused, Kate saw his throat working. It was the first time he'd said his sons' names since he'd shoved his way into her home. Apparently, it had affected him deeply.

But Kate couldn't afford to sympathize, couldn't afford to glamorize or glorify his appearance on her doorstep. She didn't dare feel anything for Wyatt Shaw. She was fighting for her children's lives. If Shaw had his way, she and her sons would be imprisoned behind high stone walls. She wasn't about to let that happen.

"Legally, J.D. Pendleton is my sons' father. You provided the seed. That was all. You have no legal rights where Lucky and Chance are concerned. None. I don't need your help. I don't want your help. My sons—yes, *my* sons," she repeated in a fierce voice, "have managed fine without you in their lives for eight years. And they're far more likely to grow into fine young men if you never come anywhere near them."

Shaw's face blanched.

Kate felt a pang of remorse for hurting him. And ruthlessly quelled it. What did he expect? His reputation had preceded him. No mother would willingly expose her children to a man like Wyatt Shaw. He was the antithesis of Jack McKinley. One man was an outlaw, the other a lawman. There was no question in her mind who would make the better father.

She took a deep breath and said, "I'd like you to leave."

Kate expected Shaw to argue. Expected him to threaten. Expected him to point out all the reasons why his suggestion was the best way, the only way, to keep her children safe. But he did none of those things.

He simply said, "Goodbye, Kate." Then he turned and walked to the door. He opened it, glanced back over his shoulder, and said, "I'll be in touch."

Kate hurried across the living room to close and lock the door behind him. But she didn't feel the least bit safe.

I'll be in touch.

What did that mean? Kate's stomach cramped as she realized how vulnerable her sons were. All Shaw had to do was intercept them at school. Or after they got off the bus.

Kate's heart was lodged in her throat. She had to call the boys' school. She had to warn them that her sons weren't safe. She had to retrieve Lucky and Chance before Wyatt Shaw made his move. Because she was certain that once Shaw had her sons behind high stone walls, he would never give them back.

3

Jack McKinley had a knot in his belly. He wasn't looking forward to the next half hour. He had a confession to make that was going to break Kate Pendleton's heart.

He sat in his SUV, parked on the curb in front of her house, trying to put a smile on his face before he headed for her door. His mouth wouldn't cooperate. She was going to see the truth in his eyes, so why pretend everything was all right? Nothing was going to be right for a very long time.

Well, not for the next four months, anyway. In four months his not-quite-ex-wife Holly would give birth to an unplanned baby. Unplanned because the sex between them had been unplanned.

Last November, Jack had traveled to Holly's home in Kansas to have Thanksgiving dinner with his six-year-old son, Ryan. After Ryan had gone to bed, he'd had a terrible row with Holly over visitation rights.

The sharp blows they'd exchanged had all been verbal, but Holly knew exactly where to strike to hurt him most. He was equally adept at hitting below the belt and got in a few good licks of his own. They'd both been furious, hissing and snarling insults because Ryan was asleep down the hall.

They'd ended up having sex.

She'd scratched and bit. He'd left bruises. Neither had minded.

It was how they'd resolved most of the quarrels during their fractious nine-year marriage. There had been a lot less sex—and a lot less trust—toward the end. But he'd never imagined Holly could, or would, keep something as important as a child they'd created a secret from him.

But she had.

Jack had met Holly Gayle Tanner when he was fifteen and she was thirteen. She'd been on the junior cheerleading squad. He'd been the high school football quarterback. He'd already had sex with more than one girl when he'd met Holly, but he'd never been in love.

He'd taken one look at Holly, with her long, curly auburn hair and leaf-green eyes, her freckled nose and wide, friendly smile, and fallen hard and fast.

They'd been inseparable from the day they'd met. Until Holly had broken up with him at Christmas his senior year. He'd still been deeply in love with her, sifting his football scholarship offers as he planned their future together, when she'd told him, "I want a chance to date other guys. I want to see what else is out there. You're going off to college, so we'll be separated anyway."

He'd been devastated.

Once he'd left the small town in the piney woods northeast of Houston where they'd grown up and headed to the University of Texas at Austin, they hadn't crossed paths again until his 15th high school reunion. Holly was in town for the birth of her youngest sister's first child and had come to the reunion with a friend from the cheerleading squad.

He'd felt his heart jump when he'd seen her stroll into the Kountze High School gymnasium. Felt it thump hard in his chest when he realized that she'd never married. And that he still loved her.

Holly had become a renowned pediatric oncologist. He was a pro football quarterback who'd been driven from the game, accused, but never tried and convicted, of shaving points in the Super Bowl. He'd lost the restaurant he'd opened in Austin, the Longhorn Grille, to the IRS for unpaid taxes.

Because of his suspected involvement in a national gambling scandal, he'd been offered the chance to work undercover as a Texas Ranger to bring down a mob-controlled gambling syndicate. Jack was proud of his work with the Rangers and had struggled, mostly successfully, to put his checkered past behind him.

He and Holly had both been in a good place in their lives, happy to see each other, eager to share old memories.

To his surprise, they'd ended up in bed that night. He remembered how shy she'd been with him. How tender he'd felt toward her. His heart in his throat, he'd proposed the next morning. And she'd accepted.

Despite the difficulties in their marriage, Jack would never have abandoned his family. His tall-for-his-age, chestnut-haired, green-eyed son was the joy of his life. Holly was the one who'd asked for the divorce eleven months ago.

For the second time, and for reasons that were not entirely clear to him, she'd forced him out of her life.

Holly had taken Ryan with her to Kansas while they waited for the divorce lawyers to work out the financial arrangements between them and for the divorce to be finalized in court. Holly had wanted to live close to her parents, so they could help her with child care while she spent long hours at the hospital.

Jack had argued with the family court judge that he could only be a Texas Ranger in Texas, and that Holly shouldn't be allowed to take his son so far away. The judge had replied that law enforcement was law enforcement, and Jack could take a job as a Kansas City cop if he wanted to be closer to his son.

But the Texas Rangers weren't the same as other law enforcement agencies. Rangers worked as lone wolves, independent lawmen whose ingenuity and courage and determination made them the best at what they did. When Jack became a Ranger, he'd become part of a history that reached back to a time when the Texas Rangers provided law and order for the brand-new Republic of Texas, formed in 1836 with its own president and its own army and navy.

Despite his plea, the judge had given Holly permission to take Ryan and leave the state. His heart had ached for the loss of Holly. It had bled for the loss of his son.

He'd moved on with his life. He'd allowed himself to fall in love again, with Kate Pendleton. He'd enjoyed the time he spent with her sons, Lucky and

Chance, in the months they'd lived with him and his parents at Twin Magnolias, his ranch west of Austin, while Kate was in a coma. He'd even arranged for Ryan to come stay with him and meet Kate's sons during Christmas vacation.

Fortunately, Ryan had sent him a Valentine's Day card with a drawing of "Mommy" showing Holly with a swollen belly. He figured Holly's mother must have accidentally mailed it. Holly knew he'd always wanted more children. It was difficult to accept the fact that she'd schemed to keep this second pregnancy from him.

Even after he'd confronted his nearly-ex-wife, she'd lied.

"The baby isn't yours," she'd said, facing him with her chin tilted upward in a gesture of defiance he recognized all too well.

"You willing to prove that?"

She'd frowned. "We're getting a divorce, Jack. What does it matter whose child this is?"

"I'm not having a son of mine born a bastard. It's a burden no innocent child should have to bear. I can stand to be married to you long enough to give my son—"

"Or daughter," she'd interjected.

"Or daughter," Jack had said, imagining a little girl with Holly's green eyes and red hair, "my name."

Holly's eyes had brimmed with tears as she said, "I don't want to spend the last few months of my pregnancy with us at each other's throats. And that's what happens lately whenever we're together."

It had hurt to hear her say it, even though their marriage was within a few weeks of being over. "Too bad," he'd retorted. "I'm not giving you a divorce until the baby's born."

"I want this fighting to be over with, Jack." Her voice was angry. But her eyes were agonized.

"No problem," Jack said. "The day you give birth, we're quits. But the papers don't get signed until then."

"All right, Jack. You win."

He'd won the argument, all right, but lost the war. At least, that was how it felt. Instead of being free to pursue a relationship with Kate, whom he loved, he'd tied himself to Holly for four more long months.

Of course, he and Kate couldn't get married anyway until they found her errant husband. She'd only admitted J.D. was alive after Jack had said, "I love you"—to explain why she wasn't completely free.

The world believed her husband was dead, but Kate knew J.D. was alive. How could she get a divorce from a man who was legally dead? And it took seven years after his "disappearance" to have J.D. declared dead— again.

But he'd bought a ring, anyway. He'd planned to go down on one knee tonight and propose to her.

Instead, he had to confess to Kate that while she'd been in a coma, he'd gone to bed with his wife. And gotten her pregnant.

That wasn't the worst of it.

Holly had made demands of her own before she would agree to postpone their divorce until the child was born.

"I'll stay married to you on one condition," she'd said.

"You're in no position to make conditions," he'd shot back.

"You have to live with me and Ryan until the baby is born."

He'd been so stunned that for a moment he hadn't been able to speak. Fury had quickly followed. "Why are you jerking me around, Holly? You're the one who asked for the divorce. You're the one who kicked me out on my ass. And you're the one who pointed out that all we ever do anymore is fight. Why in hell would you want us to live together for the next four months?"

"I want us to use this time to mend what was broken between us."

"You've got to be kidding." Jack was pretty sure they couldn't mend what was broken between them if they lived together for the next forty years.

"I want us to become friends again," she explained, her leaf-green gaze focused on his.

He'd always been a sucker for that pleading look, and she knew it. But he wasn't about to let her manipulate him. "Why make this any harder than it is?"

In a soft, throaty voice that he couldn't remember hearing Holly use in recent memory, she said, "We were best friends once, Jack."

"That was a long time ago," he replied, his voice harsh. "We can't go back, Holly. What would be the point?"

"The point is, we're going to have two children who'll need us to be able to talk without arguing," she said reasonably. "Two children who'll need us to be friends in order to make custody arrangements without hurting them or each other."

He hated to admit it, but she was right. Over the past year, every discussion they'd had about Ryan had been laced with animosity on her part and resentment on his. But there was a sticking point that made what she suggested impossible for him.

"I'm not giving up my job."

"You won't have to do that," Holly said. "I've accepted a position at M.D. Anderson in Houston. I'll be doing research at the Children's Cancer Hospital on a grant through the end of my pregnancy. All you'd need to do is ask for a transfer across the state."

He could hardly believe his ears. "When did all this happen?"

"I've been working on it for a couple of months."

"You were intending to come back to Texas and you never told me?" He was angry again.

"It wasn't any of your business."

"My son's whereabouts isn't my business?"

She flushed and her green eyes sparked with anger equal to his own. "I know about you and Kate Pendleton. I didn't want to come back to Texas until the divorce was final. It would have been humiliating to have my colleagues know my husband was involved with another woman, especially someone as high-profile as the governor's daughter-in-law."

He could see her point. Again. "How soon do you want to do this?"

"I've already rented a house near M.D. Anderson. Ryan and I will be moving there over the weekend."

"*This* weekend?" he'd asked incredulously.

"The furniture's being delivered Saturday morning. So, do you think you can get a transfer?"

His undercover assignment was located in Houston. He was investigating a businessman there. "That won't be a problem."

"When can we expect you to join us?"

"I can be there Saturday morning. Do you want help moving?"

He saw the astonishment on her face. She hadn't been expecting him to manage a transfer so soon. Or maybe not at all? Had this all been another trick?

"That would be a big help," she said. "I won't tell Ryan you're coming until you show up. It can be a nice surprise."

Was she hoping he wouldn't show up? "What are we going to tell him? He's going to think we're getting back together."

"We can worry about that after the baby is born."

And that was that.

Jack was distracted from his thoughts when Kate stuck her head out her front door and asked, "Are you all right?"

He shoved his way out of the SUV and headed down the sidewalk. "I'm fine." As he closed the distance between them he said, "I have some news I need to share."

He was surprised when her smile of welcome disappeared and she replied, "I have some news, too."

4

Kate wanted Jack's arms around her. She'd been seriously rattled by Wyatt Shaw's visit. She'd realized she would never get to the twins' elementary school before class let out for the day, so she'd called a friend who lived near the school and asked her to pick up Lucky and Chance. Her friend had called to let Kate know she had the boys in hand, so at least Shaw hadn't intercepted them before they got on the bus. The boys were going to stay at their friend's house and play for a while before her friend brought them home.

Then she'd paced the floor, waiting for Jack to arrive.

Jack represented comfort. And security. He arrived at her front door dressed like the lawman he was in the only "uniform" the Texas Rangers wore: a crisp, long-sleeved white western shirt with, in Jack's case, a bolo tie with a silver clasp, Wrangler jeans, a western hat and cowboy boots.

As he stepped inside, he set his gray felt Stetson on a nearby table with the crown down. As soon as he did, she wrapped her arms tightly around his waist. "I'm so glad you're here."

He shoved the SIG Sauer P226 in a slide holster on

his belt out of the way. But she could feel the cold imprint of the Texas Ranger badge, a star within a circle stamped out of a silver Mexican *cinco peso* coin which he wore over his left breast pocket, against her cheek.

She waited anxiously for his arms to close around her. Finally they did. But it wasn't enough to quiet her fears.

"Hold me tighter, Jack."

His grip tightened at last, but only for a moment, just long enough for her to hear that his heart was thumping surprisingly fast. Then he grasped her shoulders and pushed her away.

Kate raised her face, thinking Jack wanted to kiss her. She was confused by the anxious look in his dark brown eyes. For a moment, it seemed he wouldn't kiss her. And then he did.

Kate welcomed the passionate meeting of tongues and caught fire as Jack yanked at the buttons on her cotton blouse. He shoved a hand inside her blouse, then inside her bra, and palmed the naked weight of her breast. He used his other hand to press her hips tight against his erection.

The abrasive brush of his callused thumb caused her nipples to peak. His tongue mimicked the sex act, withdrawing, then seeking honey again.

Kate shoved her hands up around Jack's neck and into his hair, raising herself on tiptoe so their bodies would fit better, feeling the hot, hard length of him through the layers of denim they both wore. He wasn't nearly close enough. She wanted him inside her.

Her hand shoved its way back down between them. She traced the shape of him, the length of him, the heat of him, and heard the guttural groan that told her he liked what she was doing.

Which made it all the more shocking when he tore his mouth from hers, yanked his hand out of her bra and grabbed her shoulders with both hands. He held her at arm's length, his eyes tortured, his lungs heaving.

Kate could feel Jack's body trembling with need. Felt her own knees buckling, as nature did its best to get her supine to procreate. "Jack?" she gasped.

"We have to stop. We can't do this."

"Why not? I love you." It was the first time she'd said the words. "And I know you love me." He'd told her so in the days before she'd been shot. He'd proved it by coming to the hospital every day while she was in a coma, and by taking care of her sons when her mother-in-law might have seized the opportunity to steal her children away.

Jack closed his eyes. His jaw worked as though he were fighting some great emotion. "Oh God, Kate."

When he opened his eyes at last, there was a hopeless look in them that made her breath catch. Kate could think of only one reason why Jack wouldn't want to make love. She looked earnestly up at him and sought the words that would ease his troubled mind.

"It's okay, Jack. I know we can't get married right away, maybe not for a long time." J.D. might never be caught.

"But being shot, being in a coma, has taught me that none of us knows how long we have in this world. My heart is yours, Jack. I think it has been for a very long time. I want to make love to you. With you."

Jack made a low, growling sound in his throat, but he kept her at arm's length.

"We've waited long enough," she said. "I want to start our lives together now. We can worry about J.D. when—or if—he ever shows up again."

Kate tried to reach out and touch Jack, but his grip tightened painfully. "Ow. Jack, you're hurting me."

He let go of her abruptly and took a quick step back. When Kate reached out again, he put his hands up and snapped, "No. Don't touch me."

Kate recoiled. "What's wrong?"

He shoved a hand through his sun-streaked chestnut hair and looked down and away.

Kate recognized the move. J.D. had done it often enough. That was guilt. But guilt about what?

Jack stalked past her to the wet bar on the far side of the living room. He found a bottle of Jack Daniel's, poured himself a stiff drink and gulped it down in two swallows.

Kate watched him warily, stunned by his rejection. All she could think was that something had changed while she was in a coma. That he didn't love her anymore. That he'd kept on watching over her sons because he'd felt an obligation to do so. He'd gotten carried away by the kissing and touching, but he wasn't interested in anything permanent. Which explained why he'd seemed so upset by her profession of love.

"Have you changed your mind about loving me, Jack?" she asked, struggling to keep her chin from quivering.

"No!" His voice was loud. Harsh. As guttural as his groan of pleasure or his growl of guilt.

"Then why did you stop? Don't you want to make love to me?"

"My balls ache, I want you so bad," he said through gritted teeth. "I love you. I want to marry you."

Kate shook her head in bafflement. "Then why—"

"Holly's pregnant."

It took Kate a moment to process what Jack had said. She was trying to figure out what Holly's pregnancy had to do with Jack not making love to her. And realized what he hadn't said.

"It's your baby."

Jack didn't bother to confirm what she'd said. He just stood there looking sick at heart.

"When...? How soon...?"

"She got pregnant over Thanksgiving," he said. "The baby's due in mid-August."

Kate felt the heat grow in her cheeks. While she'd been in a coma, Jack had been having sex with his wife.

"I'm sorry, Kate."

"For what?" she snapped. "Holly's your wife. She *is* still your wife, right?"

"She is. But—"

"Does this mean you've reconciled? That you're not getting a divorce?"

"It was an accident," Jack blurted.

Kate laughed. It wasn't a nice sound.

"We were arguing and..." He rubbed a hand across his nape. "Aw, hell. That's how Holly and I settled every argument we ever had during our marriage. It was just...habit."

"You didn't take any precautions?"

"She's forty-one. Neither of us thought she could get pregnant because she's been... What's it called?"

"Menopausal?"

"Yeah. She started missing periods and said that was the end of kids for us. So I didn't think—"

"That's the understatement of the year," Kate muttered.

"Look, neither Holly nor I planned for her to get pregnant. It just happened. And now that it has…"

He paused again, and Kate waited to hear the death knell to her dreams of a life with Jack. "And now?"

"I don't want my child born a bastard."

Kate's breath soughed out of her. "I see."

He didn't explain further. He didn't need to. She could see where he was headed.

"I presume that means you're not getting a divorce."

"We're still getting divorced. We're just not going to sign the papers until after the baby's born in August," Jack qualified.

"What if I'm willing to have you live here and make love to me while you're still, technically, married to Holly?"

He was already shaking his head. "I can't do that, Kate."

"Why not?"

"Holly set conditions on us staying married until the baby is born, one of which is that we live together in Houston for the rest of her pregnancy. She has a job at M.D. Anderson."

Kate felt dizzy. "You're moving to Houston? To live with Holly?"

"And Ryan."

Kate felt an awful ache in her chest, felt her eyes brim with sudden tears, as though someone she loved had just died. She fought the sorrow with anger. "Why would Holly want you to live with her? She's the one who asked for the divorce!"

"She wants to use these few months together to work out some of our differences, so we can be friends again."

"Friends?" Kate snorted the word as though it was an epithet.

"Holly and I won't be sleeping together, if that's what you're worried about."

"Why the hell not?"

"Because I'm in love with you."

Kate moaned and swayed. She covered her face with her hands and fought back a sob.

Jack crossed the room in three strides and gathered her in his arms. His cheek was pressed close to hers and his voice was gruff as he said, "This is just a hiccup, sweetheart. We'll be together soon. But I have to do this."

Kate opened her mouth to tell Jack about the threat she faced from Wyatt Shaw and closed it again without speaking. It would tear Jack in two if he thought she was in trouble and needed him while he was stuck living with his wife in Houston.

"When do you leave?"

"Tonight. I'm helping Holly move in tomorrow."

Kate startled herself when she burst into tears.

"Honey, sweetheart, please don't cry," Jack crooned.

Kate felt him kiss her closed eyes, felt him kiss away the hot tears on her cheeks.

He put a finger under her chin and tipped her face up. "Look at me, Kate."

He waited patiently until she opened her eyes.

She looked up at Jack through a veil of tears. "It's not fair, Jack. It's like fate is conspiring against us."

"Our day will come, Kate. Sooner than you think."

But Kate wasn't so sure. What if Jack fell back in love with his wife? And she'd been counting on Jack to be a buffer between her and Wyatt Shaw.

She swallowed over the painful knot of sorrow— and fear—in her throat and said, "I can't believe this is happening."

"Hey," Jack said, tucking a stray curl behind her ear. "It won't be so bad. We can talk on the phone every day, and I can visit sometimes on weekends. We have the Internet and texting. If you love me as much as I love you, we can get through this together."

She didn't want to be coaxed into compliance. She stiffened in his arms. "You're still planning to woo me while you're living with your wife?"

"My very pregnant wife," Jack pointed out.

"Pregnant women are beautiful."

"I'm sure you were," Jack said with a grin. "And I hope you will be again."

Kate flushed. She was only thirty, with many more childbearing years, she hoped, ahead of her. She laid a palm against Jack's cheek, which was rough from an early five o'clock shadow, and said, "I would love having a child with you."

"Give me four months, Kate," he said, "and we can start to work on it."

The kiss he gave her was soft, tender, loving. And brief. His gaze was still focused on her mouth as he said, "I'm sorry I have to break our date tonight. I'll make it up to you. I'd better get out of here before I do something I'll be sorry for in the morning."

Kate knew she could tempt him. Even though Jack

had said he ought to leave, he was still holding her close. It wouldn't take much to push him over the edge. He was aroused again—or still. His dark eyes were heavy-lidded, with an avid look that made her pulse leap.

"You'd better go." But she made no move to send him on his way.

"I love you," he said again.

"And I love you."

Which made what he was about to do all the more insane, Kate thought. Maybe if she told him about Shaw he would stay. But that would mean telling Jack who'd really fathered the twins. He was going to learn the truth sooner or later, and surely it would be better if he heard it from her than found out some other way.

"Jack…"

"Hmm," he said as he nuzzled her throat.

She leaned her head back to give him better access, feeling the shiver roll down her spine as he sucked on the tender skin beneath her ear.

"I have a confession, too," she whispered.

"Hmm," he said, trailing kisses across her cheek, headed for her mouth.

"I…"

He caught her lower lip in his teeth and nibbled gently. She returned the favor. Soon, Kate was breathless, as desire spiraled upward through her body.

"I have to go, Kate," he said. But he sought her mouth with his, and they were caught up once more in the pleasure of kissing and touching each other.

With the sixth sense every mother has, Kate heard the front door opening. She pulled free of Jack's embrace and pressed a quick hand to her mouth before she turned to greet her sons with a bright smile.

"Mom, we're home!" Lucky said as he flung the door open.

"Hi, Jack. How's Ryan?" Chance said.

The twins had met Ryan at Christmas and talked about him often. According to Jack, Ryan had been jealous of the twins spending time with "his" father and had rebuffed their attempts at friendship at first. But before the holiday was over, the three boys had become "Best Buds."

"Ryan's fine," Jack said. "In fact, I'm glad I have this chance to let you boys know I'll be living with Ryan for the next couple of months."

"You're going to Kansas?" Lucky asked.

"Ryan and his mom are moving back to Texas," Jack said. "I'm going to live with them in Houston for a little while."

Kate held her breath, hoping Jack wouldn't mention Holly's pregnancy.

Chance frowned and glanced from Jack to Kate. "I thought you and Mom liked each other."

"We did," Jack said. "We do," he corrected. "But Holly's—" Jack stopped and looked at Kate, seeking guidance.

"Ryan's mother is pregnant," Kate explained. "Jack's going to live in Houston to help her out until she has the baby."

Kate waited with bated breath for one of the twins to ask how Ryan's mother had gotten pregnant, but neither did.

"You're coming back though, right?" Chance asked.

Jack playfully ruffled his black hair. "You bet!"

"There are chocolate chip cookies in the kitchen," Kate said, hoping to distract her sons and prevent more awkward questions.

The twins gave a yell and headed for the kitchen.

"Be sure to leave your book bags on the counter," she called after them. She turned to Jack and barely stopped herself from walking right back into his arms. "We'll miss you."

"I'll miss all of you, too."

Kate waited for a last kiss, a final hug. But Jack was keeping his distance. She needed to tell him about Wyatt Shaw's ultimatum and ask for his help. "There's something I need to talk to you about."

"Can it wait, honey? I need to check in with my captain before I leave town and I've got some packing to do. We'll have three hours to talk while I'm on the road to Houston tonight. If I don't get out of here, I'm going to want to hold you again." He grabbed his Stetson from the table by the door and settled it low on his forehead.

Kate was torn. Her fear of Wyatt Shaw warred with her fear of what Jack would think of her when he knew the truth. "Jack, I wish—"

"Goodbye, Kate." He kissed her hard and walked out the door.

And ran right into Wyatt Shaw.

5

"Did my father send you here?" Wyatt snarled at Jack, as the two men faced off on Kate's covered front porch.

"Hell, no!" Jack retorted. "What are you doing here?"

"None of your damn business," Wyatt said.

Kate's blood ran cold as she watched Wyatt and Jack face off like vicious junkyard dogs claiming the same territory. She was shocked by their verbal exchange, which suggested the two men knew each other.

Wyatt shot Kate a veiled look, then said to Jack, "You tell D'Amato to keep his nose out of my business."

"Tell him yourself," Jack said as he backed his way down her front steps, never taking his eyes off Shaw.

Kate felt like she was watching a movie in a foreign tongue with no translation under the picture. She was both confused and terrified. It seemed Wyatt thought Jack, a man wearing the uniform and badge of a Texas Ranger, took orders from his father, the mob boss. And Jack was playing along.

The explanation came to her in a flash.

Jack is on some kind of undercover assignment for

the Rangers. Wyatt has seen him talking in private with D'Amato and made the assumption that Jack is on his father's payroll.

It was the only thing that made sense. Jack had to be working—or pretending to work—for D'Amato, collecting enough information about the mobster's criminal activities to put him behind bars.

Why hadn't Jack simply told Shaw that he and Kate were romantically involved?

Because if Jack is working undercover for the mob, it might put me and my sons in danger.

Kate shuddered at the thought of what D'Amato might do to Jack—or to those Jack loved—if he learned the Texas Ranger was still one of the good guys.

"Did he hurt you?" Wyatt asked.

"Of course not!"

"Did he ask you any questions about the twins?"

"Why would he?"

Wyatt frowned. "You said you were dating a Texas Ranger. Is he the one you're seeing? The one you're planning to marry?"

Kate's heart pumped a burst of adrenaline into her bloodstream. Should she tell Shaw the truth? Or lie? She decided on the literal truth. "I may have exaggerated my relationship to Jack," she said. "Under the circumstances, it seemed safer to say I was involved with another man."

"You're not engaged?"

"No. I'm not involved romantically with anyone at the moment. Jack's just a friend."

"What was he doing here?" Wyatt demanded.

"He came to see how I'm doing, now that I'm home

from rehab. Jack and his parents were kind enough to take care of the twins at his ranch while I was in a coma and for the past six weeks while I've been recuperating. You do know that I was shot in the arm and the chest last October, and that I was in a coma for four months?"

He nodded curtly. "I assumed your parents kept the twins."

Kate shook her head. "My mother was in delicate health—pregnant with a late-in-life baby—so Jack stepped in."

Wyatt followed Jack's progress, his eyes narrowed, till he reached his SUV, then turned back to face her. Jack shot her an anxious look behind Wyatt's back that asked, *What the hell is he doing here?*

Apparently, he couldn't stay and demand answers from her without blowing whatever cover he'd established for himself as one of Dante D'Amato's minions.

In a raspy voice too soft for Jack to hear, Shaw said, "Did you tell him?"

"Tell him what?"

"Don't play dumb. Did you tell him the twins are mine?"

"No, I didn't." But she'd come very close.

"Thank God for that."

Kate blanched as she realized why Shaw was so upset. He thought Dante D'Amato had also discovered the truth about who'd fathered the twins and sent Jack here to get Kate to confirm or deny what he'd heard.

"By the time my father knows for sure that Lucky and Chance are my sons," Shaw said, "I'll have you all somewhere he can't get to you."

"I'm not going anywhere with you," Kate said, her voice sharp with fear. "Neither are my sons. Why should your father be any threat to us? I would think he'd be glad to know he has grandchildren."

"You don't know Dante D'Amato."

Kate glanced toward where she'd last seen Jack, but his SUV had already disappeared down a small hill under a canopy of live oaks. Why had he abandoned her with Shaw? Was protecting his cover more important than protecting the woman he loved and her children from someone with Wyatt Shaw's reputation?

It must be.

Or maybe the best way to protect her was to pretend not to be romantically involved with her. Which gave her way too much food for thought.

Kate stood with a hand on either side of the doorway, blocking Shaw's entrance, and said in a cold voice, "I told you not to come back."

"Let me in, Kate."

It was a command, pure and simple. Kate's neck hairs rose. "Go away. I don't want you here."

"I know the twins are home. I intend to see them."

She tried slamming the door in his face, but he caught it again with his hand.

"We're not going through this again, are we?"

Kate realized she wasn't physically capable of keeping him out. She was trying to think of an argument that would convince him to go away when Lucky and Chance came barreling into the living room.

"Mom! Chance is cheating at Mario Brothers Galaxy on the Wii!" Lucky complained. "He won't give me my turn."

"I was not!" Chance said, shoving Lucky in the back. "You're just afraid I'll beat you."

Lucky turned and socked Chance in the shoulder.

Kate left Shaw standing where he was to intervene between her sons. "Chance! Lucky! Stop that right now!"

Shaw moved into the open doorway behind her, where she knew he could see the fracas.

Kate grimaced. Her sons weren't making a very good first impression on their father. "We have company," she announced.

But Chance had already tripped Lucky, who turned and grabbed Chance's school uniform shirtfront on the way down. Both boys landed hard on the floor. They rolled, hitting at each other with their fists and knocking into the furniture with their thrashing feet.

Kate wished she could tell Shaw that this behavior was unusual. But ever since she'd come home from rehab, they'd roughhoused like this at least once a day. She supposed Jack must have tolerated this sort of behavior over the past four months while the boys had been living at his ranch house.

"That's enough."

Kate watched as her sons' heads snapped toward the door. She wondered whether it was the mere sound of a male speaking, or the stern, no-nonsense tone of Wyatt's voice, that had gotten their attention.

They untangled themselves and sat up, staring at the stranger who'd spoken.

Wyatt closed the door behind him and crossed to stand beside her. She knew he was waiting for her to introduce him to her—their—sons. "Come over here," she said gently. "There's someone I'd like you to meet."

That wasn't true. She didn't *like* anything about this situation. But she figured this traumatic moment in her sons' lives would be less devastating if she orchestrated it.

The twins never took their curious gazes off Shaw. A quick glance at Shaw revealed that his gray eyes were focused intently on Lucky and Chance. His impenetrable gaze gave nothing away, but Kate could see the tension in his shoulders, the muscle that worked in his jaw. She felt a moment of guilt for depriving him of knowing his sons and quickly squelched it.

Wyatt Shaw was a ruthless man capable of anything, maybe even murder. Just because the police hadn't found enough evidence to arrest him didn't mean he wasn't guilty of strangling that poor woman with his bare hands. Could he possibly be as innocent as his expensive lawyer had told the press he was? If Shaw hadn't killed that woman, who had? And why had she been found in his bed?

Kate couldn't believe the direction her thoughts had taken. She was realizing, far too late, that just because this stranger had been gentle with her during the night they'd spent together, didn't mean he wasn't a killer.

"Mom?" Chance said anxiously.

Kate flushed when she realized she'd been staring at Shaw—perhaps with the fear she was feeling showing in her eyes. She took a deep breath and said, "This is Wyatt Shaw. Mr. Shaw is…"

Kate's throat suddenly constricted. How was she supposed to introduce him? It seemed too abrupt to baldly announce to her sons that this man was their biological father. She turned to Shaw, looking for help. She found no sympathy in his steel-gray eyes. She realized she would rather tell the boys herself than have Shaw say the words, which he surely would, if she didn't speak them soon.

Kate turned back to her sons and saw the innocence Shaw was forcing her to steal. She took a deep breath and said, "Mr. Shaw is—"

"I'm an old friend of your mother's," Shaw interrupted.

Kate shot a surprised—and grateful—look in Shaw's direction.

"I'm Lucky," Lucky said, holding out his hand to be shaken.

Kate watched as Wyatt solemnly took his son's hand. Shaw's hand completely enveloped the smaller one. His hold lingered long enough that Lucky pulled free.

"I'm Chance." Chance thrust his hand out to be shaken.

This time Wyatt let go before the boy felt the need to pull away.

"Is it all right if we go play on the Wii again, Mom?" Lucky asked.

Kate turned to Wyatt, wondering if he wanted to talk further with the boys. He met her gaze, the look in his eyes still obscure, and gave the slightest nod of agreement. She turned back to her sons and said, "Can you do it without fighting?"

The twins exchanged grins, then turned to her and simultaneously said, "You bet."

"All right. Another half hour. Then you need to go wash your hands for supper."

Kate waited for the boys to disappear before she turned back to Shaw. "You've met them. Now I'd like you to leave."

"Is that normal behavior?"

Kate bristled at the implied criticism but forced herself to stay calm. She refused to care what Wyatt Shaw thought. He wasn't going to be around long enough for it to matter. She shrugged and said, "They're boys."

"You allow them to fight like that in the house?"

She opened her mouth to explain that the twins' behavior was more rambunctious now than it had been before her accident and snapped it shut again. She would *not* apologize to this man for anything her sons did.

"I've made arrangements to fly the three of you to Houston tonight," he said. "You'll be living with me. You should pack a few bags with whatever you need for tonight and maybe tomorrow. I'll be providing everything you need from now on."

Kate felt as though he'd punched her in the gut. It took a moment to recover enough air to speak. "You can just tear up the tickets, because we're not going anywhere."

A smile flickered across his face. "We're traveling on my private jet."

"I have a job here. I have to earn a living."

"Not anymore. I'll be taking care of any expenses associated with my sons. And their mother, of course."

"I enjoy my work," Kate said angrily.

"You enjoy providing physical therapy to amputees at Brooke Army Medical Center?"

"Yes!" she said, unsettled that Wyatt knew what she did and where she worked. "You can see how special—and unique—my work is. I can't do it just anywhere or with just anyone."

"You can find a comparable job at M.D. Anderson."

Kate gasped. "Jobs like mine don't grow on trees."

"They'll give you a job."

"What makes you so sure?" she demanded.

"I'm a benefactor."

"Oh, so you'll *buy* me a job, is that what you're saying?"

"You're the one who said you wanted to work. I told you, there's no need."

"I don't want your money. I make enough to support us."

"My sons are entitled to whatever I can give them," Wyatt said. "And I can give them more than this." He gestured around her tiny living room.

She could understand the male need to be the provider. But she was stung by his disdain for her home, which was filled with love, even if it was small. She lifted her chin and said, "There's more to being a good parent than living in a big house."

"Thanks to you, I wouldn't know about that," he shot back.

"What makes you think you can be a good father to my sons?" she challenged.

"I'm sure you'll let me know where I go wrong."

"You have an answer for everything."

"There's nothing you can say to make me change my mind."

Kate made a rumbling sound of frustration. There

was another very good reason she didn't want to go anywhere near Houston and M.D. Anderson. Holly would be living and working there. But she wasn't about to mention that to Shaw.

"The boys attend a good school."

"There are good schools in Houston."

"Their friends are here."

"They can make new friends."

"You mean they're going to be allowed to socialize with other human beings," Kate said sarcastically. "I thought we were going to be hiding behind high stone walls."

"Now you're being absurd."

Kate fought the tears that threatened. She gripped her hands together to keep him from seeing how badly they were trembling. "I'm happy living here. I don't want to move."

"You can't stay here," Wyatt said flatly. "It's not safe. Your Texas Ranger friend isn't going to be any help to you. He's proved his loyalty to my father."

Kate wondered what Jack had done to prove his loyalty to the mob boss. It didn't bear thinking about. "I can hire protection," she said.

"It won't be enough."

"Who says?"

"You don't even have a garage for your car. It would be easy to put a bomb in it."

Kate felt gooseflesh rise on her arms. "Who would do such a thing?"

He didn't answer her, just lifted a brow and let her imagine the worst. Which she easily did.

Kate was startled by a hard knock on the door. Her

heart leapt with the hope that Jack had returned. His name was already on her lips, when the door swung open with a bang.

A giant with the face of a gargoyle stepped inside.

"Oh, God!" Kate cried. She turned to run toward the bedroom, where the boys were playing, but Shaw grabbed her around the waist and yanked her back tight against his chest. His other hand came up to cover her mouth but never closed over it.

"Don't scream," he warned.

Kate whimpered, but she didn't scream. She wasn't sure she could have, because all the air had been frightened out of her lungs. She remained silent because she didn't want to draw Lucky and Chance into the living room to witness her death.

"If you're going to kill me," she said in a shaky voice, "I'd rather you didn't do it in front of my sons."

"Boss?" the big man said, his scarred brow furrowing.

"It's all right, Bruce," Shaw said. "I think Mrs. Pendleton thought my father sent you to take care of both of us." He angled Kate's chin so she could see his face and said, "I asked Bruce to join us."

Kate sagged in Wyatt's arms and put a hand to her mouth to hold back a sob of relief. Tears brimmed in her eyes and she blinked them back. "Why?" she gasped.

"What?"

"Why did he burst in here like that?"

"Bruce was waiting outside in the limo with my driver. I told him to give me fifteen minutes and join us."

"It's all right, ma'am," Bruce said. "I'm here to

protect you. Actually, I'm going to be keeping an eye on the Boss's kids." He glanced at Shaw, smiled crookedly and said, "I think the Boss is going to be keeping an eye on you himself."

A polite giant. Who knew?

Kate would have laughed, except her throat was still choked with leftover terror.

"Can you stand if I let you go?" Shaw asked, easing her feet back onto the ground.

Kate's legs were limp noodles. The instant Shaw set her down, she stumbled away from him and turned to face both men. "You had this planned from the beginning," she said bitterly. "I never had any choice in the matter, did I?"

"No."

"What if I refuse to go with you?"

"You can stay. But the boys are coming with me."

Kate was horrified. "They won't leave the house without me, not without a fight."

"Whatever it takes, they're coming with me."

Kate realized what he was saying. "You'd use force on your own sons?"

"I'd rather not," he admitted.

But he would. He'd obviously brought the big man in to help him manhandle the twins, if that became necessary. Kate felt panicked. She glanced toward the landline in the living room, but knew she wouldn't have time to dial 911 before Shaw stopped her. Maybe she could call for help when she was in her bedroom supposedly packing.

"Don't even think it," Shaw said.

"What?"

"Don't think about calling the police. Or anyone else. I promise you, you'll regret it."

It was a threat that left everything to her imagination. Which was working overtime.

"Call the twins back in here," Shaw said. "We need to tell them what's going on. Then Bruce will help them pack."

"What about me?"

"Are you coming?"

Her mind was racing, trying to think of a way out of the trap Shaw had sprung. But she—and her sons— were well and truly caught. "What's to keep me from calling the police later? I mean, if I'm going to be allowed to work, I'm not always going to be stuck behind high stone walls."

He didn't even dignify her question with an answer.

He would have an explanation ready that would satisfy the police. And he had a secret weapon. He was the twins' father. He could prove it, if need be. He might seek joint custody or, if she became too troublesome, sole custody of the twins.

And he had the money to make it all happen.

Her family was wealthy, and she knew both her grandfathers would be happy to fight Shaw. But a nasty legal fight like that was bound to impact her sons' lives. And not in a good way.

She met Wyatt's implacable gaze and said, "Suppose I go with you willingly and give Lucky and Chance a reason for this visit that will keep them from hating your guts. When is this forced imprisonment going to end? When is it going to be safe for my sons to come back home?"

His answer was blunt and uncompromising. "From now on, their home will be with me."

6

"I need cash, Mother. I'm tapped out."

Ann Wade Pendleton pursed her lips as she stared at her wayward son. She'd received some shockingly bad news this morning and had abandoned the campaign trail for her ranch in Midland, Texas, seeking solitude to think about what she should do. Surprise, surprise, she'd discovered J.D. hiding out at the ranch, which boasted far more oil wells than cattle.

Luckily, she'd kept her Secret Service contingent out of the house, so knowledge of her "dead" son's presence, and the public relations disaster that would have resulted, had been narrowly averted.

She could remember being glad, as her only son grew from a boy into a man, that he'd inherited his father's good looks and athletic ability. J.D. was tall and blond and blue-eyed. He'd become a star football player. He'd also learned at the master's knee how to charm a woman, how to lie to her and cheat on her and still smile at her without a hint of guilt.

She almost didn't recognize the gaunt figure with shaggy blond hair and sunken blue eyes who sat slumped in the studded black leather chair across from her. The charm was long gone. What she saw in her son's eyes was desperation. And despair.

She contemplated the road to J.D.'s downfall from her seat behind the ancient oak desk where her deceased husband had kept track of his dwindling fortune. Dwindling because Jonas David Pendleton, Jr. had gambled his oil money on every half-assed harebrained investment scheme that came along. Another trait he'd passed along to his son.

J.D. had married a woman with enough money to keep them living in luxury their entire lives and had frittered it away in a few years. It was her son's enormous unpaid gambling debts that had gotten him into trouble with D'Amato, and given the mobster the leverage he needed to involve J.D. in the brokering of guns for heroin that had led to her son's ruin.

Ann Wade settled farther back into the oversize chair made of polished cow horns and covered in black-and-white spotted cowhide and asked her son, "What happened to the quarter million I gave you last fall?"

"It's expensive to stay invisible, Mother. Bribes. Payoffs. Blackmail. And the sons of bitches found me in Brazil anyway. I was lucky to escape with my life."

Ann Wade's insides wrenched when her son reached toward the festering scab on his face where a bullet had gouged a path through his flesh. Fortunately, he dropped his hand before touching it.

"Actually, getting shot is the least of my worries," J.D. said. "I think Dante D'Amato has something far worse than a bullet to the brain in mind if he ever runs me down. Probably a bullet in each knee and two in my balls—for a start."

"Why don't you give him back the heroin he told me you stole from him?" Ann Wade said.

"He's already made it clear it's too late for that. Besides, I don't have it anymore."

"What happened to it?"

"I stowed it in a cargo container on the deck of a tramp steamer. The container went overboard during a hurricane. What are the chances?" he said ruefully.

Ann Wade knew her son wasn't as nonchalant as he was trying to appear. Besides the infected-looking scab across his left cheek, he had another bullet wound in his thigh that hadn't yet healed. The hitmen D'Amato had sent to hunt him down had left her son wounded and shaken.

She wasn't so sanguine herself. She was practically a shoo-in to be selected as her party's next presidential candidate. Everything could fall apart in a heartbeat if J.D.'s criminal activities, not to mention the fact that he'd faked his death and deserted his post in wartime, became known. God forbid the public learned that she'd paid her son an extortionate amount of cash to disappear.

She could understand why some mothers ate their young.

"This can't continue, J.D. You have to come to some accommodation with D'Amato."

"You have twenty million dollars to spare?"

"No, I don't!" she snapped. "It's bad enough that I've had to keep the Texas attorney general off D'Amato's back since that mobster found out you're still alive. I was able to justify that by saying D'Amato is the federal government's problem, not ours. I even managed to reassign Jack McKinley, the Texas Ranger hottest on D'Amato's trail, as a bodyguard for my grandsons. But I don't like being blackmailed by that conniving bastard."

Ann Wade patted at her short, perfectly coifed blond hair and pressed her lips together to smooth her pink lipstick, both activities that helped her to calm down. It was never a good idea for a woman in politics to show too much emotion. But she was seriously annoyed with her son.

"I shudder to think what that scoundrel might expect from me once I'm president," she said. "You need to disappear, J.D. Somewhere I can be sure D'Amato will never find you."

So long as her son was alive and about in the world, D'Amato had a very large sword to dangle over her head. Once she was president, any accusations D'Amato made without J.D.'s body in hand could be explained away.

J.D.'s casket in Arlington Cemetery was empty because there had supposedly only been enough of his body left after the ammo dump explosion to identify his remains through DNA. J.D. had given the sample of his DNA, along with a great deal of cash, to the lab tech making the identification. So, no body, no proof her son had survived.

J.D. made a disgusted sound in his throat and shoved himself onto his feet, limping over to the wet bar. "So nice to know you care, Mother."

Ann Wade watched as J.D. poured himself a Dewar's and drank it down, then poured another double shot, drank it and carefully set down his glass.

He turned to her and said, "What did you have in mind for me to do? I tried disappearing. It didn't work."

"Then perhaps you should stop running and start fighting back."

"How?"

"You're the demolitions expert. Figure it out." If D'Amato was dead, it would solve both their problems.

"D'Amato has a half-dozen bodyguards around him at all times. His home in Houston is impregnable. His cars are kept in underground garages. He has no family left except that bastard son of his, and Wyatt Shaw has security even tighter than his father's." He cracked his knuckles, then added, "Well, there may have been a loophole or two, but those have been closed since that hooker was found strangled in his bed."

"And you know all this how?"

"I'm not as dumb as you think, Mother. You're not the first one to consider blasting the problem out of existence." He poured himself another drink and gulped half of it down.

Ann Wade almost smiled. There were some things J.D. had learned from her. Shrewdness. Guile. And a willingness to do the hard thing.

She loved her son, but right now, J.D. was a loose end that could cost her the presidency. And his situation was unfraying before her eyes.

She debated whether to tell him the shocking news she'd heard this morning from Harry Dickenson's assistant, who was going through his deceased boss's open files to make final reports to Harry's clients. She should've known that her bitch of a daughter-in-law would find a way to stab her in the back. Her grandsons, who'd been such assets in the political arena, had become definite liabilities.

Her eyes narrowed. "I have some unpleasant news I need to share with you."

J.D. groaned. "Save it."

"This is important. It relates to our other problem." She smiled as she realized her own play on words, "In fact, it's *directly related* to our other problem."

He swallowed the rest of the Dewar's in his glass and said, "Get to the point, Mother."

Upset at his rude interruption, Ann Wade said bluntly, "Lucky and Chance aren't your sons."

"The hell you say!" J.D. limped his way over to her from the bar, his unshaven face blotchy with the blood that had rushed there. "That isn't funny, Mother."

"No, it isn't," she agreed, curling her hands around the smooth horn arms of the chair. "And you haven't even heard the best part." She sat forward and looked up at him. "Wyatt Shaw is their father."

The glass dropped from J.D.'s hand and rolled across the Turkish carpet under the desk, before clattering along the pegged oak floor all the way to the wall.

"You're shitting me," J.D. said.

"I promise you, it's the truth. I found out the twins weren't your sons when Lucky needed a blood transfusion earlier this year. Kate was in a coma, so the hospital sought permission from me to treat him. Which is how I found out his blood type is A positive, an impossibility if the twins were yours."

"How did you find out Shaw is their father?"

"I hired a very good private investigator, Harry Dickenson. Harry's assistant called me this morning to tell me he found copies of DNA tests that prove Shaw fathered the twins. The assistant was calling because Harry was killed after he met with Shaw."

"Shaw had him killed?"

"Who knows? He was hit by a garbage truck that ran a red light outside Shaw's office in downtown Houston."

"Has Shaw contacted Kate?"

"I don't know that he has, but we have to presume that he will."

"Oh, shit."

"What has me concerned is the possibility that Dante D'Amato has—or will—discover the truth."

"Holy shit."

"Precisely my feeling," Ann Wade said.

"Goddamn it all to hell," J.D. said angrily, stomping back to the bar, where he found another glass and poured himself another double shot of Dewar's.

"I'm not any happier about this than you are," Ann Wade said. "Do you realize what this means?"

"My wife was fucking another man the same time she was fucking me."

"I was thinking more about the additional ammunition this will give D'Amato when he comes asking for more favors."

"This is all that bitch's fault," J.D. muttered.

Ann Wade didn't bother to point out that J.D. had been playing the same game as his wife. Except, no unexpected children had shown up on his doorstep. Yet.

"What happens now?" J.D. asked, shoving a hand through his stringy blond hair.

"I think the solution to both our problems is obvious."

"Kill D'Amato. Kill Shaw. Kill both the bastards dead."

"Can you do it?" she asked. "Or arrange to have it done?"

"Sure. If I had enough cash."

"How much?"

"Fifty thousand," J.D. said. "But the minute you make a withdrawal like that, D'Amato's going to hear about it and start looking over his shoulder for a hired assassin."

"I've got that much in the safe here at the ranch."

"Then I can manage the rest. I plan to—"

"I don't give a good goddamn how you make this all go away, J.D.," she interrupted brusquely. "Just get it done."

Because if he didn't, she would take care of the problem herself. The entire problem.

7

"This plane is *bad!*" Lucky said, grinning broadly as he stepped inside Wyatt's luxurious Gulfstream 550 business jet.

By which Wyatt knew his son meant the plane was "neat" or "cool" or one of the myriad other phrases his generation had used to sound "hip."

"It's a jet, stupid," Chance said as he clambered onto the camel-colored leather couch that took up part of one wall toward the rear of the plane. He leaned over to peer through a porthole window and said, "How far can we fly before we have to stop, Mr. Shaw?"

"She'll go seven thousand seven hundred and fifty nautical miles without a fill-up," Wyatt replied with a smile. He was going to have to think of something else to have his sons call him besides "Mr. Shaw." And he would rather his sons didn't call each other stupid. But there would be plenty of time to correct them, after they learned he was their father.

And that he loved them. Had loved them from the moment he'd seen their images in a photograph and learned of their existence. And that he would always love them. For themselves, of course, and because they had brought him back together with their mother.

Wyatt had felt poleaxed when he'd realized that the mother of his children was the woman with whom he'd spent a single, life-altering night nine years before. That woman had shared herself without holding back, then stolen away like a thief in the dark, taking his heart with her.

He shouldn't have been surprised when the anonymous woman disappeared or when she was impossible to find. He'd felt the rings on her finger the moment she'd grasped his hand. He'd known she was someone else's wife, that she'd chosen him at random for a night of sex. He hadn't asked her reasons and she hadn't offered any.

He hadn't asked her name or given her his.

She'd nearly chickened out when the elevator doors opened on the penthouse floor. Her chin had wobbled, and she'd looked up at him with anxious blue eyes. He'd led her directly to the bedroom, hoping that her nerve would hold a little longer.

The bed had already been turned down, and the only light on the pure white sheets had come from the full moon outside. He'd taken her in his arms while she was still fully clothed and felt her tremble in his embrace. She'd made a mewing sound as he slid his open hand down to her hips and pulled her close enough to feel the heat and hard length of him.

But she didn't try to pull free. Instead, she breathed in the scent of him as she slid her palms up over his shoulders. He could remember feeling gooseflesh rise on his arms as she teased her fingers through the hair that fell onto his nape and then tugged his head down toward hers.

He remembered the soft weight of her breasts, and then their pebbled tips against his chest, as she leaned into him and raised her lips for his kiss.

That first kiss—

"Wow!" Chance said, tugging on Wyatt's hand and putting an abrupt end to his erotic daydream. "We could probably go all the way to China in this plane!"

"Yes, we could," he agreed. Before he could say more, the boy was off to investigate more of the plane.

Wyatt's gaze shot to the door. He'd boarded after the twins but before Kate, who'd stayed behind with Bruce to remove some items from her luggage before it was loaded into the baggage compartment. He wondered what was holding her up.

He'd taken off his suit jacket and tie, loosened the top couple of buttons on his shirt and folded up the sleeves. He was standing slightly hunched near the cockpit door, so his head didn't hit the 6'2" ceiling. It was the only thing he didn't love about the sixty-million-dollar jet, which had actually taken him to China and back several times over the past six months. Unfortunately, the next size up jet with the headroom he needed was a Boeing 737.

Kate suddenly appeared in the doorway. She glared at him—a far cry from the yearning look he'd been re-membering—then glanced over her shoulder at Bruce, who was bringing up the rear, a massive obstacle Wyatt had put there to keep her from grabbing the boys at the last minute and making a break for it. Now that he knew Jack McKinley was the man Kate had expected to protect her, it was even more important to keep her behind high stone walls. Jack had already proved his willingness to kill for Dante D'Amato by eliminating a snitch.

"Mom, wait'll you see this!" Lucky said from the aft section of the 550. "There's a whole kitchen. And a bathroom with a counter and a mirror and a closet for clothes."

"The kitchen on a plane is called the galley," Wyatt said.

"Mom, come see the galley." Lucky scampered back to grab Kate's hand and tugged her all the way inside the plane, then got behind her and literally shoved her down the aisle so she could see the galley, which was designed for hot meal service. For the very short flight, Wyatt had stocked hot Papa John's pizza and ice-cold Cokes for the kids and chilled Cristal Champagne he planned to offer Kate.

"Lucky, look!" Chance exclaimed as he spotted several screens mounted near a tabletop. "A computer! And a DVD player!"

Lucky pounded back down the center aisle between the couch and a row of two facing seats with a table between them, to the front of the jet. He looked up at Wyatt, his blue eyes bright with excitement, and said, "Do you have any games we could play or movies we could see, Mr. Shaw?"

"I have both," Shaw said. "They're in that cupboard." Wyatt pointed to a cupboard built in along the wall near the tabletop above which the DVD screen was mounted. "I think there might be a few movies in there you'd like." He'd picked them out himself, based on what he remembered liking as a kid and what the reviewers said were appropriate movies for young children.

The two boys dropped to the carpeted floor, yanked open the cupboard door and riffled through the games and DVDs.

Wyatt was entranced by their exuberance. He glanced up and met Kate's stark gaze at the opposite end of the plane. He saw the flicker of panic in her eyes and followed her gaze to where Bruce was locking the door to the Gulfstream, barring Kate's last avenue of escape before they landed at the private airstrip near his compound north of Houston.

"Folks, we're cleared for takeoff," the pilot drawled over the intercom in a thick East Texas accent. "Please take your seats and buckle your seat belts."

The twins ignored the announcement.

"You boys need to buckle in so we can take off," Wyatt said, tapping each boy on the shoulder. "The pilot will let us know when it's safe to move around again."

The twins each had a handful of DVDs when they stood.

"I'll hold those for you." Wyatt held out both hands.

Lucky looked to his mother, who nodded, before he handed over his loot. Chance followed suit. Wyatt stowed the DVDs they'd selected in an overhead compartment.

"Where should we sit?" Lucky asked Wyatt.

"I want you both where I can see you," Kate said, pointing to facing seats on the same side of the plane as the couch. Each boy grabbed one of the seats on opposite sides of a table and reached for the seat belt. Kate helped Chance, while Wyatt helped Lucky.

Kate shot him an aggravated look but didn't say anything.

She took a seat across from the twins. Wyatt took the seat opposite her, with a table separating them.

Bruce headed to the back of the plane, where he sat on one of the four club seats around what would be the dining table near the galley.

Wyatt tried to meet Kate's gaze, but she turned her face toward the boys and ignored him. She'd barely spoken a word since he'd given his ultimatum at her home, except to explain to the boys that they were going on a little vacation. Which suited him fine. At least she wasn't saying or doing anything to make Lucky and Chance dislike him.

Once they were at altitude, he got the boys settled watching *WALL-E,* where they were quickly engrossed. Bruce was in the galley fixing plates of pizza and handed Wyatt a can of soda for each of the boys.

Kate stepped into the aisle and intercepted him close to the galley. "I don't allow them to have carbonated beverages."

Wyatt grimaced. "What do they drink?"

"Water. Or lemonade, if you have that."

"It'll have to be water. Even with pizza?" he asked.

"Water is the perfect beverage, Mr. Shaw."

He set the Coke cans down on a nearby table and stuck his hands on his hips. *"Mr. Shaw?"*

She flushed. Her voice was low and intense and full of resentment. "How about Mr. Kidnapper? That fits."

"Look who's talking," he shot back, keeping his voice equally low, fighting the rage that rose every time he thought of all the years he'd lost with his sons.

"You're the one who kept my children hidden from me."

She didn't excuse herself again. Or argue the point. "What am I supposed to call you?"

"Wyatt. It's my name. Or Shaw, if it suits you."

"All right, Shaw. There, is that better?"

"Much. And I'd like my sons to call me something besides *Mr. Shaw.*"

"Please, Shaw, don't tell them you're their father," she pleaded. "Not yet. They're too young to understand all of this."

"I don't want the twins upset or frightened any more than you do. I can wait."

"Thank you."

He saw another flash of resentment before she lowered her gaze. Before he could express the resentment he was feeling at her resentment, she raised her eyes to his and said, "Why not have them call you Shaw, too, without the mister?"

He supposed that was a good compromise. "All right," he said grudgingly. At least until they knew the truth. By then he hoped they would want to call him Dad or Papa or Daddy. Because he was planning to spend the rest of his life being their father.

"Make yourself comfortable," he said to Kate, indicating one of two seats on either side of the table near the galley. He waited until she sat, then traded the Cokes for bottled water, crossed back to the boys, took off the caps and dropped the bottles into the recessed glass holders on each side of the table between them.

"Pizza's ready, Boss," Bruce called from the galley.

Kate rose. "Can I help?"

"Bruce and I can handle it," Wyatt said, returning down the aisle and putting a hand on her shoulder to encourage her to sit again.

She jerked away from his touch, crying out as she hit her hip against the table.

Lucky turned around in his seat. "Mom, are you all right?"

"Just bumped into the table," she called back in a falsely cheerful voice.

Wyatt was amazed that the boy was so aware of his mother. Not nearly so surprised that Kate had kept her injury from her sons. She was still obviously in pain, holding her lower lip in her teeth to keep from crying out again.

"You're hurt," he said softly.

She shook her head. "I'm fine. It's nothing."

He glanced at the spot on her hip she was rubbing gently with her fingertips. He could remember what that exact spot of skin near her hipbone looked like. He'd kissed it. And caressed it.

He met her gaze and saw from the troubled look in her eyes that she remembered, too. She shook her head as though to deny what she was feeling. Or perhaps to warn him that she had no intention of letting what had happened between them once happen ever again.

She sank back down, but he could feel her eyes on him as he headed the few extra steps to the galley to get the plates of pizza Bruce had prepared for the boys.

He wondered if Kate would be more amenable to the idea of him being a father to Lucky and Chance if she knew that he intended to spend the rest of his life with her as his wife.

Probably not.

Everything she'd said or done had made it clear that the sooner she was shed of Wyatt Shaw, the better. So how was he supposed to woo her? How was he supposed to win her heart?

Especially when he'd been accused of murder.

He wondered what she would do if he told her who he believed had actually strangled the woman found dead in his bed.

Likely call him a liar.

Until he found enough evidence to cast a giant shadow on that other party, he was going to remain the prime suspect in a murder investigation. So he could understand how she might be leery of him. He was ready for the fight he knew was coming when she realized what their sleeping arrangements were going to be at his ranch.

"How did you know pepperoni's my favorite, Mr. Shaw?" Lucky asked.

"It was a 'Lucky' guess," he said, ruffling the boy's hair. Amazing what a little detective work of his own had turned up about his sons. "And you can call me Shaw, without the Mister."

Lucky pointed with his pizza, which he'd picked up in his hands and said, "Oh, I get it. A 'Lucky' guess. Very funny, Shaw." He glanced at his mother and said, "That's all right, Mom, isn't it? He told me I could just call him Shaw."

"It's fine, sweetheart," Kate said.

Her voice sounded choked to Wyatt, and when he looked, he saw tears had brimmed in her eyes. What was that all about?

"You're missing the movie," Chance warned his brother.

Wyatt crossed back to Kate and said, "Hungry?"

"I think if I ate anything right now I'd throw up."

"How about something bubbly to settle your stomach," he suggested.

"Club soda sounds good."

He smiled wryly. "I was thinking of a glass of champagne."

She looked at him stony-faced and said, "I can think of nothing—*nothing*—about this moment I want to celebrate."

He leaned down and said through tight jaws, "There were two of us in that bed. You were as much responsible as I was for what happened there. We became parents that night. And you are not going to make me feel guilty for wanting to be a father to my sons!"

He stood up and said, "Bruce, pop open that bottle of champagne." When he looked down, he saw her eyes were once more brimmed with tears. He swallowed past the sudden lump in his throat and said, "I feel like celebrating."

8

The impressively high river-rock walls that separated Wyatt Shaw's ranch compound from the outside world were every bit as daunting as Kate had feared they would be. Her sons seemed not to notice when the beautiful black wrought iron electric gates, with the elaborate S in the center, closed behind them.

Lucky and Chance sat on either side of Shaw in the black stretch limousine that had picked them up at his private airfield, talking a mile a minute as they quizzed him about what he had planned for their "vacation."

"I have a stable full of horses," she heard him tell the boys. "But we can have your horses—"

"Big Doc," Lucky interjected.

"And Little Doc," Chance supplied.

She watched Shaw smile indulgently as he finished, "Big Doc and Little Doc can be trailered here from San Antonio by tomorrow, if you'd rather ride your own mounts."

"You'd do that? Really?" Lucky asked.

"Of course," Shaw said.

As though it cost nothing to trailer a couple of

quarter horses halfway across the state. It *was* nothing
to a wealthy man like Shaw, Kate realized.

"Can we bring our dog here, too?" Lucky asked.

"And our cat?" Chance added.

Shaw glanced quickly at Kate. "You have a dog
and a cat?"

"We got them for our birthday last year," Lucky
said. "We had them with us at Jack's ranch while Mom
was in the hospital. Jack's mom and dad, Uncle Frank
and Aunt Rose, have been taking care of them for us.
Harley and Scratch were supposed to come home this
weekend. They must be missing us like crazy—"

"Because we're missing them," Chance finished for
his brother. "Please say they can come stay with us here."

"I don't see why that couldn't be arranged," Shaw
said. "If it's all right with your mother."

"She doesn't mind, do you, Mom?" Lucky said.

"She loves Harley and Scratch," Chance said.

"Harley and Scratch?" Shaw repeated, eyeing Kate
dubiously.

"Harley's our black Lab," Lucky said. "He runs
really fast, like our dad's Harley-Davidson motorcycle."

"And Scratch…" Chance exchanged a chagrined
look with Lucky, then glanced up at Shaw. "Well, you
can guess how she got her name."

Shaw laughed. "I can't wait to meet them."

Kate was beginning to understand there was far
greater danger in having her sons spend time with Shaw
than she'd ever imagined. He was going to spoil them
rotten by giving them anything and everything their
hearts desired. Including the attention from a father
figure they were soaking up right now like sunshine.

He was going to make them love him.

They were never going to want to leave.

Several times since this journey had started, Kate had contemplated grabbing the twins and running as far and as fast as she could. But even now, the giant who'd introduced himself as the children's bodyguard followed in a smaller black limo behind them. There was no escape from this nightmare.

At least, not yet. She wrapped her hand around the cell phone in her Levi's pocket. She'd secretly tucked it there when she was packing. As soon as she had a moment alone, she was going to call Jack and tell him everything.

He would understand. And he would help her...if he could. Kate wasn't sure how Jack's undercover assignment was going to affect his ability to intervene. Especially in light of the fact the twins were Wyatt Shaw's biological sons.

She and her sons were captives for the moment, but Shaw wasn't going to be able to keep them behind these walls for long. The boys had to go to school. And Shaw had promised she could work. There would be opportunities for escape.

It might take some planning, but Wyatt Shaw would discover that she had weapons of her own with which to fight the war between them. Her grandfathers would help her. And her father and mother. And Jack would be there for her...when he wasn't taking care of his wife and son.

Kate felt sick. Did she dare bring the wrath of Wyatt Shaw down on her family? Or on Jack?

Maybe the best thing to do was wait Shaw out. Being a father was a novelty right now. How would he react if the two little boys got sick all over his carpet or were cranky because they were feverish? He might not find it so much fun playing parent when the twins turned stubborn and defiant. How would he respond if they were mischievous? Or downright mean to him? All of which she'd experienced with her sons in their short lives.

Once Shaw realized what being a parent was *really* all about, he might be as anxious to be rid of the twins as he'd been to have them come and live with him.

She could always hope.

The limo rolled to a stop in front of a sprawling, single-story house with white adobe walls and a red, barrel-tiled roof. Shaw's home was half-hidden by flowering bougainvillea and draped by gnarled live oaks that provided cool shade from the hot Texas sun.

Kate looked for windows, but didn't see any. She felt her heartbeat ratchet up. How could anyone bear to live in a place so shut off from the light? She would feel suffocated in a house like that.

A barrel-chested man in a long-sleeved plaid, western-cut shirt, worn blue jeans and cowboy boots opened the door to the limo and stood back as Shaw got out, the boys tumbling after him. Her sons headed straight for the German shepherd sitting beside him.

Kate's heart was in her throat, afraid the large dog would snap at them. When Shaw reached a hand back inside for her, she took it as the fastest way to get out of the limo.

"Be careful!" she warned the boys.

"Wolf won't hurt 'em, ma'am," the heavyset man said.

Despite his dangerous-sounding name, the dog sat

unruffled as her sons "oohed" and "aahed" and ran their hands over his furred head and back.

"This is Micah," Shaw said, introducing the man to Kate. "He takes care of the house. He's a terrific cook."

"Good to see you, Boss." The hired man turned to Kate and said, "You need anything at all, ma'am, just let me know."

"Thank you," Kate said.

Micah excused himself to help Bruce with their bags, which were in the trunk of the second limo. Wolf rose and followed him.

"Let's go inside," Shaw said to the twins. "I'll show you your rooms."

As though it was the most natural thing in the world, he slid an arm around Kate's waist and headed down the winding walkway that led to the front door. She went with him willingly, because her other choice was to make a scene in front of her sons.

The boys hop-skipped on the lush lawn beside Shaw to keep up with his long strides.

"You said *rooms,* Shaw," Lucky pointed out. "Does that mean I don't have to share a room with Chance?"

"Is that all right with you?" Shaw asked.

"It sure is!" Lucky backpedaled beside Kate as he crowed, "Mom, I'm gonna have a room of my own!"

"Me, too!" Chance shouted, running in circles on the lawn with his hands held out like an airplane.

Kate made a distressed sound that Shaw must have heard because he leaned close and said, "Any reason why that isn't a good idea? I just thought—"

"It's a fine idea," she snapped. "Any other wishes you plan to fulfill while we're here?"

"As many as I can," he snapped back. "I've got a lot of making up to do, as you well know."

"You're going to spoil them, Shaw."

"By giving them their own rooms?"

"And bringing their horses and their dog and their cat here."

"That doesn't sound like a hell of a lot," he said. "I would have liked to be the one to give them their first horse. Or their first dog."

"Or their first cat?"

"I hate cats."

Kate couldn't help it. She laughed.

"What's so funny, Mom?" Lucky asked.

"I tickled your mother's funny bone," Shaw said.

"I know Mom's really ticklish in the ribs," Chance said. "I didn't know she had a funny bone. Where is it?"

She looked helplessly at Shaw and laughed harder. It beat the heck out of crying.

Shaw chuckled. "I'll show you sometime." He opened the door to his home and gestured his sons inside.

Kate saw why there were no windows on the outside. The interior walls in the U-shaped house were made of windows that brought the outdoors inside. The patio in the center of the courtyard was shaded by a giant oak and graced with a waterfall burbling over stones into a pond dotted with blooming white water lilies.

Kate watched her sons move through Shaw's earth-toned bachelor living room, past the saddle-leather, man-size chairs and the plush, man-length couch, both situated in front of a stone fireplace that ran up to the cathedral ceiling, as though they were bird dogs hunting down the scent of a covey of quail.

They touched everything, the odd-shaped lamps, the Hopi Indian dolls, the pillows on the couch, letting their curiosity take them from item to item. They scuffed their feet across the colorfully patterned rug.

She waited for Shaw to tell them to back off, not to handle this, to leave that alone. But he said nothing. She searched his face, trying to discern what he was feeling. But he had his emotions well contained.

When the boys finally headed down a wide hallway off the living room, he followed them as though he were attached by an invisible string. She thought he might have forgotten she was there, so entranced was he with his sons.

She stood bemused for a moment, wondering if she should follow him or stay where she was.

He returned to the doorway and said, "The bedrooms are down this hall."

He waited for her, and she was grateful the hallway was wide enough for her to walk beside him without touching. She saw the boys had stopped and waited for him.

"Which room is mine?" Lucky asked.

"Which one is mine?" Chance asked.

"This is yours," he said to Lucky, pointing through a doorway. "And this is yours," he said to Chance, indicating the doorway next to it.

At first Kate thought there was a mirror in the wall between the two rooms. Then she realized that a double door had been cut in the wall between the two rooms, and that they were mirror images of each other. The boys could shut the door between their rooms for privacy, or leave it open if they wanted to play together.

While Kate watched, the two boys met in the doorway, then turned and grinned at Shaw, acknowledging the perfect beauty of the connecting doorway. Then they turned again to explore their separate rooms, which each held a twin bed, an end table and lamp and a desk with a computer. Flatscreen TVs hung on the wall of each boy's room, with a DVD player on a table beneath it stacked with many of the same movies she'd seen on the plane.

Kate smelled fresh paint. "When did you do all this?"

"I had a doorway cut between the rooms the day I found out about the twins."

Kate felt a shiver run down her spine. He'd planned this moment. He'd intended to have his sons living here. This was no *vacation* he'd organized for them. This was forever.

Kate glanced up at Shaw and at last saw some of the emotions he'd been so careful to hide. Triumph. And satisfaction.

"I hope my room is near the boys." So she could grab them when the time came and make her escape.

"You're sleeping in here." He opened the door to the room at the end of the hall and waited for her to enter.

Kate's heart skipped a beat when she realized he'd invited her into what was clearly his bedroom. A mystery novel lay half-read facedown on the end table. A picture of a woman with a young boy who she thought might be Shaw and his mother sat atop the chest of drawers. A shiny pair of black lizard cowboy boots, one a fallen soldier, sat at the base of a wardrobe.

"What is this?" she demanded.

"Didn't I mention it? You'll be sleeping with me."

9

When the boys began to bicker, Kate knew they were finally exhausted from the excitement of the day.

"Time for bed," she said.

"Aw, Mom," Chance said.

"I'm not tired," Lucky argued.

"Showers. Now."

"Do we have to, Shaw?" Lucky asked.

Kate was incensed that her son was looking to a stranger for permission. "Yes, you have to," she said sharply.

"You heard your mother," Shaw said.

Kate realized it wasn't until Shaw confirmed her demand that her sons obeyed her and trotted off to take showers in the bathroom across the hall. "I can handle this," she told Shaw, hoping he'd take the hint and leave.

"Let me stay."

He didn't plead, just stood there looking vulnerable. And virile. She knew she was being a fool. He was manipulating her again, using her soft heart against her. She put herself in his shoes and imagined what it would be like to discover you had two children you'd never known existed. How you'd want to be a part of everything they did from now on. It would take someone more cruel than she was to exclude him.

But that meant she was going to have to share the bedtime ritual she performed each night with her sons. She fought back the jealousy she felt. Her sons craved a father, and Jack had taken himself out of the picture for the next four months. She should be grateful Shaw was willing to step into the role.

"All right. Stay," she said.

"What should I do?"

She was amazed that a man as powerful as Wyatt Shaw could look so helpless. She retrieved a pair of boy's white briefs and a set of Batman pajamas out of the overnight bag she'd brought and handed them to him. "When Lucky comes out of the shower, dry him off and put these on him."

It occurred to her suddenly that Shaw might not know which twin was Lucky. She hadn't yet heard him address either one by name. She eyed him askance, wondering whether he would be able to tell which twin was which, since they were truly identical physically.

A moment later, the boys came running into the bedroom, naked and shrieking, towels flying behind them, tracking wet footprints on the tile floor.

Shaw turned to her, scowling, and said, "You had them circumcised?"

Kate had a sudden vision of a naked Shaw, who wasn't. J.D. had insisted on it. Flustered, she said, "Yes. And it's too late to undo it now. So live with it!"

Shaw grabbed Lucky and began briskly toweling his hair.

Kate called to Chance and began patting him dry. She glanced at Shaw and said, "How did you know which twin was Lucky?"

"It's obvious, isn't it?"

"Not to most people," she said, waiting while Chance pulled up his underwear, then holding out Superman pajama bottoms so he could step into them. The twins had often fooled their teachers and even their friends.

"Did you brush your teeth?" she asked Chance.

"Not yet."

"Both of you, back to the bathroom. Brush your teeth," Kate ordered.

"Aw, Mom," Chance said.

"Jeez, Mom," Lucky said. "Do we hafta?"

"Go," Shaw said.

They went.

While the twins ran back to the bathroom to brush their teeth, Kate asked Shaw, "So tell me, how did you know which twin was Lucky?"

"He was the first one in the room. He always leads. He's more confident, more brash. Chance thinks more, feels more, argues less."

Kate was surprised and pleased that he'd noticed those vital differences between the two boys. "I suppose those extra five minutes Lucky spent in the world before Chance arrived gave him a little more self-assurance."

"Or maybe you treat him differently because you know he's the elder," Shaw said.

"Maybe," Kate conceded.

When the boys returned from the bathroom and

bared their teeth in grimaces that passed for smiles, Shaw said, "Now what?"

"I usually read them a story."

Shaw's gaze slid anxiously to the bookcase. "Which one?"

"I want the one about Winnie the Pooh and the honey pot," Chance said.

"I want the one about Tigger," Lucky said.

Kate took out one book from A. A. Milne's four-book *Winnie-the-Pooh* collection for herself and handed another one to Shaw. "Lucky will show you which story he wants."

Both boys pulled down the covers and climbed into the twin beds on their own. Kate sat on the edge of Chance's bed, then looked over and nodded, to indicate Shaw should do the same. Then she began to read. She heard Shaw's raspy voice rise in falsetto as he pretended to be a bouncy Tigger.

The door between the two rooms remained open. Neither boy had wanted it closed.

Kate was disturbed to see that Shaw had her sons' favorite books shelved in both rooms. It frightened her that he knew so much about their likes and dislikes. His knowledge felt like an intrusion. These weren't his children.

Yes, they are, a nagging voice reminded her.

And it was clear he wanted—intended—to be a part of the twins' lives. He'd maneuvered her into coming here by hanging the threat of danger over their heads. But Kate was sure no physical danger from Dante D'Amato could be as ominous to her and her sons as Wyatt Shaw's desire to make a happy family out of them.

He planned to have her sleep in his bed, even though she'd told him she was involved with someone else. How could he expect her to feel safe closing her eyes at night, when he'd been accused of strangling the last woman who slept in his bed?

What else did you expect from the son of a mob boss, a man who's arrogant as sin and wealthy as hell?

Fortunately, Kate had known her share of arrogant, wealthy men. Her grandfathers, Blackjack and King, had given her good practice in coping with such behavior. The secret was to hold your ground. Because the minute you gave a man like that an inch, he took a mile and a quarter.

She was going to have to confront Shaw and lay down her own rules for what she was and wasn't willing to put up with while she and her sons were living in his house. And the sooner the better.

She finished the story she was reading, then stood and tucked the covers more firmly around Chance, up one side and down the other. Finally, she leaned down to kiss him on each cheek as she said, "Good night. Sleep tight."

He answered, "Don't let the bedbugs bite."

Ordinarily, that was the signal to turn out the light. But as she straightened, Chance said, "I want Shaw to tuck me in, too."

Kate felt forsaken. Her sons hadn't even met Wyatt Shaw twenty-four hours ago. Now their mother wasn't enough for them. They wanted Shaw's attention. The man had clearly ensorcelled them.

She kept the betrayal she felt out of her voice as she said, "I'll let him know."

She stood in the open doorway between the two bedrooms and watched as Shaw tucked the covers snugly around Lucky's body, first down one side and then the other, as Lucky had apparently instructed him to do. She observed her son, whose gaze stayed focused intently on Shaw, as though the man were an apparition that might disappear from his life, as J.D. had, if he closed his eyes.

When Shaw reached for the light, Lucky grabbed his wrist. "First you have to say, 'Good night. Sleep tight.' And then I have to say, 'Don't let the bedbugs bite.'"

She felt her breath catch as Shaw brushed a dark curl from his son's forehead and said, "Good night, Lucky. Sleep tight."

"Don't let the bedbugs bite, Shaw."

He reached over and clicked off the light. When he turned, Kate saw his eyes glistened with unshed tears.

Her voice was choked as she said, "Chance would like you to say good night to him, too."

Shaw crossed past her into the light as she stepped into the darkened room. She leaned over and kissed Lucky on each cheek. "Good night. Sleep tight," she whispered.

"Don't let the bedbugs bite," he whispered back.

Kate didn't wait to see Shaw perform the ritual again with Chance. She headed down the hall to the bedroom they were supposed to share. When she got to the door, she realized confronting Shaw in his bedroom would put her at a distinct disadvantage. She turned around and headed back to the living room, which was more neutral ground.

There was enough light from the hall to make her

way to a chair near the fireplace. She turned on a single lamp on an end table and sat down to wait.

It didn't take long for Shaw to find her.

"Why are you sitting in the dark?" He struck a long match and bent down to light the kindling in the fireplace, which crackled to life, creating flickering shadows of light. Then he crossed to a bar in the corner, hit a switch that created a soft light above it and poured himself a drink from a crystal decanter. "Can I make something for you?"

"No thank you."

He took a sip of whatever he'd poured before he returned and sat in the chair next to her. He sighed as he settled one ankle over the opposite knee.

"Are you comfortable now?" she said irritably.

"Yes, I am."

She stood and paced to the fireplace, where she turned and faced him, her arms crossed protectively over her breasts. "What is it you really want from me, Shaw? What has this charade today been all about? Are we really in danger? Or did you just make that up?"

He took a deep breath and let it out. He put his foot back on the floor, then leaned forward with his forearms on his knees, rolling the glass of liquor between his hands. He focused his gray eyes on **her** when he spoke. "I'm not sure what my father is going to do when he finds out about the twins. If it's anything like what he did when he found out about me, then yes, the danger is very real."

"What are you talking about?"

"My mother wasn't a bad woman, she just fell in

with a bad man. When she got pregnant, she realized she didn't want to raise her child anywhere near Dante D'Amato. So she ran.

"My father found her and kept her a virtual prisoner while she raised me. Eventually, he decided he didn't like the things she was teaching me—like the difference between right and wrong. So when I was twelve, he had my mother killed."

Kate hissed in a breath. "How do you know that?"

"I don't *know* it," he said bitterly. "I never even suspected it at first. It was only later that I realized what he'd done and why."

Kate didn't speak, didn't breathe, for fear he'd stop talking.

Shaw drank the rest of the alcohol in his glass and set it on the coffee table in front of him. He sat back in the chair and brushed his fingers through the wings of silver hair on either side of his head. "The moment my mother was dead, D'Amato took control of my life. He sent me to the most exclusive prep school he could find, then to Harvard."

He stood abruptly and walked the few steps to the fireplace, where he shoved the burning wood around with a metal tool, making sparks fly, then adjusted the screen in front of the fire. When he was done, he leaned back against the mantel and said, "I studied hard because I wanted to make him proud of me." He snorted. "I was pitifully starved for male attention. And I thought he cared about me."

"How do you know he didn't?"

She could feel the animosity radiating off of him as he snarled, "He just needed someone he could trust—

someone related to him—to keep his books doctored. His two legitimate sons were already running businesses for him. It wasn't until I graduated from Harvard that he told me what he expected from me.

"When I refused to be a part of his dirty business— it seems my mother had 'infected me' with a belief in the value of truth and honor—he called me 'an abomination' and cut me off without a penny."

Kate frowned. "But you're rich."

Shaw laughed nastily. "I had something to prove. The best part is, I never broke the law making my fortune. And he hates me for it."

"So D'Amato would hurt Lucky and Chance to get back at you?"

"Not in the way you're probably thinking. But right now, he doesn't have anyone to inherit his business. He didn't succeed with me, but he might see the twins as possible heirs. And I don't intend to give him the satisfaction."

"Oh, my God."

The fire was suddenly too warm. Kate moved away from the heat—away from Shaw—to sit on the couch. "So this is a game between you and your father, and we're the pawns?"

"Maybe I want to keep those two trusting boys from being victimized like I was."

"And maybe you just want to keep D'Amato from winning the game," Kate accused.

"Think what you like. You're here now, where I know you're safe."

He was too close. Too overpowering. *Too tempting.* She rose again and paced to the row of shelves containing a collection of Native American artifacts. With the distance of the room between them she turned and said, "I'm not going to sleep with you, Shaw."

"I doubt either one of us will get much sleep," he said with a lazy grin, as he sat on the arm of the couch.

"I don't find that the least bit amusing," she snapped. "This is a big house. I'm sure you have another bedroom I could use."

"Actually, I do."

Kate sighed with relief. "Good. Just point me in the right direction."

When Shaw stood, Kate thought he'd given in gracefully. But instead of directing her to another bedroom, he crossed to the shelves where she was standing and ran his fingers over the intricate beading on a pair of buckskin moccasins. Then he turned to her and said, "How about a little experiment before we go our separate ways?"

Kate was instantly wary. "What did you have in mind?"

"A kiss."

"No. Not just no, but hell no."

"What are you afraid of, Kate?"

"I'm not in the habit of kissing men I hardly know."

He raised a sardonic brow.

She flushed. "I was out of my mind with anger at J.D. the night you and I met."

"And yet you stayed with him for eight more years."

"He threatened to take my sons away from me if I tried to divorce him," she shot back. "I couldn't take that chance."

"There wasn't a night I didn't think of you," he

said as he closed the distance between them, "and imagine where you were. What you were doing."

"I don't believe you," Kate said, refusing to back away.

"I wondered if our night together was as transcendent for you as it was for me."

Kate gave an unladylike snort. *"Transcendent?* It was just damned good sex."

His eyes narrowed in anger and a muscle worked in his jaw.

So what if she'd made him mad? She had to belittle his memories. Otherwise, he might realize that she'd experienced the same thing: something rare and remarkable. And that knowledge would give him too much power over her.

One word from her about how *transcendent* their evening had been and Shaw would realize how vulnerable she still was to his animal magnetism. When she was anywhere near the man, she experienced an undeniable—and inexplicable—carnal response. It had to be some sort of evolutionary anomaly that made her extraordinarily susceptible to him sexually. To misquote a phrase, "His pheromones had her surrendering at hello."

As far as she was concerned, their *transcendent* night together was nothing more than a case of nature run amok.

Shaw was standing so close she could feel the heat of him, smell the alluring male musk that had filled her nostrils nine years ago. Those damned sexy pheromones! She closed her eyes and inhaled.

He made a guttural sound of need deep in his throat.

Kate felt her body come alive, every nerve ending

poised in expectation of his touch. She hungered for it. Had imagined it a hundred thousand times since the night they'd spent together. Would it—could it—possibly be as magical as she remembered?

She opened her eyes and looked up. His heavy-lidded gaze was focused on her, his gray eyes dark with barely tethered desire. She gasped as he roughly grasped her hair in his fist, angled her head back and captured her mouth with his.

It was a kiss of domination. And possession.

She could feel his need, taking her deep. An iron band circled her hips, and he held her captive as he plundered her mouth. She welcomed the rush of sensation that took her under. Her fingernails dug crescents in his shoulders as she held on for dear life.

Waves of feeling crashed over her, overwhelming rational thought. She was sucked down by a riptide of emotion that held her under for long, terrifying moments. She was afraid she would drown if she didn't claw her way back to the surface.

Shaw broke the kiss, and Kate gasped life-giving air. And then he took her under again.

She wasn't sure who reached for whose belt buckle first. She worked frantically on Shaw's while he yanked her belt free. They shoved off shoes as zippers slid down. Hands tore past layers of clothing searching for naked flesh.

Shaw stepped away from his clothes as he backed her against the wall. She kicked her jeans and underwear away, then wrapped her arms around his neck and latched on to his shoulder with her teeth as he lifted and impaled her. It took only a few thrusts before she felt herself cresting on a high wave of passion. She buried a cry of exultation against his throat and heard his guttural sound of satisfaction as he spilled his seed.

They clung to each other to keep from falling down, his lungs heaving like bellows, hers gasping for air. Then he eased her legs back down from where she'd wrapped them around his hips. Her legs were so boneless she might have slid down the wall if he hadn't held her upright with an arm around her shoulder.

Kate suddenly felt cold, as a draft of air-conditioning reached the sweat that dotted her skin. She raised a trembling hand to Shaw's stubbled cheek, but before it got there, he turned his head and kissed her palm.

It was the gesture of a lover for his beloved.

But this wasn't the man she loved.

She wondered if her eyes showed the despair she felt. She swallowed over the knot of misery and guilt in her throat and said, "I don't know why this happens with you. It isn't love. It can't be anything good, because—"

"Because I'm a bad man?"

"Let go of me," she said. "I want to get dressed."

Instead, he scooped her up in his arms. "There's no sense putting on clothes, when I'll just want to take them off again."

Kate knew she should kick and scratch. She should shriek and rage. But she lay her head on his muscular shoulder and let him carry her down the hall to his bedroom. For the second time after making love to this man, tears brimmed in her eyes and slipped onto her cheeks.

She'd tried to resist him. And failed. Tomorrow would be soon enough to begin the fight again.

10

Jack tried several times to reach Kate by phone as he drove the two hundred or so miles from San Antonio to Houston Friday night. Before he'd left the house that afternoon, she'd mentioned she wanted to talk to him, so he was surprised that she hadn't answered his calls. He'd left three messages on her answering machine, one each hour of his drive.

He had some things he wanted to ask her. Like why Wyatt Shaw had turned up on her front doorstep. It was possible she'd met the billionaire at some charity function sponsored by her family. Her grandfather, Jackson Blackthorne, had his fingers in a great many pies. But if so, why hadn't she mentioned her acquaintance with such a notorious man?

He was also sure Kate was going to want an explanation of what he was doing for Dante D'Amato, since Shaw had insinuated he worked for his father. Jack hadn't yet figured out what he could—or should— safely say to explain his connection to the mob.

Jack tried to imagine why Kate might still be out of the house at half past ten. Maybe she or one of the boys had been hurt and she was at a 24-hour clinic. Or maybe her mother, Libby, was in labor with the late-in-life baby she was expecting. Kate had promised to travel to Austin to take care of her much younger siblings, Houston and Dallas, while her father, Federal District Court Judge Clay Blackthorne, was at the hospital with her mother.

Once Jack reached the small apartment that he kept for work on the outskirts of Houston, he left three more messages on Kate's cell phone, one every half hour, the last one at midnight, all of which went directly to voice mail. Where the hell was she?

He was tempted to call her father, but if Kate's mother wasn't in an Austin hospital delivering the baby, there was no sense putting her parents in a panic. Kate might have gone out to get ice cream with the boys, or maybe she'd been in the shower, or maybe she'd gone to bed early and silenced her cell phone, and now it was too late to call her home phone without waking up the twins.

He couldn't help being worried about what might have happened after he'd left her alone with Wyatt Shaw. He'd had no choice. It would have been worse if he'd hung around. The less Shaw—and Kate—knew about what he was doing for Dante D'Amato, the better.

For almost twenty years Jack had been hunting the party responsible for demanding that he shave points in the Super Bowl. His foolhardy father had amassed gambling debts in the amount of $321,800, with no hope of repaying such an amount. The syndicate holding his father's markers wouldn't take cash in payment from Jack. They wanted the Super Bowl fixed instead.

No one could prove Jack had cheated to keep his father's throat from being cut by the mob. In fact, he'd refused to cooperate.

But he'd fumbled the ball on the opposing team's five-yard line. He'd gotten an intentional grounding call on fourth and short. He'd thrown an interception in a spot where he had no receiver within a dozen yards.

And they'd lost the game.

His teammates had refused to play with him. He'd been forced from the game of football, and his name had been forever blackened.

After his professional football career was destroyed, Jack had sworn he was done rescuing his father, who'd gambled away every penny he'd ever earned and more, for as long as Jack could remember. Every time they lost their home, his father had wept and promised he would quit gambling. But he never had. Jack had hated his old man for so long he didn't know what it was like to feel any other way.

But his mother had refused to walk away, and Jack was sure that if the bookmakers ever came after his father again, they wouldn't leave any witnesses. So last October, when his mother had called him because his father was crying and ashamed and in trouble again, Jack had come.

When he'd arrived at the tiny house where his parents lived, he'd found his father locked in the bathroom. When he finally got him to open the door, his old man had stared at him from haunted brown eyes and said, "They're threatening to slice me in half from eyebrows to balls, Jack, if you don't back off of your investigation."

For the second time in his life, Jack had seen himself losing everything—losing himself—if he gave in to extortion.

So he'd packed up his parents and safely parked them at Twin Magnolias, the ranch west of Austin he'd invested in with Kate's uncle, FBI Special Agent Breed Grayhawk, giving him the freedom to finish what he'd started.

And then, out of the blue, Governor Pendleton had arranged for him to be taken off the case he was working and assigned as a bodyguard for her grandkids. Making it look, once again, like he'd kowtowed to the mob.

Jack had been furious and frustrated. But there was nothing he could do.

A surprising amount of good had come out of that transfer. Most importantly, he and Kate had been thrown back together.

Kate's fascination with him—and his with her—had begun ten years ago when she was a nineteen-year-old University of Texas student, and he was a thirty-two-year-old former pro football player trying to put his life back together. He'd been friends with her uncle North, who'd asked him to keep a watchful eye on Kate during the high-profile "Bomber Brown" trial her father was adjudicating.

Jack had known Kate liked him, maybe even thought she loved him. But he wasn't about to inflict himself and all his dirty linen on someone as lovely and innocent as she was then.

Ten years had changed a lot of things. Their attraction had flickered back to life at a time when she was supposedly a widow and his marriage seemed to be at an end.

At about the same time, Jack had been approached by a representative of Dante D'Amato. The mobster apparently believed, because of Jack's behavior on two previous occasions when extortion appeared to have worked, that he could be bribed or bought.

"Mr. D'Amato hopes you will be useful in helping him to solve a little problem," D'Amato's attorney said. "He is willing to pay you well for your trouble. And of course," the lawyer continued, "your father's debts would be forgiven, and there would be no reason for any further action against him. The utmost discretion will be required. Are you interested?"

Jack was incensed and insulted. But he'd quickly realized the value of going to work for the very man he'd been investigating. He'd told the lawyer, "I'm interested."

Then he'd gone to his Ranger captain. They'd agreed to keep what Jack was doing strictly between the two of them, since D'Amato was known to have long tentacles that reached into every area of law enforcement and the courts.

"It's going to be dangerous enough working for D'Amato," his captain had said, "without him finding out that your main goal is still to put him behind bars."

"He's likely to suspect that anyway," Jack said.

"Just make sure he doesn't catch you sniffing around where you don't belong," his captain warned.

"Shouldn't we tell the FBI what's going on?"

"I'm sure the FBI has someone of their own on the inside that we don't know about. Better to do it this way," his captain said. "That way there are no 'accidental' leaks. The FBI will be happy to make use of whatever evidence you collect."

Jack had insisted on meeting D'Amato in person, and the lawyer arranged it. Jack showed up at the lawyer's office in a mirrored high-rise in downtown Houston and found D'Amato waiting for him in a wood-paneled conference room lined with legal tomes.

He'd been surprised at how unthreatening Dante D'Amato looked. He stood nearly as tall as Wyatt Shaw but his body was reedlike. His receding hair was silver, his heavy brows black. His eyes were a piercing blue, set deep in a narrow, wrinkled face. He had arthritis in his fingers, with knobs at every joint. Jack doubted he could curl his index finger around a trigger.

But mob bosses didn't usually have to do their own killing. D'Amato had surrounded himself with a half-dozen brutes of various shapes and sizes who were clustered near the coffee urn and pastries at the other end of the room. Jack was glad when the mob boss sent all but one of them from the room.

D'Amato gestured Jack into a swivel chair, then took a seat himself at the head of the table, while the remaining man, thick-chested and stocky-legged, with a significant bulge under his jacket, stood sentinel near the door.

"I always wondered if you threw that game, or just played badly," he said. "Which was it?"

If the man's point had been to disconcert Jack, he'd succeeded. "It hardly matters now."

"I would like to know."

Jack debated whether to tell D'Amato the truth. Finally he said, "I didn't plan to lose. I just..."

"Made a few too many mistakes?"

Jack shrugged uncomfortably.

"The subconscious mind is more powerful than we imagine. You did what was necessary to save your father. That sort of devotion is hard to find these days."

Jack bit his cheek to keep himself from saying he hated his old man. "What is it you want me to do?"

"I'm looking for someone who took something from me. He faked his death and disappeared. I need you to find him. And I need you to find what he stole from me."

"That sounds like something any competent private investigator could do. Why do you need me?"

"Because you have special access to this man's home. And to his wife and children. I'm speaking of J.D. Pendleton."

Jack hissed in a breath. He'd known that J.D. was alive, because Kate had told him her husband had shown up in her kitchen last fall. But he was appalled to discover J.D.'s connection to D'Amato.

D'Amato pressed the balls of his fingers together and said, "That son of a bitch stole a package from me worth twenty million dollars. The California party involved in this transaction is holding me accountable for both the money and the package."

Jack had a pretty good idea who the "California party" was. The FBI had evidence that D'Amato was involved in drug trafficking with the Mexican Mafia, which had started as a California prison gang and morphed into a ruthless and violent nationwide drug trafficking, auto theft and gambling operation. But no witness had ever hung around, or lived long enough, to testify against D'Amato.

"So, this other party wants forty million from you?"

"They'll settle for twenty million and the bastard who stole the package. I want you to find J.D. Pendleton. And I want you to find the package."

"Are we talking drugs?"

D'Amato laughed softly. "Sergeant McKinley, I'd hardly be likely to admit to a Texas Ranger that I'm looking for twenty million dollars' worth of heroin. Even if that Ranger had accepted a great deal of cash to work for me."

Jack realized he needed to find J.D. before D'Amato did. Once in protective custody, and with desertion and drug trafficking charges looming, Kate's husband just might be the witness the FBI needed to take the mob boss down.

D'Amato's eyes narrowed and his voice hardened. "I know Pendleton has been in touch with his wife. Maybe he told her where he's planning to hide. Maybe he left something in the house that will tell you where he's headed or where he hid my package. You're guarding the woman's children. Make friends with her. Find out what you can."

Within days of his meeting with D'Amato, Kate had been shot and spent the next four months in a coma. But because of his earlier conversations with Kate, Jack had been able to tell D'Amato that J.D. had gone to South America. D'Amato's men had finally found him in Brazil ten days ago, shot at him, apparently wounding him, and then chased him back to California.

As far as Jack knew, Kate hadn't heard from her wayward husband since she'd recovered from her coma.

It was bad luck that Wyatt Shaw had seen Jack with D'Amato at the lawyer's office, where they usually met, and then run into him at Kate's. It was one thing for her to deduce he was working undercover for D'Amato. He just hoped Shaw didn't tell Kate he was helping D'Amato locate her husband so the mob boss could kill him.

She would be upset. And he couldn't explain.

To be honest, Jack had never thought D'Amato's men would find J.D., based on the information he'd given them. South America was a huge continent. Jack could only assume J.D. hadn't concealed himself very well.

Jack figured there was only one person J.D. could be certain would hide him, now that he was back in the States: his mother. Since Ann Wade was currently traveling around the country campaigning, J.D. could link up with her anywhere. That is, assuming he could get anywhere near the Texas governor and presidential hopeful, who was protected by both Texas Department of Public Safety officers and Secret Service agents.

It was far more likely J.D. would head to the ranch his mother owned in Midland, Texas. With Ann Wade traveling, the ranch house was probably empty. Midland was flat country, and the ranch house was in the middle of vast acres of land, so it wouldn't be easy to sneak up on him unawares.

Jack felt sure he'd have better luck finding J.D. in Midland if he looked for him himself, but he wasn't sure he wanted to be the one to find Kate's husband. He didn't imagine J.D. was going to come in without a fight. And he absolutely didn't want to be the one who killed him.

Kate no longer loved her husband, but since Jack planned to become the twins' stepfather, he didn't want to have to tell them someday that he'd killed their father.

He decided to suggest to D'Amato that he have his men look for J.D. at Ann Wade's ranch, because he was sure the mob boss would already have thought of it for himself. And because Jack hoped eventually to bring J.D. in alive, he would make a call to Ann Wade's ranch himself to ensure that J.D. knew the hitmen were coming.

There was something much more important he wanted to discuss the next time he saw Dante D'Amato: Wyatt Shaw's visit to Kate. Maybe D'Amato had some idea why his son had come visiting J.D. Pendleton's wife.

11

"You should be sleeping."

Kate turned over in bed so she was facing Shaw. She could see his eyes shining in the soft moonlight that streamed through the wall of sliding doors in his bedroom. One glass door was open, the space covered by a sliding screen, so she could hear crickets chirping and the burble of the waterfall in the courtyard. But those sounds weren't what was keeping her awake.

"Would you sleep if you were me?" she asked. "I mean, considering the fact that the last woman who closed her eyes in your bed never opened them again?"

"I didn't kill her."

"Why should I believe you?"

"If I'd killed her, I wouldn't have left a body for the police to find."

That made sense. "I guess the son of a mob boss would know how to hide a body."

He lifted a sardonic brow. "But you aren't totally convinced."

"Your security seems pretty airtight. Maybe you just hadn't hid the body yet when your maid walked in and found you."

"I came home and found an unconscious woman in my bed. I checked for a pulse and didn't find one. That's the closest I got to her throat."

"Why did the police arrest you?"

"The question you should be asking is why they let me go."

Kate was dumbfounded, because it had never occurred to her to ask why the police hadn't kept Shaw in jail. She'd simply assumed he'd paid some stupendous bail. "Why did they let you go?"

"Because another man's DNA was found inside that woman—and on the sheets of my bed."

"Why haven't the papers published the fact that there's another suspect?" Kate asked.

"The police don't know who the real killer is yet. They don't want to scare him off before they can catch him."

"His DNA doesn't match a criminal who's already in the system?"

"Apparently not."

"Who could have gotten into your apartment?"

He started to speak. And then didn't.

"Who?" she persisted.

"Your husband."

Kate pushed herself upright and grabbed a silk-covered pillow, hugging it to her naked chest. "That's absurd. That would mean J.D. is back in the States. And that he's a murderer."

"Yeah. So?"

That was terrifying news if it was true. "How could J.D. get into your suite? Why would he want to? And why kill that woman?"

Shaw slid a hand under his head to prop himself up and said, "The woman got in by telling the concierge I'd asked her to come."

"Did you?"

He made a face. "No."

"But you must have in the past, otherwise the concierge would have known better," she concluded.

He didn't confirm or deny. He simply said, "I think J.D. figured out I knew her and paid her to help him get in."

"You're guessing about everything," Kate accused.

Shaw nodded. "Making educated guesses. Yes. I don't think J.D. intended to strangle the girl, because otherwise he wouldn't have left his DNA inside her. Maybe she changed her mind about helping him when she realized he was bent on murder, so he had to shut her up. And even if he didn't manage to kill me, he'd still be making a lot of trouble for me by leaving a murdered woman in my bed."

"So why aren't you dead?"

"I had other plans that night that kept me away from home."

"You slept in some other woman's bed?"

Again, he didn't confirm or deny.

"Have you told the police what you suspect?"

His lips twisted ruefully. "I tried. As far as the Houston cops are concerned, Texas Governor Ann Wade Pendleton's son is a war hero buried in Arlington Cemetery. The governor made sure the investigation of J.D. got shut down before it went anywhere."

"Why would J.D. want to kill you?" she asked.

"Because I gave the FBI the evidence they needed to

start asking questions about his activities in Afghanistan."

Kate stared at Shaw wide-eyed. "You're an FBI informant?"

Shaw's mouth twisted. "The person I wanted to help the FBI take down was my father. J.D. got caught in the same net."

"How did J.D. find out it was you who sent the FBI after him?"

"I wouldn't be surprised if his mother told him. After my father told her."

"How did D'Amato find out what you did?"

"He has his own sources of information in the FBI."

"Why would you want to turn in your own father?" Kate wondered aloud.

"It's a long story. Suffice it to say, there's no love lost between me and Dante D'Amato."

"Ann Wade seemed as surprised by J.D.'s return from the dead as I was," she mused.

Shaw sighed. "There's a lot you haven't been told."

Kate gripped the pillow tighter, as though it could protect her from another unexpected blow. "Such as?"

"My father has your mother-in-law in his pocket. He's been acting the puppeteer for years."

Kate shook her head in denial. "That's impossible."

"Is it? Political campaigns cost money. You aren't the only one whose pockets J.D. drained. My father was standing there waiting when Ann Wade put out a call for cash."

Kate felt her body trembling. She turned her naked back to Shaw, then shoved her way off the bed, dropping the pillow behind her. She searched for a white cotton nightgown in her suitcase and slid it down over her body. The simple garment had narrow straps, a ruffle of lace across the bosom and covered her to mid-thigh.

She could feel Shaw's eyes on her, almost feel the magnetic pull of her attraction to him, urging her to return to bed. Instead, she crossed to the screen door, eased it open and walked out into the night air. She crossed a redbrick patio that led down to the reflecting pool.

Kate wanted to run away from the sordid facts she'd just been told. And from the knowledge of her sexual betrayal—twice in one night—of the man she loved.

It was bad enough that she'd made love to Shaw in the living room. She could almost forgive herself for allowing him to kiss her—and for kissing him back. She'd been curious whether her memories of what two perfect strangers had done together that long-ago night, in bed and out, could possibly be real.

She hadn't realized how powerful their attraction to each other still was. Hadn't realized how much she would want to touch him, and to be touched by him. There had been no rational thought involved by the time he joined their bodies.

Mindless. Thoughtless. Helpless.

Stupid. Idiotic. Self-indulgent.

Those words described her behavior the first time they'd made love. But how could she explain letting Shaw make love to her a second time?

Cruel. Disgraceful. Treacherous.

Kate felt ashamed of what she'd done. She wondered if Jack would ever be able to forgive her. Assuming she told him what she'd done. The bigger question was whether she would ever be able to forgive herself. She was still confused by her behavior.

After they'd made love—had sex, she corrected with ruthless honesty—in the living room, Shaw had carried her back to his bedroom. The moment he laid her down in his bed, she'd turned her back on him and curled her body into a fetal ball, still shaken by their lovemaking in the living room.

Lovemaking. She was using euphemisms again.

She couldn't help it. Because even if she wanted to call what had happened between them *sex,* there had also been an element of *something*—a tenderness, a gentleness—in the way Shaw touched her. Except, the passion between them had been so savage, so devastating, that she wondered at her selection of those particular words.

Tender? Gentle? *Shaw?*

She realized it was the knowledge that he desired her, above all other women, that gave his savage lovemaking its human tenderness. The knowledge that he revered her, above all other women, that made his possession gentle, despite the bruises he'd left on her flesh. And on her soul.

Kate had been drowsing in his bed, struggling against sleep, which hadn't seemed safe considering the fact that Wyatt Shaw was a suspected murderer, when he'd kissed her naked shoulder.

Naked shoulder.

That was another thing she didn't understand. Why hadn't she immediately gotten out of bed when he'd brought her to his bedroom from the living room and put on a nightgown? Then she would have had some protection from the exquisite sensation when, as she was drifting in a state somewhere between waking and sleeping, he'd cupped her naked breast in his palm.

Why hadn't she slapped his hand away? Why hadn't she done something—anything—to stop him? She'd allowed him to caress her. To send shivers down her spine. To awaken her body to pleasures she'd never imagined possible. Again.

She'd been unable to stop herself from wanting him. Again.

And succumbing to temptation.

What did it mean?

Kate had believed, when she was nineteen and met thirty-two-year-old Jack McKinley, that they were soul mates. Which was why she'd been so devastated when he'd walked away from her without looking back. The most he'd been willing to concede was that there had been an attraction between them.

He'd told her that he'd been roped into watching out for her by her uncle North, and that the time he'd spent with her had merely been a *job.*

Which made her attempt at seducing him by baring her breasts to him a humiliating memory.

He'd told her he was done with the job. And with her.

She'd promised to make him eat those words.

Kate hadn't seen Jack again until her parents' wedding day later that summer. As her mother's brides-maid, Kate had been dressed in a full-length, peach-colored chiffon dress that looked like something she might have worn to the prom. Jack had called her "cute as a button."

She could remember their conversation as though it had happened yesterday.

"I'm not a child, Jack. Don't talk to me like I am one."

"I was hoping to avoid you," he'd admitted.

When he made no move to touch her, to take her in her arms, she'd found herself fighting tears. It was a battle she lost. She'd turned to run, but Jack caught her. She'd clung to him, trembling, waiting to hear words of love.

Instead, he'd said, "I'm no good for you, Kate."

She'd answered naively, honestly, "I love you, Jack."

"I know."

With those two words, instead of the three she'd wanted to hear, Kate had felt the death knell to all her dreams of a life with Jack.

He'd tipped her chin up and tried to explain. "It wouldn't work, Kate."

She'd known little and cared less about Jack's troubled life before she'd met him. She'd preferred to ignore the fact that his fabulous career as a pro football quarterback had gone down in flames when he was accused of shaving points in the Super Bowl. Or that his restaurant in Austin, the Longhorn Grille, had gone belly-up for unpaid taxes.

All she knew was that he was giving up on any hope of a relationship between them before they'd even tried. "I don't care about anything you've done. I only care about being with you."

"You're being naive, Kate. You have no idea—"

"I love you, Jack! Please. Please—"

He'd stopped her pleas with a kiss. A closemouthed kiss. The kind you gave someone you were placating.

She'd moaned against his mouth, wanting more.

He'd opened his mouth to her in a searing kiss—only to grasp her shoulders and force them apart. "I'm not the white knight you think I am," he'd said in a harsh voice.

She'd protested again that she didn't care what he'd done in the past, didn't care about his unsavory reputation.

"You're too young to know what you want," he'd replied. "And I'm old enough to know better. This isn't going to happen, Kate."

"Why not?" she'd demanded. "You know you want me."

"That's lust. Not love."

She'd been appalled to hear him say such a thing. "I don't believe you. You do love me. I know you do."

"If I did, that would be all the more reason to keep my distance."

If I did...?

That hadn't made sense to her, and she'd told him so.

He'd tried another argument. "You deserve better."

"I want *you!*" she'd protested.

"We don't always get what we want," he'd said flatly. "Or what we deserve."

Then she'd made her threat. "I'm not going to wait around for you to come to your senses, Jack. I've got a life to live, and I'm going to live it. You'll be sorry—"

"I'm already sorry I showed up here," he'd said. "I'm outta here."

"Go!" she'd cried to his retreating back. She was panting with fury and frustration and tears were streaming down her cheeks. "See if I care!" she'd shouted after him. "Don't expect me to come running after you. Grayhawks don't beg. Or plead. Or go down on bended knee for anyone."

He'd never hesitated. He'd never looked back.

She wondered now why she hadn't taken him at his word. Wondered now why she'd been so surprised when he'd married his high school sweetheart within the next year.

Then, last fall, Jack McKinley had once again entered her life as a bodyguard, this time for the Texas governor's grandchildren—her children. He'd been a man at his lowest ebb, having just lost his wife and son, who'd moved to Kansas while he waited for his divorce to become final.

And she'd been a desperately unhappy woman.

She'd been the widow of a man she'd no longer loved by the time he was killed—or supposedly killed—in an ammo dump explosion in Afghanistan. A woman with two fatherless, rambunctious sons. A woman exhausted by the emotional demands of a job she loved. A woman who'd spent the crippling months since her husband's death leaning on a man three years her junior, her best friend and uncle Breed Grayhawk.

She'd been desperate and unhappy enough to suggest that she and Jack comfort each other by "having sex." "Making love" wasn't a possibility, she'd said, because she no longer loved him.

Jack had brutally rejected her offer.

"If you're looking for a fuck buddy, I'm not your man."

Whereupon Kate had confessed that she'd never stopped loving him. And pleaded for forgiveness.

He'd taken her in his arms and kissed her the way she'd imagined him kissing her for so many years. They'd been on their way to the bedroom to consummate their relationship when Jack had been called away.

They had never made love. J.D. had turned up that same night, making it clear she was not a widow, as she'd believed. And she'd used her husband's reappearance as an excuse not to pursue her relationship with Jack.

None of that had mattered with Shaw. It had never even come up. He'd touched her. And she'd melted in his arms.

"It's a lovely night," Shaw said into the quiet.

Speak of the devil... "Don't touch me," she said sharply. She'd warned him away because she feared that, despite her feelings of shame, she wouldn't be able to resist him.

He crouched down and wiggled his fingers in the water. Koi in all the colors of the rainbow came swimming up out of the darkness, their orange and red and green and blue and black and white scales reflecting in the moonlight. She realized they must be used to Shaw feeding them.

He stood and wiped the water off on the thighs of the jeans he pulled on to cover his nakedness. The top button was undone and the denim hung low, revealing his hipbones and the line of black down that led from his navel to a thick pubic bush.

She inhaled the musky smell of him. And remembered the taste of the single drop of liquid she'd licked away before taking him in her mouth.

Kate ached with need for him. She suppressed a

moan of desire. Frightened by her feelings, she met Shaw's gaze in the moonlight and said, "I want to go home. I want to leave here. You have to let me go."

"No."

"I don't want to be with you."

"Your body says differently."

"There's nothing else between us except this... physical...thing," Kate said fiercely. "We're as much strangers as we ever were. I won't have sex with you again, Shaw. Not until I'm free to make that decision, not until I can do it with honor."

"Not until your husband is dead?"

Kate could see he would happily kill J.D., if he could just find him. "J.D. made the choice to abandon me. There's another man involved here besides my husband," she said softly.

"Who?"

She'd already told him Jack was just a friend. That had been a lie of convenience. Now it was imperative to tell the truth. "Jack McKinley."

Shaw snorted. "Your *friend?*"

Kate flushed. "Jack is more than that."

"Your *lover?*" Shaw snarled.

She ignored the question. "I won't deny you can seduce me. *Have* seduced me. I'm asking you not to do it again."

He shoved both hands through his hair in frustration. "Then how am I supposed to get to know you?"

She wondered what it was he really wanted from her. She knew he wanted his sons. She knew he enjoyed having her in his bed. But there wasn't much else they had in common. Or much future for them as a couple, considering that she was in love with another man.

Are you in love with Jack? Or did you grasp at Jack as a lifeline?

Kate was angry because it seemed she was looking for a way to excuse her behavior. It would be fine to make love to Shaw if she wasn't really in love with Jack.

But she *did* love Jack, had loved Jack for ten years. Yes, they'd gotten together last fall at a moment when they'd both been vulnerable. But the need—and the love—had been real. On both sides.

Wyatt Shaw was causing this crisis in confidence. Before he'd come along, there had been no doubt about her feelings for Jack. She loved him.

What about his feelings for you? Why would a man who's in love with one woman agree to move back in with another?

Jack had a good reason for what he was doing. He wanted his child to have his name. It was the circumstances that were forcing him to behave as he was.

And there was no other choice he could have made? No other way to convince Holly to postpone the divorce? Are you sure he didn't want to move back in with his wife?

Kate hated that she was doubting herself. Doubting Jack. Jack loved her. His feelings and sensibilities deserved more consideration in this situation than she had given them.

It was one more thing to blame on Wyatt Shaw.

Kate shivered.

"You're cold. Come back inside," Shaw said. He reached for her hand and she let him take it and lead her back into his bedroom, where he took her in his arms and held her close. His lips found a spot between her neck and shoulder, pushing aside the nightgown to reach more of her flesh.

Before Kate could stop him, Shaw stripped the cotton nightgown up over her head, leaving her bare. He tossed it behind him and reached for her again.

"What are you doing?" Kate demanded.

"Making love to you."

Kate realized she would have to get past Shaw to retrieve her nightgown. It seemed safer to conceal herself under the sheets. She retreated and slipped into bed, her back against the headboard, her knees drawn to her chest, the covers pulled up to her neck, and said, "This has to stop."

"Is there a better way to get to know each other?" he asked.

"We can talk. We can—"

"Kiss? Touch?"

She lifted a brow. "Can you kiss and touch without doing more?"

"Can I control myself? I think I can manage."

"I need a better guarantee than you *think* you can," she said with asperity.

He slid into the other side of the bed. "I won't make love to you again until—and unless—you tell me you want me," he said through tight jaws. "Is that good enough?"

"If that's your best offer," she said. "I'll take it."

12

Jack's cell phone woke him up. He saw it was 3:04 a.m. and that Kate was calling. He flipped open the phone as he switched on the bedside lamp. "Are you all right?" he said anxiously. "I called you six times and never heard back from you."

"I'm fine, Jack," she whispered. "I found the messages you left on my cell phone. That's why I'm calling."

"Why are you whispering?"

"I don't want Shaw to hear me."

"Wyatt Shaw's there? Where are you?"

"I'm in the bathroom. He's in the bedroom down the hall."

Jack was confused. And concerned. "Shaw's still at your house?"

"No."

She paused so long he thought he'd lost the connection. He looked at the phone to make sure the duration of the call was still ticking off, then said, "Kate?"

"I'm here," she whispered. "At Shaw's compound in Houston."

"Where?"

"He flew me and the twins here in his jet earlier this evening. He said we'd be safer here."

"Safer? From what? From whom?"

She sighed. "It's a long story, Jack. Where are you?"

"I'm in Houston."

"With Holly?"

"No. In an apartment I keep here for work. Why would you agree to go anywhere with Wyatt Shaw?"

"There's something I have to tell you, Jack. Something important."

"I'm here for you, Kate, no matter what."

"I hope you still feel that way after you hear what I have to say."

He thought he heard her sob. "What is it? What's going on, Kate? You're scaring me."

Jack was out of bed, pulling a pair of jeans up over his boxers while he talked to her on the phone, expecting any minute to need to get into his SUV and come after her.

"Wyatt Shaw is the twins' biological father."

Jack tripped on the leg of his jeans that was only halfway up and went rolling on the carpet. He dropped the phone when he hit the floor and it slid under the bed. He grabbed for it and said, "Kate? Are you still there?"

"Jack?" he heard her cry softly. "Jack?"

"I'm here," he said, sitting on the carpet in his boxers with his back against the side of the bed. He shoved his jeans the rest of the way off with his bare feet. He put a hand over his eyes. "I don't think I heard you right."

"Wyatt Shaw is the twins' biological father," she repeated.

"That's what I heard. I'm just finding it a little hard—impossible—to believe."

"It's true. I…picked him up in a bar. I didn't know who he was. I was trying to get back at J.D. for… It doesn't matter now why I did what I did. The point is, Ann Wade got suspicious and hired a private investigator and Shaw found out the truth. He's worried his father will do something to hurt the twins if he discovers they're his grandsons. And he's afraid J.D. will be a threat to the twins, and you know that's one of my fears, too. So he brought us here to live with him."

"You and the twins just…moved in with Wyatt Shaw?"

"It's only for a little while," she said.

"How long?"

"Long enough for me to take a job at M.D. Anderson, and for the boys to go to a private school in The Woodlands," she admitted. "Shaw is having the boys' horses trailered here, and he's arranging for Harley and Scratch to come, too."

Jack was reeling. "What about us?"

"You'll be living with Holly for the next four months. This seemed like the smart thing to do, under the circumstances."

"When I left this afternoon, you told me you love me. Suddenly, you're living with another man. Just how well do you know Wyatt Shaw?"

Jack was furious, because he felt so helpless. His love life kept whirling out of his control. First J.D. showing up alive, keeping him and Kate apart. Then Holly getting pregnant, keeping him and Kate apart. And now the twins turning out to be Wyatt Shaw's sons, keeping him and Kate apart.

"I hate what's happening to us," he said.

"This hasn't been easy for me, either, Jack," Kate said in a small voice. "I spent one night with Wyatt Shaw nine years ago and never saw him again until today."

"You shouldn't have gone with him, Kate."

"I had no choice! Just a minute…"

He watched the seconds tick off on his phone. It took her twenty-eight of them to return. She was whispering again.

"I thought I heard someone in the hall, but Shaw's still asleep."

"You went into his bedroom? Are you crazy?"

She hesitated. "No. I'm…"

Jack drew in a sharp breath. "You're sleeping with him?" *Having sex with him?*

She didn't answer. Which was the wrong answer.

"Do you love him?" Jack choked out.

"No! But…it's complicated."

"I damn well guess it is. What am I supposed to do now, Kate?"

"Go take care of your wife."

"What about us?"

"From your conversation this afternoon with Shaw, it sounded like you're working for his father."

"I can't talk about that, Kate."

"I figure you must be involved in some kind of undercover assignment for the Rangers. The best thing you could do for 'us' is to put Dante D'Amato behind bars. The sooner the better."

"Shaw's the one accused of murder," Jack pointed out.

"I don't believe he strangled that woman."

"And you base that on what?"

She didn't answer, and he checked his phone again to make sure they hadn't been disconnected. "Kate? What makes you so sure Wyatt Shaw isn't a killer?"

"I asked him. And he told me he didn't do it."

"When was this?"

"Earlier tonight. Or rather, this morning."

"He could have been lying. He probably was."

"I believed him."

"Were you in bed together at the time?"

She didn't answer.

"What is it between you and him?" Jack said angrily. "What kind of hold does he have over you, to make you do things so out of character? This isn't you, Kate. What am I supposed to think when you tell me you're sleeping with some strange man?"

She started to cry. "I can't help it. When I'm with him, I feel—"

"I really don't want to hear this," Jack interrupted.

"I don't love him," she insisted. "I love you."

"But you're fucking him." He was shocked at the ferocity of his reply. And its viciousness. He'd never experienced jealousy before. He didn't like the way it made him feel. Or the way it made him act.

Kate wasn't his wife. He wasn't her husband. He had to back off. He had to support her choice. At least until he was free to pursue her himself.

"That was out of line," he said at last.

"I'm tired," she said.

He could hear it in her voice. She'd probably been up half the goddamn night having sex with Shaw. He bit back the jealous retort at the tip of his tongue and said, "Me, too."

"Do you still want to stay in touch?" she asked.

"Do you?"

"Maybe we could have lunch sometime, once I'm working at M.D. Anderson."

"I'd like that," he said. "Give me a call."

"Good night, Jack."

"Good night, Kate." He closed the phone. And threw it against the wall.

13

Jack hadn't slept well after he talked to Kate. He was still pissed off the next morning that she'd kept her secret about who was really the twins' father even from him.

Of course, it was a doozy.

He got a call at the crack of dawn from Dante D'Amato's attorney arranging a meeting with the mob boss in his *home* at nine-thirty that morning. It was the first time Jack had been invited inside D'Amato's private residence, so he wanted to go. Besides, how would it sound if he said, "I can't come because I'm helping my wife move today."

He tried phoning Holly to let her know he was going to be late, but the only number he had was her cell and the calls kept going directly to voice mail. "Damn it!" He turned his phone off, snapped it closed and stuck it in the pocket of his Wranglers, then knocked on the front door of D'Amato's condominium.

D'Amato's suite took up the entire top floor of a downtown building that had been put in the shade when Shaw Tower went up across the street. Jack wondered if Wyatt Shaw had purposely built in that location just to ruin his father's view.

Jack had never been vetted by so many guys with guns. He was ushered into D'Amato's opulent study by a broad-shouldered, thick-trunked man with long arms, big ears, small black eyes and a flat, bald head. Long Arms had not been at the lawyer's office. Jack saw prison tatts on the man's knuckles. He figured he was looking at the man who did D'Amato's wet work.

Jack felt dwarfed by the twelve-foot ceiling and hemmed in by the walls lined with bookcases of first editions that must have been worth a mint. A plush, red-and-black oriental rug was centered on the shiny black marble floor.

D'Amato was sitting in one of two gold brocade wing chairs facing a black-marble-faced fireplace, where a gas fire was burning. Wall sconces and judiciously placed gold floor and table lamps provided soft light, since the room had no windows.

D'Amato gestured Jack into the other chair. "Sit down. Make yourself comfortable." He turned to Long Arms, who'd stationed himself beside an exquisite antique burled walnut desk, and said, "Leave us, Roberto. Close the door."

The minute Jack sat down, D'Amato handed him a Montecristo cigar.

"What's this for?"

"I'm celebrating," the old man said. "May I trim that for you?"

Jack held out the cigar, and the mobster used a gold double blade guillotine cigar cutter to clip off the cap, which fell into a crystal ashtray on the round parquet table between them. The cutter was so sharp, Jack wondered if the mobster had ever used it to snip off a finger. Or two.

The old man clipped his own cigar, then stuck it in the corner of his mouth. He set down the cutter and picked up a small gold Aladdin's lamp, which he used to light Jack's cigar.

Jack puffed on his cigar and blew out the smoke, then waited while D'Amato lit his own cigar. He was both anxious and curious to know what they were celebrating. Had D'Amato caught J.D.?

"I took the liberty of having a drink poured for you." D'Amato gestured to the crystal glass on Jack's side of the checkered tabletop. "Jack Daniel's Black Label. Straight up."

"Thank you."

"A toast," the old man said, picking up the glass of liquor on his side of the table.

Jack picked up his whiskey and waited for the older man to tell him what was going on.

"I'm delighted to tell you I've become a grandfather. It seems my son Wyatt is the father of twin boys. *Salud!*"

Jack felt his heart pound harder in his chest. How had D'Amato found out? Who'd told him? "Congratulations," Jack said, lifting his glass.

D'Amato clinked his cut-crystal glass against Jack's and drank.

Jack nearly choked trying to get a swallow of liquor down his constricted throat. He didn't like the self-satisfied look on D'Amato's face. He couldn't believe Shaw had told his father anything. So who had? D'Amato must have spies in Shaw's household.

"I'm hoping to meet the mother of my grandsons soon," D'Amato said. "She moved in with my son yesterday."

"Who is it?" Jack said, playing his part in D'Amato's little drama.

"You know her well."

Jack lifted a brow. And waited with clenched teeth for what he was pretty sure was coming next.

"It's a very small world, after all, Sergeant McKinley. Imagine my surprise when I learned that the mother of my eight-year-old grandsons is your very good friend, the governor's daughter-in-law, Kate Pendleton."

The mob boss paused but Jack didn't rise to the bait.

"It doesn't please me to think you knew the truth and never said anything to me, Sergeant McKinley," D'Amato said in a hard voice.

"This is as much a surprise to me as it is to you," Jack said.

"But it wasn't news to you just now."

Jack hesitated, then said, "Kate called me last night."

"Ah," D'Amato said. "Interesting. She called you from Wyatt's house?"

Jack gave a jerky nod.

D'Amato continued, "The timing of this development couldn't be better for our purposes."

"Our purposes?"

"Capturing J.D. Pendleton and retrieving my package," the mob boss said, all humor gone from his voice.

"How so?"

"I imagine that bastard is going to be one angry man when he finds out his wife cheated on him. He may even think he can kidnap the twins and use them as a negotiating tool with me, since they're my grandsons.

"At the very least, that son of a bitch will want to confront his wife. We can only hope he'll take a shot at stealing the kids. Whichever move he makes, when he finally makes his move, you will grab him."

Jack wasn't surprised that D'Amato was planning to use Kate and the twins to lure J.D. Pendleton into the open, but he said, "I would think you'd rather keep your grandsons—and their mother—*out* of the line of fire."

"They'll be fine. One of the Texas Rangers' finest will be there to keep an eye on them."

"How do you figure that? As you pointed out, the three of them are now living with Shaw."

"There's no need for pretense, Sergeant. I know about your relationship with J.D.'s wife. I won't mind at all if you ruffle my son's feathers by getting as close to her as you can—and staying there."

Jack felt a cold shiver knife down his spine. "I don't know where you got the idea that Kate and I are together."

"You're in love with her. And she loves you. Although I'd question the latter, if I were you, considering the fact she was fucking my son last night."

Jack came halfway out of his seat, saw the smirk on D'Amato's face and forced himself to sit back down. D'Amato was quoting back Jack's conversation with Kate yesterday afternoon at her house. The mob boss must have J.D.'s home bugged. Obviously, there were a lot more players than Jack and the hitmen assigned to track down J.D. Pendleton.

"J.D.'s wife will be untouchable so long as she's

behind Shaw's walls," D'Amato said. "But I understand she has insisted on working. Which means she'll be alone for long periods at M.D. Anderson."

"Is there anything you don't know about Kate's life?"

"I know all there is to know about your girlfriend. Just as I know all there is to know about your wife. Including the fact you're *not* fucking her. At least, not lately," D'Amato said with another smirk. "Although, you can always hope that will change, now that you're moving in with her and your boy."

Jack clenched his fists and managed, barely, to hold on to his temper. D'Amato was like a bully poking a chained dog with a stick through a fence. He felt safe rattling Jack's chain from outside the bars. Jack consoled himself with the thought of what it would be like to sink his teeth into D'Amato's hide, figuratively speaking, of course.

Watch out for your throat, old man, because one of these days I'm going to rip it out.

"I will contact Mrs. Pendleton and introduce myself and ask if I may meet my grandsons," D'Amato continued. "Wyatt will try to stop her. Being a stubborn woman, she will then insist upon it. I will make sure I meet the boys where J.D. will be tempted to make a try for them."

"And I'll be there to catch him," Jack finished.

"Precisely." D'Amato's eyes narrowed to slits. "And Roberto will make sure that the son of a bitch tells me what I want to know."

Jack knew the plan would work, because both Shaw and Kate were likely to react exactly as D'Amato had predicted. Jack felt the blood throbbing in his temples and consciously relaxed his hands. His job was to capture J.D. before D'Amato did. That was turning out to be even more of a challenge that he'd thought.

So far, D'Amato had stayed five steps ahead of him. It was about time he took the lead.

14

Holly Gayle Tanner had always loved Jack
McKinley. But she'd never trusted him. She'd held
him close and loved him well when he was with her.
But every time he headed out the door, she wondered
if he'd be coming back. From the time she was knee-
high to a grasshopper she'd known the way of the
world: Men left. And women wept.

Growing up in a small East Texas town like
Kountze hadn't been easy for a girl with big dreams
and a drunk for a father. As the eldest of five, Holly
couldn't remember a time when she wasn't trying to
figure out how to keep the little ones from going
hungry. Food stamps only went so far.

So at ten years old she'd planted tomatoes and
string beans and watermelon in the rich red earth
behind their shanty in the piney woods, better known
as the Big Thicket, located so far east in Texas that it
was practically in Louisiana.

They'd eaten stewed tomatoes and string beans over
rice, and sliced tomatoes and string beans, and pickled
tomatoes and string beans, and tomato soup and string
beans, until she expected her skin to turn red and

green. In the late summer they gorged on sweet, juicy watermelon that left their fingers sticky, and made a contest of spitting the seeds as far as they could.

All the while she hoed weeds and picked off caterpillars, Holly was planning how she'd have a different life than her mother. She'd learned early that her brains could get her a scholarship to college—and her beauty could get her just about anything else. The wealthiest man she knew in Kountze, the one with the biggest house, anyway, was Doc Benton. So she decided to become a doctor.

Holly had no intention of getting married. Ever. But she'd been fascinated to discover how much feminine power resided in her hourglass figure. She had a tiny waist set off by both generous breasts and sexy hips, exotic green eyes, a pretty smile, a pert, lightly freckled nose and curly red hair that she enhanced, unbeknownst to the boys or her mother, with a henna rinse.

While she was making the most of her looks, she was also getting straight A's and planning her escape from Kountze. She never told anyone about her plans to go to medical school. The kids in her tiny high school would have laughed at the idea of Holly Gayle Tanner—with boobs and a butt that were heaven on earth—becoming a doctor.

Kountze was a basketball championship town in a football crazy state. Because she was the prettiest girl in school and could have her pick of the boys, she'd had her eye on the high-point basketball forward. She'd been caught off guard when the Kountze Lions' football quarterback, Jack McKinley—with a mediocre team record of four wins, four losses and a tie— had asked her for a date.

Since Jack was just as tall, and better-looking, than the basketball forward, she'd said yes. She'd never expected to like him so much. He was thoughtful and kind. His kisses left her breathless. And he'd been gentle when he'd taken her virginity. Actually, it had been as much give on her part as take on his.

Best of all, Jack understood what it was like growing up with a father who made your life hell.

Jack's father gambled away his paycheck every Friday night betting on whatever sport was in season, so Jack knew what it was like to scrounge food for himself and his two younger sisters. He understood what it was like to want a life beyond the boundaries of an old railroad town of two thousand mostly white, mostly lower income residents, where the labels you got at sixteen stayed with you the rest of your life.

Jack had been a refuge from the stark reality of her life.

It wasn't just that her daddy was mean when he was drunk, calling names and striking out with his fists. When he was on a binge, he'd slam the screen door on his way out and disappear for days or weeks at a time. Once he was gone for a year, two months and three days. Her mother had cried bitter tears and languished all the while he was gone.

But she took him back.

Holly couldn't see the point. Why set yourself up for that kind of disappointment again?

She had never wanted to hurt Jack. But when she saw him making plans for their future his senior year that included a walk down the aisle, she'd broken up with him.

Holly had kept her eye on the prize. First a high school diploma. Then a college degree. Then medical school. Internship and residency. And finally a specialty.

Eventually, she'd become a pediatric oncologist. She'd found herself wanting to understand more about the cancer that too often won the battles she fought. She began to do research into new treatments for childhood leukemia and made several breakthroughs that brought her notoriety.

She'd still been unmarried at thirty-one, when she'd met Jack again at his 15th Kountze High School reunion. They'd spent the night talking and laughing and making love. She'd listened as he told her how his father's gambling vice had ruined his football career. How he'd found work that made him happy and proud of himself with the Texas Rangers.

He'd listened to how she'd made her escape from Kountze just a few years after him. How much she enjoyed her work healing children and investigating the diseases that took their lives. And how lonely she was.

He'd comforted her. He'd made her feel cherished. And she'd finally understood why her mother had always taken her father back.

Holly wasn't sure why she'd agreed to marry Jack, when she knew how it was going to end. Ryan, born three years after they married, had been an accident. She'd been determined not to bring a child into the world to suffer as she had in her youth. But she never thought of ending the pregnancy, and from the moment she held her son in her arms, she'd loved Ryan with her whole body and soul, the way she'd never been able to love Jack.

It hadn't been a comfortable marriage. She and Jack had loved hard. And fought harder.

She'd never given Jack her whole heart because she hadn't trusted him not to break it. For long periods she could keep her fears at bay, but they never really disappeared.

Whenever Jack was a minute-and-a-half late, she started worrying he was gone for good. She looked cockeyed at him if he had more than a single shot or a couple of beers. And it wasn't only her own father's vices she feared. She waited and watched for signs in Jack of his father's compulsive gambling.

Finally, it had seemed easier to send Jack away herself. That way she didn't have to keep waiting for the other shoe to drop. Once he was gone for good she could grieve and get over him and move on with her life.

Only it hadn't worked out that way.

Holly had learned something unexpected during their year of separation. She was miserable without Jack. She loved him, and she wanted to spend the rest of her life with him.

She was afraid her revelation might have come too late.

Because sometime during the eleven months when she'd been figuring out why she'd shoved Jack out the door and learning how to let him more fully into her life and becoming a more trusting—and less neurotic—person, Jack had fallen in love with another woman.

Holly certainly hadn't planned to get pregnant again, but she blessed the child in her womb, because it gave Jack a reason to move back in. It had taken a lot of courage to mail Ryan's Valentine's Day card, with the drawing of her extended belly, but all had turned out well. She'd been given one last chance to win back her husband's love.

Holly ran her hands over her five-months-pregnant curves and smiled wryly. She wasn't even going to be able to use her beauty to lure him back. She was going to have to do it with a protruding stomach and fat ankles.

Her plan was simple. She would offer Jack her whole heart. And trust he would accept it.

"Mommy, Daddy's here!" Ryan called from the living room.

Holly knew her son had been on his knees on the couch looking out the front picture window waiting for his father for the past hour. Jack was late. But she was not going to make an issue of it. She was *not.*

"Let him in, please, Ryan."

Holly looked around the kitchen at packing boxes she'd purposely left half full. One of the ways she'd excluded Jack was by being extremely self-sufficient. She had to let him help her. She had to learn to depend on him.

Which wasn't easy for a woman who hadn't dared rely on the adults in her life when she was a child.

You're a grown-up now, Holly Gayle. And Jack is reliable and responsible. He won't let you down.

And that was another thing. She'd been *Holly* all through high school. It was only when she'd moved away that she'd dropped her first name and begun calling herself *Gayle,* because she thought Holly sounded too much like a Christmas decoration. Jack had balked at calling her Gayle, except when he was mad at her, preferring the name he'd called her when they were kids.

She'd already written to him, telling him that she was using Holly again. It was a small thing, but she needed all the reminders she could get of a time when Jack had loved her.

Holly left the kitchen and stepped into the living room, where she found Jack hefting Ryan, who was really getting too big for it, into his arms for a hug.

"I missed you!" Jack said, rubbing noses with his son.

"I missed you, too," Ryan said, wrapping his arms tight around his father's neck and pressing his cheek against Jack's throat.

And then Jack saw her. His eyes never left hers as he set Ryan back on his feet. Holly felt breathless. She always forgot how good-looking Jack was, and how far she had to look up to meet his gaze. The sight of him made her pregnant body coil in expectation of his touch.

Ryan grabbed his father's hand and tagged along beside him as he crossed to her.

She swallowed down the sudden lump of emotion in her throat and said, "Hello, Jack."

"Hello, Holly." His gaze dropped to her burgeoning belly.

She could see that he wanted to touch. He'd been fascinated by the way her abdomen grew when she'd been pregnant with Ryan. How taut it was, like a drum, when the rest of her was so soft. She reached for his hand and laid it on her belly and said, "She's been moving around a lot today."

"She? Do you know the baby's sex?"

"No. I just have a feeling that this time it's a little girl." She felt her smile grow until it was so big it crinkled her eyes.

And he smiled back. His hand moved reverently over her belly, which was framed by a clingy white knit maternity top. "I'd like having a daughter to spoil." He jerked his hand away. "She just kicked me," he said with a laugh.

"Let me feel," Ryan said.

He put his small hand on her belly, and Jack put his larger hand over it. The two men in her life waited with bated breath for the baby to move again.

"She's obviously found a comfortable spot to sleep," Holly said a few moments later, when the child inside her stayed quiescent.

Jack reluctantly removed his hand and took a step back. Ryan followed suit. Jack turned and looked around the living room, which held the hodgepodge of furniture the two of them had bought a piece at a time during their marriage.

They'd collected items they liked, without any thought to how they would look together, with mixed fabrics, mostly in blues and browns and beiges. A glass-bottomed lamp. A pine end table. A corduroy chair with an ottoman for him. A silk, flower-print upholstered rocker for her. And a long, wide, durable leather couch for making love.

"I'm sorry I'm late. I couldn't get here sooner," Jack said. "I had a meeting this morning. Work. I tried calling, but you didn't pick up."

She slapped her forehead. "I stuck my purse under

the sink in the bathroom while the movers were here. I'm sorry you couldn't reach me."

"I left a message that I'd be late."

Which was precisely why she hadn't checked her voice mail after the movers left. She'd been too afraid she'd find a message that said he'd changed his mind about coming. "I'm just glad you're here."

An awkward silence followed, when he could have said, "I'm glad to be here." And didn't.

He glanced around. "It looks like someone's already done all the heavy lifting."

"Not me," she assured him. "The movers stayed long enough for me to figure out where I wanted things."

She could see he was disappointed. She'd shut him out of so much during their marriage. Now it was happening again. "There is something you could help me with," she said, quickly looking around the living room to see what she could move.

She pointed to the rocker in which she'd sat for so many hours nursing Ryan. "I think my rocker is too far from the fireplace."

"You always did like to roast your toes," he said with a wry grin, heading across the room. "Come here and let me know when I've got it right."

"I'll help you, Daddy," Ryan said.

"Thanks, son."

Holly bit back a warning to Ryan to be careful. She'd noticed the other day that he had a few bruises on his legs and one on his elbow. He was a boy. He needed to run and play. And she knew Jack wouldn't let him get hurt.

As Jack lifted the chair and moved it forward, she

could see Ryan's hold on the opposite side was probably adding weight, but Jack only said, "Good job, Ryan."

"Three or four inches is plenty," she said.

Jack adjusted the rocker, angled it and said, "How's that?"

"Yeah, Mommy," Ryan said, putting his hands on his hips in imitation of his father and surveying the rocker. "How's that?"

"Perfect." She smiled at him. At them. Beamed, actually. Was she overdoing it?

Jack cocked a brow, and she knew he was waiting for the *but* that usually followed anything he did for her. He was going to be waiting a long time.

"I could use some help unpacking in the kitchen," she said. Was that surprise she saw in Jack's eyes? Had she really been so critical? And so independent? Was it so very strange for her to ask for his help? Apparently, it was.

"Come on, Ryan," he said, "Let's go help Mommy unpack."

Holly had already unpacked enough dishes and pots and pans and silverware to show Jack where she wanted everything. They worked together for the next hour in perfect harmony.

"What's your schedule like at the hospital?" he asked.

"Believe it or not, I'm working nine to five."

"I'll believe it when I see it," he said.

In the past, Holly had often become so engrossed in her work that she'd forgotten the time and ended up missing supper, and sometimes even Ryan's bedtime. That was another thing she planned to change.

"Did you get as sick the first couple of months as you did with Ryan?" Jack asked.

She shook her head. "But I've needed a lot more rest during this pregnancy, so I've been taking a break in the middle of the day for a nap. I've turned forty-one, you know."

"Gee. I guess that makes me about forty-three." He tottered across the kitchen like an old man, nearly dropping a serving dish before he got it up on the top shelf.

"Laugh at me all you want," Holly said. "But you try growing a baby and see how you feel."

"Are you all right? I mean, is there something wrong you're not telling me about?"

He suddenly looked worried. She put a hand on his forearm—the first time she'd touched him since he'd walked in the door—and felt the muscles tighten beneath her fingertips. She looked into his dark brown eyes and said, "My doctor says I'm fine, Jack. But I'm not a kid anymore, so I have to take better care of myself and the baby."

"I can't believe M.D. Anderson agreed to a nine-to-five workday interrupted by naps."

"I told them those were the only terms I'd accept."

He turned away to drop some serving spoons into a drawer, breaking the contact between them. "That's going to be a real change for you."

"Yes, it will." In the past she'd put her work first, because it was the one thing she'd been certain she could count on. In the future she envisioned, she would be spending a lot more time with Jack and the children. From now on, they were her first priority.

It didn't take long to finish putting everything away. When they were done, she said, "How about some iced tea and grilled cheese sandwiches for lunch?"

"Sounds good," Jack said.

"Would you help Ryan set the table?"

"No problem."

While Ryan and Jack put out silverware and place mats on the dining room table and poured icy cups of the sun tea she'd brewed that morning, Holly made grilled cheese sandwiches and cut up some strawberries.

She felt the tension ease out of her shoulders as she and Jack and Ryan sat down to the first meal of their new life together. After they said a quick grace, she asked, "How was your meeting this morning?"

"I can't talk about it," Jack replied curtly.

"How was I supposed to know that?" she retorted. Holly realized she was ready to tear into Jack and brought herself up short. She made a face. There would be plenty of things to fight about that mattered. "Is there any part of what you're working on that you can share with me?"

He chewed a bite of sandwich and swallowed it before he answered. She thought maybe he was reining in his temper in much the same way she had, which she took as a good sign.

"I'm not sure how much I *should* tell you," he began tentatively.

"Is what you're doing dangerous?" she asked.

He snorted. "You know I wouldn't tell you that, even if it were the case."

"I'm curious, Jack."

"That's nothing new."

"I'm kind of tired, Mommy," Ryan interjected. "Can I go play with my Wii?"

"You haven't eaten much of your sandwich," she noted.

"I'm not hungry. Can I go?"

Holly figured her son was too excited by Jack's return to have much appetite and tired from all the unpacking they'd done. "Go ahead," she said.

Ryan shoved his chair back and left the dining room on the run.

"Must be a good game," Jack said as he watched him go.

"It's one he learned from Lucky and Chance at Christmas." She was watching Jack's face, so she saw him wince at the mention of Kate Pendleton's sons. "How are the twins?"

"Fine, the last time I saw them."

"When was that?"

"Yesterday. But things have changed a lot since then," he muttered.

Holly raised a questioning brow. "Has something happened?"

"You might say that."

She made a "spill it" gesture with her free hand.

"Kate and her sons have moved in with the twins' biological father, Wyatt Shaw."

Holly's jaw dropped. "Wyatt Shaw? J.D. isn't their father?"

Jack shook his head. "Kate picked Shaw up at a crowded bar nine years ago. And got pregnant with the twins."

"Lord have mercy. Those poor boys."

Jack snorted. "He's supposed to be a billionaire. There's nothing *poor* about those boys now. They're living in the lap of luxury."

"Why did they move in with him?" Holly asked. "I thought you and Kate were practically engaged."

"I planned to propose to her this weekend."

Holly felt her heart contract. She'd come *that close* to losing Jack forever. But something had happened to throw a monkey wrench into his plans. Something dire from the look on Jack's face. She didn't say she was sorry, because she wasn't. "I know you must be upset," she said instead.

"To say the least."

"What's going on, Jack? Can you tell me?"

One good thing that had come of their childhood together was that she and Jack had always shared their troubles. She'd been a discreet sounding board for him when he was working cases for the Texas Rangers and sympathized when he was frustrated by his parents' behavior. He'd held her in his arms when she cried for a dying child and sympathized when her search for a cure seemed stymied.

"I've missed having my best friend to talk to, Jack," she said into the silence.

He let out a soughing breath. And began to talk. "Shaw convinced Kate the boys would be in danger the moment his father found out the truth, and that they'd be safer living behind stone walls with him."

"Why would Dante D'Amato want to hurt his own grandsons? That doesn't make any sense."

"As it turns out, there's a kernel of truth in it. You're just missing a big piece of the puzzle."

She lifted a brow and said, "Which is?"

"J.D. Pendleton isn't dead."

"Then how were you going to marry Kate?" she blurted.

"We can't marry until he shows up, dead or alive."

"Who all knows J.D.'s alive?" Holly asked. "I mean, we all went to his funeral at Arlington, for heaven's sake. I cried when they played taps. They gave him a twenty-one-gun salute. They folded the flag and handed it to Kate."

"The circle in the know is small. Kate knows, because J.D. showed up in her living room alive and well a year after he'd supposedly died. I know because she told me. D'Amato knows because J.D. double-crossed him. I don't know how Shaw found out, but he knows, too."

"Does Ann Wade know?"

"She knows."

"Then why hasn't she made it public? She's running for president. What's going to happen when word gets out about this?"

"I think she plans to keep it quiet."

"Can she?"

"She can if J.D. doesn't show up alive."

"She hopes her own son will end up dead?" Holly said, aghast.

"He's got a lot of bad men after him."

Holly watched Jack stop himself from saying more. She wanted to know as much as he would tell her about his business, which was why she always listened without interrupting. But he'd apparently realized just how much he'd told her about J.D. Pendleton, because he changed the subject.

"The twins are looking forward to seeing Ryan when they can."

"I'm sure he'll enjoy spending time with them, too." Holly barely managed not to grimace. She'd been focused on how great it was that Jack and Kate weren't engaged, and the fact that Kate was living with the biological father of her sons. It hadn't occurred to her that instead of being halfway across the state, Kate and the twins were now living in the same city.

"Did Kate have to quit her job at BAMC?"

"Yes, but she's going to work at M.D. Anderson."

Holly bit back a gasp. She and Kate were going to be working in the same hospital! She wasn't sure what she would do if she encountered her nemesis face-to-face. She consoled herself with the thought that the University of Texas M.D. Anderson Cancer Center was such an enormous complex, with so many buildings taking up so many acres of land, their paths might never cross.

"This is bizarre," she murmured.

"You said it," Jack agreed.

Holly named her greatest fear. "Since Kate's going to be so close, are you planning to keep seeing each other?"

"I'm not sure how the situation with Kate is going to shake out," Jack said evasively. "It might be awkward, don't you think?"

"You mean, considering the fact that you're living with me?"

"I mean, considering the fact that she's sleeping with him."

Holly couldn't believe what Jack had just said. It was wonderful news if it was true.

He must have seen the shock on her face because he said, "Forget I said that."

"It's forgotten." But she was doing a little jig in her head.

"I don't think the living arrangements between Kate and Shaw are going to last very long."

"Really?" Holly hoped he was wrong.

"I think D'Amato is right. I think as soon as J.D. finds out who fathered the twins, he's going to make a move. When he does, I'll be waiting for him. Once he's caught, Kate and the twins can move back home."

Holly stood and picked up Ryan's plate and her own and headed for the kitchen, so Jack wouldn't see her face blanch. She hoped J.D. Pendleton didn't act as quickly as D'Amato thought or Jack hoped. Because once J.D. was out of the picture for good, Kate would be free to marry Jack.

"I've got some things in the back of my SUV I'd like to move in, if you can show me my bedroom," he said, setting the rest of the dishes on the counter beside Holly.

She stopped filling the dishwasher and looked coyly up at him. "I guess this means that, even though she's sleeping with him, you're not going to be sleeping with me."

Jack surprised her by chuckling. But he didn't suggest that they share the same bed. He gave her a friendly swat on the fanny and headed out the door.

"You can have the bedroom across the hall from Ryan," she called after him.

It was going to be a lot harder to seduce her husband if he was determined to sleep in another bedroom. Not that it couldn't be done. And not that she didn't intend to do it. It was just that, Kate Pendleton had set the bar very high, and with all the extra baby weight, Holly might have a little harder time getting over it.

But somehow, some way, she would.

15

"**M**om! Mom!"

Kate sat bolt upright, awakened from a deep sleep. It was morning, and she was alone in Shaw's bed. Where was he? What was going on? One of the boys was in trouble!

She leapt out of bed, stumbling on the sheet that caught her foot, started for the door—and realized she was naked. She turned and did a quick search for her nightgown but couldn't find it. She was headed for her suitcase to get something to wear when she heard another frenzied cry for help.

"Mom! Come quick!"

She yanked the top sheet free and wrapped it around her haphazardly, tripping over the silk cloth as she stumbled from Shaw's bedroom.

"What's wrong!" she cried. She hit the walls on one side and the windows on the other, as she raced down the hall, her black hair and the black sheet both flying.

She lurched through the first doorway she came to and slid to a stop, her heart beating like a frightened bird in her rib cage.

"Harley's here!" Lucky said, a wide grin on his face.

The black Lab sat in the center of Lucky's bed, tongue lolling, Lucky's arms slung around his neck.

"And Scratch!" Chance sat on Lucky's bed clutching the calico cat, which was hissing and ripping at the boy's pajama top to get free. Chance yowled as claws reached skin and let go, and the cat leapt off the bed straight for Kate.

Kate nearly dropped the sheet to catch the cat.

Fortunately, large male hands intercepted Scratch's leap.

"Gotcha!" Shaw said.

The boys laughed.

"You should have seen your face, Mom," Lucky said.

Kate was staring wide-eyed at Shaw, admiring the broad shoulders and six-pack abs revealed by the tight black T-shirt he wore. Her glance slid down to the Levi's that fit him like a glove and left hardly anything to the imagination. Not that she needed help remembering exactly what was cupped so lovingly in the front of his butter-soft jeans.

"I'm sorry they woke you up," Shaw said sympathetically. "I was going to let you sleep."

Kate shoved a belated hand through her tangled hair and blinked eyes clumped with mascara. She tightened the silk sheet around her naked body when she recognized the avid look in Shaw's eyes. That turned out to be a mistake. She looked down to see her nipples poking out like headlights beneath the black silk.

"I need to get dressed," she said.

"Mom, wait!" Lucky said, clambering off the bed, Harley climbing down after him. "Shaw says Big Doc and Little Doc are here, too, and that we can all go riding to a pond where we can swim and have a picnic as soon as we get dressed. Can we?"

Kate shot a perturbed look at Shaw, who said, "I suggested it, but I told them they had to ask you."

"Can we, Mom? Please?" Chance begged, joining his brother.

Kate could see her life spinning completely out of her control. "I thought you brought us here to keep us safe," she said to Shaw. "How safe are we going to be riding around the countryside on horseback?"

"The trails we'll be riding, and the pond, are on land I own surrounding my compound, all of which is fenced with barbed wire and patrolled by men with guard dogs."

"Like a prison," Kate muttered.

She saw Shaw's mouth tighten.

"Mom?" Lucky said. "Please, can we?"

She felt like throwing her hands up in defeat, but considering the circumstances, that was a bad idea. Instead, she tightened her hold on the black silk sheet, put a smile on her face and said, "That sounds like a lot of fun. As soon as you make your beds and straighten up these rooms—"

"Aw, Mom."

"Jeez, Mom."

"I have a housekeeper—" Shaw began.

She glared Shaw into silence and turned back to her sons. "After you make your beds and straighten up these rooms and get dressed and brush your teeth and comb your hair and eat your breakfast, we can go."

"Yippee! We're going on a picnic!" Lucky began jumping up and down, which set the dog to leaping and barking.

The cat made a horrible snakelike spitting sound and raked Shaw's forearm with its claws. Shaw began muttering imprecations that ended with, "A curse on all cats!"

Kate quickly transferred her two-handed grip on the sheet into one fist and rescued the cat from Shaw, who was about to squeeze the feline into submission.

The agitated cat crawled halfway up Kate's chest until it was hanging over her shoulder like a calico fur shawl.

She scowled at Shaw, who was shaking his head at her in disbelief. "I'm going to get dressed." She kicked the silk sheet out of her way, then turned and tripped on it.

Shaw caught her before she fell. His hands brushed across the crests of both nipples before they landed at her waist.

"Sorry," he said as he steadied her.

She glanced at his face and saw a mischievous look that reminded her of her eight-year-old sons. She realized he wasn't the least bit sorry! She straightened her spine, lifted her chin, kicked the sheet from around her ankles and stalked back down the hall.

When she reached Shaw's bedroom, she discovered he was right behind her. She whirled and barred the door with her body. "If you take one step into this room before I'm dressed, I'll sic this cat on you."

Shaw laughed and held up both hands in surrender. "Since that truly is a fate worse than death, I think I'll go see if I can help the twins get ready."

"Shaw," she said.

He turned and walked the few steps back to her. "Yes, Kate?"

She felt a shiver of pleasure at the sound of his raspy voice saying her name. But she had a point to make. "You shouldn't spoil them. They have to do their own chores. And they're perfectly capable of dressing themselves."

His brow furrowed. "I..."

It took her a moment to realize what he wasn't saying. What he would never admit. He was starved for the sight of his sons. He'd missed so much, and he was afraid he'd never catch up.

The sad thing was, he could never get those years back. And spoiling her sons would only make them brats.

"I know it's tempting to give the twins everything their hearts desire," she said. "But they need a little adversity in their lives. It's good for their character."

"They need a father in their lives," Shaw said. "Let me find my own way, Kate. If I make mistakes, I'll learn from them."

In other words, *Back off.*

"Then check and make sure Lucky brushes his teeth. He wets the toothbrush because he knows I check, but he doesn't use toothpaste."

Shaw smiled. "Will do."

She shut the door and leaned back against it. Wyatt Shaw was turning out to be not at all what she'd expected.

She dropped the sheet, then crossed the room, gently lifted the cat off her shoulder and settled her on Shaw's pillow. "Make yourself comfortable, Scratch," she said with a grin.

With any luck, Scratch would make Shaw's pillow

her home away from home, and he would have to re-move the obstreperous cat every time he wanted it back.

Kate headed for the shower, feeling achy all over. She glanced down at her body and saw a bruise on her inner thigh, one at her waist and a love bite low on her neck. She hadn't been aware of Shaw making any of the marks, which was a sign of how passionate their two bouts of lovemaking had been.

And yes, she'd needed the extra sleep this morning, because after they'd returned to bed, Shaw had pulled her close. He hadn't made love to her—because she hadn't asked. He'd simply spooned her body against his and held her close.

She'd lain awake, her body tense with expectation—and aching need—waiting for him to break his promise. Waiting for him to take her to the heights of ecstasy again. And finally cursing him for having the self-control to lie with her and not take what she knew, from the press of his body against hers, he desperately wanted.

It was no wonder she felt tired and sore and sick at heart.

She'd hurt Jack badly last night. Then she'd lain in the circle of Shaw's arms actually regretting the fact that he hadn't made love to her again. What was wrong with her?

Maybe Jack's not the right man for you. Maybe Shaw is.

It was not a comfortable thought, considering everything she knew about the mob boss's son. Nor was it comfortable to look at her behavior with Shaw in the stark light of day. She couldn't keep giving in to his charm. Otherwise, she'd be begging him to make love to her before the week was out. She was going to have to grow a backbone—one so straight and strong it couldn't be easily spooned into Shaw's enticing embrace.

16

Wyatt kept a sharp eye out as they rode north from the stable through shortleaf and loblolly pines, post oaks and black hickory, toward the pond on his property. He trusted his men to do their jobs. But he wasn't taking any chances with his sons' lives. Or with Kate's.

It was hard not to get distracted. He was as fascinated by Kate now as he had been for a single night nine years ago. She was a riddle he planned to solve.

The challenge was convincing her that he was the man of her dreams, when she believed it was some other guy. His charm wasn't enough, though he could briefly enchant Kate. She enjoyed matching wits with him, though she gave in whenever the battle cut too close to the heart of their differences. He knew she was physically attracted to him, though she'd protested she was not.

Today, he would find out the truth. There would be opportunities to touch when they were playing in the pond. The brush of his lips against hers. A breast grazed in passing. Or cupped with his hand. Each would tell a tale. He would let Kate's body answer honestly, since he couldn't trust her lips.

He glanced surreptitiously at the woman riding across from him. She was poetry on horseback. And her sons—their sons—were well on the road to becoming good horsemen. Wyatt often rode horseback on his land when he wanted peace and quiet to think. But the twins bubbled with energy and excitement and their chatter competed with the morning calls of the bluejays and chickadees.

"Don't they ever wind down?" he asked Kate.

"I'd be worried if they did," she replied.

When they reached an open field with an outcropping of rock on the opposite side, Lucky shouted to Chance, "I'll race you to that rock!"

He dug his heels into Big Doc's sides as Chance shouted, "Go!" and both quarter horses leapt into action.

Wyatt shouted, "Stop!"

Chance reined his mount to a stop so fast the quarter horse was practically sitting on his rump. Lucky must not have heard his shout, or simply ignored it.

Wyatt kicked his horse into a gallop that quickly overtook the boy. He leaned down and grabbed the reins near Big Doc's mouth and jerked the animal to a stop so abrupt that Lucky was thrown forward out of the Western saddle halfway up the horse's neck.

Wyatt came off his horse before it had completely stopped, yanked a startled Lucky off his mount and dropped him on the ground, leaning over him to shout, "What the hell were you thinking!"

Lucky looked back at him from wide, frightened eyes and burst into raucous tears. His horse whinnied and skittered away.

A moment later, Kate came flying off her horse and put herself between Wyatt and her son, her teeth bared. "Leave him alone!"

Wyatt balled his hands and stuck them on his hips because he didn't want Kate to see how badly he was still shaking from the overdose of adrenaline that had fed into his bloodstream when he'd realized how much danger his son was in.

His heart was still thundering in his chest, and the damned woman was giving him hell for saving her kid. By God, for saving *his own damned kid!*

"The boy nearly got himself killed and his horse lamed," he snarled.

"Lucky's a good rider. He can stay in the saddle just fine at a gallop," Kate retorted.

"That field is riddled with groundhog holes," Wyatt said through gritted teeth. "One wrong step and the horse stumbles and breaks a leg and the kid goes flying and breaks his neck."

"Couldn't you just have said that?" she shot back.

"He should know better than to go galloping off where he isn't familiar with the terrain."

"Lucky and Chance have been doing all their riding in an *arena* in a *city.* You're the one who brought them out here in the middle of nowhere," she pointed out. "And they're only eight years old!"

"Yeah, well at this rate, they'll be lucky to make nine."

Kate made a frustrated sound in her throat, turned her back on him and went down on one knee to pull the crying boy into her arms. "It's all right, Lucky. Dry your tears."

Lucky wiped his tears with the tail of his T-shirt, then swiped at his runny nose with his arm and wiped that on his T-shirt as well. Wyatt had a monogrammed handkerchief in his back pocket, if the boy had asked. But with Kate on a tear, he wasn't about to say anything.

To his amazement, Kate said, "Of course, Shaw is right, sweetheart. You need to be more careful when you're riding in country you don't know."

Wyatt felt his gut wrench when the boy hiccuped away another sob. "I could gallop anywhere at GeePa's ranch."

"That's because GeePa has waged his own private war on gophers at Bitter Creek," Kate said, wiping away the last of the tears with her thumbs. "Now go get Big Doc."

She turned the boy and headed him in the direction of his horse, which had stopped a short distance away to munch on some buffalo grass.

"I'm sorry I yelled at him," Shaw said to Kate as he watched the boy's slump-shouldered shuffle to his horse.

"Don't tell me, tell him," she said as she remounted. "Come on, Chance," she said as she kicked her horse into a trot and headed back along the trail they'd been following.

Chance frowned at Shaw over his shoulder, shot his brother a sympathetic look, then hurried to catch up with his mother.

Shaw grabbed the reins and threw himself into the saddle. He stuck his feet in the stirrups and walked his mount over to Lucky, watching to see if the boy could get back on his horse on his own.

The kid looked over his shoulder once at Shaw, his expression pretty much the same sour look as his brother had worn, then stuck his foot in the stirrup and climbed his way up into the saddle.

Shaw said nothing, just turned his horse and followed after Kate and Chance. Lucky caught up and rode beside him.

The boy's cheeks were still flushed and his eyes were red from crying. "I'm sorry, Shaw," he said.

Wyatt was surprised to hear Lucky apologize to him when Kate seemed to think he needed to apologize to the boy. "You didn't know about the groundhogs," he said gruffly.

"Yeah, but I heard you shout to stop and I kept on going." He glanced up at Shaw to see what effect his confession would have.

Shaw struggled not to smile. He'd been a lot like Lucky growing up, never taking no for an answer. "I'm sorry, too," he said.

"What are you sorry for?" Lucky asked.

"I shouldn't have yelled at you."

"My dad used to yell at us all the time and he never apologized."

Shaw clamped his teeth to keep from telling the boy what he thought of a man who yelled at his kids "all the time." Especially when the kids at whom that son of a bitch J.D. Pendleton had been yelling were *his* sons.

"There's an old wagon trail near the pond where it's safe to run your horse," Wyatt said. "When we get there, you and your brother can have that race."

Lucky shrugged, apparently no longer interested in racing.

Shaw realized he would do just about anything to bring back the excitement and joy in his son's demeanor that this incident seemed to have quelled. "If it's any consolation," he said. "I think you might have won that race."

The boy brightened. "Do you really think so?"

"You were first off the mark. And you've got a good seat. You just need to hang on a little tighter with your thighs. But those muscles will get stronger with time."

He watched as his son tested the muscles in his thighs with his free hand and said, "Yeah, they're getting stronger every day."

"Come on," Wyatt said. "Let's catch up with your mom and your brother."

They loped their horses along the path until they caught up with Kate and Chance, who'd slowed their horses to a walk.

"Is that the pond?" Chance asked Wyatt, pointing to a shiny pool of water in the distance.

"That's it," he confirmed.

"Can we ride ahead to look?" Lucky asked.

"Go for it," Wyatt said.

Lucky gave a yip, and the two boys loped off down the trail toward the pond.

"It looks like you and Lucky made up," Kate said.

"I was scared he was going to get hurt," Shaw admitted. "That's why I yelled at him."

"I've done the same thing myself."

"You have?"

"Sure," Kate said. "As much as you promise yourself that *next time* you'll be calm, you lose it all over again. Parenting is a hair-raising proposition."

"I'm beginning to see that."

When Wyatt and Kate arrived at the pond, the boys were already off their horses exploring the flora and fauna.

"Can we swim now?" Chance asked.

"If it's all right with your mom."

"Are there any dangers we should know about?" Kate asked, cocking a brow.

Wyatt smiled ruefully and said, "Just one that I know of."

"What's that?"

"The pond's spring-fed."

"So it's cold," Kate said.

"Icy," he replied with a grin. "It feels good though, when it's hot, like it is today."

"So can we swim or not?" Lucky asked.

"Have fun," Kate said.

The boys hurriedly unstrapped the saddlebags on their horses that contained swimsuits and towels and stripped down where they stood. As soon as they yanked up their suits, they raced into the pond, shrieking as the cold water turned their skin into gooseflesh.

Shaw noticed Kate made a point of picking up their clothes and folding them and setting them on a nearby rock. "I thought they were supposed to pick up after themselves."

"There are exceptions, like now, when I know these clothes will end up soaking wet if I don't move them. They won't care. But I'll worry that they might catch a chill later."

"I see," Shaw said. "So you're doing this for your own peace of mind."

"Exactly."

When she made no move to change her clothes he asked, "Aren't you going to swim?"

She eyed him sideways from beneath lowered lashes. "I can't remember the last time I put on a swimsuit."

"But you brought one?"

She nodded.

"I will, if you will," he said with a coaxing smile.

She looked around and said, "Where can I change?"

He pointed to some thick blueberry bushes and said, "Plenty of cover, and you're safe from bears until the berries ripen."

Kate laughed and headed behind the bushes.

Wyatt stripped down right where he was. He saw Kate sneaking peeks at him from behind the bushes but noticed she kept herself well hidden.

He waited for Kate because he thought she might sit on the banks of the pond rather than joining him and the boys in the frigid water. He whistled in appreciation when she came out from behind the bushes.

Kate's arms were up over her head as she finished putting her hair in a ponytail. The black tank swimsuit was designed to reveal a woman's flaws, but Kate didn't have any that he could see. The suit hugged her hourglass figure, and the high cut emphasized the slender length of her legs.

"Wow," he said softly.

"You're remembering the way I looked a long time ago. My waist isn't nearly as small and—"

"You're beautiful."

He wanted to touch. But he wasn't really sure that he could touch without wanting a whole lot more. And with the boys here, that couldn't happen, even if he could coax her into asking him to make love to her. So he just looked. And imagined what it would be like to hold her in his arms.

There was no hiding the moment her nipples peaked beneath the skintight swimsuit. He tried to meet her gaze, but she wouldn't look at him. Maybe it wasn't going to be as hard as he'd thought to get her to say yes to making love to him.

"Let's swim!" she said, suddenly turning and heading for the pond.

He followed after her, enjoying the sexy sway of her hips—and her tight ass—in the swimsuit.

When the water reached her waist she glanced at him over her shoulder, her teeth chattering, and said, "I'm freezing!"

"Better to get in all at once." Wyatt put his hands on either side of her waist, lifted her high and threw her toward the center of the pond. He dove into the water after her, caught her by the waist again underwater and threw her up into the air a second time.

The boys shrieked with laughter as their mother erupted from the water, her arms and legs akimbo, and came splashing down.

Wyatt was paddling in the water beside the boys when Kate came up spluttering water and scrubbing her eyes.

"Now you're in trouble," she said. "Get him, boys!"

Both twins launched themselves at Wyatt, one grabbing each shoulder and shoving him underwater. He was tangling with the twins when he felt a jerk on his swimsuit and realized it was now hanging around his ankles.

Kate came up grinning, and she and the boys shared high fives.

Wyatt laughed and ducked underwater to pull his swimsuit back up. But he didn't immediately resurface. He swam over to the twins and threw first one, and then the other laughing boy, high into the air.

He came up beside Kate while the boys were still swimming their way to the surface, pulled her nearly naked body against his naked chest and stole a quick kiss.

"Don't!" she said, shoving at his shoulders. "I told you I don't want to confuse the boys."

"They didn't see a thing. And you liked it. I can tell," he said with a grin meant to charm her.

Her eyes sparkled with laughter, but she bit it back and tried to look stern. She couldn't chastise him further because the twins had bobbed back up.

Chance swam over to him and said, "Shaw, can you teach me how to float on my back? Lucky can do it, but I can't."

"Sure," Wyatt said.

"Why don't you and I play a game of Marco Polo?" Kate suggested to Lucky.

"Yeah!" Lucky agreed, swimming away as Kate closed her eyes and yelled, "Marco!"

Lucky shouted, "Polo!" and swam away from the location where he'd been, so his mother couldn't find him in the water.

Wyatt was amazed at how skillfully Kate had maneuvered the situation so he and Chance would have time alone. He was going to have to remember that trick.

"What seems to be the problem?" Wyatt asked Chance.

"When I float on my back, I think I'm going to sink," he explained.

"Give it a try, and let's see what happens."

Chance turned onto his back, lifted his head out of the water and began frantically splashing with both hands and feet to stay afloat.

Wyatt put his hands under the boy to support his back and said, "Relax. I've got you."

He was surprised when the boy didn't immediately relax.

"I've got you," he repeated.

He saw the mistrust in Chance's eyes, which questioned whether he could rely on the man holding him not to let go.

He put a little more pressure on his hands under Chance's back, so the boy could feel his support, and he started to relax. But he kept his head out of the water.

"Relax your head."

"I'll get water in my ears," Chance said.

"Is that a problem? Do you get earaches or something?"

"I just don't like it," Chance said.

"Well, that might be part of your problem," Wyatt said. "Kind of have to get your head in the water to be able to relax and float."

Chance grimaced. "Do I have to?"

"I'll tell you a secret," Wyatt said. "I don't like getting water in my ears, either. But everything sounds kind of neat once I do."

Chance leaned his head back slowly until it was floating and made faces as his ears filled with water.

"Can you hear how funny my voice sounds now?" Wyatt said.

"Yeah," Chance said.

Once the boy wasn't struggling to keep his head out

of the water, he was able to relax his arms and legs, which helped him to float.

"How are you doing?" Wyatt asked.

"I'm floating!" Chance said with amazement.

"Try waving your arms and legs a little bit to move yourself around," Wyatt said.

The boy waved his arms and scissor-kicked his legs and went floating away.

Wyatt stayed beside him, ready to catch him if he started to sink.

"I'm floating," Chance said with a grin.

"And I sound funny, right?" Wyatt said with a smile.

"Yeah, you do," Chance agreed. He turned himself over and swam freestyle to his mother shouting, "Mom! I can float!"

Wyatt swam after him and ended up joining the game of Marco Polo. Kate called an end to the game when Wyatt caught her—actually, one of her breasts in the palm of his hand—underwater.

"Time for lunch!" she said.

She had a tight grip on his wrist underwater when she spoke, so he stayed behind when the boys swam like crazy for shore.

"You have to stop this!" she hissed. "I don't like it."

"You're lying," he said, staring down at her peaked nipples.

"I'm cold," she snapped.

"I'm not." He let her see the heat she created in him and watched her throat and cheeks flush with warmth.

"When are you going to give up?" she said, exasperated.

"Not until you give in."

17

Kate was determined to keep her distance from Shaw the rest of the afternoon. To her chagrin, he never came near her. He focused his attention entirely on the twins.

The three of them seemed to have a wonderful time playing word games while they consumed the chunky peanut butter and grape jelly sandwiches—how had he known that was the twins' favorite?—he'd brought for their lunch. She'd been faced with the choice of either joining in the fun or sitting on the blanket like a lump, and she wasn't that much of a spoilsport.

The result was an afternoon that felt far too much like a happy family outing. In fact, she would have enjoyed herself tremendously if she hadn't known Shaw had an agenda.

He'd already succeeded in seducing Lucky and Chance, who admired and respected him and sought his approval. There was nothing wrong with the boys liking their biological father. She just didn't want them getting too attached, because despite Shaw's hopes and plans, this situation wasn't permanent. She didn't want her sons to be hurt when Jack replaced Shaw in their lives.

Won't they be hurt when they find out that Shaw is their biological father, and that you took them away from him? They've attached themselves to Shaw in a way they never did with Jack. Why is that? Is it something Shaw is doing? Or something Jack didn't?

"Kate? Are you ready to go?" Shaw asked.

Kate had been so caught up having fun, she hadn't noticed how much time had passed. She only realized the sun was headed down when Shaw said, "We need to get started, or it'll be dark before we get back."

On the ride home, she stayed at Chance's side, forcing Shaw to ride with Lucky behind them on the narrow trail. She could feel his eyes focused on her almost like a caressing hand.

She felt aware and alive. And aroused. And angry because Shaw knew what he was doing to her.

She was the "other half" of his agenda.

Kate refused to be captivated by Shaw as her sons had been. She'd refused his sexual advances throughout the day, which hadn't been easy. She'd made it as plain as she could that she was in love with another man. She didn't know what else she could do to convince the stubborn fool that she would never—could never—fall in love with him.

It had very little to do with whether Shaw was a person she could love. He had a number of admirable qualities, among which was the amazing rapport he'd managed to develop with their sons in such a short time.

She wasn't going to deny that she found him physically attractive. He was and she did.

His wealth was evidence of his intelligence, his inventiveness and his integrity—if he wasn't lying about being an honest businessman, she thought cynically.

And Kate could appreciate Shaw's determination to do whatever was necessary to get what he wanted: the woman he'd spent the night with nine years ago.

But he was fighting a battle he couldn't win. Because that woman no longer existed.

Kate had given her heart to Jack McKinley when she was only nineteen and had it handed right back to her. It had been broken during her marriage, challenged by her single night of sin and eviscerated during the year she'd spent as a widow. There was hardly enough left of it to give to anyone.

But what there was, she had offered to Jack. She wasn't about to rip it out of his grasp and offer it to anyone else. Especially not to some rogue who laughed with relish while he did his best to steal it from her.

She was done playing Shaw's game, because it was a contest neither of them could win.

When they arrived back at the stable, she unsaddled her horse without help from Shaw. She ate what was put in front of her on the dining room table and made sure she and the boys helped with the dishes. She got the twins ready for bed on her own, although Shaw came to bid them good night.

She didn't allow him to make a battle out of where she would sleep. She simply put on her most concealing nightgown, pulled down the covers of his bed and hopped into the side she'd slept on last night.

She brought a book to bed with her, a Regency-era romance novel, where the Duke of Whatever was a blackguard, until the heroine reformed him. Kate had known from page one that, after a great many trials and tribulations, the duke and his new duchess would live happily ever after. Kate desperately needed the fantasy because her own experience was so far from it.

Once again, Shaw undressed without a thought to her modesty, showing off his splendid physique in the soft light from the lamps on either side of the bed.

She reread the same paragraph three times because the hero in her book didn't have abs or a flat stomach or lean hips that could compete with Shaw's. She finally gave up and snapped, "Put on some clothes!"

He grinned and sauntered over to his wardrobe. He pulled on a pair of black, thigh-length briefs that did absolutely nothing to hide any of the assets she was trying not to admire.

He laughed. The blackguard.

Kate was fuming by the time he joined her in bed. She was expecting another fight, but he surprised her by switching off the light on his side of the bed, turning his broad and impressively muscular back to her, and saying, "Good night. Sleep tight."

She absolutely, positively refused to say the rest.

She heard him chuckle and whisper, "Don't let the bedbugs bite."

Actually, it was a pretty good exit line. At least, it left her with nothing to say.

Kate doggedly kept reading the same paragraph, frustrated by her awareness of the man pretending to sleep next to her. *Pretending* because she could tell by the uneven rhythm of his breathing that he was faking it.

He'd left her itching for a fight, which she refused to provoke, because she knew that was exactly what he wanted.

It dawned on her that she hadn't spoken with Jack today. She should call and ask him how the move had gone yesterday and how he was getting along with his pregnant wife.

His pregnant wife.

Kate refused to be daunted by what now seemed to be overwhelming odds against any kind of "happily ever after" with Jack. She marked her page and set down her book, then got out of bed and located her cell phone, after a search through her purse and her overnight bag and the pockets of her jeans. She jumped back into bed, crossed her legs, plumped a pillow up behind her and called Jack.

Let Shaw *pretend* to sleep through this, she thought with devilish glee.

"Hi, Jack. Yes, I'm sorry to be calling so late."

She heard the silk sheets rustle on the other side of the bed. "Yes, I'm in his bed. But I've run a coil of barbed wire down the center of it, a sort of no-man's-land he's afraid to cross for fear of losing important body parts."

Shaw rose up the length of his arms like a waking tiger and glared at her.

She winked at him. "You're lucky to have a room of your own," she told Jack. "I did ask. He said no, so I'm making do."

She pursed her lips. "Well, yes. I did kiss him again, but not because I wanted to." She glanced at Shaw and said, "We were swimming, and he just…took it."

Shaw muttered, "You bet I did. And I'd do it again."

"No, I don't think I have to worry about it happening again."

Shaw's eyes narrowed, and Kate knew she was walking a fine line. If she pulled the tiger's tail too hard he was liable to whirl and pounce on her.

"How are things with you?" she asked Jack. "Ryan's sick?" she said anxiously. "A hundred and two? Are you sure it's just the flu?" She glanced at Shaw, sharing the worry she felt, and saw he was sitting up, listening attentively.

"Shouldn't you take him to the emergency room?" Kate asked. "Yes, I did forget you have a doctor in the house. Be sure to call me tomorrow and let me know he's all right."

She held her hand over the phone and said to Shaw, "Jack wants to know when I start work."

"Tomorrow, if you like."

She took her hand off the phone and said, "I start at M.D. Anderson tomorrow. I'm not sure yet where in the hospital I'll be working."

"With pediatric cancer patients," Shaw said.

Kate turned and stared at Shaw with horror. "I've got to go, Jack. I'll talk with you tomorrow."

She snapped the phone closed and said, "You've got to be kidding! You have me working in the same department as Jack's wife? Am I in the same building? On the same floor?"

"I have no idea. You'll find out when you get there."

"What makes you think I'd take a job under those conditions?"

"The amputees who need your help are kids who've lost a limb to osteosarcoma. The hospital is making great strides in treating bone cancer without amputation, but they're not always successful in saving limbs."

"Isn't there somewhere else in the hospital I could work?"

"I thought you wanted a job similar to what you were doing with disabled vets at BAMC."

She did. She would love the job if she wasn't afraid of running into Holly every day. But if Holly was going to be doing research, and she was going to be doing physical therapy, and as big as M.D. Anderson was, there was a good chance they'd be working nowhere near each other.

Better to wait and see. She could always quit and find another job on her own. She carefully set down her phone and picked up her book.

"How long are you going to read?" Shaw asked. "I can't sleep with the light on."

She raised an eyebrow. "I'll be more than happy to go sleep in another bed. In another room."

He lay back down and turned his back to her. "Just remember we all have to be ready to go tomorrow morning by seven."

"We have to *leave* by seven? The boys usually *wake up* at seven."

"Then it should be an interesting morning," Shaw said.

Kate was still staring at the same page without seeing the words written on it when she heard Shaw snore. She thought he was faking it, so she gave him a little shove. He turned over and the snoring stopped, but he was clearly asleep.

She was wide-awake.

She was going to need her wits about her tomorrow, so she should try to get what sleep she could. She marked the page in her book, turned out the light, punched the feather pillow into submission and closed her eyes.

But she didn't find any peace, because there was nothing she could actively do to end the situation she was in. She was waiting for Jack's wife to have her baby. She was waiting for Shaw to get tired of hearing her refusals. She was waiting for J.D. to get caught.

She sighed and started counting backward from one hundred. Maybe that would work.

Ninety-nine. Ninety-eight.

How had her life gotten so far out of her control?

Eight-three.

When she thought about it, every bad thing that had happened to her could be traced back to her decision to marry J.D. Pendleton.

Seventy-six.

She wondered what that son of a bitch was doing tonight.

18

J.D. was cold and scared and pissed off. His day had started well and ended badly.

His mother had loaned him his father's two-seat Piper Cub to fly himself from the airstrip on the Pendleton Ranch to a small county airport south of San Antonio. J.D. loved flying. As a bonus, for the few hours he was in the air, he knew he was safe.

The illusion was false and fleeting. When he landed, D'Amato's hitmen were waiting for him.

J.D. couldn't figure out how they'd found him, unless his mother had said something to D'Amato. It was a sad state of affairs when your own mother wanted you dead. He had no intention of helping her by killing D'Amato. When he was done with his business here in Texas, which included getting rid of Shaw and that bitch wife of his, he intended to disappear for good—courtesy of the federal government and the witness protection program.

J.D. had a certain video of a certain mobster committing a certain crime, which he intended to use to start a new life. Of course, he still had the twenty million dollars in heroin that hadn't really gone overboard, which would make his life in witness protection more comfortable.

Somehow, he'd stayed one step ahead of D'Amato's men at the airport. He'd pulled the Piper Cub in behind the hangar, slipped into the back of one of the delivery trucks supplying materials for a building under construction on the site and made an ignominious escape.

The truck had made a delivery stop at the Hilton Palacio del Rio on the River Walk in the middle of downtown San Antonio, a couple of blocks from the Alamo. He'd remained hidden behind a stack of boxes until the deliveryman headed inside with his load and simply walked away.

Enough tourists thronged the River Walk, restaurants and shops along the San Antonio River that were recessed below street level, that J.D. felt comfortable blending into the crowd. He sat down at one of the riverside café tables shaded by a brightly colored umbrella and had an enormous lunch of his favorite Mexican foods—flautas, chalupas, tacos, rice and beans, with some sopapillas doused in cinnamon and soaked with honey for dessert.

He also consumed a king-size frozen margarita, which helped to slow down his ratcheting heartbeat. The alcohol buzz kept him sitting longer than he probably should have. He got antsy and started making note of the people walking by. He saw a lot of men and women wearing military uniforms, not really surprising when San Antonio was home to five military bases, both army and air force.

Some of the soldiers had visible prosthetic limbs, also not surprising when Brooke Army Medical Center had a whole floor devoted to patients with appendages severed by IEDs—improvised explosive devices.

Thinking of soldiers with severed limbs reminded J.D. of his wife, who worked giving physical therapy to disabled vets at BAMC.

J.D. set down his frozen drink. And smiled.

IEDs. And his wife.

Why not use an IED to take out his bitch wife and her lover? He could simply plant a powerful IED on the roadside where he knew Shaw and the bitch would be traveling and detonate it remotely.

He would have to make sure the kids weren't in the car with them. Lucky and Chance were the only ones who knew where his "extra insurance"—a cell phone video of D'Amato killing a hireling who'd double-crossed him—was hidden.

A friend of J.D.'s in the Mexican Mafia, Lou Ferme, had sent J.D. the cell phone for safekeeping. The video showed D'Amato personally executing the man by shooting him in the back of the head.

Before he left for Afghanistan, J.D. had given a small box containing the cell phone to his sons and told them to bury it. His life depended on keeping the location of the box a secret, he'd told them seriously. They were not to tell anyone but him where it was. And he didn't want to know where they'd hidden it until he came home from the war.

While J.D. was in Afghanistan, Lou flapped his mouth, and D'Amato discovered the existence of the video. D'Amato's enforcer, Roberto, tortured Lou—toenails and testicles were both involved—until he confessed that he'd given the cell phone to J.D.

D'Amato had demanded that J.D. give up the video if he wanted to live. Of course, J.D. was certain that the in-

stant he handed over the cell phone with the incriminat-
ing evidence, he was a dead man. Which was when he'd
come up with the brilliant idea of stealing the twenty million dollars in smack, faking his death and disappearing.

As far as the kids knew, he was dead. They might
already have dug up the box. But he knew they hadn't
given it to Kate, because if they had, she would already
have turned it over to that Texas Ranger she'd been
kissing when he'd shown up in her kitchen last fall.

Maybe having the kids hide the cell phone hadn't
been the smartest move he'd ever made. But at least
he could get to it without D'Amato's guys following
him to a bank safe deposit box. Just thinking about the
condition Lou was in when Roberto was done with
him had J.D.'s heart hammering hard in his chest. So
far, he hadn't been caught by D'Amato's wise guys.
But if his luck ran out, he was going to need that cell
phone to buy his life.

J.D. felt eyes on him and trusted his instincts
enough to throw some money on the table and head
back up the stairs to the world above. Looking down
from the waist-high stone wall at street level, he saw
the hitmen moving along the River Walk below him,
showing his picture to waiters and waitresses.

He hailed a taxi and got a ride up Broadway to a used
car dealership, where he paid cash for a white Lexus SUV.
Then he headed north to the I-410 beltway around the city.

J.D. had stolen munitions all during his tour in the
Texas National Guard and shipped a few more home
from Afghanistan, all of which he kept in one of the
thousands of storage units located along I-410 North
used by transient military families.

He had plenty of explosives to build an IED. He just wasn't sure it was absolutely safe to retrieve them.

J.D. was almost certain D'Amato didn't know about the storage unit. He'd used a fellow soldier's name—the man he'd traded places with when he'd faked his death, actually—and paid cash in advance each year for the unit.

He'd chosen an unattended storage facility, with no surveillance video camera, where all he had to do was key in a code and a metal gate would open, allowing him access to the outdoor storage unit.

Today he found something new, and therefore suspicious.

The discreetly located video camera was focused on the entrance, where it would get a picture of both the car tag and the face of the driver.

J.D. stopped his Lexus out of range of the camera. The last time he'd been to his storage unit was six months ago, when he'd dropped off the twenty million dollars of heroin, before he left for Brazil.

Maybe the storage company had installed the camera since then to deter theft.

And maybe D'Amato took the time and trouble to mount video cameras in every storage facility in the city and has someone watching the tapes, so he'll know when you're back in town.

That might sound paranoid. But he wouldn't put it past that devious bastard. D'Amato knew J.D. had shipped arms to San Antonio from Afghanistan, which he'd needed to store somewhere other than his home. San Antonio was where J.D. lived, where his family was located. It made logical sense that he would have shipped the heroin to an address here, and that he would have a storage unit somewhere in the city so the arms—and the smack—would be easily accessible.

Which, of course, he had and he did.

If D'Amato had arranged for the surveillance, how soon after the camera captured his picture was someone liable to show up at the facility? Did he have time to get in and out?

J.D. could buy the explosives he needed somewhere else. But he needed to retrieve the heroin, now that he'd found a buyer for it in South America.

He grimaced. He was going in. He would save himself time and trouble by using his own explosives. And he wasn't leaving without those precious plastic bags of smack.

He couldn't hide behind the tinted car window, because he had to key in his code to get the metal gate to open. He tugged down his white ball cap with the embroidered burnt orange University of Texas logo and pulled his hair forward as best he could to cover the scab on his cheek.

He had no way of knowing whether someone reviewed the surveillance video concurrently or once an hour or once a week, so he decided to get in and get out as fast as he could.

He punched in the numbers and waited impatiently for the gate to open. He drove to his storage unit, keyed open the lock and held his breath as he rolled up the door.

He didn't know what he'd expected. That the government had come in and taken everything, maybe. That D'Amato had confiscated the munitions and heroin. That his wife had somehow discovered the existence of this storage unit and told her Texas Ranger boyfriend about it.

But everything was exactly as he'd left it.

J.D. grinned. He stepped inside and rolled the door most of the way down while he went through the munitions to see what he could use to make his IED. He collected some Composition C-4 (RDX), some trinitrotoluene (TNT), a couple of grenades and some Semtex—RDX and pentaerythritol tetranitrate (PETN).

He debated whether to take along a claymore mine. He wasn't sure he could incorporate it in his IED, but he decided it couldn't hurt to have it on hand. He collected a couple of throwaway cell phones he kept in storage, one of which he could use as a detonator.

J.D. planned to use an Explosively Formed Penetrator (EFP), or shaped charge, with his IED to produce a jet of high velocity superheated gas to burn through whatever protection Shaw might have welded under his armored, bullet-proof, chauffeur-driven car.

He was careful to put the various explosive substances and detonators in separate cardboard boxes when he loaded them into the back of the Lexus. He loaded the heroin in the backseat.

He would need to obey all road signs on his way to Houston. It would be too ironic if the cops pulled him over for running a stop sign.

J.D. was almost done when he saw another car arrive at the front gate. He was instantly wary, because the car just sat there. The gate didn't go up. And the car didn't back away.

He didn't hesitate. He pulled the door of his unit

down and locked it, got into his Lexus and headed for the exit, which was on the opposite side of the storage facility. He needed to punch in his code again to get out. He waited with his hands clutched on the wheel for the railed wrought-iron gate to slide open.

He was already on the exit road when he realized it led right back around to the front entrance. He was going to be passing by whoever was stopped at the front gate. For the moment, he was hidden by the storage building. He had about five seconds to make up his mind what he was going to do.

J.D. tugged his hat down, gripped the wheel even tighter, and kept the Lexus traveling at the 15 mph speed limit posted in the parking area, as he made his way back out to the main road.

He glanced anxiously in the mirror and watched as a squat man with a bald head got out of the car parked at the entrance.

It was Roberto.

J.D. felt a spurt of terror but managed to resist stepping on the gas. He didn't want to do anything to look like he was running, because if he did, that monster would come after him. He was so focused on the image in the rearview mirror that he nearly ran into another car coming off the main road. The driver honked angrily.

And Roberto looked to see what all the noise was about.

J.D. hit the gas.

He was afraid to stay on I-410, so he took U.S. 281 out of San Antonio headed north. Which he realized was foolish, because he was going to have to head east sometime if he wanted to get to Houston. He was afraid to stay at even the cheapest motel, certain D'Amato had sent pictures of him to all the places in South Texas where he would be liable to pay cash.

He couldn't afford to underestimate the mob boss. He'd seen what was left of men—and women—in Brazil who hadn't spoken quickly enough when they'd been questioned by Roberto concerning his whereabouts.

So he spent the night sleeping under a tree. It seemed safer than sleeping in a car full of C-4 and TNT and Semtex. There was enough dew on the grass and enough chill in the air to make him miserable.

He took solace from the knowledge that it was just one more thing his bitch wife was going to pay for with her life.

19

Ryan was still running a fever of a hundred and two when Jack checked at three in the morning. He sat on the edge of his son's bed, debating whether to wake Holly, who'd been sure the Tylenol she'd given their son at midnight would bring his fever down. She had to work in the morning and with her pregnancy, she needed all the rest she could get. So maybe he should let her sleep.

"Daddy?" his son croaked.

"I'm here, Ryan. Can I get something for you?"

"I don't feel good. It hurts."

Jack flipped on the bedside lamp. "Where do you hurt?"

Ryan put a hand on his right shoulder. And his left elbow. And his right knee.

Jack unbuttoned Ryan's pajama top, which was damp with sweat, and moved it aside to see if there was a rash or some other visible symptom of what was wrong with his son. The only thing he found was a bruise on the kid's elbow. He tugged the leg of his pajama bottom up and found a small bruise on his knee. Nothing out of the ordinary. Nothing you wouldn't find on just about any normal six-year-old boy.

So should he wake Holly, or not?

Ryan moaned.

That did it. "I'm going to get your mother. I'll be right back." Holly was the doctor. Maybe she would see something wrong that he didn't.

He put on the hall light and left Holly's bedroom door open so the light could stream in, rather than turning on her bedside lamp. She was lying on her back, her five-months-pregnant belly pushing out the sheet. Maybe it was the uneven illumination from the hall, but he thought he saw dark circles under her eyes. He really hated to wake her. But he was afraid not to.

He touched her shoulder and said, "Holly?"

She came awake slowly, a sign perhaps of how tired she was, or how deeply asleep she'd been. She shoved herself up onto her elbows with effort and said, "What time is it?"

"It's about three."

"In the morning?" she said, blinking herself awake as she pushed herself completely upright.

"Ryan's fever is still a hundred and two."

She shoved the covers out of the way and dropped her feet onto the floor. She was so concerned about Ryan that she forgot what she was wearing.

Jack was treated to the sight of powder-blue silk sliding down over her breasts and belly the way his hands might have. He could see the shadow of her dark pink areolas. Static cling kept the silk attached to her belly and legs, revealing her navel and the dark cleft between her naked thighs. He was still standing where he was when she was gone from the room.

Fully aroused.

He muttered a foul oath and hurried after her. It was a simple physiological reaction. It would have happened with any pretty woman he'd seen in a revealing nightgown.

Any pretty *five-months-pregnant* woman?

He consoled himself with the thought that his body didn't know he was getting a divorce, so it was reacting as it always had to his wife.

When he got to Ryan's doorway, he found Holly sitting beside their son, using her fingertips to check the glands on either side of his throat.

"Could it be mumps?" Jack asked.

"He's been immunized against mumps, but there's an infinitesimal chance the MMR vaccine didn't work."

"MMR?"

"Measles, mumps and rubella," Holly explained. "Have you had mumps, Jack? If you haven't, you shouldn't be around him. The mumps can cause really unpleasant complications in grown men."

"I had the mumps when I was eight."

"As far-fetched as mumps seems, Ryan has all the symptoms—fever, achiness, loss of appetite. His lymph nodes are even swollen. They weren't last night."

"Should we take him to the emergency room?"

"He doesn't have any abdominal or testicular pain," she said. "I think tomorrow's soon enough to take him to the doctor. If it is mumps, he's going to be uncomfortable for three or four days. There isn't anything the hospital can do for him tonight that we can't."

"I can stay home with him tomorrow," Jack volunteered.

"Are you sure?" Holly said. "I can call the hospital and tell them I can't come in for another week."

"I can handle it," Jack said. "How do you suppose he got infected?"

"He must have run into someone with mumps at school before we left Kansas," Holly said. "I'll call the principal tomorrow and let her know, so the school can watch for symptoms in other kids."

"Mumps. I can't believe the vaccine didn't work," Jack mused.

"Maybe it isn't the mumps," she murmured.

She ran Ryan's pajama top through her fingers and muttered, "Night sweats. Night sweats."

"What?"

"No. No," she said. "It couldn't be. Not Ryan."

"What is it, Holly?"

She hurriedly removed Ryan's pajama shirt, then tugged off his pajama bottoms so he was lying there wearing only a tiny pair of jockey shorts.

Jack took a step closer and watched as she examined their son from top to bottom, pausing at the bruises on his shoulder—which he'd missed—and on his elbow and his knee. She then turned him over and found another bruise on his hip that Jack hadn't seen.

"No. No," she said, shaking her head. "Not possible." She stood and crossed to Ryan's chest of drawers, pulled out a dry pair of pajamas and carefully dressed Ryan again. When she was done she turned to Jack and said, "Will you bring him some Pedialyte? I store a couple of bottles in the fridge. We need to keep him hydrated."

Jack headed to the kitchen to retrieve the drink,

which was specially formulated to replace fluids when a child had been vomiting or had diarrhea. But Ryan had neither symptom. So why had Holly asked him to get Pedialyte for their son?

He grabbed the plastic bottle from the fridge and hurried back to Ryan's room. Holly wasn't there. He followed her voice back to her bedroom. She was pacing away from him, her body arched backward against the weight of her pregnancy, one hand pressed against her hip as though her back ached.

She was talking on her cell phone.

"He has all the symptoms, the fever, the night sweats, the bruises, the petechiae. He has aching joints and he's been feeling tired. I thought it was mumps." She sobbed and let go of her hip to thread her fingers through her hair, shoving it away from her wan face. "I wanted it to be the mumps."

"It's not?" Jack said sharply.

She whirled and put a hand to her mouth. He could see her eyes were wide with fright. Which scared him.

"Who are you talking to?"

She held on to the phone with both hands, as though she needed them both to keep from dropping it. "It's a colleague in Kansas. A specialist."

His hand tightened on the bottle of Pedialyte. "What's wrong with Ryan? Do we need to get him to the emergency room?"

Her eyes stayed focused on Jack's as she told the person on the other end of the line, "I'll call you tomorrow when we get the results of the blood tests." She snapped her cell phone closed and set it down on the end table beside the bed.

When she turned back to Jack, he saw her face was bleached nearly white. She looked like she was about to fall down.

He hurried across the room and caught her around the waist as her knees collapsed.

She clutched him around the neck and began to weep.

Jack's throat was constricted with fear. "What's wrong with Ryan?"

"I don't know for sure."

"Then what do you *think* it is?" he persisted.

She took his face between her hands. "I don't want you to panic, Jack. Treatments have come a long way."

He reached up and shoved her hands away and held her shoulders as he pulled her face close to his and said savagely, "Just tell me what the hell is wrong with him, Holly."

She pulled free and took a couple of uneven steps backward, wrapping her arms around herself, since his were no longer there to comfort her. She looked up at him, her chin trembling, and said, "I think Ryan has leukemia."

20

Holly sent Jack into the waiting room of the Robin Bush Child and Adolescent Clinic at M.D. Anderson's Children's Cancer Hospital, while a technician drew enough of Ryan's blood to test whether his white blood cell count was elevated. Jack was fine when he was the one injured, but he'd nearly fainted the first time Ryan fell and cut his lip and blood dripped down his two-year-old chin.

Holly sat beside her brave son, who hadn't cried when the needle went into a vein in his arm. She felt tears sting her eyes and burn her nose. If Ryan's white blood cell count was high, as she feared, her son would be anesthetized tomorrow morning in order to withdraw a sample of bone marrow from his hip and do a spinal tap. Other tests would be done to check his liver and kidney function.

Ryan would learn to hate needles. To hate the smell of the hospital. To hate the chemotherapy treatments that would be needed to save his life. He would hate the fatigue and the nausea and the painful sores in his mouth and digestive tract. He would hate being bald at the age of six. And he would hate the seeming endlessness of it all.

Except, there would be an end. When he went into re-mission. Or when the disease accelerated and he needed a bone marrow transplant. Or when the disease won.

Holly couldn't believe she hadn't recognized Ryan's symptoms immediately as leukemia. But they were similar enough to flu that she'd been inclined—needed—to believe the less serious cause for his illness. When she'd looked more closely last night and found the petechiae, the tiny red spots under Ryan's skin, her heart had skipped a frantic beat.

It was inconceivable that her own child could be stricken with the disease she'd spent her entire profes-sional career fighting to cure. Especially when she knew that, despite the best doctors' best efforts, children still died from the disease.

The only comfort she had was the knowledge that *if* he had leukemia, Ryan couldn't have been sick for very long. His pediatrician had given him a clean bill of health before he started school last fall. So *if* he'd developed leukemia, it had happened sometime during the past six months. Hopefully, *if* he was sick, the disease hadn't spread to his spinal fluid. Finding the disease at an early stage could mean better management and control of it.

Holly gnawed her lower lip worriedly. The swollen lymph nodes were a bad sign. *If* it was leukemia.

"I appreciate you running these tests for me so quickly," she said, stepping aside with the technician as he labeled the last vial of blood he'd drawn from Ryan.

"You're welcome, Dr. Tanner. It's a privilege to meet someone who's come up with so many breakthroughs to fight leukemia. Welcome to M.D. Anderson."

"It's Dr. McKinley," she corrected him.

"You got married? Congratulations," the techni-cian said.

"Just not getting divorced, after all," Holly ex-plained with a smile.

The technician eyed her pregnant stomach and said, "Sounds like a plan."

She turned and saw Jack standing in the doorway. His eyes were wary and anxious and his face was lined with weariness. He looked every one of his nearly forty-three years.

"Not getting divorced, after all?" he said cynically.

Holly had planned to use her maiden name at M.D. Anderson, since she'd expected to be divorced from Jack by the time she started work. Many of her journal articles and much of her initial research had been done as Dr. Tanner, so it was a name by which she was rec-ognized in the medical community.

She shrugged and said, "My grant application and all my paperwork here at M.D. Anderson was done as Dr. Tanner. I'm making the correction on the go."

"How's Ryan?" Jack asked.

"He did fine. He's hanging out in the playroom with the other kids, while we wait for the results of his blood test."

"How long is that going to take?"

"Not long. I could use a cup of coffee," Holly said, not because she needed it, but because she could see Jack did. "I saw a coffee shop downstairs near where we got on the elevator."

"Should we take Ryan with us?"

Holly saw the panicked look in Jack's eyes and said, "There's someone keeping an eye on the kids in the playroom. Just let me tell Ryan where we'll be. I'll meet you at the elevator."

Holly found her son sitting at a table coloring. He looked up and said, "Can we go now?"

Holly's heart constricted with sympathy for her child. "Not quite yet." He probably wouldn't be going home tonight, but there was no sense telling him that now. "Daddy and I are going to get some coffee. Do you want to come with us, or will you be all right here?"

He shrugged, too tired to make a choice.

"We'll be back in a little while. If you want us, just tell the lady with the pink top. She'll know where to find me and Daddy."

Holly told the caretaker where she would be and joined Jack, who was pacing by the elevator like a dangerous animal in a too-small cage. "Let's go," she said.

Holly went through the line at the coffee shop with Jack, then sat down across from him at a table for four that another ravaged-looking couple had just vacated. She'd picked up a pastry, knowing that her pregnancy required energy, but she was afraid that if she ate anything she would throw it back up. For the first time in months she felt nauseous. But she was more sick at heart than physically ill.

"How could this happen?" Jack asked as he stared at his steaming coffee without drinking it. "How does a child get infected with this disease?"

"That's one of the mysteries we haven't solved yet," Holly said.

His dark brown eyes met Holly's leaf-green ones as he said, "Do you find this as ironic as I do? I mean, what are the chances that our son might get this disease?"

"Maybe thirty-five hundred kids a year—out of how many millions in the U.S.?—are diagnosed with leukemia. You do the math."

"If he's sick, what are Ryan's chances of getting through this?" Jack asked bluntly.

"If he's sick," Holly said, "it depends on what kind of cancer he has and whether it's chronic or acute and what stage it's in."

"Okay, give me a best-case scenario," Jack said.

"Stage one chronic leukemia. White blood cells are more mature when they're released into the blood-stream and grow at a much slower rate. If he has acute lymphoblastic leukemia, ALL, white blood cells are released from the bone marrow into the bloodstream before they mature, and they reproduce rapidly.

"In both cases," Holly said, "survival rates are high."

"High?"

"Ninety percent."

"So ten percent still die," Jack said somberly.

Holly nodded, because her throat was swollen with the emotion of trying to clinically discuss leukemia when the patient was her own son.

"Worst case?" Jack asked.

"Acute myelogenous leukemia. But only twenty percent of kids who get leukemia have AML."

"So his chances of having it are less. What about his chances of surviving it if he has it?"

"They're less, too," she admitted.

"How much less?"

"We're coming up with new treatments all the time."

"Give me a number, Holly."

His voice had risen so much Holly was aware of

people from other tables looking at them. "Shh. Keep your voice down, Jack. I don't want to give you a number, because you're going to focus on that instead of on the fact that children with AML do survive."

He leaned across the table, his lips drawn back in a snarl and said, "Give me a fucking number!"

"Less than half."

"How much less?"

"Damn it, Jack! We don't even know if Ryan has leukemia. Let it alone."

"It must be bad if you won't give me a number."

It was, but she wasn't even going to think the number in her head, for fear she would jinx Ryan's blood test results.

"Maybe you should go to work," she suggested.

"Work can wait." He picked up his coffee and put it back down again. He hitched in a breath, huffed it out and said, "I'm terrified, Holly."

"So am I."

"You look so calm and collected. I don't know how I'm going to handle this. I can't imagine how Ryan's going to handle this." Jack rubbed a hand across his face.

Or how our marriage is going to survive this, Holly thought. Devastating illnesses like leukemia either tore couples apart or brought them closer together. She wondered which it would be for her and Jack.

Holly's cell phone rang. She'd set it on the edge of the table when she'd sat down, so it was a simple matter to answer it. But she stared at it without picking it up.

"Answer it, Holly."

She met Jack's gaze as she picked up the phone. "Yes, this is Dr. Tanner. I see. Thank you."

She closed the phone and looked at Jack. She knew the answer was already visible on her face, but she said the words anyway. "His white blood cell count is sky-high. The doctor wants Ryan to spend the night. He's scheduled for a bone marrow biopsy and spinal tap first thing tomorrow morning."

Holly half expected Jack to jump to his feet and stalk away. He did something she hadn't anticipated.

He reached for her hand and held it in his as he changed seats, moving from the chair across from her to the one beside her.

Holly felt a tear spill onto her cheek and blinked furiously to stem the tide for Jack's sake.

He wrapped his arm around her shoulders and leaned close. He kissed the tear from her cheek and caught the next one that spilled with his thumb and said, "We can get through this, Holly. Ryan's going to be fine. We're not going to let our son die."

That was when Holly finally lost it. She turned her face into Jack's shoulder and burst into tears.

21

Kate found it hard to sleep when Shaw was in bed beside her. She was aware of every male sound. Every male scent. Aware of him in a way she'd never been aware of Jack.

Of course, she'd never been in bed with Jack. Never had his callused hands roaming her flesh as she returned the favor. Never felt his bristled jaw against her belly. Never experienced the joining of bodies that changed everything between a man and a woman.

Kate made a frustrated sound in her throat and turned her back to Shaw. And felt the luxury of silk sheets surrounding her.

That was another thing. Shaw was a hedonist.

He loved fine wine. He enjoyed good food. He had silk sheets, for heaven's sake. She couldn't imagine Jack sleeping on silk sheets. A sleeping bag on the ground was more his style.

Not that there was anything wrong with that.

Kate rustled the silk sheets as she turned over and tried, unsuccessfully, to get comfortable.

"Go to sleep," Shaw murmured.

She no longer protested that she couldn't sleep. He

knew the problems she had lying in bed with him. He didn't care. He wanted her in bed with him, and that was that. She'd actually tried moving to the guest bedroom, located between the boy's room and Shaw's bedroom, the fourth night she'd spent in Shaw's home.

That had been a disaster she'd never repeated.

She'd gone to bed early that night, knowing Shaw wouldn't confront her—if he intended to confront her—until the boys were asleep. She'd lain in bed with bated breath, thinking of all the arguments she would use to convince him this was the right thing to do.

But he never came. She'd already started to drowse when he kicked open the door, scooped her into his arms and headed toward his bedroom.

She'd struggled silently—but violently—as he carried her down the hall, pulling his hair, biting his naked shoulder, scratching and kicking and writhing to free herself from the prison of his arms. Once he had her inside his room, he kicked the bedroom door closed behind him and threw her onto the bed.

"This is where you sleep. Tonight and every night."

"I don't want to sleep with you!" she'd raged, crawling off the bed and standing toe-to-toe with him. "Don't you get it? I don't want to be here!"

"Fine. Leave the boys and go."

"You know I won't do that," she snarled.

"Then go to bed. It's late. We've both got work tomorrow."

She eyed the door, met his obdurate gaze, then tried an end run around him. She had her hand on the doorknob when he slung an arm around her waist from behind, pulled her back tight against him, stalked back across the room and dumped her onto the bed.

"This is ridiculous," he said, his hands on his hipbones, which were visible above a pair of low-slung jeans.

Kate was incensed. "You're the one insisting that I sleep with a man I don't know. A man I don't like." None of that was provoking a response, so she said, "A man who makes my stomach turn."

That did it.

He shoved her flat on the bed and came down on top of her, restraining her kicking legs with his thigh while he manacled both her hands in one of his and held them on the pillow high above her head.

"Let me go!" she gritted out between bared teeth.

He used his free hand to grab her chin, while he captured her mouth with his, staking his claim. She got one hand loose and yanked his hair. He grabbed her breast, pinching the nipple hard enough to make her cry out with the pain—and the pleasure—of it. She bucked against him, desperate to get free.

Arousing him.

And inflaming herself.

The fingers that were pulling his hair threaded through it, and she thrust her tongue into his mouth, making him grunt with surprise. He let go of her hand so he could trace the healed surgical scar on her chest, where the bullet had nearly taken her life, then twisted his hand in her hair to haul her close for another soulful kiss.

She shoved her free hand between them and slid it down inside his jeans, past a slicing scar on his hip, making a growling, angry sound in her throat when the sturdy cloth didn't give way. She reached for the snap and shoved down the zipper before her wrist was caught in a vise of steel.

Kate was gasping for breath, panting for air, excited and aroused and frustrated, biting at Shaw's lips and tasting him with her tongue.

He lifted his head and she saw his eyelids were heavy, his gray eyes avid, his lips full. "Say you want me," he said in a guttural voice.

"I—" She wanted him. It must have been obvious to him. Her nipples were painfully peaked, her breasts sensitive to his touch. Her body arched into his hips, seeking the heat of him. Wanting to be impaled. Needing him inside her.

"Say it," he muttered.

"I want—"

"Who do you want?" he rasped. "Say it, Kate."

"I want—" she grated out. "To go home."

He dropped his forehead to her shoulder. She felt him collecting himself, felt the tension ease from shoulders and biceps, felt his breathing slow. Then he rolled off of her and pulled her into his arms, holding her close. "Lady, you sure know how to kill a mood."

That was when she knew for certain that he was going to keep his promise not to make love to her unless she asked him to. And that she might as well sleep in his bed, because even though it wasn't a comfortable place to be, it was where she wanted to be.

Somehow she'd managed to get through a very long, very celibate week in Shaw's bed.

Why hadn't Jack called her back to tell her Ryan was okay? She'd tried to reach him throughout the week, but the calls had all gone to voice mail. Why hadn't she kept calling until she reached him? Or left a message? Or e-mailed him?

That was easy. Too much to tell. Too much to explain. Too much that was inexplicable.

She'd barely dropped off to sleep when she heard her cell phone buzz on the bedside table. She grabbed for the phone and flipped it open, noting the time on the bedside clock—12:23 a.m. Because Jack had been on her mind as she fell asleep, she presumed it was him.

"Jack? Why are you calling so late?"

"It's Dad. Your mom's in labor."

"Daddy? Isn't it too early?" Kate said anxiously.

"Just three weeks," her father said. "You were early, too, so I'm trying not to panic."

But she could hear the worry in his voice.

"Who is it?" Shaw asked as he turned over in her direction. "What time is it?"

Kate shushed him and said, "But Mom's all right?" Her mother's late-in-life pregnancy had kept her bedridden, so Kate knew she would be glad for the early delivery, so long as both she and the baby were okay.

"Libby's fine," her dad said, "but I need you here in Austin. We're at Brackenridge Hospital. I tried calling your home phone but you didn't answer."

"I…couldn't get to the phone," Kate said.

"I've got a neighbor staying with your brother and sister until you get to the house."

Kate glanced at Shaw, who was stirring, and said, "I'll be there as soon as I can, Daddy."

"Thanks, sweetheart. I love you."

"I love you, too, Daddy. Tell Mom I can't wait to meet my new brother."

Shaw flicked on the lamp beside the bed, then rubbed the sleep from his eyes. "Your mom's in labor?"

"Yes, and I need to get to Austin. I was—am—supposed to take care of my younger sister and brother while my father's at the hospital with my mom."

"How much younger?" Shaw asked.

"Dallas is six. Houston's eight." She didn't want to ask Shaw for help, but the drive from Houston to Austin would take more than three hours. And she'd have to rent a car. "Can you fly us there?"

"By *us* do you mean you and me?"

"I planned to bring the twins with me, so they can spend time with my siblings. Then we'll all go to the hospital together to meet our new brother—and the twins' new uncle—once he's born."

"Your parents know it's a boy?"

Kate nodded. "Because it's a high-risk pregnancy, Mom had to have a lot of tests. One of the nurses let it slip. They've already named him Austin."

Shaw snickered. "How are they coming up with these names?"

"For your information, smarty-pants, my mom told me the kids are named for the city where they were conceived."

He arched a dark brow and said, "What are we supposed to do when we need a name, and Houston's already taken?"

Kate flushed. "Don't be ridiculous."

"The twins could stay here," Shaw said. "That way they wouldn't miss school."

She shook her head. "I'm not comfortable leaving them behind." Because she might never get them back.

"I wouldn't steal the twins from you, despite the fact that you kept them from me," Shaw said.

Kate pushed the black silk aside and got out of bed. "Nevertheless, they're going with me."

"Then so am I," Shaw said, shoving his way out of bed on the other side.

Kate turned to face him, her hands perched on her hips. "My father's a federal judge. He isn't going to appreciate having Dante D'Amato's son in his home while he's at the hospital with my mother."

"Dante D'Amato is my father by an accident of birth," Shaw snapped back at her. "And you're not going anywhere without me."

Kate didn't argue. She went into the bathroom, where she wouldn't have to worry about Shaw following every move she made and eating her with his eyes, got herself dressed and went to wake the boys. The twins had been looking forward to spending time with Houston. Dallas always joined in because she refused to be left out when the three boys were playing.

Shaw woke up Lucky while Kate woke up Chance.

Scratch stretched languorously at the foot of Chance's bed, then hopped off and left the room with her tail held high, seeking somewhere else to sleep. Kate figured she was headed for Shaw's pillow, from which he'd evicted her when he'd gone to bed.

Harley jumped off the foot of Lucky's bed and trotted into Chance's room. He stuck his cold nose in Kate's palm, as though to ask why they were getting up in the middle of the night. She was glad Shaw had help at the house so they didn't have to take the pets with them.

"What's going on, Mom?" Chance asked, rubbing

the sleep from his eyes in much the same way Shaw had. Heredity? she wondered. Or environment? Perhaps Chance had seen Shaw rub sleep from his eyes early one morning last week and copied him.

"Gram is having the baby," she told her son. "Shaw is going to fly us to Austin to see Houston and Dallas."

"That sounds really confusing," Shaw said from the other room. "Flying to Austin to see Houston? Or to see Dallas? Of course, we're actually flying to Austin to see Austin, so I guess it all works out."

"Stuff it," Kate replied.

"Yippee!" Chance said, bouncing out of bed. "We get to fly in Shaw's plane again!"

"It's a jet, stupid!" Lucky called back, as he came barreling into Chance's room, his arms spread wide, making jet noises as he pretended to be Shaw's Gulfstream.

"Your brother isn't stupid," Shaw said. "But he does make a pretty good jet," he said as he watched Chance mimic his older brother.

Shaw stood in the doorway that divided the two rooms with his arms crossed over his chest and grinned as he said to Kate, "I always wanted twin jets."

Kate was chagrined to realize that the boys were more excited about riding in Shaw's 550 than about the new baby, or even the opportunity to have a playdate with their youthful aunt and uncle.

"Just intercept Lucky and get him dressed, please," Kate said.

Shaw saluted and grabbed Lucky on his way past, lifted him up, tipped him sideways, balancing a hand under his chest and one under his legs, and soon had him flying back toward his room high in the air.

"Do me!" Chance insisted as Lucky came to a laughter-filled landing on his bed.

Shaw picked Chance up and flew him back to his own bedroom, where Kate was waiting for him.

Kate's eyes brimmed with tears.

Shaw set Chance down and came back to her, using his body to shield her from the twins. "What's wrong? Why are you crying?"

Kate shook her head and scrubbed at her eyes with her knuckles. "It's nothing," she said, forcing a smile. "Really. I'm fine."

"Shaw," Lucky yelled. "I can't find my other tennis shoe."

"Lucky needs help," she said.

Shaw clearly didn't want to leave her, but she gestured him away and said, "I need to get Chance dressed."

How could she tell this man that he'd been more of a father to her sons in the past week—playing with them spontaneously, as he had just done, listening to them at the supper table, helping them with their homework, reading to them every night—than J.D. had in the eight years he'd been their father.

She'd often wished J.D. was more interested in doing things with the twins. When the boys had been younger, he'd considered them a bother. By the time they were old enough to amuse him, he'd been gone, first serving in Afghanistan, then away the year he'd supposedly been dead, and in South America the past six months.

Her sons were starved for a male in their lives. No wonder Shaw had been so successful in winning them over. Jack had played with them, of course. But

Shaw's eyes focused intently on them every time they spoke. He touched them every chance he got, ruffling their hair or patting their backs in approval. And he indulged their whims and whiny behavior the way no one except a parent would.

Kate knew Shaw was making up for lost time. Watching to see the minuscule changes he'd missed as they'd grown up. Touching to reassure himself that they were really here with him. And giving his sons all the time and attention from their father that they'd been deprived of when Shaw hadn't known of their existence.

The twins absorbed every bit of love he bestowed like sponges soaking up seawater. It was a heady time for them, and they were thriving under his approving gaze.

During the short flight to Austin, the twins fell asleep on the couch on either side of Kate, who was having trouble staying awake herself. Bruce moved to the front of the plane to give Shaw and Kate privacy.

"You should quit that job," Shaw said. "You end every day exhausted."

"But invigorated," Kate said.

"That doesn't make sense."

Kate shrugged. "It does to me."

Kate loved her new job at the Children's Cancer Hospital, but over the past week she'd learned the subtle difference between working with veterans of battle and kids battling cancer.

She'd always been amazed by the courage of the soldiers she'd worked with at BAMC. Wounded in war, she'd helped them learn how to manage with one or more prosthetic limbs. In almost every case, soldiers met the challenge with determination and tenacity.

But they were merely adjusting to a new way of life. The kids with sarcoma she'd met during her first week at the Children's Cancer Hospital weren't sure how long that new way of life was going to last.

Kate's physical therapy patients were still fighting the sarcoma, even though they'd given up a limb to combat the disease. Nevertheless, they almost always had smiles on their faces.

They believed they were going to get well. They believed they were going to have a bright future. It was hard not to catch their infectious enthusiasm, even though Kate knew that some of them wouldn't survive.

She came away humbled and inspired. And grateful that Lucky and Chance were so healthy.

She brushed a dark curl away from Lucky's forehead, then straightened Chance's sleeve.

"They're so angelic when they're sleeping," Shaw said, "it's hard to believe they can get into so much trouble when they're awake."

Kate frowned. "What kind of trouble are you talking about?"

Shaw made a face. "I wasn't supposed to tell you."

"What kind of trouble?" Kate insisted.

"Just a little fracas at their new school in The Wood-lands. Nothing serious."

"I'm listening," Kate said.

"Maybe Bruce should tell you. He was there." Shaw called to the big man, who bent his massive shoulders and head to avoid bumping into the ceiling as he walked down the aisle. Shaw had arranged with the private school the boys attended for their bodyguard to park his car on school property during the day. Bruce kept an eye on entrances and exits to the school and monitored the boys' activities anytime they were outside.

"Tell Kate what happened at school today," Shaw said.

Bruce settled into one of the cushioned seats at the table across from her and said, "It wasn't nothing, ma'am. I stopped it as soon as I saw what was going on."

Kate glanced at Shaw who said, "Go ahead and tell her, Bruce."

"After school today one of the kids made fun of the twins, ma'am. Said he thought he was seeing double. So your two boys, they looked at each other, and then one hit the bully on the left side of his face. And the other hit him on the right. And then the boy who hit first—"

"That would be Lucky," Shaw interjected with a grin.

"He said, 'Just so you know, there's two of us.' The kids around them laughed, which is when I hustled them out of there."

"Thank you, Bruce. I appreciate that."

"No problem, ma'am. Whoever taught 'em those left and right crosses did a good job."

Kate waited until Bruce had returned to his seat at the front of the plane before she spoke. "Take that grin off your face," she said to Shaw. "You're acting like what they did was a good thing."

"You can't run from a bully," Shaw said. "Only makes him meaner."

"And you would know this how? Don't answer

that." She didn't need him to answer, because she already suspected what he would say. He must have had a terrible time without a father, might even had been called a bastard. Children could be cruel. "Even so, you don't have to settle everything with your fists."

"Who taught them how to fight?" Shaw asked.

"Your husband."

"No." J.D. couldn't be bothered.

"The Texas Ranger?"

Kate heard the edge in Shaw's voice and was glad she could temper it with her answer. "If you must know, It was their GeePa."

"Your father? Their grandfather?"

"Their great-grandfather," she said with pride. "Jackson Blackthorne, better known as Blackjack."

"An old man taught them that?"

Kate laughed. "Don't let Blackjack hear you call him *old*. He can't rival you for dollars, but Jackson Blackthorne owns the biggest spread in Texas, a ranch the size of Vermont called Bitter Creek, with a thirty-thousand-square-foot house called The Castle, filled with original Tiffany and Chippendale and Hepplewhite and cowhide and horn and western art that will steal your breath away.

"Blackjack and his second wife, Ren, raise some of the finest quarter horses and Santa Gertrudis cattle around. What's more, Bitter Creek has been owned by Blackthornes since the Civil War."

"With a heritage like that, why isn't your dad a rancher?" Shaw asked.

"My dad was the eldest son, but his mother had different plans for him. Sort of like J.D.'s mother had other plans for him." She shrugged. "Dad went into politics.

He was the U.S. attorney general before he was accused of a murder he didn't commit. He was cleared, but the shadows on his reputation ended his political aspirations. I know he likes being a federal judge.

"My dad's twin, my uncle Owen, became a Texas Ranger. He and his wife live in Fredericksburg with their twin sons.

"The baby of the family, their sister Summer and her husband Billy Coburn, ended up running Bitter Creek."

"You've mentioned two sets of twins, and you have twins. I take it twins run in your family?"

"There are lots of Blackthorne twins, going all the way back to the first Blackthorne in Texas. I've heard family stories that suggest he was the ninth or tenth Duke of Blackthorne, born a twin in England, and became just 'Blackthorne' when he ended up in Texas during the Civil War."

"Have you ever checked to see if he really was a twin? Or a duke? I'd want to know whether his twin inherited the dukedom if his brother stayed in Texas."

"I've always wondered," she admitted with a laugh. "But not enough to find out. Forebears can be fascinating, but what matters is who we are. And who we become."

"Do you really believe that?" Shaw asked.

She nodded.

"Then why do you keep bringing up Dante D'Amato."

"I suppose because I saw you coming out of a federal courthouse with him by your side. Your father didn't look like part of your past, Shaw. He looked like part of your present."

"I haven't had anything to do with my father since I found out he had my mother killed. It's the FBI who keeps throwing me in the same pile of dung with him."

"If you know your father conspired to murder your mother, why haven't you helped the government put him in jail?"

His lip curled wryly. "My father doesn't tend to leave a lot of witnesses."

"But you've been tarred by the media with the same brush. How can you stand to have people thinking the worst of you?"

His lips quirked. "It isn't what other people think of you that matters. It's what you think of yourself."

Kate laughed at the way he'd turned her words around to express the same sentiment.

She was still concerned about what her father was going to say—or do—when she showed up with Shaw at the hospital. As the twins' father, Shaw had the right to be there. But her father wasn't privy to the adversity that had caused her life to turn so many unexpected corners.

Oh, God. She was going to have to tell her parents the truth. Her father was going to have a fit when he learned who'd really fathered the twins. Her mother wasn't going to be too pleased, either.

"We're going to have to lie to my parents," she said suddenly.

"Why is that?"

"They don't know J.D. is alive. They don't know Jack has moved back in with his wife. And they don't know you're the twins' biological father."

Shaw shook his head in disbelief. "That's a lot of

secrets, Kate. Wouldn't you rather tell them what's going on?"

"They have their plates full with Houston and Dallas and the new baby. I don't want them worrying about me and the twins."

"And showing up with me isn't going to worry them?"

"Not if you tell them you love me."

He put a hand to his ear. "I don't think I heard you right. What did you say?"

"Look, we can tell my parents about the other suspect in that murder, right? And we can tell my parents that Jack went back to his wife. And we can tell my parents—"

"The truth, Kate. That's the best way to go. I'm not going to tell them I'm in love with you. Not when they still believe you're in love with another man. If your parents are as astute as you say they are, one or the other of them is going to take a look at the twins and me in the same room and notice the physical resemblance. Why lie, when the truth will serve you better?"

She hadn't bothered her parents with all the changes that had made her life so complicated because she hadn't wanted to burden them. But Shaw was wrong. They would never understand why she hadn't turned to her rich and powerful—and loving—family for succor when things started going wrong.

She would just have to convince them that she'd fallen in love with the mobster's son.

"Time to buckle up again, folks," the pilot drawled. "We've arrived at our destination."

22

"Isn't he beautiful?" Kate said to Shaw. She was standing in her mother's private hospital room, the afternoon sun shining through the window, holding her baby brother in her arms. "How are you feeling, Mom?"

Her mother scooted up in her hospital bed and said, "I'd forgotten how much childbirth hurts. Fortunately, Austin decided to make his entrance quickly, if not painlessly."

"Next time use some anesthesia," Kate said with a laugh.

"There isn't going to be a next time. I've had my quota. Your turn," her mother replied.

Kate glanced up at Shaw and felt the heat in her cheeks when she recognized the sudden flare of desire in his eyes. She quickly lowered her gaze to the baby in her arms. "I'll think about it."

Her father had marched the four kids, who'd taken one excited look at the baby and then started roughhousing, down to the cafeteria. Shaw kept looking anxiously over his shoulder, waiting for his sons to return.

"Why don't you go down and join them?" Kate

said. His mind was with them, even though his body was still in the room.

"I think I will," Shaw said. "Nice to meet you, Mrs. Blackthorne."

"Libby, please," Kate's mother said.

"Libby," he said with a fleeting smile. "Congratulations again on the birth of your son. I think I'll go catch up with your husband and the boys. And Dallas. She's a pistol."

"Yes, she is," Kate's mother agreed.

Once he was gone, Libby said, "What are you doing here with Wyatt Shaw?"

"I love him?" Kate realized that making it a question wasn't exactly going to convince her mother she meant it. She took a deep breath and plunged. "He's the twins' biological father."

Her mother gasped. "I noticed the resemblance, but I thought I must be imagining it. I don't know what your father's going to think when he finds out."

"I can imagine," Kate said. "Which is why I haven't said anything before now."

"I presume there's an explanation for how that happened. I didn't even know you knew Wyatt Shaw nine years ago."

Kate sat on the foot of her mother's bed and watched as Austin closed his tiny hand around her little finger, gripping it tightly. "Shaw was a stranger I picked up in a bar."

Her mother gave Kate the look of disapproval that had cowed her ever since she was six.

"It's a long, sordid story, Mom. I'm not proud of what happened, but I had my reasons."

"J.D. provoked you, of course."

Kate nodded.

"I never liked the son of a bitch."

The comment startled a laugh out of Kate. "Why didn't you say something to talk me out of marrying him?"

"Whatever your father or I said would only have made you cling to J.D. more tightly. You tend to be stubborn when you want something."

Kate met her mother's sympathetic gaze and said, "I caught him in bed with another woman."

"I might have suspected as much. How did Wyatt Shaw get in the picture?"

Kate shrugged. "I chose him at random, believe it or not."

"He's very handsome."

"And surprisingly kind."

"That's a strange thing to say about a mob boss's son."

"Why does everyone judge Shaw by who his father is?" Kate said with asperity. "It's so unfair! There's so much you don't know about him."

"That sounds almost like you admire him. Like you weren't really joking when you said you loved him."

Kate saw the worried look in her mother's eyes and said, "Shaw said I should just tell you the truth. But I didn't want to admit what a shambles my life is in right now."

"Start at the beginning and tell me everything."

The baby started to fuss, and Kate placed him back in his mother's arms. She watched as her mother opened her nightgown and offered Austin a breast. The baby began to suckle.

And Kate began to talk.

She sat at the foot of her mother's bed and explained how she'd slept with Shaw and then learned she was pregnant. How she'd hidden the truth from J.D. How she'd discovered Shaw's true identity. How she'd fallen in love with Jack again last fall. How J.D. had returned alive and well a year after his supposed death and asked for money to disappear.

How Ann Wade had found out the twins weren't J.D.'s sons when Lucky had been injured while she'd been in a coma. How her mother-in-law had hired a private investigator, who'd found Shaw and told him the truth.

And how Shaw had insisted on taking her and the twins to his compound in Houston to keep them safe from J.D., who was back and more dangerous than ever, and from his own father, who might threaten their safety.

"This is all so unbelievable," her mother said, clearly agitated. "I still don't understand why you didn't turn to Jack for help, if you're in love with him."

"Jack is living in Houston with Holly. They…got back together."

"I'm so sorry, darling," her mother said. She brushed at the fine black hair on Austin's head. "I know how much Jack cared for you. And he was so good with the twins while you were in a coma."

"Holly's pregnant."

"Oh, dear."

"So you see, I wasn't kidding when I said my life's a mess."

To Kate's amazement, her mother grinned.

"What's so funny?" Kate demanded.

"I'm wondering how Wyatt Shaw is faring downstairs with your father."

Kate was on her feet in an instant. "I'd better go rescue him."

Her mother laughed. "I'm wondering which one you think needs rescuing, your father or Shaw."

Her mother held up a hand to keep Kate from answering. "Sit down, Kate. I think it might be better if we let those two sort things out for themselves."

Wyatt had been fighting his emotions ever since he'd taken his first look at Kate's baby brother. Because all he could think was how much he'd missed when his own sons had been born. He'd never counted their tiny fingers or toes. Or marveled at their tiny eyelashes and fingernails.

He'd been angry at Kate all over again.

At the same time, seeing that baby had made him wonder what it would be like if they made another child together. What would it be like to watch Kate's belly grow? To watch her struggle to give birth? To cradle their newborn child in his arms?

Fat chance of that happening.

Ever since that first shattering night together in Houston, Kate had kept her distance. He might as well have been a lump of clay on the other side of the bed, for all the attention she paid him at night.

On the other hand, he was aware of her every second. Heard every breath in and out of her lungs. Heard every sigh and snuffle. Heard the sheets rustle over her beguiling body as she turned in her sleep.

It was torture. But he wouldn't have given up a moment of it.

He didn't have any trouble finding Judge Blackthorne and the kids. They were making plenty of noise in the corner of the cafeteria. The little girl was crying. The boys looked subdued. Kate's father was chastising them.

As Wyatt watched, Blackthorne abandoned the boys and picked up the little girl to comfort her, awkwardly brushing her tears away with his thumb. He watched as Dallas looked up at her father from beneath tear-clumped dark eyelashes. And saw Clay Blackthorne melt at one look from those dewy blue eyes.

Wyatt barely kept himself from grinning. Judge Blackthorne had a reputation for making mincemeat of incompetent and unprepared attorneys in his courtroom. But he was helpless in the face of a six-year-old girl's tears.

Wyatt glanced at his unrepentant sons, who were already making trouble again, and understood exactly how Clay Blackthorne felt. "Hey!" he called. "Stop that."

Lucky and Chance froze and turned in his direction.

"He started it," Lucky accused, standing and pointing at Chance.

"No, he started it," Chance retorted as he rose to face his brother.

"I'm ending it," Shaw said, putting a hand on each boy's shoulder and settling them back in their seats. "Drink your lemonade and behave yourselves."

Blackthorne was still holding the little girl in his arms. He seated her beside her brother and said, "Leave your sister alone."

Then he turned back to Shaw, keeping his eyes on all four children, watching for rebellion in the ranks. The boys began comparing how much was left in each of their glasses and started a contest to see who could finish first, slurping lemonade loudly through their straws.

Blackthorne joined Shaw, who'd backed a short distance away from the table where the kids were sitting.

"You did that masterfully," he said to Shaw. He hesitated and added, "Just like a father."

Wyatt also hesitated, then said in a voice quiet enough that the boys couldn't hear, "That's because I am their father, Judge Blackthorne. Although they don't know it. Yet."

Wyatt had to give him credit. Kate's father took the news without swearing, in fact, without making a sound.

"I don't even know where to start asking questions," the judge said. "I'm concerned first and foremost for my daughter, Mr. Shaw."

"Please, call me Wyatt."

"I'd rather not be on a first-name basis with Dante D'Amato's son. Or a man accused of murder."

Wyatt bit back the retort that came to his lips. Instead he said, "I'm nothing like my father. And the police have another suspect for that murder."

"So you say."

"Kate believes I'm innocent."

"Kate's a fool for love. I can see from the way she looks at you that she's head over heels."

"You might want to check your eyesight," Wyatt

said. "Kate's in love with another man." Kate never looked at him with anything resembling love. He would have noticed. "I'm D'Amato's son by an accident of birth," he said. "You don't hate your grandsons because I'm their father, do you?"

Blackthorne eyed him askance. "When you put it that way, I can see your point. Wyatt."

Wyatt swallowed over the painful lump in his throat. It was a small hurdle to win Judge Blackthorne's approbation, but he was glad to have gotten over it. "I only found out that I have twin sons a few weeks ago. I've been doing my best to make up for lost time."

"And doing a good job of it, from what the twins say," Kate's father said grudgingly. "Why did you move Kate and the boys to Houston?"

"To keep them safe."

"From what?"

"From my father. And Kate's husband."

Blackthorne frowned. "J.D. is dead."

Shaw shook his head. "He's alive and well and causing plenty of trouble. He was trading munitions for heroin in Afghanistan. He's being hunted by the drug dealers he stole from, including my father, which is why I wanted Kate and the twins out of the way."

"Does Ann Wade know J.D.'s alive?"

"Kate says she does."

Blackthorne swore under his breath. "I have to thank you, then, for keeping my daughter and grandsons safe, Wyatt."

"You're welcome, Judge Blackthorne."

Kate's father hesitated, then said, "Call me Clay."

23

Acute myelogenous leukemia. The bad one. That's how Jack thought of Ryan's AML diagnosis. Ten days had gone by—it was May already—and he hadn't spoken once to Kate, not even to tell her the calamity that had befallen his family.

They'd been playing phone tag, neither of them apparently willing to leave a message for the other. He couldn't bear to leave a message describing the situation. He wondered how she was, how the boys were doing, but there had been no time to arrange a visit, either. He'd been spending every spare moment he could find at the hospital with Ryan and Holly. There hadn't been many, because J.D. Pendleton had finally surfaced.

Jack had gotten a call from his friend—one of Kate's many uncles—FBI Special Agent Breed Grayhawk, suggesting that he check in with Sheriff Freddy Fredericks of Alvin, Texas. Alvin was an agricultural community that produced rice and fruits and vegetables located twelve miles southeast of Houston.

Sheriff Fredericks had responded to a call from a local junkyard about a loud explosion during the night and discovered a bombed-out junked car. The sheriff had called in the Houston FBI because it looked like something a budding terrorist might have done.

Breed, who'd recently been transferred to the Houston FBI office from his position as Supervisor of the Joint Terrorism Task Force at the University of Texas at Austin, was on-site when Jack arrived at the junkyard in Alvin.

The two lawmen, who each owned half of Twin Magnolias, performed the male shoulder slap that substituted for a hug between men who were glad to see each other. Breed had moved from Twin Magnolias to a condominium in Austin, where he lived with his girlfriend, Grace Caldwell.

"Long time, no see," Jack said. "Did Grace ever say yes?"

Breed had proposed to Grace Caldwell for the first time in December of the previous year. At the time, the couple had only been acquainted for two months. Grace had insisted that they spend more time getting to know each other before she gave Breed an answer.

Personally, Jack thought that made a lot of sense. When the couple had met, Grace was a twenty-two-year-old convicted double murderer—in violation of her parole—who was suspected of planning a terrorist attack against the president of the United States. Breed was the twenty-six-year-old FBI special agent sent out to catch her.

Grace turned out to be innocent of everything, including the double murder, but while they'd been chasing the real culprit, Breed and Grace had fallen in love.

Breed grinned. "You're looking at a happy man, Jack. I've been asking that woman to marry me at least once a week for four months. On Sunday she finally said yes."

"Congratulations!" Jack reached out and shook Breed's hand. He could see from the look on Breed's face how delighted he was to be marrying the woman he loved. Jack's throat was choked with envy. His own life was such a mess right now, he didn't know if he was ever going to find that happy ending.

He cleared his throat and asked, "Have you set a date?"

"August twenty-seventh at the First Methodist Church in San Antonio. I'm counting on you to be my best man."

"You've got it," Jack said. And then realized his wife was due in mid-August, and that if the baby was late, he might not be available.

"What's happening with you and Kate?" Breed asked as they headed into the junkyard.

"Things are crazy right now." Jack wouldn't have known where to start explaining the situation between Kate and Wyatt Shaw, let alone Ryan's illness and his own predicament with Holly. The past week, he'd barely been hanging on by his fingernails. He didn't have the emotional control to tell his friend what was going on without breaking down completely. Better just to keep it all to himself.

Thinking about Ryan's leukemia reminded him that Breed's father—and Kate's grandfather—King Grayhawk, had recently been diagnosed with cancer.

"How's your father?"

"He checked into M.D. Anderson. They're giving him another round of chemo, but it's not looking good."

"You never told me what kind of cancer he has."

"Leukemia."

"Really? What kind?"

"ALL. That's acute—"

"Lymphoblastic leukemia," Jack finished for him.

Breed gave him an odd look. "How do you know that?"

"Ryan was just diagnosed with AML," Jack said.

"Oh, God. How is he?"

"He's getting chemotherapy at the Children's Cancer Hospital," Jack said, unwilling to share more than that. "You should have your father talk to my wife. To Holly, I mean," he corrected. She was still his wife, but not for long.

"Do you have her number in Kansas?"

Jack grimaced. In an effort not to talk about Ryan's situation, he'd revealed other information he hadn't been ready to share. "She's working at M.D. Anderson."

"When did this happen?"

"Recently. She's pregnant. It's mine, so we're holding up on the divorce until after the baby's born. I've been staying with her in Houston."

Breed huffed out a breath. "Wow."

"Yeah," Jack said. He could see the questions in Breed's eyes, but like most western men, he didn't ask for information that wasn't volunteered. "Anyway, Holly's up-to-date on all the latest research being done on leukemia. She would know if there's some cutting edge clinical trial your father could join."

"Thanks, Jack. I'll pass the word to King. By the

way, he still hasn't told anyone else in the family that he's sick, so keep this under your hat."

Jack frowned. "Your brother North doesn't know?"

"No. And neither do King's Brats."

Jack whistled. Because of his relationships with both Kate and Breed, he was one of the few people privy to the strange Grayhawk family tree. King Grayhawk had been married four times looking for a woman he could love as much as he'd loved Eve DeWitt, the woman Jackson Blackthorne had stolen from him and married.

Kate's mother Libby, and her uncles North and Matthew, were the children of King's first wife, Jane. Matthew had left home at seventeen and no one had heard from him since. He could be dead for all anyone knew.

King's marriage to his second wife, Leonora, had been annulled.

King's third wife, Sassy, was Breed's mother.

King's fourth and last wife, Jill, had presented him with three kids in five years before she ran off with one of King's cowhands. Taylor, Gray and Victoria were better known as King's Brats. They were all in their twenties and spent their time at Kingdom Come, King's ranch in Jackson Hole, Wyoming.

"I'm sure if Kate knew about King's cancer, she would want to visit her grandfather and bring the twins to see him, especially since he's so close. When are you going to tell everyone what's going on?" Jack asked.

"When King gives the okay," Breed replied. He pointed to a cordoned-off, burned-out vehicle that sat at the rear of the junkyard and said, "That used to be a 1988 Cadillac Seville."

"Not a whole lot left of it," Jack said. The Cadillac had been shredded.

"The junkman gave me a description of a guy hanging around yesterday that fits a certain fugitive we both know and dislike," Breed said. "Tall, thin, shaggy blond hair, toothy smile."

"Come on, Breed, that could fit a hundred thousand vagrants."

"It also fits J.D. Pendleton. Except, this guy had a sore on his face and a limp. Any reason to think J.D.'s been hurt recently?"

"Actually, yes." Jack thought of the report Roberto had made to D'Amato, that he'd seen blood on the ground in Brazil, and that J.D. had run with a limp as he'd escaped. "Have you said anything to your boss about J.D.?"

"Come on, Jack. You know better than that."

Because of his close relationship to both Kate and Jack, Breed had become privy to the close-held information that J.D. Pendleton was still alive. He also knew that Jack was hunting J.D. for Dante D'Amato.

The FBI did not.

"How are you going to handle this?" Jack asked.

"I've already handled it," Breed said. "I called you. The FBI will put out a warrant for anyone matching the description we have from the witness at the junkyard. But they won't be looking for a man the military supposedly buried with honors at Arlington Cemetery more than a year ago. I think I can trust you to hunt down J.D., if that's where this trail leads."

"Thanks, Breed." Jack was excited because this was the first decent clue he'd gotten to J.D.'s whereabouts.

"J.D. was a demolitions expert in the National Guard, wasn't he?" Breed asked.

"Yeah."

"So he'd know how to put together a bomb like this. The FBI bomb tech tells me it was actually a pretty sophisticated IED. Military munitions were used, stuff J.D. would have had access to in the Guard and in Afghanistan."

"J.D. used to brag about how good he was," Jack said.

"Looks like he's trying to figure out exactly how much C-4 he needs to blow up a car," Breed said. "Who do you think J.D. would like to obliterate?"

"D'Amato for sure," Jack said. Or maybe Kate, if J.D. had found out from his mother that his wife had cheated on him, and that the twins weren't his kids. Jack felt a shiver roll down his spine at the thought of a bomb like this one aimed at Kate.

Would J.D. wait until Kate was alone to try and kill her? Or would he be mad enough to want Shaw dead, too. And what about the twins? Would he care if Lucky and Chance were in the car with his wife and her lover?

Who knew what rang J.D. Pendleton's chimes?

Jack hunkered down to get a closer look at what was left of the Cadillac blown up by the IED. The remaining shards of metal were small and burned black. He looked up at Breed and said, "This looks like overkill."

"He wants to make sure whoever is in the car ends up dead. He used a shaped charge on the ground, Jack. It burned a hole clear through the bottom of the chassis and allowed the C-4 to do a helluva lot more damage to the interior of the vehicle. The FBI bomb tech said this IED was remotely detonated."

Jack stood and pulled off his Stetson and ran a hand through his hair, then tugged it back down again. "That son of a bitch is making a roadside bomb."

Breed nodded. "If it's anything like this one, it'll be one hell of an IED."

Jack looked into the distance, where rice grew in wet paddies. "Assuming this was J.D., any clues where he went from here?"

"He didn't use any local means of transportation—bus or taxi or rental car—so he's probably got his own vehicle. Nobody saw or heard a motorcycle last night, so probably a car. He could easily disappear in any one of the gazillion small communities surrounding Houston."

"Gazillion?" Jack said with a twist of his lips.

"Houston is dotted with tiny towns and minuscule municipalities, too many to name in a single breath. Lots of farm workers, oil workers, transients. Easy to disappear if you have a little cash and a car, which I presume J.D. does."

"I guess the question is whether I should warn D'Amato."

And Kate and Shaw.

"Might win you some points with the mob boss, but it won't keep him safe. A roadside bomb like this one can take out an armored military vehicle. It's going to make mincemeat of an armor-plated bulletproof limousine."

"Guess it can't hurt to let D'Amato know what's coming," Jack said. "Knowing D'Amato, he isn't going to let a threat like this keep him from going where he wants to go."

"Just make sure you're not in the car with him," Breed said wryly.

"No problem. Give Grace a hug from me. And say hello to King."

"Will do."

Before he left Alvin, Jack talked with Sheriff Fredericks, confirming the description of the suspect who'd caused the explosion and getting one additional piece of information.

"Had lunch today at the drugstore counter in town," the sheriff said. "The waitress, a pretty little girl named Betty Jean, said she served a man yesterday who matched the description of our bomber. Flirted with her, if you can believe it."

Knowing J.D., Jack believed it. "Did he say anything to her that would help us figure out where he might have gone?"

"Depends. Said he was married now, but he was going to be a free man soon. Does that help you?"

"Yes," Jack said. "It does. Thanks, Sheriff. I'd like to show her a picture, see if she can identify it, if that's all right."

"Sure is. You got some idea who did this?"

"I'll know more after Betty Jean takes a look at the photo."

The young blond waitress stared at the photo of J.D. that Jack handed to her and said, "Holy cow! That's him, 'cept he didn't look nowhere near this nice. If I'd known he would clean up like that I'd have thunk twice about maybe takin' a ride in that car of his."

"You got a look at his car?" Jack said.

"Nothin' fancy," the girl said with a shrug. "Some white SUV. Looked new enough, tinted windows. I like sporty cars, the ones with the tops that come off."

Jack thanked the girl and the sheriff. At least he knew J.D. had been in town, which made it a good bet he was the one who'd blown up the car in the junkyard. It was interesting to know he was driving a white SUV, but that information wasn't going to be much help finding him.

On the drive back to Houston, Jack decided to call Kate. Which was when it occurred to him that they hadn't communicated once during the past ten days. He'd seen a couple of phone messages but hadn't returned her calls. He wondered if she'd been distracted by something equally catastrophic in her life. His call went directly to voice mail. "Hi, Kate," he began.

Jack didn't want to leave a message about his convoluted personal life. Or a warning about J.D. that he couldn't really explain in a short voice message. So he simply said, "Call me. It's important."

24

Kate felt relieved that she'd told her parents the truth. She was surprised when her father agreed that she and the twins would be safest staying with Shaw. It was strange to see her father shake hands with Shaw the day her mother came home from the hospital and they parted ways. And to have her mother whisper in her ear, "I like him."

"Just because my parents accept you as the twins' father doesn't change anything between us," she warned him on the flight back to Houston.

He'd kept his distance during the flight home. But the first night they were back in Houston, she caught him watching her in the bathroom mirror as she changed into her nightgown in the bedroom.

She clutched her nightgown to her naked body and said, "Stop that."

He came out of the bathroom wearing a pair of the formfitting, thigh-length briefs she found so attractive and said, "Why shouldn't I look at what's pleasing to the eye. You're beautiful, Kate."

"Flattery will get you nowhere," she said, turning her back and pulling her nightgown over her head.

When she turned back around, he was right behind her.

"Like I said, beautiful."

"Jack, I—"

The smile on his face froze when he heard what she'd said.

She didn't know why Jack's name had come to her lips. She hadn't been thinking of him. She'd been looking at Shaw's lips and remembering how soft they felt and how good his mouth tasted.

His jaw flexed and he started to turn.

She put a hand to his cheek, turned his face back toward hers and lifted herself on tiptoe. "I'm sorry," she whispered. And kissed him.

His lips were rigid but quickly softened and pressed back against hers. Urging her to succumb.

Kate backed up quickly. "No, Wyatt." She put her fingertips to her mouth and stared at him, shocked at how badly she wanted him.

She thought maybe it was the use of his name that made him pause long enough for her to escape.

"I can wait, Kate. However long it takes. I can wait."

He turned and got into bed. "I figure we can all sleep in tomorrow."

"I can't," she told him as she got under the covers on her side of the bed. "I have patients who need to see me."

"You're tired, Kate. You need to sleep."

"I sleep just fine." Which wasn't entirely true. Having Shaw on the other side of the bed disturbed her rest. Especially when their arms or legs got tangled during the night. She thought of the exquisite friction when her smooth leg collided with one of his hairy ones. Her mouth went dry.

"Stay on your own side tonight," she said, "and maybe I'll be able to get some rest."

Despite the fact he stayed on his own side, or maybe because of it, Kate didn't sleep well. Unfortunately, she had a particularly troubling patient first thing the next morning at the Children's Cancer Hospital, so she was grateful when lunchtime came and she could take a break.

Kate left the Main Building where she worked at a brisk walk, headed for the Waterfall Café on the second floor of the Mays Clinic. The journey took less than ten minutes, but it was like leaving a dark planet for some bright star.

She caught the elevator down to the third floor, near the Gazebo, then headed for the Skybridge. She usually walked the quarter of a mile or so across the Skybridge to the Mays Clinic instead of taking the mini-shuttle, because she needed the extra few minutes to decompress.

She'd slowed her pace, so she was surprised when she started to gain on the tall man walking in front of her. He reminded her of Jack. Considering she was in Texas, and a lot of men wore Wranglers and western shirts and Stetsons and boots, she didn't think it was him, especially when she noted the droop of the man's shoulders and his listless stride.

She suddenly realized she hadn't spoken to Jack for ten days. She'd left messages asking him to call, but he hadn't contacted her. She figured he needed time to work out the kinks of living with Holly and Ryan. She realized she hadn't checked her cell phone for messages today. If he hadn't called, she'd call him tonight and see how things were going.

And tell him what's going on between you and Shaw?

Probably not. He knew the worst—that she'd slept with Shaw. She wasn't sure how much of the rest she would ever tell him.

The guy in front of her *really* looked like Jack. Kate shifted her angle to look for a SIG at his waist. And found it.

"Jack?" she called. When the man didn't respond, she hurried forward and said, "Jack? Is that you?"

When he turned, she drew up short at the anguished look in his dark brown eyes. It was clear something dire had happened. Jack looked almost dazed as he stared down at her.

She put a hand on his stiffly starched sleeve and said, "What's wrong? Are you all right?"

"What are you doing here?" he asked.

"I work here," she said, laughing to mask her discomfort. "Remember?"

He put a hand to his brow. "Yeah. That's right."

"What are you doing here?" she asked. "Were you looking for me?"

"No. But, God, I'm glad to see you." He pulled her close and hugged her tight.

Kate had trouble catching her breath and pushed against Jack's shoulders so she could inflate her lungs. She searched his features, wondering what disaster could have wreaked such havoc in such a short time. His red-rimmed, sunken eyes were proof he wasn't sleeping. His concave cheeks told her he wasn't eating. His bowed posture spoke for itself.

"What's going on, Jack?" she asked. "What are you doing here?"

He stepped back and let her go. "It's a long story. Let's go find a place to sit down, and I'll tell you everything."

"I was headed to the Waterfall Café for lunch."

"Sounds good." Jack took her arm and walked her across the Skybridge.

Once they were seated in the café, Kate with a bowl of chicken noodle soup and some iced tea and Jack with a ham and Swiss sandwich, a bag of corn chips and a Dr Pepper, Kate asked, "What's going on, Jack?"

"Ryan has cancer. Acute myelogenous leukemia."

"My God." She reached out and squeezed his hand. "I'm so sorry!"

"He's already had his first few rounds of chemo, but he's been having such a bad reaction to it, his doctor is keeping him in the hospital to be monitored. He gets so sick, I can't stand to watch."

"Oh, Jack." Kate reached up to caress his cheek, but he caught her hand before it got there and pushed it away. That seemed odd, but she figured he was too overwrought to know what he was doing. She realized that neither one of them had touched their food.

"Ryan keeps asking when he can go home." He swallowed hard, then continued, "If he could tolerate the chemicals better, he could go home between treatments. But his cancer is aggressive so he needs the larger dose, and it's killing me to watch him suffer."

He pulled free of her touch, balling his hands into fists on the table. "I feel so goddamned helpless."

"Take a breath, Jack." Kate had never seen him so

rattled. The lack of sleep was obviously taking its toll. "I know things may seem out of control right now, but Ryan's a fighter. He's going to come through this just fine. You have to take care of yourself so you'll be able to take care of him. How's Holly holding up with all this additional stress?"

"She's a trooper," Jack said. "Her strength is amazing. I don't know how she does it. She's working in between spending time with Ryan at the hospital, since she can get back and forth pretty easily from the lab where she does her research to his room."

Kate heard the admiration for his wife in Jack's voice. "I'm glad Holly's there for you and Ryan."

Because I can't be.

Kate felt selfish even thinking about what Ryan's illness meant to her relationship with Jack. But she couldn't help it. Jack had already committed to staying with Holly until the baby was born. Ryan's illness meant he might be staying with his wife and son for far longer than that.

"What's going to happen to us, Jack?" she asked.

"I don't know," he admitted. "Feels like a real uphill climb from here, doesn't it? Maybe we should just cut our losses."

"I'm not ready to do that."

"Ryan's fighting for his life, Kate. I can't leave him until…things are resolved."

Kate knew that nothing was certain with childhood cancer. Some kids lived for six or seven years, fighting cancer the whole time, until it killed them. Some kids lost the battle in a few months. Some kids battled the cancer bitch for years before they finally won.

"Why didn't you call me?" Kate said. "I would have been glad to provide a shoulder to lean on."

He made a face. "At your home in Houston or mine?"

Kate returned the face with interest. "Metaphorically speaking, of course."

"I left a message on your cell phone today," Jack said.

"I haven't listened to it yet. What did you say?"

"Just to call me. I have some news about your errant husband."

"Have you found him?" Kate asked hopefully.

"I know where he's been," Jack said. "What's more important, I know what he's planning."

"What's that?"

Instead of answering her, Jack said, "Can you fix it so I can talk to Wyatt Shaw today?"

Kate blanched. "Is that a good idea?"

"I think maybe it is. Especially with what J.D. has planned."

"Exactly what does J.D. have planned, Jack? Tell me," Kate insisted.

"Can you set up a meeting with Shaw?"

"He's picking me up after work. Will that be soon enough?"

"He picks you up? Every day? Same time, same place?"

"Of course."

"Jesus, Kate. You're making it easy for J.D."

"Making *what* easy? What are you talking about, Jack?"

"J.D.'s been down in Alvin practicing how to blow up a car with an IED. His target could be D'Amato, since D'Amato's after him. But he might not stop there. He might also want to get a little revenge and target you and Shaw."

"With an IED?"

"A remotely detonated roadside bomb, to be precise. So it's important that you and Shaw vary your schedule and pickup locations, so you don't make yourselves an easy mark."

"There are only so many places Shaw can pick me up," Kate said. "Only so many routes we can take to the heliport where Shaw's helicopter waits for us every day."

"Heliport? Helicopter? You *fly* back and forth to his compound?"

Kate flushed. "What's wrong with that?"

Jack snorted. "Nothing, I guess, if you're filthy rich."

"Shaw earned his money honestly," Kate said.

"So he says."

"I believe him."

"All the money in the world isn't going to help either one of you, if J.D. figures out a convenient spot to plant a roadside bomb along your route."

"I told you, there are only so many ways we can go."

"Then get creative," Jack said.

"Is that why you want to talk to Shaw? To warn him J.D. may be after us?" Kate asked. "If so, I can tell him that."

"Thanks for the offer, but I need to speak with him about another matter, as well."

"I'd be glad to give Shaw a message," Kate offered. "If you don't have the time to meet with him in person."

Jack's lip curled cynically. "Don't want us comparing notes?"

"That's not fair, Jack."

"None of this is fair," he shot back. "It's not fair that my son might die. It's not fair that my wife is pregnant with a child I'll never really know because I'm divorcing her the day after it's born."

His gesturing arm accidentally knocked over his glass of Dr Pepper. He picked up the glass with one hand and grabbed sliding ice cubes with the other. He glared at her as he raked the soda off the table, where it splattered on the floor, and dumped the ice cubes back in the glass. "It's not fair that the woman I love is living with another man, and I have to rely on him to protect her, because I can't."

Kate tugged the glass out of his hand and set it on the table. "Jack, please—"

"No, Kate," he finished, grabbing a napkin and wiping his hands savagely. "Not a goddamn thing in my life is fair right now." His chair scraped on the floor as he shoved it backward. He threw the napkin on the table and stood. "I'll be waiting when you're done with work. You can take me to wherever you're meeting Shaw."

Kate reached out and caught his arm before he could take a step away. She saw before her a man pushed not just to the edge, but all the way over it. She looked up at him and said, "Sit down, Jack. You haven't eaten your lunch."

"I've lost my appetite."

"You need to eat. Please, sit down." She spoke softly. Gently. He resisted the tug on her arm, so she stood and put herself in front of him. "If you don't sit down, I'm going to make an awful scene."

"Go ahead."

When she opened her mouth to yell, he grabbed his chair, pulled it toward the table and sat back down.

Kate gave a silent sigh of relief as Jack picked up his sandwich and took a bite that consumed a third of the sandwich. She forced herself to pick up her spoon and eat a bite of her chicken noodle soup.

"Would it be all right if I bring the twins to visit Ryan while he's an inpatient at the hospital?" she said.

"I'll ask Holly, but I think he'd like that."

"Give me a call and let me know what Holly says. And, Jack?"

"What?"

"Don't let so much time go between calls. If we're going to survive this separation, we need to stay in touch."

He was chewing and had to swallow before he could speak. "That works both ways. How are the twins?"

Kate realized it would be cruel to tell Jack how well the twins were getting along with Shaw. "They're doing fine. Shaw enrolled them in a private school in The Woodlands."

"I don't think J.D. would hurt them, but you might want to employ the same precautions with their commute back and forth to school that you use with your own."

"I'm sure Shaw will have Bruce do whatever's necessary to keep them safe."

"Bruce?"

"He was Shaw's bodyguard. Now he watches the boys." Kate saw the look on Jack's face and said, "Bruce looks like a gruesome giant, but he's polite to me and kind to the twins. They like him."

"Do you find all this as strange as I do?" Jack said. Kate found herself smiling. "Weird and fantastical."

"Yeah," Jack said, finishing the last of his corn chips and noisily crushing the bag into a tight ball. "Bizarre and peculiar. That describes my life perfectly."

Kate wondered how soon their lives would get back to normal. And what normal would look like when they did.

25

"Hey, Boss. We got trouble."

"I see it, Jimmy. Be ready to get us out of here in a hurry," Wyatt said to his limo driver.

When Jimmy reached toward the glove compartment, Wyatt said, "Leave your Glock where it is."

Wyatt's gaze was riveted on Kate, whose arm was linked with Jack McKinley's as they exited the Main Building at M.D. Anderson. His heart was racketing in his chest. His shoulders were tensed, his hands fisted expecting bloodshed as he stepped out of the limo.

You can't have her. She's mine.

The couple stopped two feet in front of him. Kate looked up at Jack, as though waiting for him to speak.

Wyatt wasn't afraid of any man. But he was terrified that Kate was going to leave him. He felt sure she'd brought Jack here not as an officer of the law, but as the man she loved, and that the two of them intended to prevail upon him to return the boys and allow Kate to go home.

Which he would do when it snowed in hell. It had taken him too long to find her. He had no intention of letting her go anywhere. Especially not with a two-faced son of a bitch like Jack McKinley.

"What's going on?" Wyatt asked in his calmest, deadliest voice.

He could see the Texas Ranger was anxious and edgy. He half expected the lawman, who was wearing both badge and gun, to arrest him for kidnapping. Or make some plea on behalf of D'Amato. Instead, McKinley put a courteous finger to the brim of his Stetson and said, "Shaw."

Wyatt lifted his chin, returning the greeting. "Sergeant McKinley." Then he focused his turbulent gaze on Kate and asked, "What's he doing here?"

"We need to talk," the Ranger said.

"Kate, get in the car," Wyatt ordered.

He saw her body stiffen, watched her shoulders square and her eyes narrow, and knew he'd made a mistake.

She let go of the Ranger's arm to shift the strap of her purse higher on her shoulder, and said, "Jack has something he wants to tell you."

That sounded ominous. Wyatt wanted Kate where he could make a quick getaway if things between him and the Ranger got nasty. He took a step forward, forcing Kate to take a step to her right, closer to the open door to the limo, where broad-chested Jimmy now stood, powerful arms akimbo, looking like the bodyguard he was.

Wyatt turned to the Ranger and said, "Talk."

"J.D.'s been practicing how to make a roadside bomb. It may be for D'Amato. Or he might decide to use it on the two of you."

Shaw lifted a surprised brow. He felt some of the tension ease out of his shoulders. It seemed McKinley was here as a lawman, all right, but not to help Kate get away from him, or on some mission for D'Amato.

"I saw what was left of the Cadillac J.D. practiced on," the Ranger said. "There wasn't a piece left bigger than a sandwich. No amount of armor is going to protect your limo if he plants an IED along the route you've been using to get back and forth to your compound."

Wyatt had seen the results of the sort of devastation McKinley was talking about up close and personal when he'd gone to Iraq to investigate a military security business in which he'd planned to invest. He'd been in a convoy moving along Highway One when the armored personnel carrier directly in front of him had been blown up by a remotely detonated IED.

Four out of the six soldiers in the carrier had been killed outright. The fifth had lost his right leg and arm and had a skull fracture. The sixth had been burned so badly that his skin sloughed off when Wyatt tried to move him to safety.

Wyatt had a scar on his hip where he'd been hit by shrapnel, but he'd come away essentially unharmed. Except for the indelible mark the experience had left on his psyche. For months afterward he'd jumped every time he heard a car backfire. It was horrifying to imagine Kate as the victim of such a destructive weapon.

"Kate told me the two of you have been using a pre-dictable route back and forth to a heliport here in Houston," Jack said.

Wyatt nodded. "That's true." He wasn't used to

being a target. That was more his father's bailiwick. "What do you suggest?"

He saw Kate tilt her head, as though she hadn't expected him to ask or accept the Ranger's advice. But he was willing to do whatever was necessary to keep her safe, even if it meant swallowing a little pride.

"Vary your route around Houston, and in and out of your compound, so it's unpredictable," McKinley said. "It would be better if you weren't traveling the highways at all."

"You mean we should stay in the city?"

The Ranger shrugged. "You've got a place here."

Kate looked at Jack as though he'd betrayed her. "The boys are in school in The Woodlands. It would be too much of a commute for them if we were staying in downtown Houston."

"Just until the police or the FBI can locate what they think is a terrorist with a bomb," McKinley said to her. "I want you safe, Kate."

"I appreciate the warning," Shaw said, irritated by the intimate looks the two of them were exchanging. "Please get in the car, Kate."

Wyatt could see she was angry—at the Ranger and at him. For a moment he thought she was going to turn around and walk back inside the hospital. Instead, she took the few steps to the limo, threw her purse inside and stepped in after it. Wyatt turned back to the Ranger and said, "Thanks for the warning."

"Take care of her."

"I intend to do just that." He turned his back on the Ranger and joined Kate in the limo. Jimmy closed the door behind him and headed around the rear of the limo. When he was back behind the wheel, Wyatt said, "Take us to Shaw Tower."

"You got it, Boss."

"Cancel that, Jimmy," Kate said.

The limo driver met Wyatt's eyes in the rearview mirror, his bushy brows raised in question.

"Hold on a minute, Jimmy," Wyatt said.

The limo driver found a safe place to stop the car and pulled it to the curb.

Wyatt turned to Kate and said, "You heard what McKinley said. It isn't safe to be traveling back and forth on the highway."

"I have to get back and forth to the hospital every day through the city. That's going to leave J.D. a way to get to us the same as if we drove to a heliport every day. Why not just use a different heliport every day or simply make the drive all the way home sometimes?

"We can even stay in the city on the weekends occasionally, when the boys can be with us," Kate said. "J.D. can't be everywhere. If we vary the route we take, and where we spend the night, he'll never know where to find us."

"Unless he picks an intersection we'll be likely to cross and simply waits for us there."

"If both the FBI and the Houston city cops are on the lookout for a terrorist with a bomb, he couldn't really hang around the same place every day without getting noticed, could he?" Kate asked.

Wyatt saw her point.

"And he's not likely to hang around close to your compound, because he'd stick out like a sore thumb. Not to mention the fact he'd have to sleep on the ground. I don't see J.D. inconveniencing himself if he can help it."

"I don't like playing Russian roulette with that son of a bitch," Wyatt said.

"I lived with J.D. long enough to know he'll take the path of least resistance. If we vary our routes in and out of the city and make it difficult for him to predict where we'll be, he'll get tired of waiting and give up."

"You want me to gamble with your life."

Kate met his gaze and said, "I can't be away from my sons, Wyatt. J.D. has already caused enough disruption in their lives."

He noticed she'd used his first name again, which made him feel more attached to her. And more vulnerable. He was sure that was why she'd done it. "Skip the heliport and drive us home, Jimmy," Wyatt said at last.

"You got it, Boss."

He met Jimmy's gaze again and the limo driver closed the glass privacy window between the front and back seats.

Kate released a breath Wyatt hadn't known she'd been holding, leaned her head back against the comfortable leather seat and closed her eyes.

"You're exhausted again," Wyatt said. "And it's only the middle of the week."

"I had a new patient today," she replied, "a ten-year-old boy named Simon. He lost a leg to sarcoma. I've been helping him do exercises with his stump to get ready for his prosthetic limb."

"One little boy tired you out?"

"He thinks the exercises are pointless, because he

doesn't think he's going to live long enough to need the prosthetic limb that's being made for him."

No wonder she was tired, Wyatt thought. He could never do what she did. He didn't know where she found the emotional strength to consistently face that sort of challenge.

"The sad thing is," Kate continued after a moment of silence, "he's probably right. Simon's cancer was so far advanced when he was diagnosed that he may very well die."

Shaw didn't know how to comfort her. The opportunities to offer comfort had been few and far between in his life. So he offered the only suggestion he thought might help. "You need to get more sleep."

"I would sleep better if you gave me my own bedroom," Kate said acerbically.

Shaw looked out the window, ignoring the request. She was staying in his bed, where he could hold her close at night. He felt the same need to make up for lost time with Kate that he did with his sons. There were years they'd spent apart that he could never get back. He planned to make the most of every day from now on.

They'd been riding in silence for quite a while when Kate said, "Jack's six-year-old son Ryan has leukemia."

Expressing sympathy wasn't usual for him, either. He wasn't sure exactly what expression was appropriate. He imagined how he would feel if his sons were ill with a life-threatening disease. And felt sick in the pit of his stomach. "I'm sorry to hear it," he said in a gruff voice.

"That's why Jack was at M.D. Anderson. Ryan

hasn't reacted well to the chemotherapy he's been getting. He's an inpatient at the Children's Hospital. I'd like to take Lucky and Chance to visit him over the weekend."

"I didn't know they were acquainted with McKinley's son."

"The boys met over Christmas, when Jack was taking care of the twins and Ryan came to visit from Kansas."

"Is that a good idea?" Wyatt asked hesitantly. "Taking them to see a kid who's so sick he has to be in the hospital?"

"I'm sure the boys would enjoy seeing Ryan. And, if he's feeling well enough, I think Ryan would enjoy having visitors."

"I meant…" Wyatt wasn't sure how to express his concern about what the boys might suffer when they saw their friend in a hospital bed.

Kate opened her eyes and searched his face. "What is it?"

"I was just wondering how they'll handle seeing their friend so sick."

"I didn't say it would be comfortable for them. Not at first, anyway. But I wouldn't like to think Lucky and Chance would abandon their friend just because it's difficult to see him hurting or in unusual surroundings."

"What's the boy's prognosis?" Wyatt asked.

"I don't really know, but he has one of the more deadly forms of leukemia."

Wyatt felt that same ball of panic in the pit of his stomach. "That's too bad."

"So you'll let me take them to visit on Saturday morning?"

"I'll even come with you."

"Don't feel like you have to come. We'll be fine without you."

"I'm coming," Wyatt said. "And that's the end of it."

"Because you want to? Or because you don't trust me?"

"Does it matter?"

"It does to me."

"I want to come. Satisfied?"

"But you don't trust me."

"Should I?"

She rolled her eyes and huffed out a breath. "We're going and you're going. Fine. End of discussion."

"You and that cat of yours," he murmured.

"What?"

Shaw's lips quirked. "You both show your claws when you get upset."

26

Holly's ankles were swollen the size of grapefruits. She'd been on her feet all day at work—on a Saturday—without a break. Not the smartest move for a stressed-out woman who was almost six months pregnant. But Ryan had been expecting afternoon visitors, and Jack wasn't around, so she'd decided to go to the hospital a bit before visiting hours and meet with some of the patients in her clinical trial.

She sat down on Jack's oversize chair in the living room and put her feet up on the ottoman. She'd missed having a mid-morning break because she'd used the time to visit Ryan, who was cranky and miserable.

"Please, Mom, I want to go home!" he'd begged, his lips scabbed and giant tears rolling down his pale cheeks.

"Soon, sweetie," she'd soothed. "Soon."

But her throat had swollen tight as she spoke the lie. The first treatment phase, which was intended to induce remission of the cancer, had consisted of a drug cocktail of daunorubicin and cytarabine, given over a course of seven to ten days. The chemotherapy was supposed to leave the patient clinically free of the disease and with a normal white blood cell count.

Ryan had completed his tenth day of chemotherapy with his blood count nowhere near normal. He was definitely *not* in remission. His doctor would be adding more drugs, perhaps thioguanine or etoposide, before trying again.

Sadly, Ryan had been too sick to spend more than a few minutes with Lucky and Chance when they'd come to visit. Since her son's immune system was so compromised, the twins had worn gowns, masks and gloves. Nevertheless, it had been an awkward few minutes, because their mother, and a man she recognized from TV coverage as Wyatt Shaw, had come with them.

"Thank you for bringing the boys to visit Ryan," Holly had said politely to her nemesis.

"I'm glad you allowed them to come," Kate replied with a smile. "They've been worried ever since they heard Ryan was sick."

Holly glanced at the three boys. Ryan was lying weakly on his hospital bed while the twins stood on the bed rails hovering over him. Shaw was standing beside them, also gloved, masked and gowned. "I'm not sure seeing Ryan like this is going to reassure them."

She'd watched the three boys long enough to see that Lucky and Chance were enjoying the novelty of wearing gowns, masks and gloves, and that Ryan had a smile on his face for the first time since he'd been admitted to the hospital.

"I was surprised to hear from you," Holly admitted.

"Didn't Jack tell you? I'm working here at M.D. Anderson," Kate replied. "With pediatric sarcoma patients."

"I think Jack did mention you would be working

here." *Which made me wonder whether the two of you might be making plans to see each other.* "How do you like working with kids instead of soldiers?"

"It's different," Kate replied. "Sadder in some ways. Because they're still fighting for their lives."

Holly was surprised at Kate's frankness. And how quickly she'd put her finger on what was also the hardest part of Holly's job. She didn't want to like Kate Pendleton. Holly considered the woman a serious threat to her marriage. She wished Kate weren't so empathetic. And so beautiful. What chance did Holly have— with her thick waist and her thick ankles—competing with such a slender, absolutely stunning woman?

As though she'd read Holly's mind, Kate said, "In case you were wondering, our move to Houston didn't have anything to do with Jack moving in with you. The twins and I are staying with Mr. Shaw for a little while."

"So you changed jobs?" Holly asked, her brow furrowed. That didn't sound very temporary. She was dying to ask how Kate had gotten involved with such a notorious man in the first place, but she didn't want to open a new can of worms, afraid of what would spill out.

Kate shrugged. "The opportunity to work here presented itself, so I took advantage of it."

One of the twins interrupted them to say in a surprised voice, "Mom, Ryan fell asleep."

"We should go," Kate said. "May we come again?"

"Of course," Holly replied. She wouldn't deny her son anything that made him happy, despite her own discomfort with the situation.

Especially since there was no telling how long

Ryan's recovery would take. Because of his increased risk of infection and other side effects from his chemotherapy, he might be in the hospital anywhere from four to six weeks. And that was if the second round of chemotherapy was successful.

If chemotherapy didn't work, Ryan would need a bone marrow transplant. Holly leaned farther back in Jack's chair and hissed in a breath. The most successful bone marrow transplants were done using a human leukocyte antigen (HLA)-matched sibling—a brother or sister—rather than a mother or father.

Unfortunately, Ryan was an only child.

That's not true, Holly. Ryan has a sibling. A sister.

Blood suffused her face as she remembered how it had felt to discover she was pregnant at fourteen. The terror. And the joy. And the horror at what she must do. There was no way she could raise a child on her own. She'd still been a child herself. So she'd given away the baby she and Jack had made. Only God knew where their daughter—a twenty-six-year-old woman—was now.

It hadn't been an easy decision. She'd made list after list of the pros and cons of keeping the baby. She always came up with the same rational answer. She couldn't. Her parents would be no help, and if she married Jack, she might never escape her mother's fate.

So she'd done what she thought was best for the three of them. First, she'd broken up with Jack without even hinting that she was pregnant. Then she'd gone to visit a nonexistent "sick aunt" in Houston until the baby was born. Finally, she'd given up their baby for adoption.

Holly had held their little girl long enough to see through a blur of tears that she had chestnut curls, like her father, and very green eyes, like her mother. She'd quickly counted all ten fingers and all ten toes. Then the nurse had come and taken her away. Letting go was the hardest thing Holly had ever done.

Holly didn't know what had become of their daughter. Didn't know her name. Had tried to forget her birthday. But for the past twenty-six years, she'd never yet made it through the entire day on April 10 without crying.

If it became necessary to save their son's life, she would tell Jack the truth. She shuddered to think what he would do. What he would say. How he would react to her deceit.

In hindsight, she knew what she'd done was wrong. She should at least have told Jack she was carrying his child. But she'd feared he wouldn't want to give up the baby. She wouldn't have been able to resist his entreaties to marry him and raise their child. And she hadn't believed he would love her forever and ever, as he'd always claimed he would.

Every day she prayed that their daughter had found a good home with loving parents. She'd endured a great deal of guilt over her decision. And second thoughts. And regrets.

But what was done was done. There was no going back—unless Ryan needed his sister's help to stay alive. Then Holly would have to face her daughter—and her husband—and account for the choices she'd made so long ago.

Assuming their daughter could be found.

Holly closed her eyes and sighed. She'd come to

Houston with such high hopes such a short time ago. It was hard to stay optimistic under the circumstances.

When she'd left Ryan's hospital room after bidding Kate, Wyatt Shaw and the twins goodbye, she'd felt too nauseated to eat anything. Now her stomach was rebelling because it had been empty for too long. And she was just too tired to get up and cook something.

Especially since she wasn't sure Jack would be home to share the meal. He was spending long hours trying to track down J.D. Pendleton, who seemed to have disappeared from the face of the earth. Jack was sleeping in a separate bedroom and had a separate bath, so she'd hardly seen him in the nearly two weeks since Ryan had gone into the hospital.

Which was probably a good thing. Her hair needed washing. Her eyes had dark circles from lack of sleep. Her figure was gone, taken over by the growing baby inside her. How was she supposed to compete with a woman like Kate Pendleton?

"Holly? Are you all right?"

Holly opened her eyes and realized Jack had come in without her being aware of it. He was sitting on the ottoman, a masculine hand wrapped around one of her massively swollen ankles. "I'm sorry, Jack. I meant to make us some supper. I must have dozed off."

"I'll cook. You need to stay off your feet."

She could see he was eyeing her ankles. She tried to pull the one he was holding out of his grasp and get the ugly things out of sight, but he caught her foot.

"Hold it," he said. "Let me help you get your shoes off. I forgot how much trouble you have reaching your feet when you're pregnant."

He untied her tennis shoes, loosened the laces and eased them, one after the other, off her feet, along with the tennis socks she wore. It had been too much effort to bend over her enlarged belly and remove them herself.

Holly felt emotional tears in her eyes and blinked them back. Removing her shoes and rubbing her feet was something Jack had done for her when she was pregnant with Ryan. This was the first time he'd touched her since he'd moved in.

Holly moaned as Jack used his knuckles to massage her arches.

He glanced up and their eyes met. And he smiled.

It was a rare sight because they'd had so little to smile about lately. She smiled back and said, "You have no idea how good that feels."

"I wish I could be here every day when you get home. I might as well be here," he added ruefully. "That son of a bitch Pendleton has been as elusive as an eel."

"There's some ground sirloin defrosted in the fridge. How about sloppy joe's?" She'd suggested the meal because she knew it was easy to make, and because it was one of Jack's favorites.

"Sounds good." But he made no move to stop what he was doing.

"If I weren't so tired I'd offer to help with supper," she said.

"How was Ryan today?" Jack asked.

"The same. Except he had visitors."

Jack lifted an inquiring brow and Holly said, "The twins showed up with their mother. And Wyatt Shaw."

Holly was watching closely, so she saw the slight

grimace that crossed Jack's face before he said, "I can't believe Kate and the twins are still living with that man."

"He was good with Ryan and the twins," Holly said.

"He would be," Jack muttered in disgust, as he laid her right foot down on the ottoman.

She was sorry she'd mentioned Kate's visit, because it seemed to have put Jack in a bad mood. Bad enough to quit what he was doing, anyway. He'd probably been mentally comparing her swollen ankles to Kate's more delicate ones.

To her surprise, he picked up her left foot, this time starting his massage with her toes. She'd never told him that the tips of her toes were an erogenous zone, that when he ran the callused pads of his fingers across them, she felt her womb contract.

But this was no time for foreplay, even if it was unintentional. She wasn't feeling particularly attractive, especially when she compared herself to Kate Pendleton. Besides, she didn't think she could stay awake for sex, even if Jack were interested.

"You're tickling me," she said with a forced smile, tugging at her foot. She persisted in wriggling until Jack left her toes to work on her arch with his knuckles.

"Lord have mercy," she murmured. "That hurts so good."

Jack chuckled.

She leaned back and closed her eyes and moaned at the pain/pleasure. "Don't stop," she said, when it seemed he would.

"How soon before Ryan will be able to come home?" he asked.

She opened her eyes and met his gaze. "It's going to be a while, Jack."

He stopped what he was doing and asked, "Why isn't that damned chemo working?"

"The doctor hasn't found the right combination of drugs. But he will."

"How much more of this torture is Ryan going to have to endure before the doctor figures out he can't stand it?" Jack grated out.

"You'd be surprised what Ryan can stand."

"Well, I can't take much more of this."

Jack let her foot drop back onto the ottoman as he rose and headed for the bar in the living room. He poured himself a bourbon and stood at the bar while he emptied the glass, then poured himself another drink. "I never realized how hard it would be to see my son suffering, especially when I'm helpless to end it."

Holly shoved her feet off the ottoman, hefted herself out of the comfortable chair with a great deal of effort and crossed to Jack. She took the glass out of his hand and set it aside. "This isn't going to solve anything."

Inebriation hadn't made things easier for her father. And it wouldn't make things easier for Jack. "We have to stay positive for Ryan's sake."

"Say something hopeful," he urged. "Say something that will make me believe our son will get well."

But the statistics weren't on Ryan's side. Instead, she took a step as close as her burgeoning belly would allow, wrapped her arms around her husband's waist and laid her head against his chest. "Hold me, Jack," she said quietly.

She was certain he needed to be held as much as she needed his arms around her. She waited with bated breath until his arms tightened around her shoulders. He rocked her, comforting both of them.

"God, Holly. Who'd have thought we'd end up like this? How did we get so far from where we started? I can remember a time when I couldn't wait to get home to share my day with you, to hold you like this, and be held like this."

"I have to take the blame for a lot of what went wrong," Holly admitted.

"I think I started a few of those arguments," he said gruffly.

"Back then, I was afraid to love you, Jack," she said quietly.

"What?" He leaned back and said, "Holly, look at me."

She leaned her head back and looked up into his serious brown eyes.

"What are you saying? That you didn't love me?"

She saw the confusion in his gaze and wondered how much she should tell him about her fears all those years ago.

Everything, Holly. If you want a chance at a life together, you owe him that.

"You know what my dad was like, Jack."

"He walked out on you and your family. A lot," Jack said. "What does that have to do with me?"

"I was always afraid that you'd do the same thing. So... I never let myself trust you—love you—completely. I was always waiting for the other shoe to drop."

He let go of her and reached behind him to remove her hands.

She tightened her grip. "Please don't let go of me, Jack. I'm telling you this because I've changed."

His hands remained at his sides, but Holly kept her arms around him. She focused her eyes intently on his, which were shuttered now. "I forced you out of my life a year ago because I thought it would be easier to have you gone once and for all than to wait for you to leave on your own."

"What the hell—"

She stood on tiptoe and used her mouth to shut him up. The kiss was brief and shocked him into silence.

"I don't know if you still have any feelings for me, Jack. I just wanted to let you know that I still have feelings for you. And that I'm willing to take the risk that if I welcome you back with open arms, you'll stay."

His arms closed around her slowly, but they tightened until she squeaked. He loosened his hold as he searched her eyes, perhaps looking for proof that she was no longer hiding the truth from him.

"I love you, Jack," she said. "I've missed you. I need you."

Holly didn't know what else she could say. She felt exposed, vulnerable, as she waited for his response.

Jack bent and slid one arm behind her knees. He lifted her as though she weighed nothing. She marveled anew at the play of muscle and sinew in his powerful arms and shoulders. A moment later, he was headed down the hall.

"Where are you taking me?" she asked.

"Unless you have an objection, I'm going to make love to my wife."

Holly was suddenly wide awake. "I have no objections at all, except…"

He stopped in his tracks and said, "Tell me now if you don't want this."

"I don't feel very pretty right now," she confessed, peeping up at him from beneath lowered lashes.

"You've never been more beautiful to me than when you're carrying my child. Don't you know that, Holly?"

She slid her fingers into the hair at his nape and lifted her mouth to his for a kiss that was as arousing as it was satisfying. "Take me to bed, Jack," she murmured against his lips.

She needed the reaffirming closeness, the solace that they had always found in each other's bodies. It seemed tonight Jack needed her as much as she needed him. She would hold him tight and love him well. There was no telling when it might be the last time.

Because the day was coming when she might have to choose between saving Ryan by revealing the existence of a sister, or saving her marriage by continuing to keep her secret. She was pretty sure that if that happened, only one of them would survive.

27

Jack had forgotten how easy it was to make love to Holly. How well they fit together. How much the smell of her and the taste of her and the feel of her skin appealed to him. He supposed that, like all rejected men, he'd convinced himself that he could fall in love with another woman just as easily as he'd fallen in love with Holly.

But it hadn't happened.

He wondered if his feelings for Kate were different because they'd never made love. He supposed that was part of it. There was something soulful about joining the male body to the female body. At least, there always had been with Holly.

He was spooned behind her, because that was the easiest way for him to enter her when she was pregnant, something they'd learned when she was carrying Ryan.

Jack forced his thoughts away from his son. He palmed one of Holly's breasts, large and heavy from her pregnancy, and used his forefinger and thumb to tease the nipple into a tight bud.

"I don't know how you do it," Holly said.

"Like this," Jack said as he slid himself inside her.

Holly moaned as Jack kissed her nape and said, "I meant, I don't know how you make me feel so beautiful, when I'm huge like an elephant."

"You're huge with my baby, which makes you a very beautiful elephant." His hand was caressing her taut belly when he felt their child kick him. He chuckled and said, "The Little Slugger wants you all to himself."

"The Little Ballerina is dancing again," Holly replied with a lilting laugh of her own.

He felt her hand cover his own and guide him, telling him what she liked, where she wanted him most. It was something he'd always admired about Holly, that she helped him to know how best to satisfy her. He could feel her breaths becoming shallow, see the pulse race at her throat, feel the tension in her body as he touched her, as he moved inside her, and as she began to climax.

He loved the sounds she made in her throat as her body convulsed around him. He felt his orgasm joining hers, and the mounting ecstasy tore a groan of exhilaration from his throat.

The aftermath of sex with Holly was sweet. The total relaxation of their sated bodies, the sweat cooling their skin as it evaporated, their heaving lungs gradually quieting, their heads resting close beside one another on pillows as their eyes slid closed.

"I love you, Jack."

"Love you, too."

It was what he'd always said. The words were out before he could stop them. He realized he didn't want to call them back. He would always love Holly, even if he didn't spend the rest of his life with her.

"Do you, Jack?" she asked. "Do you still love me?"

Jack disentangled himself from his wife and reached over to turn on the lamp in her bedroom, since the light of the day had gone while they'd been making love. He shoved a pillow behind him and sat up. From nine years of marriage, he knew when his wife wanted to talk. This was the wrong time, as she very well knew. But he'd learned from past experience that she wouldn't rest until they'd discussed whatever it was she had on her mind.

Holly sat up next to him and used the sheets to cover her breasts knowing, again from past experience, that he would find the sight of them distracting. Jack arranged pillows behind her so she would be more comfortable.

"Do we really have to talk about this?" he said in an effort to head off what he was afraid would be a quarrel that would negate the peace they'd found in each other's arms. "Can't it just be what it was?"

"What was it?" Holly asked.

Jack sighed. "Sex, Holly. Damned good sex."

"All right," she said.

Jack frowned. That didn't sound like the argumentative Holly he knew. "All right?"

She smiled. "I agree. It was damned good sex."

Jack relaxed. "Now what?"

"I don't know about you, but I could use some supper. Followed by a good night's sleep."

Jack felt relieved and delighted by Holly's reply. "We're already in bed. How would you feel about ordering a pizza?"

"Sounds delicious. Pepperoni?"

"Half mushroom, half pepperoni?" he countered.

"There's a coupon for half off by the phone in the kitchen," she said.

"I'll order the pizza and get us something to drink while we're waiting." He got out of bed without thinking about his nakedness. He turned to Holly and said, "What would you like to..."

He paused in mid-sentence, arrested by the look in his wife's eyes as she surveyed his body—face, chest, waist, hips, genitals. He felt his body respond to the intensity of her gaze and watched her pupils dilate as the blood surged through his body, causing a powerful reaction.

"What would you like?" he repeated in a voice hoarse with need.

She met his gaze with the hint of a smile and said, "You?"

"Let me order the pizza," he replied with a grin. "Then I'll see what I can do before it arrives."

"They deliver in thirty minutes or less."

He laughed. "I think I can manage that." Then he sauntered from the room. It wasn't until he hung up the phone after he'd ordered the pizza that he realized he was feeling happy. With his wife. Whom he was divorcing.

And who was waiting for him in bed.

Was he a bastard for making love to Holly when he still planned to leave her after this child was born? After all, they were still married. They still cared for each other. *Loved* each other, he amended. So where was the harm?

The harm was that he would be hurt again when they separated at last. They had a long history together, which was both good and bad. Holly had already rejected him twice in his life. He wasn't sure he could survive being forsaken for a third time.

So don't give her your heart.

That was more complicated than it sounded, because the truth was, he didn't think he'd gotten it back when he'd left her the last time.

"Jack? Is the clock ticking yet?"

He didn't want to consider the past. Or think about the future. He just wanted to make love to his wife.

"It's just starting now, Holly," he said as he headed down the hall. "Here I come, ready or not!"

He heard her giggle like the girl he'd known a long time ago, as he launched himself onto the bed.

28

"What do you mean, you have to go to China?" Kate said as she watched Shaw pack his suitcase, which was laid out on his bed. She was pacing on the opposite side of the room.

"I've been facilitating a construction project for the past six months. There's a hitch and I need to be there."

"After telling me how dangerous J.D. is, you're leaving us to fend for ourselves?" Kate said incredulously.

"Bruce will keep an eye on the boys. I called Sergeant McKinley to ask him to watch over you."

"I would like to have been a fly on the wall when you had that conversation," Kate muttered. "What did Jack say?"

"He agreed to keep an eye on you, of course."

"Of course. Can't someone else do this for you?"

He threw another crisply starched and folded white shirt into the suitcase and added a couple of silk ties. He stuck his hands on his hips and said, "Do you think I want to make this trip? I don't have any choice."

"I understand you have to make money."

"It's not about the money," he snapped. "It's about

the political ramifications if I don't follow through on my part of the bargain I made with the Chinese."

Kate didn't understand why she felt so agitated. She should be glad Shaw was leaving. She should be glad to have this time to herself to think about what she wanted to do with the rest of her life. "How long will you be gone?"

"I don't know."

Kate threw up her hands. "Of course you don't."

He stalked around the foot of the bed, took her by the arms and said, "I'll be back as quick as I can get here. If you're worried, you and the boys can always take a few days off from school and from work and stay here."

"You know how I feel about that," she said, crossing her arms in front of her to keep him at a distance.

He pulled her into his embrace anyway. "Kate, please," he murmured in her ear. "I'm going to be worried enough about all of you when I'm halfway around the world. Do me a favor and stay here at the compound."

"Then J.D. wins," she said stubbornly.

He pursed his lips as he looked into her eyes. "He certainly wins if he manages to explode a roadside bomb anywhere near where you are. Please, Kate, do this for me."

She nearly gave in. He sounded genuinely worried. Instead she said, "You have your job to do. I have mine. And I don't want the twins to miss any more school."

He shook his head in defeat and let her go. "Fine. You do what you have to do."

"I will," she said, suddenly feeling bereft.

He closed the suitcase and dropped it on the floor.

"When are you leaving?" she asked.

"The Gulfstream is being serviced right now."

"Are you going to wake the boys up and tell them goodbye?"

"You think I should?"

"Yes, I do."

"It's five-thirty in the morning."

"They can go back to sleep after you talk to them."

He grabbed his suitcase and carried it with him down the hall, where he left it as he entered Lucky's room. Kate followed him, waiting in the doorway as he said his goodbyes.

He went first to Lucky, shook him on the shoulder and said, "Hey, buddy, I've got to fly to China today."

Lucky rubbed his eyes, patted Harley, who laid his head back down on the other side of Lucky's pillow, then wrapped his arms around Shaw's neck and hugged him. "Can Chance and I come, too?"

"No, you have to stay here and go to school."

"Will you bring me something from China?"

"Sure. What do you want?"

Lucky grinned and shrugged. "I don't know. What do they have?"

Shaw cuffed him on the chin and said, "I'll surprise you."

Kate saw Lucky didn't want to let him go.

"It's not time to get up yet," Shaw said as he eased the boy's arms from around his neck. "Go back to sleep."

Lucky turned on his side and put an arm around the dog's neck. "G'night," he mumbled.

Shaw crossed to Chance and gently shook him awake. Chance sat bolt upright, looked from Shaw to his mother and back, and said, "What's wrong?"

The cat skittered off the foot of the bed and went running down the hall, tail held high, to Shaw's bedroom. She would end up, Kate thought wryly, on Shaw's pillow, where she could be found whenever Shaw wasn't sleeping on it.

"Nothing's wrong," Shaw told the anxious boy. "But I have to go to China."

Chance scrambled out from under the covers and launched himself at Shaw, grabbing him tightly around the neck. "I don't want you to go!"

Kate saw Shaw's surprised look when he glanced at her over Chance's shoulder.

He hugged the boy and said, "I have some business in Peking. I'll be back as soon as I can."

"When?" Chance insisted, his gaze focused on Shaw's face.

"I don't know, exactly."

"Can Lucky and I come?"

"You need to stay here and go to school," Shaw said.

Chance gripped him tightly around the neck and pleaded, "Don't go, Shaw!"

"Hey," Shaw said, sitting down on the bed and pulling Chance into his lap. "What's this all about?"

"I had a dream that you went away and never came back."

Kate met Shaw's gaze as he raised a brow, questioning what he should say next. Kate was at a loss. This was another scar J.D.'s "death" had left on Chance's psyche. She shrugged slightly, leaving the decision up to Shaw.

He pulled Chance close, tucking the boy's head under his chin, and said, "I'm coming back, Chance."

The boy clutched at him. "Are you sure?"

"I'm sure," Shaw said. "I love you and Lucky, and I'm always going to love you."

"Are you sure?" Chance asked again, leaning back to look into Shaw's eyes, as though to gauge the truth of his words.

"As though you were my very own flesh and blood."

"I love you, too, Shaw," Chance whispered. He glanced at Kate as though he was saying something he shouldn't be saying.

Kate felt her throat swell with emotion. She glanced at Shaw and saw him swallow hard. His voice wasn't quite steady when he spoke again.

"If you have that dream again," he told their son, as he tenderly brushed Chance's hair from his brow, "know that when you look for me, I'll be there."

It was harder to get Chance settled again, but Shaw stayed with him until he was lying quietly in bed with his eyes closed.

Kate met Shaw in the hall. He took her hand tightly in his, grabbed the suitcase with his other hand and headed toward the front of the house. When he got to the front door, he set the suitcase down and took her in his arms.

"I never imagined it would be so hard to leave them," he said, his raspy voice more rough than normal. "Or you."

Kate hugged him, and when he kissed her, found herself kissing him back. The passion flared fiercely between them, and she had to make herself pull away. "Be careful," she said.

"I'm the one who should be saying that." His hand lingered on her cheek after he tucked a wayward strand of hair behind her ear. "I'll be back as quickly as I can." Then he grabbed his suitcase and was gone.

Kate was surprised a moment later to find Chance standing by her side. He slipped his hand into hers and said, "Do you think he'll be coming back?"

"He said he would," she replied.

"But do you think he will?" Chance persisted.

Kate realized it was time to tell her sons the truth. Maybe if they knew that Shaw was their father, they would understand why he loved them "like his own flesh and blood." And why he would always be coming back to them.

"Let's go wake up Lucky. I have something I want to say to both of you."

It turned out Lucky had gone back to sleep. He was grumpy when Chance woke him up. But Kate wanted to give herself plenty of time to tell her sons about their father before it was time to get ready for school. She was determined they would keep as much to their regular schedule as possible while Shaw was gone.

"What is it?" Lucky said. "Why did you wake me up?"

Chance was sitting on the bed beside his brother, the dog between them. Kate sat on the edge of the bed close enough to be able to touch both boys.

"Did you hear what Shaw said to Chance?" she asked Lucky.

"Which part?" Lucky asked.

"Then you heard everything?" Kate confirmed. "About him loving you?"

"That he loved us? Yeah, I heard that part."

"There's a reason why Shaw loves you both," Kate said.

"It's 'cause we're cute," Lucky said with a snort.

"Yes, that's part of it," Kate said, smiling at the twins, who certainly could be adorable when on their best behavior.

"And fun to play with," Chance added.

"Yes, that's true, too. But there's something else, something more." Kate paused to gather her thoughts and was surprised by Lucky's next comment.

"Is it that 'flesh and blood' thing he said?"

Kate was amazed at her eight-year-old son's perception. "Yes. Do you know what that means, to be someone's flesh and blood?"

"To be like, a relative?" Chance suggested.

"Exactly," Kate said.

Lucky's young brow furrowed. "So Shaw is like, a relative?"

"Yes, he is."

"Like our uncle?" Lucky asked.

"Yes, but not your uncle." Kate took a deep breath and said, "Your biological father."

"Biolocal? What does that mean?" Lucky asked.

"Biological," Kate repeated. "It means that I provided the egg and Shaw provided the sperm that split inside me and grew into the two of you."

"So our dad was… I'm confused," Lucky said.

"I was married to your dad, so he was your father while you were growing up."

"But you knew Shaw a long time ago," Chance deduced. "Before we were born."

"Yes, I did."

Lucky was frowning again. "So…why didn't Shaw tell us he was our bio—whatever—father?"

"Because I asked him not to."

"Why didn't you want us to know?" Lucky asked.

"I was afraid it would confuse you. And I wasn't sure you would like Shaw." Or whether Shaw would be a good father.

"I like him fine," Lucky said.

"I love him," Chance said. "And he likes me. I can tell."

"He loves you," Kate said. "I heard him say so this morning." She focused on Lucky and said, "He loves both of you, as though you were his own sons. Because you are."

"So are we supposed to call him Dad or Daddy or what?" Lucky said, that unnatural furrow back in his young brow.

"That's up to you, I think."

"I don't think we should call him Dad, because Dad was Dad," Chance reasoned. "We could call him Daddy," he suggested to his brother.

"I guess I'd like to call him Daddy, if you think he wouldn't mind," Lucky said. He turned to Kate and asked, "Do you think that would be okay with Shaw? If we called him Daddy?"

Kate had never been more proud of her sons. She put a hand on each boy's shoulder and said, "I guess you'll have to wait till he gets back and ask him yourselves."

29

Kate had just sat down at a table for two in the Waterfall Café when she was joined by a very tall, very thin, white-haired man with thick black brows over piercing blue eyes.

"I hope you don't mind if I join you," the gentleman said as he sat down across from her.

Kate had seen this man before. With his son.

He confirmed her suspicion when he said, "I'm Dante D'Amato, Wyatt's father. Your sons' grandfather."

The blood left Kate's head in a rush. She gripped the edge of the table, afraid she might faint. She'd wondered whether D'Amato knew the truth about the twins. Obviously, he did. Shaw's stories about D'Amato's treatment of him and his mother had frightened her. She found it ominous that the mob boss had waited until Shaw was out of the country to introduce himself.

A glance to the side showed a table for four occupied by four very large men in bad-fitting suits, every one with something bulging beneath his armpit. She wondered how the men had gotten weapons into the hospital, which was quite security conscious. Then she remembered that Shaw had contributed a great deal of money to the hospital. Had his father done the same?

Kate stared at the food in front of her and felt acid in the back of her throat. She wouldn't be able to swallow a bite with that dangerous man sitting across from her. She felt her heart knocking around in her chest like a frightened bird caught on a wire.

D'Amato smiled and said, "I would like to meet my grandsons."

Kate lowered her hands to her lap so he wouldn't see they were shaking. All the saliva was suddenly gone from her mouth. She had to clear her throat to say, "I don't think that would be a good idea."

"Actually, I wasn't asking," he said in a pleasant voice. "I was telling you I intend to see them. I can do it under your supervision. Or not."

Kate felt a cold chill rattle down her spine. She nodded curtly and said, "Given those two options, of course I would choose to be there when you meet them." She added, "Shaw won't be happy when he hears about this."

"By then I will have met the twins," D'Amato said. "So his objection will be moot."

Kate's eyes flashed at the disdain in his voice. "Why do you want to meet my sons?" she demanded. "What purpose could it serve?"

"They're family," D'Amato said. "My family is important to me."

"Only if you can use them for some purpose of your own," she retorted.

D'Amato's crystal blue eyes narrowed.

Kate found herself wanting to taunt the cold-blooded reptile sitting across from her. She resisted the urge. This deadly snake had poisonous fangs and seemed entirely willing to use them.

"I believe you have plans to take the boys out for dinner tonight. I would like to join you," D'Amato said.

How could he possibly know that? It didn't really matter, Kate realized. The important thing was to contact Jack and make sure he was there tonight, to ensure that D'Amato didn't try to take the boys from her. And of course, Bruce would be with them. She'd never been so grateful for the bodyguard.

"Bruce is bringing Lucky and Chance to the hospital after school to visit a friend of theirs who's sick."

D'Amato nodded. "Jack McKinley's boy. A shame about that."

Kate's eyebrows rose in surprise. Was there anything he didn't know?

D'Amato smiled. "I'm acquainted with Sergeant McKinley. He's been chasing me for nearly twenty years." He winked and said, "Hasn't caught me yet."

Kate was appalled. Did the mob boss know Jack was only pretending to help him, that he was still working, even now, to put D'Amato behind bars? Was this frightening old man playing Jack like a fish on a line? Or was he the one who was in for the big surprise?

"If you know Jack, then you won't mind if he joins us for supper," she said in a cool voice.

"Should we ask his wife to join us, too?" D'Amato said.

Kate felt the flush rising up her throat to land on her cheeks. The man was diabolical. He knew everything.

And seemed to enjoy using what he knew to unnerve and embarrass her. She was determined to deny him the pleasure of seeing her discomfited.

She picked up her soupspoon, keeping her hand as steady as she could, and said, "I'll see if Jack wants to invite Holly along. The more the merrier, right?"

D'Amato scowled. "Wrong. This game has gone on long enough, Mrs. Pendleton. Bring the boys. Tell Jack to stay away. No, I'll tell him. I expect you to introduce me to your sons as their grandfather."

"They just found out a few days ago that Shaw is their father," she protested.

"I know," he said. "So they won't be surprised to discover that Shaw has a father who's their grandfather."

It was the feeling of being helplessly swept along, of things moving out of her control, that scared Kate the most. Even if she could get in touch with Shaw, she didn't think there was anything he could do from so far away. Shaw had his own share of bodyguards, but Jimmy had gone with him to China, and Bruce had orders to stay with the twins.

She'd met the men who patrolled the grounds of Shaw's compound, but she wouldn't have known how to reach any of them, and wasn't sure what help they'd be against the four truly gigantic enforcers D'Amato had brought with him today. Besides, she was afraid that if these big men started shooting at each other, they wouldn't be the only ones who got hurt.

"All right," she said at last. "We'll join you for supper. We were going to—"

"You'll come to my home."

"No!"

"I could have taken your boys at any time since they started at that school in The Woodlands. I've chosen not to do that. I want to meet them as their benevolent grandfather—"

"Which you're not!" Kate snapped.

D'Amato lifted a dark brow. "It is what I will be to them, you may rest assured. I trust you won't tell them differently."

"Why shouldn't I tell them who you are? What you are?" Kate snarled.

"Because I'm their grandfather," he said simply.

Kate's brain worked furiously to come up with some other option than taking her sons to Dante D'Amato's home. But absolutely nothing came to mind.

The mob boss rose and pushed his chair back under the table. He waited for her to look at him and said, "By the way, tell Bruce his presence won't be necessary."

"What if he won't leave the boys?" she asked, a last desperate hope for some physical bulk between herself and this malevolent man. "Shaw told him not to—"

"Shaw is gone," he interrupted. "I'm the one making the rules here. And rule number one is that you and your sons come alone. I'll send a car to the hospital at five-thirty. That should give the boys time to visit their friend."

Kate couldn't believe this was happening. She hadn't spoken to Shaw in the four days since he'd left. He'd given her a phone number to use in an emergency and made sure her cell phone was equipped with a SIM card so she could make overseas calls.

Kate got out the phone and sat with it in her hand for several minutes, debating whether to call. Wondering what Shaw could do to help from so far away. Wondering if D'Amato had the power to order Jack to stay away, and whether Jack would defy D'Amato and show up if she asked him to be there.

As her heart rate slowed and she could think more rationally, Kate realized that if D'Amato had wanted to steal the twins, he probably could have done it with impunity at any time over the past few weeks. He seemed to know everything that was going on in her life—and Shaw's and Jack's for that matter. He obviously had well-placed spies telling him their business.

It seemed that what he wanted was a chance to make a good impression on the twins, with the hope of— what?—enticing them to come into his business someday? Kate snorted. Fat chance of that with Shaw around.

The only question was whether she should contact Shaw before she and the boys had dinner with his father to let him know what was going on. That seemed only prudent. She needed to tell someone with the power to fight D'Amato about this command performance, in case the mob boss changed his mind and decided he wanted his grandsons to himself.

If Shaw was right about what had happened to his mother, D'Amato might arrange for her to disappear from her sons' lives. And D'Amato would be able to use threats against the twins as a way to keep Shaw at a distance.

Kate's body was quivering with anger and frustration. There was a reason all the nature books warned you about getting between a mother and her babies. Kate wondered if D'Amato would expect her to carry a weapon. She began planning how to conceal the small jackknife she kept in a drawer in her office. It wasn't much of a weapon, but if she got close enough to D'Amato, she could kill with it.

She picked up the phone and hit the speed dial that had been set for Shaw's phone with the preset country code for China. What time was it there, anyway? It didn't matter. If it was the middle of the night, she would just have to wake him up.

30

"I found him, Mr. D'Amato."

Dante D'Amato didn't curb the smile of satisfaction that spread on his face. "Good work, Roberto." The elusive J.D. Pendleton had finally been brought to ground. "Where was he?"

"Caught the fucker sleeping in his car on the side of the county road leading to Shaw's compound. Found this piece of shit on him."

D'Amato reached out to take the object Roberto handed him. "What's this?"

"Fucking cell phone set to detonate a fucking roadside bomb," the big man said in disgust.

"How do you know that?"

Roberto grinned sheepishly, exposing very sharp eyeteeth. "I accidentally pushed the fucking button he had under his thumb when I took it away from him and exploded the fucking thing."

D'Amato realized there were several small cuts on one side of Roberto's face. "You okay?"

"Just a few scratches," the big man said, reaching toward one of the larger cuts on his face. "Wasn't expecting anything quite so fucking big."

"J.D. all right?"

"Fucker hit the ground when I punched the button," Roberto said, chagrined. "He's just fine."

"Anybody around likely to question an explosion like that?"

Roberto shrugged. "Don't think so. We were on Shaw's property, middle of fucking nowhere. J.D. planned it pretty good."

"Where is that son of a bitch now?"

"I got him tied up in the fucking trunk of my car in the garage. I didn't want to bring him inside the building. Too many fucking eyes. Where you want me to take him?"

D'Amato really wanted to talk to the bastard who'd caused him so much trouble, but his grandchildren were coming for supper in half an hour. "Take him somewhere private, that empty warehouse down by the docks will do, and convince him to tell you where he hid that junk he stole. I know he hasn't sold it yet. And ask him about that cell phone he got from Lou Ferme. Take your time. I want him to suffer."

"You got it, Mr. D'Amato."

"Don't kill him, Roberto. I want to talk to him myself after supper."

Roberto had just left when D'Amato's cell phone rang. He checked the caller ID and recognized the number. He grunted with pleasure as he answered the call. "Hello, Wyatt."

"What do you think you're doing, old man?"

"I'm having my grandchildren and their mother over for dinner."

"Don't do it."

D'Amato grinned, enjoying the situation, since he knew Wyatt was halfway around the world. "Who's going to stop me?" He could feel his son's frustration, understood how it must gall him to be outmaneuvered. It hadn't been easy arranging the disaster in China that had required Wyatt's presence.

"If it's any consolation, I approve your taste in women," D'Amato said. "Mrs. Pendleton is stunning. I've seen pictures of her, but they don't do her justice." He kissed his fingertips. "Truly *una bella donna.*"

"What is it you want?" Wyatt spat.

"I want what you denied me," D'Amato said through tight jaws, nostrils flaring with the anger that rose every time he thought of the son who'd thrown everything he'd been offered back in his father's face. "I want someone to take over my business. If you won't do it, I have to find someone who will. And those boys are my blood and bone."

"They don't know that."

"It isn't necessary that they know who I am right now. We're just getting to know each other."

"They're eight years old."

"They'll grow up faster than you can imagine," D'Amato said.

"I'm on my way back."

"Then I'll have to do my best to make a good impression on my grandsons in the few hours I have, won't I?"

"It won't do any good, old man. I'll tell them the truth about you."

"Tell them what? That I'm a violent man? You're the one accused of murder."

D'Amato relished the silence on the other side of

the world. "You could solve the problem by coming to work for me yourself."

"I don't want or need your empire."

It was irksome to have such successful progeny. "Maybe my grandsons will."

D'Amato hung up the phone before Wyatt could reply. He glanced at his watch and saw that he only had a few minutes before his company would arrive. He was looking forward to meeting his grandsons. It would be interesting to discover what their mother had told them about him.

He put on his most benevolent smile. He wanted his grandsons to like him. He had great plans for them.

31

W yatt had finished his business in China in half the time he might have taken if he hadn't been worried about leaving Kate and the twins alone. When he got the call from Kate telling him about his father's invitation to dinner, he had just landed at the private airstrip near his compound.

"I think it might be fun if we all go to dinner with my father," he said grimly.

"Where are you?" she asked.

"The Gulfstream just landed. I'll take the helo to the city and meet you and the boys at the hospital."

"Don't forget they have a visit scheduled with Ryan."

"No problem. I have some arrangements to make before I meet up with you."

"What kind of arrangements?" Kate asked.

"I want to put some security in place so we don't run into this situation again."

"I'm so glad you're back," she said.

Was that only relief in her voice? Wyatt wondered. Or was there something else. He thought he heard pleasure, as well. Maybe he'd imagined it, because that was what he wanted to hear.

"I missed you," he said. Wyatt was amazed at how connected he'd become to Kate and his sons in such a short period of time.

"You were missed, too."

Which wasn't the same thing as saying *she* missed him. Had she missed him? Better not to ask. "See you soon." Wyatt smiled ruefully when he realized he didn't want to hang up.

"Soon," she repeated.

He waited until she disconnected the call to close his phone. Then his lips pressed flat in irritation at his father. Wyatt had been willing to let bygones be bygones. After all, he had no conclusive proof that D'Amato had arranged his mother's death. But by threatening the woman he loved and his sons, his father had stepped over a line he shouldn't have crossed. Wyatt was willing and able to make sure it never happened again.

When he reached the hospital, Wyatt called Kate to see whether the boys were done visiting Ryan.

"Come on up," Kate said. "The visit got canceled because Ryan wasn't feeling well, so we're doing an experiment in my office."

When he got to Kate's office, which doubled as a lab, Wyatt stood in the doorway for a moment watching Lucky and Chance, who stood on either side of their mother as she placed a slide under a microscope.

Lucky happened to glance up, saw him, and shouted, "It's Daddy! He's here!" He came running around one side of the long counter, while Chance came running from the other.

"Daddy! Daddy!" Chance cried. "You came back!"

Wyatt leaned down, arms opened wide for the two boys, who slammed into him at almost the same time. He ruffled Lucky's hair and gripped Chance's shoulder as he met their grinning faces with a grin of his own.

"Is it all right if we call you Daddy?" Lucky asked uncertainly.

Wyatt thought the question might have been provoked by the tears that brimmed in his eyes. He blinked them back and said, "It's fine with me."

"Mom said we should ask first," Chance said. "But I can tell it's okay because you're smiling."

Wyatt's voice was choked as he said, "I think it's great." He looked across the room at Kate and saw she hadn't been as successful as he had in containing her emotions. She was smiling, but tears streamed down both cheeks.

"Let me say hello to your mother," Wyatt said as he headed around the counter toward Kate. The boys tagged along.

There was so much Wyatt wanted to ask Kate. Why had she decided to tell the boys he was their father? What had she said to make them accept the idea so willingly? And what did it say about her feelings for him?

"Welcome back," she said softly.

It hadn't been his imagination, he saw, as he looked into her tear-bright eyes. She was happy to see him. She lifted her face for his kiss and he leaned down, first kissing away the teardrops from each cheek, then touching his lips to hers.

It finally felt like he was home.

He became aware of two interested faces on either

side of him. It was the first time he'd shown affection to Kate where the boys could see him. He lifted his head and looked from one twin's face to the other to see whether they were troubled by what he'd done.

"Are you guys getting married?" Lucky asked.

"Are you going to be our Daddy forever?" Chance asked.

Wyatt was rocked onto his heels by their frank questions. "Your mother and I haven't talked about getting married," he said. "But I'm definitely going to be your daddy forever."

"Does that mean we're going to live with you from now on?" Lucky asked.

That question was more problematic. Before Wyatt could answer, Kate said, "Boys, give Shaw some breathing space. We need to put everything away. It's time to go to supper."

Lucky grabbed Wyatt's hand and said, "We're going to have dinner with our grandfather, Mr. D'Amato. Are you coming, too?"

"Yes, I am," Wyatt said, marveling that Kate had also smoothed the path for his father to meet the twins.

Chance caught his sleeve, gestured him lower and whispered, "I don't think Mom likes him."

"What makes you say that?" Wyatt whispered back.

"'Cause when I asked if we should call him Grandpa, she said 'Absolutely not!'"

Wyatt grinned. "I vote with your mom."

"If we don't like him, why are we going to dinner at his house?" Chance asked.

"Because he's my father."

Chance's eyebrows rose in surprise. "Really?"

"Time to go," Kate said. "Or we're going to be late."

D'Amato had sent a limo to pick them up at the hospital. The driver's brows rose when Wyatt joined the other three in the car, but he didn't object.

Wyatt had never been to his father's home on the top floor of the mirrored building across from Shaw Tower. When the four of them stepped off the elevator, both boys looked up at him, their eyes anxious.

"Chance, take your mom's hand. Lucky, you take mine."

With the security of a parent's hand in theirs, both boys seemed less agitated. Wyatt rang the doorbell. He wasn't surprised when his father wasn't the one who answered the door. In fact, he'd counted on it. Once he was inside, he would be in a much better position to control what happened between his father and the twins.

The big man who greeted them said, "Mr. D'Amato is waiting for you in the living room."

"Wow. This house is even shinier than GeePa's," Lucky said.

"Everything's black and red and gold," Chance marveled.

Wyatt exchanged an amused look with Kate before they stepped into the living room. He'd seen pictures in *Texas Monthly* of The Castle, the thirty-thousand-square-foot home at the center of Jackson Blackthorne's Bitter Creek Ranch. In the photos, the priceless antiques Kate had mentioned shared space with spur-scarred wooden desks and worn leather couches that had been around for more than a hundred and fifty years.

His father's home—like his father's life—was all brand-new, shiny modern gilt, meant to hide the fact that it had been bought with very dirty money.

He put a friendly smile on his face as they crossed the threshold and greeted his father by saying, "I presume your invitation included the boys' father."

"Of course," his father said without missing a beat. The only indication of his anger was a slight narrowing of his eyes. He immediately rose from the wing chair where he'd been sitting and crossed to the twins.

The boys stood stock-still, staring up at their grandfather.

"Hello. I'm your grandfather, Dante. I see you really are identical. Which of you is which?" he asked with a smile.

Wyatt felt Lucky squeeze his hand as he said, "I'm Chance."

"And I'm Lucky," Chance said, adding his part to the lie.

Wyatt would have let them get away with it, but Kate said, "That isn't very polite."

Lucky looked up at Wyatt, his lips twisted in resignation, then turned to D'Amato and said, "I'm Lucky."

"And I'm Chance," Chance said.

D'Amato chuckled. "It's a pretty good trick, boys. You had me fooled." He focused his attention on Kate and said, "I know you had a long day at work, Mrs. Pendleton, so I thought we'd eat early. Please follow me to the dining room."

When they got to the dining room, Wyatt saw there was a place set for him at the long mahogany table.

Apparently the kitchen help had figured out that they were one more for dinner.

"Look at all the candles!" Lucky said, staring at the multi-taper silver candelabra in the center of the table.

"And red roses, Mom. You love roses," Chance said to his mother as he pointed to the clusters of cut roses in crystal vases on either side of the candelabra.

D'Amato pointed the boys to seats on either side of him near the head of the table, with Kate and Wyatt on opposite sides of the table next to each boy.

"What are we having?" Lucky asked.

"Meat loaf and mashed potatoes," D'Amato said. "I hope that's okay."

"With peas?" Chance asked.

D'Amato shot Wyatt a look—Wyatt hated peas—and said, "I can arrange for peas, if you like them."

"I don't!" Chance said.

D'Amato chuckled. "That's good, because we're having broccoli."

"Yuck! Broccoli," Lucky said.

Wyatt saw Kate frown at her son. But he agreed with both boys. He didn't like peas or broccoli. And his father knew it.

"I guess you'd like the peas," D'Amato said to Lucky, with a little less humor in his voice.

"Nope," Lucky said. "I don't like peas, either."

"Maybe you can fill up on mashed potatoes," D'Amato snapped.

Wyatt hid his smile behind his hand. His father didn't often have to accommodate anyone, and he was obviously upset that he hadn't managed to please either of the twins.

"You will both eat some of whatever is put on your plate," Kate said, cutting his—and the twins'—celebration short. "And you will apologize to Mr. D'Amato for—"

"Grandpa Dante," his father interjected.

"To Mr. D'Amato," Kate said firmly, "for complaining about the very nice dinner he's prepared for you."

"Sorry, Mr. D'Amato," Lucky said.

"Yeah, sorry," Chance said.

"Surely it would be all right if they don't eat food they don't enjoy," his father cajoled.

"No, that wouldn't be all right," Kate said. "They're guests in your home. They know better than to whine about what they're served."

"Spoiling the children is what grandfathers are for," D'Amato tried again.

"You won't spoil mine," Kate said sharply.

Wyatt had his own experience with Kate's protectiveness where her children were concerned. Nevertheless, he was surprised to see her take on his father, with his reputation for removing obstacles that got in his way.

What he found interesting was the twins' reaction to Kate's animosity toward D'Amato. The boys already had some inkling that Kate didn't approve of the older man. He watched the boys straighten in their chairs, saw their chins come up, watched their eyes narrow on D'Amato as their jaws flexed. It looked like they were about to declare war on their host.

A moment later Lucky reached for his water glass and "accidentally" knocked it over. "Oops!" he said. "Sorry, Mr. D'Amato."

The water slid in D'Amato's direction and he grabbed a napkin and stuck it at the edge of the puddle. His mouth had become a rigid hyphen.

His father must have had some sort of button under the table that called the help, because a server appeared in the doorway and asked, "How may I help you, sir?"

"One of the boys spilled his water."

"I'll take care of it immediately."

Before he'd gotten out of the room, Chance knocked the two forks to the left of his plate off the table. They hit the carpet under the table and bounced onto the marble floor with a clatter. "Uh-oh. Sorry, Mr. D'Amato."

"I'll get another set of silverware, sir," the server said.

"Serve the salad," D'Amato ordered.

Wyatt hadn't known the twins long enough to see the mischievous side of them. He got a quick lesson over the next thirty minutes, as dinner was served and eaten. Or rather, served and played with.

Chance stirred the puddle of gravy on his mashed potatoes until it dripped onto the antique lace tablecloth. Lucky chewed broccoli until it was goo and spit it back onto his plate. They blew into their glasses of water, making noise and bubbles. His sons acted like absolute heathens without manners.

And politely called his father "Mr. D'Amato" every time they apologized, after their mother chastised them for their obnoxious behavior.

"If you don't mind," Kate said, clearly at the limit of her patience, "I think we'll skip dessert."

"Aw, Mom," Lucky protested.

"Jeez, Mom," Chance moaned.

"Both of you come with me." She turned to D'Amato and said, "Could you direct me to a bathroom? I'd like to clean them up before we leave."

And give them a good talking-to, unless Wyatt was very much mistaken. He figured this was as good a time as any to let his father know the measures he'd taken to make sure he would never be a threat to the boys. As soon as the three of them were gone from the room he said, "I had a talk this afternoon with the FBI."

His father lifted a brow. "Why should that interest me?"

"I told them I had some of my father's papers and asked them if they'd be interested in having them."

His father's eyes burned with hatred. "What papers?"

"An accounting book, actually."

"Where did you get something like that?"

"My mother left it to me."

"Your mother's been dead for twenty-six years. The statute of limitations has already run out on anything having to do with those accounts," D'Amato said smugly.

"There's no statute of limitations on murder," Wyatt said.

D'Amato snorted. "I thought you said she left you an accounting book. What kind of numbers—"

"It's a book accounting for the steps you took to solidify your position as head of the syndicate," Wyatt said. "It details the men you had killed, or killed yourself, to become the boss."

"If you really had a book like that, you would have used it before now."

"I never had a reason before now to use it," Wyatt said.

"What do you want?" D'Amato said, his face flushed with anger.

"I want you to stay away from my sons," he said in a hard voice. "If you make another attempt to communicate with them—or with Mrs. Pendleton—for any reason whatsoever, you can be sure that book will find its way to the FBI."

Wyatt heard the boys talking in the hallway and said, "Do we understand each other?"

"I could have you killed."

Wyatt smiled. "I thought of that. If I die before you, the book goes to the FBI."

"Get out. And take those brats with you."

32

J.D. was in a shitload of trouble. He couldn't believe
he'd gotten caught by D'Amato's brute of the week,
Roberto. Not only that, but the idiot had detonated his
roadside bomb, using up the last of the explosives
he'd taken from his storage unit. After a blast like that,
they were lucky to be alive.

Not that he was going to live much longer, if the
brute kept up what he was doing. J.D. was tied to a
chair in the middle of a warehouse filled with boxes
of God knows what, close enough to the Gulf of
Mexico that he could smell the stench of saltwater
and oil from the tankers in port. He was bloodied and
bruised, and the monster wasn't even winded.

At least he still had his toenails and testicles.

To keep them, he'd had to admit that the smack was
hidden under the floorboards of his car, which the
idiot had left by the side of the county road near
Shaw's compound. He'd given up that information
after about an hour and a half of pretty serious torture.
He was kind of proud of lasting that long.

The brute had left him for a while to make the arrangements to retrieve his Lexus. J.D. had used the

break to work on the ropes binding his wrists behind him. He was finally making some headway when the brute returned.

He wasn't alone.

Dante D'Amato marched up to him and snarled, "You owe me twenty million dollars, you son of a bitch."

"You got your white powder back. That should make us even," J.D. whistled through his broken teeth.

"That doesn't begin to make us even. That California crowd want their product back—and they want the profit they would have made from their product. You owe me another twenty million. And I plan to take it out of your hide."

"Take it easy. I'm sure we can work something out."

"Like your eyes out of your head?" D'Amato said malevolently.

The brute grabbed J.D.'s forehead from behind, and he saw the tip of a knife slide by his nose. "Hey! Hold up a minute!"

"He's right, Roberto," D'Amato said. "You should take off your jacket so it doesn't get ruined."

"Oh, shit," J.D. muttered when the brute let go.

Roberto took off his suit jacket and laid it carefully on a nearby box, then began folding up the sleeves of his blue shirt.

J.D. squinted up at D'Amato through the slit in his puffy right eye—the left one was swollen completely closed—and said, "What put you in such a foul mood?"

"I just had dinner with those two brats of yours. Correction, those two brats my son got off your wife."

J.D. saw red at the reminder of how he'd been duped by his wife. "You shoulda killed that bastard of yours when you had the chance!"

"Unfortunately for me, that's out of the question now," D'Amato said angrily. "Fortunately for me, I can vent all that pent-up hostility on you."

"Whoa! Whoa, now!" J.D. hissed at the pain in his split lip, which had torn open when he'd yelled. He licked at the blood dripping down his chin and said, "We need to talk."

"The time for talk is over."

The brute set a tray of rusted metal instruments, creepy, horror-movie kinds of stuff, on a nearby wooden crate. "Which first, Mr. D'Amato?" he said. "The toenails? Or the testicles?"

"I still have that video," J.D. babbled. "Of you doing something I shouldn't talk about in front of the brute here. Send him away and I'll tell you all about it."

"You can't accuse me from the grave," D'Amato said.

"That video goes to the cops if I die," J.D. threatened.

D'Amato crossed his arms over his chest and said, "Where is it?"

"I'd be an idiot to tell you."

D'Amato turned to the brute and said, "Testicles."

Roberto reached down to unbuckle J.D.'s belt, pulled it out of the loops, then unsnapped and unzipped his pants.

"Stop!" J.D. shrieked as the brute reached in and pulled out his pecker and balls. "I'll give it to you. But I'll have to take you there. It's not anywhere I could give you directions."

"Cut off his balls," D'Amato said.

"All right, all right!" J.D. screamed. "I'll tell you."

"Start talking."

"The truth is, I don't know where it is. Wait!" J.D. said when Roberto hit the button on a switchblade. "I gave the phone to my sons. I told them to hide it and not to tell anyone where it was except me. They won't, either. So you'll need me to find that phone. Otherwise, those kids are going to grow up and use that phone to put you behind bars. Set me free and that phone is yours."

D'Amato walked aside with the brute. He might have thought he couldn't be overheard, but his voice echoed off the mile-high ceiling, and despite a few punches to the head, J.D. could still hear him just fine.

"I'll take care of getting the video from those kids," D'Amato said. "You take this sack of shit somewhere and sit on him. I'll call you when I get the phone. Then you kill him."

33

"Sergeant McKinley, Dr. McKinley, I'm sorry to tell you that Ryan isn't responding to chemotherapy. I think it's time to consider a bone marrow transplant."

The words hit Jack like bullets to the heart. He'd done as much reading as he could about his son's illness over the past two months while Ryan had been in chemotherapy and asked Holly questions when there was something he didn't understand. This was bad news, any way you cut it.

Holly could have quoted him statistics on their son's recovery with a bone marrow transplant, but he'd refused to consider the numbers because he found them too depressing.

"I see from the paperwork you filled out when Ryan was admitted that there's no sibling who could act as an HLA-matched donor," the doctor said. "That's unfortunate, but—"

"That's not entirely accurate," Holly interrupted.

Jack stared in confusion at his wife. Her eyes were lowered to her hands, which were threaded and clutched together in her lap. "Holly?"

"My husband and I have a grown daughter," she

told the doctor. "She was put up for adoption twenty-six years ago."

Jack's jaw dropped.

"Are you in touch with her?" the doctor asked. "Do you think she'd be willing to be tested as a bone marrow donor?"

Holly shot Jack a pleading look as she said, for the doctor's benefit, "I know the name of the adoption agency that placed her. I haven't been in contact with her since the day she was born."

"Could you excuse us for a moment, Dr. Franzen," Jack said through tight jaws.

"Yes, of course," the young doctor said.

Jack waited until Franzen had left his office and the door had closed behind him. His throat ached. His eyes and his nose stung. "We had a baby, Holly? And you gave it away?"

Holly moaned and said, "I'm sorry, Jack."

He was on his feet, standing over her, resisting the urge to grab her and shake her within an inch of her life. "Sorry?" he grated out. "Sorry? What happened to our kid, Holly?"

"I don't know, Jack."

"When did you get pregnant?"

"At the Fourth of July picnic."

They'd taken a blanket and laid it out on the grass and made love while the annual Kountze fireworks display filled the sky with glorious colors and patterns. Their lovemaking was punctuated by explosions of sight and sound that matched the explosions going on between them. It had been a truly memorable night.

And they'd made a baby.

"When was she born?"

"Our little girl was born April 10. She was six pounds, three ounces. Tiny and delicate. She was nineteen inches long. She had all her fingers and toes."

"You were pregnant when you broke up with me my senior year?"

She nodded miserably.

"Why didn't you tell me?" he said in an agonized voice. He felt the flush of heat on his throat that he knew was a sign of anger.

She kept her head down. There was no defiance in her. "I did what I thought was best for the three of us."

"It wasn't best for me! And I doubt it was the best thing for our child." He hesitated, then asked, "Is there anything else you can remember about her?"

She met his gaze and said, "She had chestnut hair like you. And green eyes like me."

"Oh, God, Holly." He covered his mouth to keep a sob from escaping. His chest hurt with the effort to keep all the pain he was feeling inside. He had a child out there somewhere in the world. A child he'd never known about. A child who might be hungry or hurt or alone.

"You never checked on her, Holly? You never tried to find out if she was all right?"

"No," she said in a small voice.

"You better hope we can find her," he said angrily. "You better hope she's all right. You better hope we can talk her into giving her bone marrow to a perfect stranger—who just happens to be her brother. Because if we can't, I'm going to blame you for making me lose two of my kids."

Jack left the doctor's office and found the physician outside, leaning against the hospital wall. "We're going to try to locate our daughter," he said. "We'll let you know if—when—we find her, whether she's willing to be a donor."

"Let's hope she's a match," the doctor said.

"Yeah." Jack hadn't even considered the possibility that their daughter wouldn't be an HLA-matched sibling. But there was no sense borrowing trouble. First, they had to find her.

He felt like an animal in pain, incapable of expressing it, needing to howl and unable to make a sound. He needed—wanted—comfort. It surprised him that he thought first of laying his head in Holly's lap and having her run her fingers through his hair. But he could hardly seek comfort from the very woman who'd betrayed him.

He was still standing in the hall when Holly left the doctor's office. She looked shaky on her feet, like she might fall down if she didn't sit down. She was nearly eight months pregnant with their child. Their *third* child.

"Come with me," he said brusquely, taking her arm and heading for the elevator. He had to get her somewhere she could sit down, and there was a café downstairs.

"I'm sorry, Jack," she said again.

He wasn't going to forgive her. He wasn't going to give her absolution. The crime against him was too great. The wrong was too deep and devastating. He had a daughter he'd never known. A grown woman now, if she'd survived all these years. He'd missed her entire life growing up.

He glanced at his wife's bent head. *Oh, God, Holly. Why did you do it? Why didn't you tell me?*

But he knew why. She'd become a noted pediatric oncologist. Where would she be now if they'd stayed together and she'd kept the baby? She might not have finished high school. It was unlikely she would have gone to college, let alone medical school.

It was equally unlikely they'd still be married, he admitted. He'd been through some very rough times over the past twenty-six years. So why was he blaming her for the decision she'd made? Why hadn't her choice been the right one for the three of them?

The elevator door opened and he gripped Holly's arm to keep her upright. He was really afraid now that she might faint. "Do you need me to carry you?" He heard how angry he sounded and didn't blame her for shaking her head.

Before he could say something less caustic, she murmured, "I can walk."

But he felt sure that if he let go of her she'd fall. He kept a hand on her arm until they reached the café. He pulled out a chair, eased her into it and said, "Are you all right?"

She nodded dejectedly.

"How about some coffee?"

"I'd rather have bottled water."

"Coming up."

As he stood in line waiting to pay for her water and his coffee, Jack realized that it wasn't giving up their child for adoption he objected to so much as the fact that Holly had unilaterally made the decision for both of them. It didn't matter that she might have made the right choice, because he hadn't been a part of it.

She was fourteen years old. Give her a break.

That was easier said than done.

He opened the bottle of water and handed it to Holly, then sat down across from her with his black coffee. "What's the name of the adoption agency?"

"The Next Generation," she said.

"Where are they?"

"Here in Houston."

He called information and got the number, then had it automatically dialed. When someone answered he said, "I need to find a baby who was placed by your agency twenty-six years ago. How can I do that?"

He listened, then said, "What's your address?" He wrote it down on a pad he kept with him and said, "Thank you."

"What did they say?" Holly asked.

"We need to fill out some paperwork. They'll check to see if our daughter has expressed an interest in finding us. Otherwise, they can't release any information."

"Oh, no."

"I'm sure there must be some sort of exception for medical emergencies like this," Jack said. "Some way for the agency to contact her and let her know we're looking for her, at least."

"That might take too long."

"I've got other resources, Holly, if it comes to that. Do you want to come with me this afternoon?"

She nodded.

"Don't you need to rest?"

"How can I rest when our son might die because of a decision I made when I was fourteen?"

"Go take your nap," he said. "An hour more or less isn't going to make a difference."

"I don't think I could sleep, Jack. Please, can't we just go?"

He saw how frail she was. The past two months had been even harder on her than on him, because she'd spent more time with Ryan. He'd been away working a lot of the time.

D'Amato had told Jack he no longer needed his help locating J.D., which he didn't think boded well for J.D.'s health. The remnants of an explosion of military munitions on Shaw's property were evidence that J.D. had been there. But there were no signs of him.

Jack had noticed that Roberto hadn't been around lately. He wondered if D'Amato was keeping J.D. prisoner somewhere, with Roberto as his guard. He wouldn't put it past the wily mobster.

"All right, we'll go now," he said to Holly. "But I'm taking you home afterward."

She bit her lip rather than protest. She'd kept her word about working more regular hours, but she spent more time at the hospital anyway, visiting with Ryan.

Holly was silent during the ride to the adoption agency, and he realized she'd fallen asleep. He drove around for an extra fifteen minutes to make sure she got more rest. She woke with a start when he stopped the car in front of The Next Generation, which was located in a storefront in a run-down section of Houston. It didn't look promising.

"Let's hope they have computerized records," he said to Holly as he parked the car out front. He felt fortunate they were still in business.

He helped Holly out of the car, noticing how big her belly was getting. He'd held her in his arms last night and felt the baby kick. And made love to her. He wondered what this newest ripple would do to their budding relationship.

He'd been falling back in love with his wife. And making love to her as often as she was willing, which was every time he asked. What was going to happen to them now?

He realized that was probably his call. In order for their marriage to survive, he had to pardon her. Could he absolve her? The answer came quickly and certainly. *What she did was unforgivable.*

The woman behind the counter at The Next Generation had skin the color of cocoa, frizzy white hair that created a halo around her face, and enough wrinkles to be Jack's great-grandmother. A pair of reading glasses hung from a beaded chain around her neck.

"You must be the gentleman who called," she said.

"Yes, I called," Jack confirmed.

"Name's Shirlee. I put the forms together for you." She handed Jack a stack of papers to fill out and said, "You could have done this on-line."

"We have a bit of an emergency," Jack said. "Our son is…dying of cancer," he managed to finish. "He needs a bone marrow transplant. We're hoping our grown daughter will agree to be a donor. We don't know if she's registered to find her parents or not. We're hoping you can help us find out."

Shirlee perched the reading glasses on the end of her nose, sat down in front of an older model computer and said, "What are the mother's and father's names?"

"Only the mother was listed on the birth certificate," Holly admitted. "Holly Gayle Tanner."

Jack felt acid in his stomach. "You didn't name me as the father?" he muttered to Holly.

She turned her back on the woman and said quietly, "I couldn't take the chance that someone would find out and tell you. I'm sor—"

"Don't bother apologizing, Holly. It doesn't make me feel any better. And it doesn't change anything."

"Date of birth?" Shirlee asked.

Holly gave her the year and the day, April 10.

"Sex of the child."

"Female," Holly said.

"Ah, you're in luck," Shirlee said. "Your daughter registered when she was eighteen to meet her biological parents. She's supplied her personal information in case you want to contact her."

"What's her name?" Holly asked, leaning across the counter.

"Savannah Whitelaw."

"That's a pretty name," Holly said.

"Where does she live?" Jack asked.

"According to the paperwork she filed, a place called Hawk's Way."

"Where's that?" Holly asked.

"It's a big ranch in northwest Texas," Jack said. "A really big ranch. The Whitelaws are almost as wealthy—and notoriously powerful and influential— as the Blackthornes. There are a lot of Whitelaws with deep roots in northwest Texas."

"Who are the adoptive parents?" Holly asked. "Can we find that out?"

"Her parents are listed as Jake and Hope Whitelaw."

"Is there a phone number we can call?" Jack asked.

"Let me print this page for you folks, and you can take it with you," Shirlee said.

Jack waited impatiently for the ancient printer to warm up and for the two pages of information to print out. Holly intercepted the pages when Shirlee handed them over the counter, read through them and said, "Here's the number."

"Let's go back out to the car," he said, eyeing Shirlee.

"Don't mind me," she said.

"It's hot in the car. Let's call from here," Holly suggested.

They crossed to a dusty table in the corner where adoption brochures had been set out and Holly sat down in a plain wooden chair beside it. Jack was too nervous to sit. "Give me the number," he said.

He dialed as she recited the numbers. "It's ringing," he said.

She stood and looked up at him with anxious eyes, waiting with him to speak to their daughter.

"Hello?" Jack said. "Is this the Whitelaw residence?" His lips quirked as he said, "I'm not selling anything. I'm looking for Savannah Whitelaw."

Jack held the phone so Holly could hear the responses.

"Savannah isn't here right now," the woman said.

"Are you her mother?" Jack asked.

"Can you tell me why you're looking for Savannah?" the woman said.

"Tell her, Jack," Holly whispered.

"I'm her biological father," Jack said. "Savannah's

biological mother and I would like to meet her, if that could be arranged."

"How wonderful! I hoped you would get in touch someday. But I'm afraid seeing Savannah may not be possible right now," the woman said.

"Why not?" Jack asked.

"Savannah's just finishing up some course work at the FBI Academy at Quantico. I think this week she's involved in various tests and examinations for a Behavioral Science class."

"It's very important that we speak to her. Can you give us a number where we can reach her?"

"I'm sorry. I don't think that's a good idea. Leave me your number and I'll get it to her. She can call you when she's free. By the way, what are your names?"

"Jack and Holly McKinley."

"You're married?" the woman said, surprised.

"We are now," Jack said. "We were kids then."

"I see," the woman said sympathetically.

Jack debated whether to tell the woman why they needed to see Savannah. But he was afraid she might talk their daughter out of becoming a donor before he and Holly even had a chance to meet her.

"Thank you for your help," Jack said. He gave the woman his cell phone number and disconnected the call.

"Is that it?" Holly asked. "What if she doesn't contact us?"

"We're not waiting for her call," Jack said. "We're going to Quantico."

34

Holly felt utter despair for the second time in her life. The first time had been when she realized she was pregnant and there was no way she could keep the baby. This time, she was sure she had lost Jack forever.

He wasn't just angry with her for what she'd done. He was furious. And unforgiving. She was certain that if she hadn't been about to fall down when she left the doctor's office, he would never have touched her again. He'd moved back into the other bedroom.

He'd spent the better part of yesterday afternoon making phone calls. With the help of his FBI friend Breed Grayhawk, he'd managed to arrange a meeting with Savannah Whitelaw at the FBI Academy at Quantico, Virginia, where she was in the Behavioral Science program.

Breed's father, who was the governor of Wyoming, had made some calls from his hospital bed at M.D. Anderson to get them the permission they needed to interrupt Savannah's course of study at Quantico.

The situation was complicated by the fact their daughter couldn't leave at this stage in her FBI training without having to start the course of study all over again. Donating bone marrow was easier now than in the past, but Savannah would probably need a couple of weeks to completely recover afterward. It was questionable whether she would want to make such a sacrifice for a brother she'd never met.

Nevertheless, Holly and Jack had gotten on a flight to D.C., then rented a car and driven the short distance through forested land to Quantico just to talk to her, in hopes she would agree to help save Ryan's life.

The chances Savannah Whitelaw's HLA genes would match Ryan's was only one in four. But Holly's doctor hadn't recommended she donate bone marrow because of her pregnancy, and Jack hadn't been a good match. The search for a matching donor from the National Marrow Donor Program took time—months and sometimes years—that Ryan didn't have. Savannah was their best hope of saving Ryan.

Holly was mentally bracing herself, unsure whether Savannah Whitelaw would be as angry as Jack had been about her decision to give her up for adoption. Certainly she would be expected to provide answers to her daughter. She hoped she could convince Savannah that she hadn't made her choice lightly.

Holly sat next to Jack in silence, while they waited in a conference room at the FBI Training Center for their daughter to arrive. She tried to imagine how the pixie face she'd briefly seen, with bright green eyes and a button nose and a rosebud mouth, might have grown into a beautiful and confident young woman.

"I wonder why she decided to become an FBI agent," Jack said.

"Why don't you ask her?"

"I hope I'll have the chance," he said. "Right now we have more important things to discuss."

The young woman who appeared in the doorway had anxious green eyes brushed by bangs and shoulder-length, sunstreaked chestnut hair. She had Holly's nose, freckled and a little upturned, Jack's high cheekbones, and a wide, mobile mouth. It was hard to see the bow, because she had her upper lip caught in her teeth. Holly held her breath waiting for her beautiful daughter to meet her gaze.

Savannah was tall, maybe 5'11", slender, but with an hourglass figure like Holly's. Poor girl, Holly thought. She knew from experience that it would be hard for any man working with her daughter to ignore such generous feminine assets.

Holly wanted to stand to greet her daughter, but her knees were trembling too badly to support her.

Jack shoved his chair back and stood, staring raptly at their daughter, eating the young woman's face with his eyes.

Savannah stepped inside and closed the door behind her. Holly saw that she was searching Jack's features as intently as he was searching hers. She watched the young woman's expressions, trying to discern her feelings. But her daughter was adept at hiding them.

Savannah turned her gaze to Holly, who found her eyes suddenly blurred by tears. She grabbed for a Kleenex from her purse and dabbed at them so she could see.

"I'm Savannah Whitelaw," the young woman announced.

"I'm Jack McKinley. Your biological father." Jack's

voice broke. He swallowed hard, turned to Holly and said, "This is my wife, your biological mother, Holly Tanner McKinley."

"It's nice to meet you both," the young woman said with a hesitant smile.

She didn't have Holly's strong East Texas accent, but her speech still possessed a soft Southern drawl.

"I'd like to give you a hug," Jack said. "Would that be all right?"

Holly's throat ached. She watched as Jack approached their daughter, who stood waiting for him, her eyes lifting the few inches to her father's.

Then they were holding each other. Holly could see that Jack's eyes were wet as his strong arms closed around his daughter. Savannah's eyes were equally bright with tears as she wrapped her arms tightly around her father's waist.

"I've wondered for so long what you would look like, who you would be," she said with a half laugh, half sob. "It's a miracle to see you both here."

Her eyes finally focused on Holly over Jack's shoulder.

Holly put her hands on the table and pushed herself upright, staggering slightly as her pregnancy sent her off balance. When she looked up again, she saw the shock on Savannah's face.

"You're pregnant?"

Holly realized in that instant that she'd lost her chance for a hug like the one Jack had received. Her daughter's eyes were shuttered, and all signs of laughter were gone from her stunned face.

Savannah pulled herself free of Jack's embrace and took a step back. "What's going on here?" she asked, looking suspiciously from one parent to the other.

Holly exchanged a look with Jack, who seemed distressed by Savannah's abrupt about-face.

"Will you sit?" Jack asked, gesturing to a chair on the opposite side of the conference table from Holly.

For a moment Holly thought the girl was going to bolt. Then her lips flattened and she sat down at the table across from Holly, who sank back into her chair.

Jack took a seat close to Holly, so Savannah could see both of her parents at the same time.

"I agreed to this meeting because I wanted answers to questions I've had all my life," Savannah said. "I spoke with my mother, who speculated that you might have some specific reason for contacting me at this time. Is that the case?"

Holly looked to Jack, imploring with her eyes that he do the talking.

He turned to Savannah and said, "We have a six-year-old son, Ryan, who has leukemia. He's going to die without a bone marrow transplant. Siblings make better donors than parents. We—my wife and I—were hoping you would be willing to get tested to see if you're a good match. If you are, we wanted to ask if you'd be willing to donate bone marrow to our son."

Savannah looked down for a moment before she met Holly's gaze and said, "I have wonderful parents. Now. But it wasn't always that way. I still have scars—emotional and physical—from the nine years I spent in the foster care system."

Holly put a hand to her mouth to keep from wailing. This was her worst nightmare come to life.

Savannah looked from Holly to Jack and asked, "Why did you give me up?"

Jack glanced at Holly and she realized he wasn't willing to paint her any blacker with the truth. But she didn't want Savannah to blame Jack when he wasn't at fault.

"I never told Jack—your father—" she began.

"Jake Whitelaw is my father," Savannah interjected. "I want it clear that I don't consider you my parents. Jake and Hope Whitelaw are my mother and father. They rescued me from hell and raised me with love. I would never have registered with the adoption agency, and I wouldn't be here today, except that my mother convinced me you must have had a good reason for what you did. I'd like to hear it. If you have a good reason, that is."

Holly swallowed over the excruciating lump in her throat and said, "I never told Jack that I was pregnant with you. He's blameless. He didn't know you existed until yesterday."

Savannah turned her gaze to Jack and said, "That must have been quite a surprise."

"I'm sorry you had a hard time, Savannah. I wish..." He shrugged. "There's no undoing what happened. I hope...that you'll let me get to know you."

"I'll think about it," Savannah said. "Would it have made a difference if you'd known about me all those years ago?"

"I don't know," Jack admitted. "Holly was very young. So was I. Neither of us had families who would have been much help to us with a baby."

Savannah turned back to Holly and said, "I'd like to hear what you have to say."

"I was fourteen when I found out I was pregnant

with you. I wanted to finish high school and go to college and become a doctor. I couldn't do that and keep you."

"So, did you become a doctor?"

"I'm a pediatric oncologist," Holly said.

"Well, that's something, at least. When did you two get married?" Savannah asked.

"Jack came back for his fifteenth high school reunion and we met again. You would have been sixteen."

"Did you ever think about me?" Savannah asked bluntly.

"Of course!"

"Really? Do you know how I feel when I see that you kept another child—that you're expecting a third child—when you gave me away? Furious, that's how I feel," Savannah said, her green eyes blazing, though she hadn't raised her voice.

Holly was afraid the next thing out of her daughter's mouth would be a denial of the help they needed to save Ryan's life. "Feel free to hate me," she said. "I'm the one responsible, ultimately, for the bad start you got in life. I just hope you won't take out your animosity toward me on your brother."

"He's no relation to me."

"You carry the same blood!" Holly said fiercely. "Which is precisely why we sought you out. Telling my husband about your existence may cost me my marriage. I did it, despite the risk of losing the man I love, to save my son's life. Ryan needs your bone marrow to stay alive. We're asking you to be tested to see if you're a match.

"So, Miss Savannah Whitelaw, it's your turn to

make a choice that can have devastating consequences. How are you going to handle it?"

Holly was surprised when Jack's hand found hers beneath the table and squeezed it. He held on while they waited for their daughter to decide what she was going to do.

A moment later, he must have remembered that she was the reason they were in this position, because he eased his hand free. Holly felt her heart sink. She was going to lose Jack. She might yet lose Ryan. And her grown daughter obviously wanted nothing to do with her. The future looked horribly bleak.

"I'm going to have to think about this," Savannah said at last. "If I leave Quantico now, I'm going to have to repeat this course. I have my own reasons for wanting to finish as quickly as possible."

"But—" Holly began.

"I understand a life is at stake," she interrupted. "But there are other lives that may be at risk if I don't finish what I'm doing here."

"Are you working a case?" Jack asked.

"I was before I came here," Savannah admitted. "A rapist who's become a serial killer. I thought I might get a better understanding of him if I learned more about psychological profiling."

"I'm a Texas Ranger," Jack said. "I'd be glad to help, if I can."

"I noticed the badge and the SIG," Savannah said with a wry smile. "Thanks for the offer, but this is personal."

"Personal?" Holly asked. "You haven't been—"

"Not me," Savannah said softly. "Someone close to me."

"Time is of the essence," Jack said. "Every day Ryan gets sicker, weaker. He needs your help, Savannah. I don't want my son to die."

"Fine," Savannah muttered.

Holly couldn't quite believe her ears. "What did you say?"

"I said fine. I'll get tested." She met Holly's gaze and said, "You realize I might not be a match."

"We'll deal with that if it happens," Holly said with a grateful smile. "Thank you, Savannah. When can you come to Houston?"

Her beautiful daughter shrugged and said, "How about right now?"

35

"She's a perfect match!" Holly sobbed to Jack over the phone.

"Why are you crying? It's good news, right?"

"The very best. I'm just happy, that's all." And overly emotional because of all the hormones her pregnancy had dumped into her system. She was in her office at M.D. Anderson. Jack was on the road in his SUV, running down another lead on J.D. Pendleton, who still hadn't surfaced. It was beginning to look like D'Amato had arranged it so he never would.

"What happens now?" Jack asked.

"Ryan gets chemotherapy for about a week."

Jack groaned. "More chemotherapy?"

"Busulfan and cyclophosphamide. It's to rid his cells of any residual leukemia. And to destroy his immune system and create space for the new immune system—donor hematopoietic stem cells—that will grow healthy white blood cells."

"Destroying his immune system sounds dangerous," Jack said.

"It is, but the hospital will keep him in a sterile environment so he won't be exposed to anything that could make him sick." One of the great dangers to Ryan between this last round of chemotherapy, and the moment when the transplanted stem cells took over and began growing healthy white blood cells to protect him, would be bacterial or viral or fungal infections, any of which could kill him.

"What about Savannah? Does she get a long needle in her hipbone, or what?"

"There's a new way of harvesting stem cells called apheresis. Dr. Franzen has decided to use the new method to transplant Savannah's bone marrow to Ryan."

"How does that work?"

Holly debated whether to try and explain and realized she was going to have to tell Jack something. She made her description as simple as she could. "A few days before the procedure, Savannah will take a drug called G-CSF. The drug forces her hematopoietic stem cells—those are the ones that will grow new white blood cells—to move from her bone marrow into her circulating blood. Once her blood is full of stem cells, it will be collected with a catheter."

"No surgery? No long needle in her hipbone?"

"No operating room, no general anesthesia. Savannah's blood will go from a tube inserted in one of her veins into a machine that separates stem cells from her other blood cells, which will go back to her. Then the collected hematopoietic stem cells will be transfused to Ryan."

"Does that mean Savannah's recovery time is quicker? I mean, can she get back to her program at Quantico sooner?"

"Maybe, maybe not," Holly said. "The drug she has to take can cause flu symptoms and bone pain in the days before and after the procedure. It'll depend on how severe a reaction she has to the G-CSF. It could take a couple of weeks before she's feeling completely herself again."

"How long before we know if the transplant worked?" Jack asked.

"It usually takes about two to three weeks for the white blood cells to recover. Within a month we should have our first inkling of whether or not the procedure was successful."

"What if it doesn't work?"

Holly was silent. Even if the bone marrow transplant worked, Ryan would have to be monitored for the next three months to see whether he developed graft versus host disease, bad infections or signs of graft rejection, any of which could result in disaster. But she didn't want to give Jack nightmares.

Jack already had enough trouble sleeping. She'd caught him sitting at the kitchen table in the middle of the night more than once over the past few weeks… when her own nightmares had woken her.

"Holly? What if it doesn't work?" Jack persisted.

If Ryan didn't recover after receiving a bone marrow transplant from what was a perfect match, there weren't a lot of other options. "Let's just pray it does."

36

"Ryan, I'd like you to meet Savannah Whitelaw," Holly said. Her glance slid from Ryan, who lay in a hospital bed, to Savannah, who stood on the opposite side of the bed from Holly, and then to Jack, who stood beside their daughter.

The frail little boy with patches of chestnut hair and sunken dark brown eyes shot his visitor a wide, gap-toothed smile. One of Ryan's two front teeth had finally fallen out. He'd been worried that the tooth fairy wouldn't find him in the hospital, but a dollar had miraculously appeared under his pillow overnight.

"Hi, Savannah," Ryan said. "You have eyes the same color as my mom's."

Considering the adults in the room were all wearing masks and gowns and gloves, about all Ryan could see were Savannah's eyes. And yet, he'd noticed the resemblance.

Savannah shot Holly a quick look before she said, "Hello, Ryan. It's nice to meet you." She reached out to shake his bare hand with her gloved one.

Holly watched her daughter's green eyes crinkle as she smiled at her younger brother.

"Savannah's donating the bone marrow you need to grow new white blood cells," Jack said.

"Wow, Savannah, that's great," Ryan said. "I can't wait to get well and get out of here." Her son's pain and fatigue and frustration were evident in his soft, hoarse voice.

A nurse pushed open the door and said, "Miss Whitelaw? We're ready for you."

"So long, Ryan," Savannah said. "Hope you get well soon."

"Thanks, Savannah."

Savannah turned to leave, and Holly said to Jack, "I'll be right back. I want to talk to Savannah."

She followed her daughter out the door and caught up with her as she joined the nurse. "I'd like to speak to my daughter a moment before you start."

"I'll be in the bone marrow transfer clinic," the nurse said to Savannah. "Join me as soon as you can."

"What is it you want, Dr. McKinley?" Savannah said, confronting her in the middle of the hospital hallway.

Holly pulled off her mask and gloves. Savannah kept hers on, avoiding contact with anything or anyone that could make her sick before she donated her marrow.

"How long are you staying in Houston?" Holly asked.

"My father's flying me home to Hawk's Way as soon as this procedure is done," she replied. "It's too late to rejoin my class at Quantico. I'm on medical leave from the FBI until I'm well enough to return to duty."

"I was hoping we'd have a chance to talk before you go." Savannah had stayed with Whitelaw relatives in

Houston until she'd checked into the hospital for the transplant procedure, refusing Jack and Holly's hospitality.

"I'm glad I can help your son," Savannah said. "But I have nothing to say to you."

"It isn't fair to punish your father—Jack—" Holly quickly corrected when she saw the mutinous look in her daughter's eyes, "for what I did. He says you won't talk to him. That you won't return his calls."

"I have a father and a mother, Dr. McKinley. Believe it or not, I even have several sisters and brothers."

"So you don't need us?"

Savannah shrugged. "The truth is, no, I don't. I love my parents. And I know they love me."

"I loved you from the first moment I held you in my arms," Holly said fiercely.

"And yet, you gave me away," Savannah snarled back.

Holly had no defense to that accusation, because it was true. "I hope you'll talk with Jack when he calls again. And he will. He's a good man. You'd like him if you got to know him."

"Are we done here?" Savannah asked.

Holly sighed. "Yes. Thank you again for—"

"I'm doing this for the little boy in that bed," Savannah interrupted. "Now I have to go."

She turned and fled.

Holly met Jack coming out of Ryan's hospital room. "How's Ryan?" she asked anxiously.

"Asleep," Jack said as he pulled off his mask and gloves. "He's so weak, Holly. It worries me."

Jack's eyes were bleak. And frightened. Holly knew

he needed words of comfort. She opened her mouth to explain how everything would be fine in two or three weeks and sobbed instead.

Because she'd been too worried to eat, her blood sugar was out of whack, and she suddenly felt dizzy. She called out "Jack!" and grabbed for his sleeve as she keeled over.

He caught her up in his arms before she hit the floor and headed for a nearby parents' lounge that was mercifully empty. He sat down on a couch with her in his arms, holding her head and shoulders against his chest.

When she came fully to her senses, Holly could hear his heart beating hard and fast. She moaned and touched her temple.

"Some girls will do anything to get a guy's attention," she heard him say as she opened her eyes and leaned back to look up into his face.

He was smiling down at her. Tenderly.

Holly felt a pain behind her breastbone in the region of her heart. "I'm sorry, Jack. So sorry. For everything."

Jack caught her head in his hands and leaned over to kiss her. Holly was so surprised she pushed him away.

He paused and stared at her in confusion. "Holly?"

She searched his gaze, looking for some explanation for his loverlike behavior. "Have you forgiven me, Jack?"

"For Christ's sake, Holly." He lifted her out of his lap and sat her beside him on the couch, then took her hands in his and looked into her eyes. "I'm as responsible as you are for Savannah being born. If there's any blame here, I deserve at least half of it."

Holly stared at him with astonished eyes. "You are? You do?"

He let go of her hands and shot her a chagrined look. "I wasn't just coming out of the door to Ryan's room when you met me. I was standing close enough to hear what you said to Savannah about not blaming me, about giving me a chance to be her father."

"Jack, I—"

"I appreciate your efforts to get her to talk to me. It's the kind of unselfish thing you've done all our married lives. Taking the blame, I mean. I've thought a lot about what happened that July Fourth. I planned to make love to you, if you were willing. I should have brought some protection. It takes two to make a baby, Holly. So, yes, I was involved in some of the decision making that led to Savannah's hard life, too.

"There's no way in hell the two of us would have been able to raise a baby. I would just have made a mess of things if I'd known you were pregnant. You did the right thing not telling me."

"Because you would have wanted to keep the baby?" Holly asked.

Jack shoved both hands through his hair, leaving it standing on end. "Hell, I don't know. Maybe. It would have been stupid and caused a lot of problems. It's too bad Savannah had a hard time with her adoptive parents and ended up in foster care. But you did what you thought would be best for her.

"In the end, she wound up with great parents. She's turned out to be an amazing woman. Imagine, our daughter an FBI agent," he said with a quick grin.

"Who won't talk to either of us," Holly muttered.

He slid an arm around her shoulders and pulled her close, then leaned back against the couch with her. "She will, Holly. Maybe not today or tomorrow or next week. But someday Savannah Whitelaw will have to make a difficult choice—maybe when she's a mother herself—and she'll understand why you did what you did. When that day comes, she'll forgive you and me and let us into her life."

"Do you really think so?" Holly asked wistfully.

"I'm betting on it," Jack said. "And since you know I don't gamble, you can damn well count on it."

"Jack!"

"What's wrong?"

She grabbed his hand and placed it low and to the right on her stomach. The baby kicked hard again with its foot, the shape of which was clearly imprinted for an instant against her skin.

Jack laughed. "He's going to be an NFL kicker, for sure."

"Oof. She's going to be the next Olympic women's soccer team goalie."

"What if the baby is a girl?" Jack asked. "What are we going to name her?"

"Hannah," Holly said softly.

"Why Hannah?"

"Because it sounds nice with Savannah. Our two daughters, Savannah and Hannah."

"Try saying that fast three times," Jack challenged. "How about Daisy?"

Holly wrinkled her nose. "Daisy? What doctor do you know named Daisy?"

Jack lifted a brow. "So now she's going to be a doctor?"

"There are two law enforcement officers in the family. I figure there might as well be two doctors."

"My mother's name is Rose," Jack said. "I thought we might name our daughter after a flower, too."

"How about Lily?" Holly said.

"Holly and Lily," Jack said, letting the sounds roll off his tongue. "Say that three times."

"I see your point. All right, you name a flower."

"Iris," Jack said.

"I knew a mean girl named Iris in third grade. I wouldn't name any child of mine Iris."

"Your turn," Jack said.

"Heather."

"Every other female born in the seventies is named Heather. The world is bloated with Heathers," Jack objected.

"Pansy."

"No."

"Petunia."

"No."

"Poppy."

"Hell no."

"Your turn," Holly said with a laugh.

"Violet."

"Hmm." Holly said it aloud two or three times. "It would probably end up being shortened to Vi."

"Or maybe 'Olet,'" Jack said.

Holly socked him in the arm. "Stop kidding. This is serious. Our daughter needs a name."

"How about Jasmine?"

"Oh." Holly sat up straight. "I love the smell of jasmine. When I was a teenager I used to have a perfume—"

"The one you wore to the Fourth of July picnic?" Jack asked, sitting up beside her. "That was jasmine?"

Holly nodded. "Yeah. That was jasmine."

"There's the connection to our first daughter," Jack said. "Something to remind us of Savannah. But giving Jasmine a name all her own."

"But which also links her to your mom." Holly sighed and leaned back again along with Jack. She laid her head on his chest as he slid his arm around her. "I'm glad that's settled."

"Holly."

"Hmm?"

"What if it's a boy?"

They played the same game with boy's names for a while, a safe way to spend the time while they waited for the next step in Ryan's bone marrow transplant, but couldn't agree on anything.

"Holly, I need to tell you something."

Lately, no news was good news, as far as Holly was concerned. She knew this wasn't good news because she could feel the tension in Jack's shoulder and hear the erratic thud of his heart.

Which now matched her own.

She tried to ease herself out from under his sheltering arm, but he tightened his grip on her shoulder and said, "Stay here beside me."

She laid her head back against his chest so she wouldn't have to look into his eyes when he told her he was leaving her. She waited for him to speak, but he remained silent.

"I'm listening, Jack," she said softly.

"I feel foolish."

At that, she sat up and looked into his eyes. His expression was sheepish. "Foolish about what?" she asked.

"I've known what I'm going to say now for quite some time. I just haven't been able to figure out the best way to tell you."

"You're leaving me," Holly blurted.

"God, no! I love you, Holly. That's what I realized. I've never stopped loving you. I want to spend the rest of my life loving you."

Holly felt herself smiling from ear to ear. "Oh, Jack." And then the hormones hit her, and she burst into tears.

Jack lifted her bulk into his lap once more, planting kisses on her eyes and cheeks and lips and murmuring love words that were a balm for her soul. "You don't have to worry about me going anywhere, Holly. I'm with you for the long haul."

They were words she needed to hear. She owed him as much. "I love you, Jack. I've always loved you. And I will love you the rest of my life."

She returned his kisses with enthusiasm, and it didn't take long for things to get out of control. When she felt Jack's hand reaching under her blouse, she broke off the kiss and, still panting, said, "I want you, Jack, so much. I can't wait to be alone with you tonight. But I think before we make love again, you should tell Kate Pendleton about your decision."

Jack sat bolt upright. "I forgot all about Kate."

Holly smiled again. Now *that* was true love.

37

It had taken quite a bit of finagling, but D'Amato managed to be at M.D. Anderson at a time when the twins were visiting Ryan McKinley and Shaw wasn't picking them up immediately afterward. He believed his son's threat. But twenty-five-year-old written evidence wasn't going to be as useful or convincing to a jury as a cell phone video of Dante D'Amato shooting a man in the back of the head.

D'Amato needed to make friends with his grand-sons so they would tell him where they'd hidden that cell phone. He knew that after they visited McKinley's son, they usually went to the same café where he'd met their mother. So he arranged to be there when they arrived.

He thought he did a pretty good job of looking surprised to see Mrs. Pendleton and sons, although he could see he hadn't fooled the woman. But so long as she didn't make a scene, he would have time to accomplish his purpose.

"Hello, boys," he said. No sense giving them a chance to misidentify themselves again.

"Hello, Mr. D'Amato," they replied in unison.

"Can I buy you some Coke? Or a bowl of ice cream?"

"We're not allowed to have Coke," one of the boys replied.

"Mom, can we have ice cream?" the other boy asked.

"It's a while before supper," D'Amato cajoled. "I'd like to do something nice for them."

"All right," she agreed, although she was obviously wary of trusting him.

"Let's go get in line," D'Amato said, ushering the boys away from their mother.

"Stay where I can see you," she said.

"No problem," D'Amato said. He just needed to get them to a place where she couldn't *hear* them.

"I like chocolate," one of the boys said.

"I like strawberry," the other said.

"Let's see what they have," D'Amato replied. "I was sorry to learn that you boys lost your dad last year."

One of the boys said, "He died in the war."

"I heard he was a brave soldier," D'Amato said. "And had a military funeral. Which one of you got to hold the flag?"

"They gave the flag to Mom," one of the boys said.

"Did you get anything to remind you of your father?" he asked.

"Some medals and stuff," the other boy said.

"I hope you put them someplace safe."

"We did."

"You need a really good hiding place, so robbers can't steal important things like that," D'Amato said.

"We know that," one of the boys said. "Our father told us we should put important things in a place where no one could ever find them."

"So where did you hide those special things of your father's?"

The boys exchanged a look that suggested they both knew where that cell phone was hidden.

"I can't tell you that," the other boy said. "Dad said we shouldn't tell anyone. Then it wouldn't be a secret."

"I just wanted to see if it was a really good hiding place," D'Amato said, knowing it wouldn't take Roberto more than a minute to convince these brats to tell him what he wanted to know. Unfortunately, he would have to return them to their father afterward, and there would be serious consequences if they showed obvious signs of wear and tear.

"It's a really good hiding place," one of the boys said.

"No one will ever find where we hid our special things," the other added.

D'Amato realized he was getting nowhere. He was just going to have to find a way to get these boys alone and convince them to tell him what he needed to know. If they still refused to reveal where they'd hidden that video, well, an "accident" could be arranged.

"What are you doing here, old man?"

D'Amato nearly had a heart attack when he realized his son was standing right behind him.

"Daddy!"

"Daddy!"

Both boys ran to his son. Wyatt leaned down to hug them and said, "I hear you're going to spoil your dinner with some ice cream."

They pointed at D'Amato and said, "He suggested it."

"Don't let me ruin your fun," Wyatt said.

"Then it's all right?" one of the boys said.

"Go for it," Wyatt replied.

When the boys were out of hearing, D'Amato said, "You can't have meant for me to stay completely away from my grandsons."

"That's exactly what I meant," Wyatt said.

"Does that go for any future grandchildren?" D'Amato asked.

"Kate's still married."

"No, she's not," D'Amato said. "J.D.'s long gone." *Or he will be, as soon as I get that video or eliminate those kids.* "I suggest you marry that woman and give me some more grandkids." *Children I can mold in my own image, not brats like these.*

"Tell the boys you have to leave," Wyatt said. "And then go."

"I'll go when I'm damned good and ready," D'Amato retorted.

"Bruce, assist my father to his car."

"Charlie, Frank, Del, Harry," D'Amato called out.

"Your men have already left the building," Wyatt said. "Assisted by mine."

D'Amato's face turned red as he realized he'd been outmaneuvered. "Very well," he said. "I'll leave. You can tell the brats I had to go."

He fumed all the way to his limo, where four very large bodyguards hung their heads and stared at the ground. During the drive home he thought of all the nasty ways four large men could persuade two eight-year-old boys to tell him what he wanted to know.

38

Kate was lying in bed with Shaw's arms around her when he announced, "J.D. is dead."

She pushed herself out of his embrace, so she could look into his eyes. "For real?"

"It's not something I'd lie about."

Shaw had woken her at dawn with a kiss, as wind-driven rain spattered raucously against the sliding glass door. He'd reminded her with a series of quiet kisses on her eyelids and cheeks and throat that it was the weekend, and they didn't have to go to work. And then he'd dropped that bomb.

Kate felt breathless. "How do you know J.D.'s dead?"

She felt Shaw's chest muscles tighten under her hands as he admitted, "D'Amato told me."

"How does he know? What kind of proof does he have?"

Shaw snorted. "If I know my father, you won't be able to find a piece of J.D. big enough to do a DNA test on this time around."

"You think he had him killed?" Kate asked, appalled.

Shaw made a face. "That would be my guess."

"Why would he tell you such a thing?"

"Honestly, I think he believes that once you know you're a widow, you'll marry me and we'll give him more grandchildren, one of whom might turn out to be more corruptible than the twins."

Kate sat up and met Shaw's gaze in the gray morning light. "If J.D.'s dead, I can go home. If I'm a widow, I can marry Jack."

"When was the last time you spoke to Jack?" Shaw asked.

"He called me yesterday."

"When was the last time you saw him?"

"That's not really any of your business." It was a defensive answer because she hadn't once seen Jack during the past month since Ryan's bone marrow transplant. He'd called regularly with news about Ryan, but the calls were brief and they exchanged no words of love. As far as she was concerned, Ryan's illness both explained and excused Jack's lack of loverlike behavior.

Yesterday, for the first time in a long time, she'd heard excitement and joy in Jack's voice when he called. The bone marrow transplant had taken, and Ryan would soon be coming home. Jack had made arrangements to talk with her today while the boys were visiting with Ryan in the hospital for what might be the last time.

"As a matter of fact, I'm seeing Jack today." Too late Kate realized the impact her words might have on Shaw.

She was surprised when he said, "If Jack McKinley's really what you want, Kate, I'm not going to stop you."

She pursed her lips. "What's the catch?"

Shaw was lying relaxed, his hands folded behind his head as he said, "I'm keeping the boys."

Kate pulled a pillow protectively to her chest. But the blow had already been struck. "I can't believe you'd threaten me like that."

"I'm not saying anything I haven't been saying all along," Shaw replied. "I'm not going to miss any more of my sons' lives."

Kate didn't like the turn the conversation was taking. "What if the twins want to leave? What if they want to go home?"

"I don't think they want to go anywhere. I think they like it fine right here."

"I'm sure they miss their friends and their school," Kate argued. "And Jack."

They'd miss their father more.

Shaw didn't say it, but Kate knew he was thinking it. To her chagrin, he was right. Would the twins be so anxious to stay with Shaw if they knew their mother wasn't part of the deal? She didn't think so. But asking them to choose between their mother and their father would tear their hearts in two.

Or maybe not. Maybe they weren't as connected to Shaw as he thought. They liked him. They liked having a "Daddy." But did they love him? She wasn't sure.

"Why don't you ask them what they want to do?" he said.

"All right," she said. "I will."

She shoved the covers aside and marched down the hall to Lucky's room in her nightgown. She was disconcerted when she realized Shaw was right behind her, bare-chested, in the cotton drawstring pajama bottoms that were all he'd worn to bed.

The boys were still asleep.

"You going to ask them, or not?" Shaw said.

"They're still asleep," she whispered. "Besides," she added irritably, "children go where they're told to go and do what they're told to do. I'm the parent. I'm the one who's supposed to make decisions in their best interests. Marrying Jack is one of those decisions."

"I'm a parent, too," Shaw pointed out. "I think our opinions about what's best for Lucky and Chance differ. I think they belong with their father."

Kate realized he wasn't saying that *she* belonged with him. He was only interested in keeping the boys. He certainly hadn't asked her to stay. She was free to leave and go marry Jack.

Of course, she'd made it clear she didn't want to stay. Was she having second thoughts about that? Second and third and fourth thoughts, she admitted. But she wasn't going to stay where she wasn't wanted. *Desperately* wanted, she amended.

Shaw wasn't acting the least bit desperate. He seemed totally calm. Relaxed. Confident…that she would take the path of least resistance and stay without being asked, she thought bitterly. He hadn't offered anything of himself as an inducement to change her mind about leaving.

Did you want him to offer his heart? Do you want his love? What about Jack? Don't you love Jack anymore?

Kate felt confused. And miserable. She didn't know

what she wanted. Certainly Jack's behavior over the past month hadn't been encouraging. Had Jack changed his mind about wanting to marry her? Was that why he'd avoided seeing her?

On the other hand, he'd asked to see her immediately once he'd found out Ryan was going to get well. Holly was within a few weeks of her delivery date. At long last, Jack was going to be free of obligations to his son and his unborn child.

Was he finally going to propose?

What would you say if he did? Are you still in love with Jack? Or have you fallen in love with someone else?

"Mom? Daddy?" Chance said, sitting up in the other room and rubbing the sleep from his eyes. "What's going on?"

The cat stretched luxuriously, hopped off the bed and trotted down the hall, heading for Shaw's pillow.

Shaw gestured with his eyes, daring her to ask whether Chance wanted to stay or go.

Kate realized she couldn't put her sons in that position. They'd accepted Shaw as their "Daddy." And they loved her. She would have to make the decision for them. She couldn't stay. But how could she bear to leave them behind? It was a dilemma for which she needed to find an answer.

"Daddy and I were just talking. I'm sorry we woke you up," she said to Chance.

"Go back to sleep," Shaw said.

It was a sign of how much the boys trusted Shaw that Chance simply lay back down and pulled the covers up over his head.

Kate left the boy's room and headed into the kitchen. She was afraid if she went back to bed, Shaw might try to seduce her into staying. She missed making love to him. She ached sometimes, wanting him. But she didn't think physical pleasure should be involved in the decision she was about to make.

She filled a mug with water and stuck it in the microwave while she rooted through the various tea bags in the cabinet to see what she wanted. A black tea with lots of caffeine, she decided. Earl Grey. She got the half-and-half out of the fridge and waited for the microwave to ding, so she could put in the tea bag and a dollop of cream.

Shaw had started the coffeemaker perking, and the strong smell of Columbian coffee made her feel nauseated. For a moment she panicked, imagining what might be causing her to feel sick to her stomach. But the situation itself was sickening enough to be causing her queasy stomach.

She tried to remember the last time she'd had a period. Not since she'd come to live with Shaw, she realized with horror. She'd made love to him twice—that first night—without a condom. And not once in the three months since then. She couldn't possibly be pregnant. Could she?

Kate shook her head. No. It wasn't possible that he could have gotten her pregnant—twice—from a single night of lovemaking. The odds must be astronomical.

Kate felt stupid. And vulnerable. And unhappy. She shot a look at Wyatt from the corner of her eye. Had that been part of his plan? To get her pregnant, so she would stay with him?

Well, it wasn't going to work. Even if she was pregnant. Which she probably wasn't.

Kate's stomach rolled with nausea. She left the cream out of her tea, because it suddenly smelled bad, and sat down in one of the two stools on opposite sides of a hightop table that looked out over the puddled courtyard patio. In the distance, the sun was breaking through the clouds, but she felt oppressed by the overcast sky. She was grateful for the plate of raisin toast Shaw set on the table between them. She grabbed a slice and bit into it and felt her stomach abandon its revolt.

"How are we going to work this out?" Kate said.

"You could stay."

As a declaration of love, it lacked a great deal. She wasn't sure Shaw ever intended to get married. His father seemed to think he would, if what Shaw had said about D'Amato hoping they would get married and have more kids was true.

Kate realized how easy her decision would have been if Shaw had said, *I want you to stay,* or even *Would you please stay?* But he'd merely offered to let her remain in his home as the "guest" she'd been since he'd coerced her into coming here with the twins.

Kate wished Jack's situation were more settled. Holly hadn't yet delivered the baby. And Ryan had to be watched closely by the doctors for several more months. Jack wasn't quite free to marry her, even if she was finally free to marry him.

But it was wrong to stay with Shaw simply because she couldn't be with Jack right now. Wrong to give the impression to her sons—and to Shaw—that they were a happy little family. Not when Shaw had never indicated that he loved her, let alone that he wanted her to be his wife.

This morning, he'd told her he was keeping the twins, even if she chose to leave. He would do nothing to stop her. He would let her walk right out the door.

Because he thinks you don't have the guts to go and leave the boys behind. Or the guts to steal the boys when he isn't looking. He thinks you'll stay because you have nowhere else to go, since Jack's still living with his wife.

He's wrong. You have a home of your own, and the will to be independent and self-sufficient. You have powerful parents and grandparents who can help you fight for custody, if it comes to that. All you need is the strength to walk away.

Kate caught her lower lip in her teeth as she considered the alternatives. Go on her own? Or try and take the twins?

"What are you thinking?" Shaw asked.

"That it's time to go home."

"I told you, the twins—"

"They can stay," she interrupted. "For now. I presume we'll have to work out some sort of visitation plan, like divorced parents do."

He looked stunned. And unhappy. And disturbed.

She wondered if she'd been mistaken. Could he possibly love her? If he did, he wasn't saying it. Were the words necessary? Weren't his actions—the passionate lovemaking that first night, the solicitous concern for her safety over the past few months, the precious time he spent with her and the twins—sufficient to tell her how he felt?

Obviously not. She wanted the whole enchilada. The words and the actions and even a romantic gesture or two. Or three. Maybe she was foolish. Maybe a man as wealthy as Wyatt Shaw, as urbane and sophisticated as he was, didn't need those sorts of gestures to attract a woman.

Maybe he was jaded by all the women who'd pursued him for his good looks and his wealth without knowing or caring who he was as a person, or what he wanted and needed from a relationship. Maybe he'd given up on love. Maybe he didn't believe he was lovable. Maybe the best he hoped for was really good sex.

Kate felt her heart squeeze with sympathy for the young boy who'd lost his mother and been betrayed by his father. Which made her wonder how many women Shaw had ever told about his past. And why he'd chosen to tell her such intimate facts about himself.

Kate glanced surreptitiously at Shaw, who was staring out the window at a cardinal that had landed in the moss-laden live oak that draped the courtyard.

"Penny for your thoughts?" Shaw said, when he caught her looking at him.

She flushed under his focused gaze. "I was just thinking."

"What?"

"It's nice when it's quiet like this." Which was as close as she could come to saying, *Be quiet and let me think.*

He was an astute man. He sipped his steaming coffee and turned his attention back out the window.

Why had he told her such intimate facts about himself? So she'd beware of his father. So she'd understand the danger to their sons from that terrible old man. Still, she'd never realized before how vulnerable he'd made himself by revealing so much. Surely that meant something.

But it wasn't words of love.

If you looked at it another way, he'd used his past as a lever to frighten her into staying with him. Had he simply been manipulating her all along to get what he wanted...his sons? And maybe another child?

It was too late to go back now and make other choices. She'd brought Lucky and Chance to Houston. She'd introduced Shaw to them as their biological father. She'd had unprotected sex with a virtual stranger—again.

She could only go forward from here.

"I'll stay until we can have lawyers draw up some kind of custody agreement," she said at last. "That will give me time to give notice at M.D. Anderson and to see if I can get my job back at BAMC. They said I could come back, but with the economy the way it is, they might already have hired somebody else."

"You're leaving?"

Was that tension she saw in his shoulders? Anxiety she saw in his eyes? "I think that's best, under the circumstances."

"You mean, the circumstances that have you pining for a married man who's about to become a father for the second time with another woman?"

Kate flushed with anger. "That's the first time you've ever been petty. It doesn't become you."

She watched a muscle work in his jaw before he said, "The truth is the truth. Even if you don't want to hear it."

She wondered if Shaw had ever apologized, even when he was wrong. Although, he wasn't wrong, was he? She was pining over a married man who was living with his pregnant wife, supporting her as they watched their son fight his way back from the brink of death. That sort of life experience was going to change Jack forever.

He might no longer be interested in being a husband to her, when he had a wife and brand-new baby living somewhere on their own. She couldn't believe how tempted she was to tell Jack to stay with his wife. That she'd found someone new. Someone who fit her better.

But she wasn't going to stay where she wasn't wanted. She'd given Shaw a dozen chances this morning to ask her to stay. He'd remained obdurate. He wanted the boys. He'd said nothing about wanting her.

She left her mug on the tabletop and slid off the bar stool. She met Shaw's gaze with her chin up and said, "I'll get my own lawyer. He can work out the details with yours."

"Kate…"

She waited for him to ask her to stay. Felt an ache under her breastbone when he didn't.

"The boys and I are going to visit their Grandpa King today at M.D. Anderson before we go see Ryan," she said. "He finally broke down and told his children he has leukemia, so a few of them might turn up there. One of his sons, my uncle Breed Grayhawk, is an FBI agent. Considering who your father is, and the fact you're still accused of murder, it would be awkward if you came along."

She watched a muscle jerk in his cheek and knew she'd annoyed him. Too damn bad. She wasn't much pleased with the situation herself.

"Bruce will go with you."

"Is that really necessary? I mean, now that J.D.'s dead—"

"I have other enemies. And I don't trust my father."

He hadn't said he didn't trust her to return with the boys. She thought it was more a case of him not believing she'd have the nerve to defy him by taking them and running. Which made her mad.

But not mad enough to do something stupid, like taking the boys and running.

"Send your bodyguard, then," she said. "We plan to see King right after lunch."

"I'll make sure the car is ready."

They stared at each other for another beat or two. Kate thought he might want to say something else. Wished him to speak the words she wanted to hear. But he didn't.

She had already turned to leave when he called out to her again. "Kate…"

She turned back and met his gaze, afraid that the longing in her eyes might give her away. Afraid it might tell him how much she wanted to hear words of love from him. She felt sick again, her stomach churning with the knowledge that she was being disloyal to Jack, the man she supposedly loved.

Disgust and anger and humiliation raised bile in her

throat. "Is there something else?" she asked when Shaw didn't speak.

His eyes were like the stone walls that surrounded his fortress, allowing no one to see behind them. At last he said, "I'll call my lawyer Monday morning."

39

Kate kept expecting Shaw to do something or say something to put a stop to the wheels she'd set in motion. He'd been in a disgustingly good mood all morning, as though nothing out of the ordinary had transpired between them at breakfast. He'd headed outside with the twins to play catch with a new baseball and gloves he'd bought for them. Then they'd tossed the frisbee for Harley.

Kate had absented herself from both activities, telling Shaw she had a new book she wanted to read. He hadn't tried to talk her into joining them, and the boys had seemed perfectly happy spending the time with Shaw.

She'd tried reading her romance novel but hadn't been able to escape into the fantasy. Reality kept intruding. She spent the first half of the morning fuming that Shaw seemed so uninterested in keeping her around.

Which must mean she wanted to stay.

Then there was the little matter of her nausea, which had returned. She was going to have ten kittens if it turned out she was pregnant. Well, actually, one baby, she thought, suppressing a hysterical giggle.

The possibility she might be pregnant was freaking her out.

Mid-morning she hunted Bruce down and told him she wanted to do some shopping, thinking she could sneak out and get a home pregnancy test, which would at least end the suspense. Maybe she just had a twenty-four-hour bug.

Oh, really? What else but pregnancy would cause you to miss two periods?

Suddenly she thought of something that might. *Cancer.*

"I'll be glad to go pick up anything you need, Mrs. Pendleton," Bruce told her.

Of course he would. Then he'd tell Shaw exactly what he'd bought for her. "I need feminine products, Bruce. I'd rather choose them myself."

Bruce blushed. "Yes, ma'am. I'll just tell the Boss—"

"I really don't want to make a big deal of this, Bruce. Couldn't we just go? You know Wyatt would want me to have what I need. And the situation is… urgent."

That was almost the truth.

Bruce blushed even redder. "Yes, ma'am. I understand. But the Boss—"

She put her hands on her hips and said with not entirely faked agitation, "Do you really need to ask Wyatt if I can go buy Tampax?"

"I guess not," he said, looking around for someone who could give him instructions about what to do in this situation.

"Let's go then," she said, anxious to get him out of the house before Shaw and the twins came in for refreshments or to use the bathroom or just to take a break.

The closest Walgreens drugstore was a half hour away in The Woodlands. Kate managed to convince Bruce to let her go inside on her own. There were several different pregnancy tests. She picked up the e.p.t. Certainty, an upgrade of the test she'd used nine years ago, when she'd determined she was pregnant with the twins. She felt the same breathlessness now as she had then.

She bought a few other things, so she'd be able to hide the e.p.t. box in the bag, including Tampax, which she might actually need if it turned out she just had the flu or food poisoning or... What else caused nausea? And two missed periods?

Bruce looked relieved when she returned to the car.

"Thanks, Bruce," she said, hugging the bag tightly to her chest.

"You're welcome, ma'am."

When she stepped inside the house, she could hear the boys in the kitchen. She presumed Wyatt was with them and hurried to the bathroom attached to the guest bedroom that had remained unused all these months, to hide the bag of toiletries under the sink. She would have liked to take the pregnancy test right away, but she was afraid she might get interrupted, so she headed to the kitchen.

"Hey, Mom, where were you?" Lucky asked.

"I went to the drugstore to buy a few things."

"What kinds of things?" Chance asked.

Shaw lifted a black brow that repeated the question.

"Girl things," she said dismissively. "What's for lunch?"

"The boys voted for PBJs," Shaw said.

"I love peanut butter and jelly," Lucky said to Shaw.

"Me, too," Shaw said, ruffling his hair.

"Me, three," Chance said.

Shaw tweaked Chance's nose and he laughed.

They love him. What she saw in both sets of blue eyes was adoration for the man who'd sired them. How naive she'd been to think they wouldn't want to stay. She felt melancholy, missing the fantasy of happily ever after, even though she knew it didn't happen that often in real life. If only she'd gone looking for Shaw when she'd found out she was pregnant with the twins, maybe they would have become a family.

That chance had come and gone. Or had it? Kate turned and caught a fleeting look in Shaw's eyes. Something astonishing.

Yearning.

For her? For the fantasy?

"While you boys eat your sandwiches, I'm going to get dressed for our trip to the hospital," Kate said.

"Don't you want a sandwich, Mom?" Chance asked. "I can make one for you."

"Thanks, sweetie," she said. "I had a snack earlier." She headed out of the kitchen before Shaw could question her more closely and hurried to the guest bathroom. She was most likely to have privacy while Shaw was helping the boys make their sandwiches. She retrieved the pregnancy test from the bag under the sink and quickly read the directions.

"The readout is 'Not Pregnant' or 'Pregnant.' Well, that's easy. Ninety-nine percent accurate. Simply remove cap and insert test strip into holder." Kate stopped to follow the directions, then picked them up to read again. "Place absorbent tip in urine stream for five to seven seconds. Test any time of day."

Kate did as she was told. "Here goes nothing." When she was done, she picked up the directions to find out how soon she'd have the results. "Three very long minutes," she muttered.

Kate set the holder on the counter and looked at her watch.

"Mom? Where are you?"

"I'm in the bathroom, Chance," she called back.

"No, you're not," he called back. "I'm in your room and the bathroom door's open and you're not here. Where are you?"

Kate grabbed the directions and the box and started to put them in the guest bathroom trash. The can was empty. The box and directions and test strip and holder were going to get noticed if she threw them in there. She put the trash she'd collected back in the plastic bag full of toiletries, then stuck it under the sink.

She heard a knock on the door and Lucky's voice. "Mom? What are you doing in there?"

Kate looked down at her watch. Two minutes had passed. Did she dare hold them off for another minute? Or should she chuck this test and take another one. She looked down at the test strip, which clearly read *Not Pregnant.*

She felt…disappointed.

She grabbed the strip and holder and dropped them in the bag under the sink. Then she flushed the toilet, waited a second and opened the door.

Shaw was standing there with the twins on either side of him.

"What are you doing in here?" he asked, looking around the bathroom like he expected to find drug paraphernalia.

"I was feeling a little sick, so I ducked in here to use the facilities. Is that a problem?" she asked in an aggrieved voice.

"You're sick?" Shaw asked.

She should have known he'd key on that. "A little diarrhea, if you must know. Must have been something I ate."

"You sure you want to drive in to Houston today?"

Kate realized the hole she'd dug for herself and said, "I had Bruce take me to Walgreens. I got myself some Pepto-Bismol, and I'm feeling much better." That would explain the trip, which she was sure Bruce would report to his boss.

"The boys wanted to know if they can take their sandwiches in the car," Shaw said. "Sort of a traveling picnic."

"That's fine with me, if it's all right with you and Bruce."

"All right. I'll pack everything up."

The boys skipped away after Shaw, who glanced back over his shoulder at her as though she might pull out that drug paraphernalia he hadn't seen the first time he looked.

Kate realized she was going to have to make an appointment with a doctor and find out what was wrong with her. Because she still felt nauseated. If she wasn't pregnant, there was some other reason she'd missed her periods.

Could be stress, you know. It doesn't have to be cancer. But if it wasn't pregnancy or stress, she had no idea what could be wrong with her. The possibility that she was seriously ill was frightening.

She had plenty of time on the ride to Houston to worry about what was wrong, while the boys ate their picnic in the backseat.

King was a leukemia inpatient on the eighth floor of the Main Building at M.D. Anderson. Ryan was an inpatient on the ninth floor of the same building. The boys gave their great-grandfather a hug and chatted with him for a few minutes, but they were anxious to visit Ryan.

"Can we go upstairs, Mom?" Lucky asked.

"I'm sorry I can't stay longer," she said to King. "The twins' friend has been very sick for a very long time. He's finally well enough for a real visit. Do you mind?"

"Go ahead," King said. "I'll be fine."

But she saw he was disappointed that she wasn't staying longer to talk. Apparently, none of his children had come to visit him. She made a split second decision to stay. "Go ahead without me," she said to the boys. "You know where to find the gowns and masks and gloves. Go ahead and put them on. I'll be there in a few minutes. Don't run! And don't get into trouble!"

"You're a trusting soul," King said with a chuckle.

"I need a few more minutes to find out how you are."

"I'm a lot better now than I was a month ago."

"Really? I thought your situation was…" The word that came to mind was *terminal,* but she didn't want to say that.

Shattered 375

"I was dying," King said flatly. "On my way out of this world and into the next."

"What happened?" Kate asked, sitting on the bed beside him.

"She happened," King said, pointing to the doorway to his room.

Kate turned and stood. She barely managed not to gasp at the sight of a very pregnant Holly McKinley.

Holly smiled at her tentatively and said, "Hi, Kate."

Kate was half in shock as she held out her hand to grasp the one Holly extended. The woman was so huge with child that she looked like a balloon ready to pop. "What do you have to do with my grandfather's recovery?"

Holly waddled over to King's bedside and checked his pulse, then used her stethoscope to check his heart. "I came here a month ago to thank your grandfather for getting the clearances Jack and I needed to visit the FBI Training Center at Quantico, where our daughter was in school.

"In the process, I discovered he was a good candidate for a clinical trial I'm conducting with adult leukemia patients. Turns out my chemotherapy cocktail put your grandfather's cancer in remission."

Kate realized her jaw had dropped and closed her mouth. "That's amazing. That's wonderful!" She crossed back to her grandfather and hugged him tight. "I'm so glad you're going to be all right."

"I'm not out of the woods yet," King said gruffly. "But this little lady says the chances are good I'll live to see another birthday or two."

Kate watched as King pinched Dr. McKinley's

cheek. The doctor smiled and threatened to put a thermometer somewhere King wouldn't like, if he didn't keep his hands to himself.

At which point Kate finally processed what Holly had previously said. "You and Jack have a daughter?"

"Her name is Savannah. She's twenty-six. I got pregnant when Jack and I were kids and gave the baby up for adoption. She was a perfect bone marrow match for Ryan. She's the reason he's alive and well today."

Kate was reeling from Holly's revelation. Jack had another child with Holly. A grown daughter. It was one more tie to bind him to his wife. And one more secret he'd kept from her.

"I can see you're surprised," Holly said. "Jack didn't know about Savannah until a month ago. I never told him I was pregnant."

"I see," Kate said. But if Jack had known for an entire month he had a grown daughter, why hadn't he mentioned it? All he'd said was that a very good donor had been found and that Ryan was getting a bone marrow transplant.

"What am I missing here?" King said, looking from one woman to the other.

"I was separated from my husband for a year," Holly said, her gaze focused on Kate. "I believe he and Kate became friends during that time."

"Yes, we did," Kate said.

But what were they now?

"Where are the twins?" Holly asked. "King told me they were coming to visit him this afternoon."

"They were here. They've already headed upstairs to see Ryan," Kate said.

"Maybe we should join them," Holly suggested.

"Go ahead," King said. "I wouldn't trust those two hellions any farther than I could throw them."

As they left King's room, Holly said, "Do you mind if we take the elevator rather than the stairs?"

"Of course not," Kate replied.

"Have you seen Jack today?" Holly asked, eyeing her askance.

Kate stared at the other woman, surprised that she knew about her plans to meet with Jack. That couldn't be good. Especially in light of the news that Holly and Jack had a grown daughter. "No, I haven't seen Jack yet."

"But you're going to see him, right?" Holly said.

"We'd planned to meet after the twins' visit with Ryan," Kate admitted.

"Then I'll let him answer all the questions I can see in your eyes."

Holly McKinley seemed confident. And sympathetic. Kate was afraid she was about to be bushwhacked by Jack. Apparently, a great deal had happened during the month he'd been out of touch. Holly wasn't acting like a rejected woman. She was acting like a possessive wife.

The elevator door opened on the ninth floor and Holly gestured Kate out before her. Kate felt angry at Jack. If he'd been a little more honest, that elevator ride would have been a great deal less awkward. She resisted the urge to head for the Waterfall Café to see him, without stopping to check on the twins and Ryan. But King was right about the twins being a magnet for trouble. She had to make sure they were all right first.

She reached the doorway to Ryan's room about the

same time as Holly. The pregnant woman filled the entire space with her girth, so Kate had to look over her shoulder to see into the room. What she found confused her.

"Where's Ryan?" she asked. The sheets on his hospital bed were mussed. The bed was empty.

"I don't know," Holly said, her voice frantic. "He's supposed to be here. He hasn't been released yet. He still has to be careful about where he goes and what he does to guard against infection."

Kate didn't see a nurse in the hallway or any patients or any parents. "Where is everybody?" she asked. "Where are my sons?"

"I don't know!" Holly cried.

Kate's cell phone rang and she fumbled in her purse for it, thinking perhaps Jack or Wyatt had intercepted the boys and taken them somewhere. She didn't recognize the number on her phone. She almost didn't answer the call, but she thought maybe it was Wyatt on a phone at one of his businesses. She wanted to let him know about this latest development, in case the boys had wandered off and gotten lost, and she needed his help finding them again.

"Hi, honey, it's me. You missing something?"

Kate went white. "J.D.? You're supposed to be dead."

"Sorry to disappoint you, honey, but I'm still kickin'. I've got some instructions for you. I need you to follow them exactly, if you want these three boys back alive."

40

J.D. thought the shocked looks on his sons' faces when they saw him in that sick kid's hospital room were priceless. Most of all, he couldn't believe his luck, finding them alone.

"Dad, is that you? What happened to your face?" A wide-eyed Lucky had looked at his brother and said, "Do you see what I see?"

"He looks sort of like Dad, but his face is…all messed up." Chance had reached out to touch J.D.'s soiled trousers. "He's real," he confirmed to his brother.

"Yes, I am," J.D. said. "We're going on a little trip, so come with me."

To his surprise, the kids hadn't wanted to come.

"We can't go with you, Dad," Lucky said. "We're supposed to wait here for Mom."

"Your mother sent me here to get you," he'd lied.

"Can Ryan come, too?" Chance asked.

Who the hell was Ryan, he wondered. "Ryan?"

"Our friend Jack's son, Ryan," Lucky said, pointing to the boy in the bed.

"I'm Ryan," the boy with the patchy hair said.

Then J.D. realized who the kid was. Ryan McKinley, Jack's boy.

"Come on, kid, if you're coming." When he'd grabbed the kid's arm, he'd started to scream.

He'd clamped a hand on the kid's nose and mouth, which shut him up pretty quick. But the twins were yanking on him, and making a shitload of noise, so he ended up having to bargain with the brats to get them the hell out of there.

He thought it was a nice irony that the Texas Ranger's kid ended up getting kidnapped along with his own. That would put D'Amato's tail in a twist. The whole damned Texas Department of Public Safety would be after D'Amato for kidnapping a Texas Ranger's kid. Not to mention the FBI, once Kate told Breed Grayhawk her sons were missing.

D'Amato was a fool. He must think J.D. was an idiot to believe he would go along with D'Amato's stupid plan to have him kidnap the twins. J.D. was kidnapping the twins, all right. But he wasn't taking them straight back to D'Amato, who promised he'd exchange the twins for J.D.'s twenty million dollars worth of smack. He was simply going to ask for cash from Wyatt Shaw, since that would save him the trouble of selling the junk.

He'd studied the diagrams of the hospital D'Amato had furnished and figured out a way to leave that took him away from D'Amato's goons. He'd counted on surprise and awe to shock the boys into going with him, and it had sort of worked.

He hadn't counted on having the sick kid come along. He hadn't gone very far before he realized the kid couldn't keep up. He'd wanted to leave him behind, but the twins had balked.

"You can't just leave Ryan here," Lucky said.

"He can't keep up," J.D. pointed out.

"Then carry him. That's what Daddy would do," Chance said.

"Daddy?" he'd questioned, squinting down at his son through narrowed eyes.

"Wyatt Shaw is our bio—whatever—father," Lucky said. "We call him Daddy."

"Yeah, well I ain't your Daddy, I'm your Dad. And I don't feel like carrying some kid halfway to hell." He'd shoved Ryan so he fell onto his knees, and both boys had raced to help him back to his feet.

"Jack's going to kill you if you hurt Ryan," Chance warned.

He'd slapped him to shut him up.

"And Daddy's going to kill you if you hurt us," Lucky shouted.

That had drawn a lot more attention than he'd wanted. The kid's threat had also been the end of any thoughts of kindness he had toward the two boys who'd been raised in his home. "Ungrateful little bastards," he'd snarled at the twins. "You help this kid keep up, or I'm going to strangle him like I did somebody else who threatened to cause me trouble."

To give them credit, the twins were strong for their size. They kept the kid upright during their escape from the hospital and got him into the old Chevy Impala J.D. stole from the parking garage. He chose a car with the parking ticket left in the window, so he wouldn't have trouble getting out. He had some money in a pocket within his pants pocket that Roberto hadn't found to pay the parking fee.

"I want my mommy and daddy," Ryan said, tears streaming down his face.

"Shut up, kid. Or I'll shut you up."

"Shh, Ryan," Lucky said, putting his arm around the younger boy in the backseat. "Be quiet."

Once they were on the road, Lucky sat forward in the backseat and asked, "Where are we going?"

"That's kind of up to you boys," he'd said.

"I want to go to Shaw's compound," Chance said.

"Is that where you hid the box I gave you?"

"What box?" Lucky asked.

"Don't play dumb with me," J.D. raged. "I gave you a box before I left for Afghanistan. I told you it was important. I told you not to tell anyone but me where you were putting it, and then I told you to hide it. Now I want to know where that box is, and I want to know right now!"

The twins exchanged glances before Lucky said, "I really don't remember."

J.D. held on to his temper. Barely. He met Chance's eyes in the rearview mirror and said, "How about you? Do you remember what you did with it?"

Chance solemnly shook his head. "No, I don't."

J.D. realized he had only himself to blame. He should have known they were too young for this sort of intrigue. Then he saw a look the two boys exchanged and realized they were lying.

He pulled the Chevy to the side of the road, opened the back door and pulled Ryan out and dangled him by one arm. "I'm going to beat this kid within an inch of his life if you don't tell me where you hid that box."

He'd already balled his fist when Chance said, "We left it at Shaw's house. We thought it was important, so we took it with us when we left San Antonio."

"Shaw's house?"

"His compound. You know. The one with the high stone walls around it."

"Son of a bitch," J.D. said.

"Put Ryan down," Lucky said.

J.D. threw the kid into the backseat and the twins put their arms protectively around him.

"All right," J.D. said. "This is what we're going to do." When he was done explaining his plan to the twins, he pulled out his cell phone and called his wayward wife.

"Hi, honey, it's me. You missing something?"

41

"Son of a bitch!" Wyatt muttered. He threw the contract back on his desk. He hadn't been able to stay at home when Kate and the twins were in Houston, so he'd headed to his office, figuring he might as well get some work done. This was the third time he'd read the same paragraph without having any idea what it said, because the scene in bed with Kate that morning kept replaying in his head. What did he have to do to convince the woman she belonged with him, rather than that damned Texas Ranger?

Did you once tell her how you feel?

If she needed those three little words, she was out of luck. He wasn't going to admit out loud that he wanted anyone, needed anyone, loved anyone.

You told the twins you love them.

That's different. They're my flesh and blood. Of course I love them.

Like D'Amato loves you? Get real. Either you love her, or you don't. Which is it?

Wyatt tried to swallow a sip of coffee, but it was cold and got caught on the lump in his throat. He felt near to tears and didn't know why. What was wrong with him?

She's going to leave you, that's what's wrong, you idiot. Unless you confess that you want her and need her and love her.

The solution to his problem sounded simple. Just tell Kate he needed her like the air he breathed. That the mere sight of her filled his heart with joy. That loving her was the greatest pleasure he'd ever known. That he wanted her to be his wife.

But Wyatt hadn't become the most successful businessman in Houston by showing his underbelly to someone with the power to rip it out. And nothing in his life previous to this had given him any reason to trust the people who were closest to him.

Maybe he'd been spoiled by the women who'd thrown themselves at him, telling him—before he asked—that they admired and loved him. He'd been appreciative. But he'd never been in love, so he'd never returned those expressions of love.

He was not just *in love* with Kate Pendleton. He *loved* her.

She was playing hardball. She wasn't offering her love when he hadn't offered his. He had to admire that. He just wished he was more certain that she felt the same way he did.

He was going to have to bite the bullet. He was going to have to take the chance that if he told her how he felt, she wouldn't kick dirt in his face, metaphorically speaking. In business terms—hell, in any terms—the reward was certainly worth the risk.

Having made up his mind to act, Wyatt couldn't sit still. He was already on his way to meet up with Kate and the twins at M.D. Anderson when he got her frantic call.

"Wyatt? Thank God I reached you. Our boys have been kidnapped! It was J.D. He—"

"J.D.?" he interrupted. "I thought—"

"He's alive! He's threatening to kill the twins—and Ryan, he has Ryan, too—if we don't do exactly what he says."

"What does he want?"

"Twenty million dollars."

"I can get it, but I'm going to have to find a banker—"

"I'm frightened, Wyatt. I need you. How soon can you get here?"

Amazing the power of those three words. *I need you.* He would have moved mountains for her, if he could. He would do everything and anything he could to bring the twins back home safe. "I came in to work this morning after you left. I'm on my way to the hospital right now. Where are you?"

"Holly McKinley and I are on the ninth floor of the Main Building, in Ryan's room. She says Ryan's health is precarious, that he's still susceptible to infections of all sorts. She's going crazy, Wyatt. I've called Jack, and he's on his way, but he hasn't arrived yet. Please hurry."

"I'll be there as fast as I can." Wyatt realized this was one time when having a Texas Ranger around wasn't going to be a bad thing. Especially since the Ranger's wife was going to be there, as well.

"See you in ten minutes," Wyatt said. After he hung up, he called a banker friend and asked him about opening the bank on Saturday to arrange a wire transfer, if that became necessary. He had his driver break the speed limit getting to the hospital and made it to Ryan's room at the same time as Texas Ranger Jack McKinley, whom he could see coming down the hall from the opposite direction.

"Who told you J.D. was dead?" Jack asked the moment he saw Wyatt.

"D'Amato."

"We need to talk to him."

Before Wyatt could say another word, Kate saw him. His arms opened wide as she slammed into him and they closed tightly around her. He could feel her trembling and vowed that J.D. Pendleton would pay for frightening her like this.

Over Kate's shoulder he could see Jack holding his wife by the shoulders. They were arguing.

"You're not coming with us," Jack told his wife.

"I'm not staying here!" she retorted. "I'm the only doctor in this bunch. If our son—or anyone else— needs medical care, I intend to be there."

"The doctor said you need to stay off your feet. You could go into labor—"

"If I do, we'll have plenty of time to get to a hospital. I'm going with you, Jack. And that's final."

She was nearly frantic by the end of her speech. As Wyatt watched, Jack pulled her into his arms and rocked her to calm her down. He was speaking into his wife's ear, quiet words that Wyatt couldn't hear, but they seemed to pacify the pregnant woman.

Wyatt met Jack's gaze and saw the Texas Ranger was every bit as angry and determined as Wyatt was himself to rid the world of their nemesis.

"Let me call D'Amato," Wyatt said, as he eased

Kate away. "Maybe he can shed some light on what's going on here."

Jack approached them with one arm still around his wife's waist. "This is my wife, Holly," he said to Wyatt.

"I'm glad to meet you at last. Just sorry about the circumstances," Wyatt said as he found the listing for his father on his phone and punched the button to dial it. He put the call on speakerphone so the other three interested parties could hear.

"I've been expecting your call," his father said when he answered.

"Where is J.D. taking those three kids?" Wyatt demanded.

"Three? He's supposed to have the twins. Who else did he pick up?"

"He's got Jack McKinley's son, as well," Wyatt said.

"Shit. That's a complication I didn't need. Does McKinley know?"

"I sure as hell do," Jack replied.

"Good afternoon, Jack. I don't think I'll be needing your services any longer. I have the situation well in hand."

"Where is J.D. going with our kids?" Wyatt demanded.

"The twins have something of mine," D'Amato said. "J.D. is going to locate it and return it to me."

Wyatt's gaze shot to Jack, who shrugged to indicate he had no idea what D'Amato was talking about.

"Don't worry," D'Amato said. "I've got my eye on J.D. He isn't going anywhere I can't follow. You'll get your boys back when I get what's mine."

"Tell us where he's going," Wyatt said through clenched teeth. "And we'll come get the kids."

"Stay out of this, Wyatt. And you, too, Sergeant McKinley. Leave well enough alone. I'll take care of J.D. and you'll all get your children back alive and well, if you just stay out of my way."

Wyatt swore when D'Amato disconnected the call. He turned to Kate and said, "What could the twins have that belongs to D'Amato?"

"I have no earthly idea," she replied. "It has to be something J.D. gave them before he left for Afghanistan the last time, because he hasn't seem them since."

"So where would the twins hide something J.D. gave them?" Wyatt asked.

"Most likely in our house on Mulberry Street in San Antonio," Kate guessed. "That's where the twins last saw their father."

"Would the boys have taken whatever it is to Twin Magnolias when they came to live with me?" Jack asked.

"Or to my compound when they came to live with me?" Wyatt asked.

"I don't know!" Kate cried.

"It's probably the key to a safe-deposit box," Jack said to Wyatt. "That explains how J.D.'s managed to stay alive this long. He's got evidence of something your father did that could put him away. D'Amato has to keep him alive until he can get it back."

"Which is why Roberto disappeared with J.D.," Wyatt said. "He's apparently been working on J.D., trying to get him to give up whatever it is he has."

"And J.D. either escaped from Roberto—" Jack began.

"Or D'Amato let him escape, so he could follow him," Wyatt finished.

"Maybe it isn't a key. Maybe it's something he gave the kids to hide, so he wouldn't have to go to a bank to retrieve it," Jack said.

"Why didn't J.D. just ask the kids where the key, or whatever he gave them, is?" Holly asked.

"Maybe they hid it somewhere that's hard to describe," Kate suggested.

"Or maybe they're refusing to tell him where it is," Wyatt said.

Wyatt wished he'd kept his mouth shut. He saw the sudden fear in both women's eyes when they realized J.D. might resort to force to get the information he wanted.

"So we have three locations where he might have headed," Jack said. "Where do we go?"

Kate grabbed the lapel of Wyatt's suit and said, "There is a way we may be able to find them."

"How?"

"The twins are wearing tennis shoes with a GPS tracking device."

"Really?" Holly said hopefully. "How does that work?"

"Are you kidding?" Wyatt said. "When did you get something like that?" And why? he wondered.

"I bought them on-line, after you moved us to your compound," she told him. "I thought..."

Wyatt made a disgusted sound in his throat. "You thought I'd steal the kids from you."

"I wasn't sure what you'd do," she retorted. "The point is, I put those shoes on them this morning."

"So how do we access the GPS tracking?" Jack said.

"That's the problem," Kate said. "The GPS device has to be activated by pushing a button on the shoe."

"Do the boys realize they can be tracked when they're wearing those shoes? Do they know where the button is?" Wyatt asked.

"I explained about the GPS chip the first time I put the sneakers on them," Kate said. "But that was three months ago. I don't know if they remember that they can be tracked with the shoes, or whether they'll be able to push the button if they do."

By which Wyatt knew she meant the boys might be restrained, tied up so they wouldn't make trouble for J.D. until they got to wherever they were going.

"Oh, no," Kate said.

"What is it now?" Wyatt asked anxiously.

"That GPS runs on batteries that only last a day or so once it's activated. The kids might have played with it—turned it on sometime in the past—and used up the battery. The GPS might not work."

"Do you have any idea how to access the GPS, so we can see if they've turned it on?" Wyatt asked her.

"If I had a computer—"

Wyatt got out his BlackBerry and said, "What's the name of the company that monitors the GPS?"

"The shoes came from Quantum Satellite Technology," Kate said. "But I think I'm paying someone else to do the monitoring."

Wyatt Googled the company and got a number to access the GPS monitoring service, which he called. Wyatt spoke with the representative and reported to the others, "The GPS is inactive."

Kate groaned.

He listened another moment and said, "But it can be activated remotely if we can provide the password. Kate?"

"Nobody said anything to me about a password," she protested. "Or if they did, I can't remember what it is. Can't we explain it's an emergency?"

Wyatt did his best to explain the problem, but the woman remained adamant. Without the password, she couldn't activate the GPS remotely. He hung up the phone and said, "We can go through the police, but that's going to take time. I suggest we split up and—"

Wyatt's phone rang. He flipped it open without looking at the caller ID. "What? Where?"

He turned to the other three parents and said, "One of the twins just activated the GPS. They're on I-410, halfway between Houston and San Antonio, headed west."

"That eliminates your compound," Jack said. "But we still don't know whether he's head to Kate's house or Twin Magnolias."

"Kate's home is the most likely place for the twins to have hidden something," Wyatt speculated. "If they buried it, which J.D. might have suggested, they probably wouldn't have dug it up to take it to Twin Magnolias. If J.D.'s headed farther west than San Antonio, we can cut him off."

"He's got a big lead," Kate said.

"I've got a big jet," Wyatt replied.

42

"When are we going to get there, Dad?" Lucky asked.

"We've got another hour to drive at least," J.D. replied. "You shouldn't have lied and told me you took the box to Shaw's compound. We'd be a lot closer to San Antonio by now."

J.D. heard what sounded like scuffling in the backseat. "You boys settle down back there." He'd considered tying them up, but he hadn't been able to make himself do it. Besides, he hadn't brought along anything to use for rope.

He wished he had that child safety feature in this old Impala that the manufacturers put in newer model cars, where the kids in the backseat couldn't open the door from the inside. He should have thought of that when he was stealing a car. But he didn't think he had to worry about the kids trying to escape at seventy-five miles an hour.

He figured no one was going to believe a couple of eight-year-olds if they said their father had returned from the dead, so maybe he didn't have to kill them, either. Better to keep them alive and well, at least until he got the twenty million from Wyatt Shaw. That had been a brilliant idea, if he did say so himself. This way, after he got the ransom, he could head straight to the FBI with his evidence against D'Amato and disappear into witness protection.

"Push there," Lucky whispered.

"Where?" Chance whispered.

"Right there," Lucky said.

"Got it," Chance said.

"Is it going to work?" Ryan asked.

"Shh!" Lucky said.

J.D. glanced in the rearview mirror and said, "What are you boys doing back there?"

"I was trying to get a really big lump out of the seat," Lucky said.

"Yeah, this is some old heap," J.D. said.

"Do you think it's working?" Ryan whispered.

"I can't tell," Chance whispered back. "It's supposed to."

"Do you think what's working?" J.D. asked suspiciously.

"Nothing," Lucky said quickly.

"Yeah, nothing," Chance said.

J.D. turned around to look in the backseat, not sure what the boys were up to, but wanting to see for himself that they didn't have a cell phone he hadn't found, or some other means of contacting their parents. "You boys got a phone back there?"

"No, sir," Lucky said.

"No, sir," Chance said.

"What about you, kid?" he said, glaring at Ryan in the rearview mirror.

"My mom says I'm too little to have a phone of my own. I have a Game Boy," he said. "It's in the drawer beside my bed at the hospital."

"What were you doing in the hospital?" J.D. asked.

"I have leukemia," Ryan said.

"Shit. You need medicine or something?"

"No. I got a bone marrow transplant, so I don't need chemotherapy anymore."

The kid was still wearing a hospital gown and slippers. J.D. had been damned lucky to get him out of the hospital without getting caught.

"I wish I hadn't changed out of mine at the last minute," Lucky said.

"Wish you hadn't changed out of what?" J.D. asked.

"Chance can run really fast in his tennis shoes. I didn't wear mine."

"Don't be thinking about doing any running away," J.D. warned. "You won't like what I'll do to you when I catch you. And I *will* catch you."

The boys were silent in the backseat. J.D. figured they were sufficiently cowed that he could pay attention to the road.

"How far now, Dad?" Lucky asked a few minutes later.

"A little less far than the last time you asked," J.D. said. "Now shut up and give me a little peace."

Five minutes later, Lucky said in a tremulous voice, "Dad, I have something to tell you."

"What?"

"After Mom told us you were dead, we dug up that box from the backyard where we buried it."

J.D. felt the hairs rise on the back of his neck. "Yeah? What did you do with it?"

"We kept it in the back of the top drawer to the chest between our beds. We wanted something of yours close by us at night," Lucky said.

"That's all right." He felt a little spurt of pride that his boys had wanted to remember him.

"We took it with us when we went to live with Jack at Twin Magnolias," Chance said.

"But we couldn't keep it in the house because Aunt Rose was always cleaning and we were afraid she'd find the box and it was pretty dirty so we were afraid she might want to clean it or maybe even throw it away so we buried it again," Lucky said all in one breath.

"Shit," J.D. said. "So we need to go to Jack McKinley's ranch, not your mom's house, is that what you're saying?"

"Yeah," Lucky said.

"Why didn't you tell me all this in the first place?" he said between tight jaws, eyeing the boys in the rearview mirror.

"We were afraid you'd be mad," Chance said.

"I'm not mad," J.D. lied through clenched teeth. "Is there anything else you haven't told me about that box? Tell me now and I won't be mad. You wait till later, I may blow a gasket."

The two boys exchanged a glance before Lucky admitted, "We opened it."

"The only thing inside was a phone," Chance said.

J.D. was holding his breath, afraid the boys had thrown out the only bargaining chip he had to get himself into witness protection, where he was safe from D'Amato, and where Wyatt Shaw couldn't find him to get his twenty million dollars back. "What did you do with the phone?"

"It didn't work," Lucky said.

"The battery was probably out of juice," J.D. said. "What did you do with it, boy?" He'd started to say "son" and stopped himself. He hadn't gotten over being pissed that his wife had cheated on him with Wyatt Shaw.

"We put it back in the box," Chance said.

It was like pulling teeth to get the two of them to talk. "What did you do with the damned box?" he asked impatiently.

"We buried it in one of the stalls in the barn."

"Well, that's a relief," J.D. said. He'd gone to Twin Magnolias before his deployment to Afghanistan for a picnic Breed had hosted for him and Kate, so he knew where he was going. If he wasn't mistaken, the barn was a ways from the house, so this most recent news was good news.

Neither Jack McKinley nor Breed Grayhawk were living at the ranch. All he had to deal with was Jack's parents, who would most likely be at the main ranch house. He could sneak into the barn and dig up the evidence against D'Amato without bothering anyone.

He could surely find rope or something else handy to tie the boys up and gag them before going on his way. They would be found sooner or later, after he was long gone. The kids' parents would stay put in Houston, per his instructions, until he told them where to deliver the twenty-million-dollar ransom.

Of course, D'Amato was on his trail. Or rather, that stupid Roberto would be following him for his boss. But he'd checked his clothes the minute he'd left the warehouse where Roberto had been working him over and found the GPS tracking device they'd put in his shirt pocket. He'd gotten rid of his belt and checked his shoes, which he'd swear were clean. Good old Roberto was going to be disappointed.

He'd told D'Amato the kids had the evidence, but he'd suggested they'd hidden it somewhere in San Antonio. Of course, he'd said, they might have taken it to Shaw's compound. Or left it at McKinley's ranch. Roberto couldn't be three places at once.

All J.D. had to do was stay one jump ahead of D'Amato's brute. The mob boss would never suspect he'd head straight—all right in a crooked line—for a ranch owned jointly by an FBI agent and a Texas Ranger.

J.D. grinned. This was all going to work out even better than he'd hoped.

43

"He's changed direction, Roberto," D'Amato said from the front passenger seat of his limousine. His enforcer was driving. D'Amato knew he should have stayed home and let Roberto finish off J.D. Pendleton, but J.D. had been such a pain in the ass he hadn't been able to resist coming along for the ride.

D'Amato had instructed Roberto to put two tracking devices in places where J.D. could be expected to look for them, so he would find them and destroy them and believe he was no longer being followed. "He probably examined his shoes, too," D'Amato said to his henchman. "But he never found the GPS chip you slipped under the left heel, and that son of a bitch is still wearing them!"

D'Amato suspected his son and the Texas Ranger wouldn't be far behind them. But he only needed to be a step ahead of them to retrieve the evidence that could send him to jail for the rest of his life and finish off the bastard who'd forced him into this wild-goose chase.

"He's heading north," D'Amato said. "Turn onto U.S. 281. I believe our mark is headed to Sergeant McKinley's ranch. Step on it, Roberto. We don't want to miss all the fun. I haven't been on a scavenger hunt in a very long time. Once we have the prize, I'm afraid you may have to do a little more digging. I intend to bury this problem once and for all."

44

"Ladies and gents, buckle your seat belts," the pilot drawled. "Our next stop is an airstrip west of Austin, Texas."

Wyatt took Kate's hand in his as they lifted off from San Antonio International Airport headed to an airstrip that her uncle, North Grayhawk, had put in halfway between Twin Magnolias and his ranch, which was a little farther west.

"How much time did we lose by coming to San Antonio instead of going straight to Jack's ranch?" Kate asked.

"Not much," Wyatt said. "Even with this detour we should get to Twin Magnolias about the same time as J.D." They'd already been on the ground in San Antonio before J.D. changed direction and headed north on U.S. 281. Fortunately, they'd managed to get clearance to immediately take off again.

"What if he's already come and gone before we get there?" Kate asked.

"J.D. isn't going to disappear until he makes sure I've wired twenty million into that offshore account he gave you. He should know better. The Feds can always trace the money and find him. Which means D'Amato can trace the money and find him. He would have been better off just making a run for it."

"Which means that whatever he's hunting for must be pretty damaging to your father," Kate guessed. "Do you have any idea what it is?"

"No," Wyatt said. "I don't." But he knew D'Amato had done his share of heinous things.

"How are we going to get from the landing strip to the ranch?" Holly asked from her seat next to Jack across the aisle from them.

"My uncle North keeps vehicles at the airstrip," Kate said. "The keys will be in a lockbox under the wheel well."

"How long to get from where we land to your ranch, Jack?" Holly asked.

"About twenty minutes."

It took thirty minutes before the main house at Twin Magnolias, which looked like an old Southern plantation, appeared on the horizon. The sky was dark with thunderclouds and streaked with heat lightning.

"Do you see anything that looks out of order?" Wyatt asked Jack.

"Let's take a drive around the property before we go up to the house. Maybe we'll see a vehicle that doesn't belong."

Wyatt was at the wheel with Jack beside him. Jack had his SIG P226. Wyatt had a Glock 22 he'd retrieved from the glove compartment of his limo. Both men checked their weapons, making certain a bullet was chambered. Thunder cracked in the distance.

Before they continued their drive, Wyatt put his

arm along the back of the seat and turned around to speak to the two women sitting in the backseat. "Maybe you two should wait at the house."

"You'll need us to take care of the kids, while you take care of the bad guys," Kate said.

"I should be there if anyone requires medical assistance," Holly pointed out.

Wyatt exchanged a rueful look with Jack and said, "All right. But you wait in the car until we call for you."

Wyatt watched the women exchange a glance that told him they'd be out of the car two seconds after he and Jack left it.

"Hell," he said. "Just be careful, both of you."

"We will," Kate said.

"There," Jack said, pointing. "That Impala behind the barn doesn't belong here."

"Behind that stack of hay," Wyatt said, his heart suddenly pounding. "That's my father's limo."

"Park here," Jack said. "They're in the barn. We'll go in through the back door."

Lightning lit up the sky as Wyatt moved toward the back door to the barn with Jack. "My father will have a weapon. So will whoever's with him."

"J.D. probably will, too," Jack said. "We don't want the kids caught in a crossfire. We need to get them under cover before the shooting starts."

"You don't have a problem with divided loyalties, do you?" Wyatt asked.

"I don't work for your father," Jack replied. He met Wyatt's gaze and said, "I never did."

"That snitch you killed—"

"Is alive and well in witness protection."

"All right," Wyatt said. "Let's go."

Wyatt felt ashamed when he saw the scene in the barn. His father was threatening Ryan McKinley—a six-year-old child—with a shotgun, while the twins stood huddled together nearby, holding each other tight, tears streaming down their faces.

J.D., or a man Wyatt presumed was J.D., was lying dead in the center of the barn floor. His face was gone. Probably the result of a blast from the shotgun his father was holding. His heart went out to his sons, who'd apparently witnessed J.D.'s death.

Roberto must have been wounded in whatever gun battle had taken place before they'd arrived. He was sitting on the cement floor, his back braced against one of the wooden stalls, a big hand pressed against his bleeding gut, while the other lay on his thigh holding a Glock.

Judging from the fresh blood pooling on the cement floor, J.D. hadn't been dead very long. Apparently, Jack's parents hadn't heard the shots. With the brewing storm, they must have mistaken the gunshots and the shotgun blast for thunder.

"Where's the damned cell phone?" his father ranted to the twins. "If you don't tell me right this minute, I'm going to blow this boy's face off, just like I did J.D.'s."

Wyatt exchanged a glance with Jack. His father had just confessed to murder. Which meant he wouldn't want to leave any witnesses. The minute they showed themselves, he was going to start shooting to eliminate them.

The twins had obviously figured out that as soon as

they told their grandfather what he wanted to know, they were going to end up like J.D. They were damned smart. And doomed unless he and Jack could figure out a way to save them.

Jack was motioning that he was going to expose himself to gunfire to save his son. Wyatt was supposed to take out his father when D'Amato turned to shoot Jack. Jack would finish off the wounded enforcer.

Wyatt shook his head. Even though his father was a monster, he couldn't kill him. He indicated that he would expose himself and Jack could take the shot at D'Amato. Wyatt would take care of Roberto.

Before either of them could act, the two women stepped inside the front door to the barn. Kate held a pitchfork. Holly held a spade.

"Let those kids go," Kate said, her teeth bared.

D'Amato was smart enough to know that the women hadn't come alone. He swung the shotgun up to stop them in their tracks. "Hold it right there!"

Which was when Wyatt leapt from his hiding place. He grabbed Ryan as D'Amato swung the shotgun back around and fired. He wrapped Ryan protectively in his arms as he ran, shielding the screeching boy from the buckshot that peppered his own cheek and shoulders and back.

The women charged, yelling like banshees as they attacked with pitchfork and spade.

"Stop those women!" D'Amato cried.

"I don't shoot women," Roberto yelled back.

"Put down your guns," Jack said, stepping into the aisle and standing spread-legged, his SIG aimed at D'Amato's heart.

Joan Johnston

Roberto lifted his gun, and Jack shot him twice in the chest.

D'Amato held the shotgun out in front of him sideways with both hands, then eased it down to the ground and put his hands up. Jack crossed to the mob boss, pulled his hands down behind him one at a time and handcuffed him.

"I've waited a very long time for this day," Jack said. "You're under arrest for kidnapping and murder."

From his position on his side on the ground, Wyatt saw Kate gather the twins in her arms.

"Come here, sweetheart," Holly said as she eased Ryan from Wyatt's clutching hands. "Are you hurt?"

Ryan shook his head. "Shaw saved me."

"Sit down here beside me while I take a look at Lucky and Chance's daddy," Holly said to Ryan. "Thank you," she whispered to Wyatt. "For saving our son."

"You're welcome," Wyatt rasped. He could feel himself fading fast. The force of the buckshot had knocked him off his feet and it felt like fire on his back and shoulders.

He was aware of Holly's hand on his wrist. He guessed she was taking his pulse.

"The old heart's still pumping," he joked.

He watched Kate use her body to shield the twins from J.D.'s corpse as she crossed to his side. "How is he?" she asked Holly.

"He's losing a lot of blood. He's going into shock. We need to get him to a hospital."

Was he dying? He felt so tired. He could hardly keep his eyes open. "Kate?" He reached for her hand, or thought he did. He felt her pick his hand up off the ground.

"I'm here, Wyatt."

He tried to keep his eyes open but they slid closed.

"Stay with me, Wyatt," he heard her say. "I love you. Please stay with me."

"I love you, too," he croaked. Had she heard him? Son of a bitch. She loved him. This was a helluva time to die.

He heard rain pattering on the tin roof of the barn. Then everything went black.

45

Kate held her sleeping sons tightly on either side of her on a couch in the surgical waiting room at Brackenridge Hospital in Austin. They'd flown Wyatt back to Austin and had an ambulance waiting at the airport. He was in the operating room, getting the buckshot picked out of his hide.

Jack sat nearby with a sleeping Ryan in his lap. He'd made a brief sojourn to the governor's mansion to inform Ann Wade that J.D. had been shot. J.D.'s "second" death couldn't be kept a secret, because Dante D'Amato was being prosecuted for his murder.

Kate was watching TV in the waiting room when a Special Report from ABC News interrupted local broadcasting to announce that Texas Governor Ann Wade Pendleton had withdrawn from the presidential race. "The governor has just learned that her son, J.D. Pendleton, did not die serving with his National Guard unit in Afghanistan. Pendleton faked his death and deserted his post.

"The governor's son was apparently brokering the sale of military weapons for heroine in Afghanistan on behalf of mob boss Dante D'Amato. D'Amato is currently in jail accused of Pendleton's murder. How much the governor knew about her son's illegal activities, and when she knew it, is currently being investigated."

"That's the end of Ann Wade's political career," Jack said when the report was done.

"I'm surprised she gave up so easily," Kate said.

"She's cutting her losses. There's a lot more for the press to uncover, which they would, if she stayed in the political arena." Jack shifted Ryan in his arms.

"How's Ryan doing?" Kate asked.

"The doctor said he's okay. We just have to watch him closely over the next couple of weeks to make sure he didn't pick up a bacterial infection."

"I wish Holly would come back," Kate said, her eyes straying to the waiting room door for the twentieth time in the thirty minutes since Holly had left to check on the status of Wyatt's surgery.

Jack met Kate's gaze and said, "You've probably already guessed, but I want to make it official. I'm staying married to Holly."

"I can't say I'm surprised," Kate said softly.

"I love her. I should have told you a month ago, but I didn't know how."

"It's all right, Jack," Kate said. "I'm in love with someone else, too."

"I sort of figured that," he said with a rueful smile.

A moment later, Holly came through the door. She had a hand pressed to the small of her back. She looked exhausted. "The wound in Wyatt's neck that was doing all the bleeding has been clamped. They'll pick out the buckshot and sew him up and he'll be fine. A little sore for a while, but he'll recover completely."

Kate put a hand to her mouth to stifle a sob. "Thank God."

"Are you all right?" Jack asked Holly. "You look like you're in pain. Were you hurt?"

Holly grimaced. "I'm in labor."

Jack stood and looked for a place to lay Ryan down.

"There's room for him here," Kate said, indicating the edge of the couch she was sharing with the twins, who were sound asleep.

Jack laid Ryan down and he curled up with his head on a sleeping twin's thigh.

"I'll keep an eye on him while you go welcome the new addition to your family," she said to Holly.

"Thank you, Kate," Jack said.

"You finally told her," Holly said as they headed down the hall toward the elevator.

"I think she figured it out for herself," Jack said. "It must show every time I look at you."

Holly looked up into Jack's eyes and felt the tears sting her nose and burn her eyes. "We were so lucky tonight. I could have lost you and Ryan. I'm glad we're all together to greet this new child."

"Do you suppose the gunfire scared him into making an early appearance?"

"I think she wants to get in on all the excitement." She put a hand to her belly. "Ooh. That was a good one."

"How far along is your labor?" Jack asked.

"Contractions are about five minutes apart."

"You're practically ready to pop," Jack said. "Why aren't you in a hospital bed?"

"That's where I'm heading now," she said as they got on the elevator. "I've already checked in."

"You have?"

"I filled out the paperwork to have the baby here at Brackenridge before I came to get you. I went to medical school with one of the OB-GYNs on call, who's agreed to deliver the baby." She stopped in place and groaned as another contraction worked its way across her belly.

"I don't like to see you in pain," Jack said. "Can't you take something?"

"Too late," she said with a grimace. "Have to do this the natural way."

Jack put his arm around her and said, "Please don't deliver here in the elevator. Let's at least get you into a bed."

Holly tried to smile and grimaced instead. "Ooh."

"It hasn't been anywhere near five minutes," Jack said. "What the hell, Holly. Where's the delivery room?"

"This way," she said, waddling down a hall after they got off the elevator. She could see Jack wanted to pick her up but thought better of it as he eyed her bulk and simply put his arm around her waist.

"There you are," a nurse said in a scolding voice. "I thought I told you it's time to deliver that baby."

"I had to get my husband," Holly said. "I didn't want him to miss the big event."

Jack shook his head. "Holly Tanner McKinley, you are one helluva woman."

"Yes, I am," she said. Since she was momentarily between contractions, she managed to smile. "I think we need to get to the delivery room," she told the nurse as she hissed in a breath.

The nurse insisted on putting her in a wheelchair to take her down the hall. She practically threw some green paper scrubs at Jack and said, "Put those on and come with us."

Holly laughed at Jack trying to walk and put paper covers over his boots in between steps. The laugh got cut off by a powerful contraction. "Damn it, Jack. Move it!" she grated out.

"She's in transition," the nurse said. "You can tell by all the bad words that pop out of very nice ladies' mouths."

They hadn't been in the delivery room for more than a few minutes when Holly announced, "I have to push."

The doctor slid into the room and said, "Hi, Holly! Long time no see. How's it going?"

"I have to push!" Holly said urgently.

"Give me a chance to check things out, will you?"

"I have to push!" Holly swore like a sailor as the baby moved down the birth canal.

"I've got the head. Lots of red hair!" the doctor said.

Holly gripped Jack's hand and heard him say, "Ow, Holly. Your nails are digging—"

Holly bit back a scream as another contraction urged her to push. She bore down to expel the child that had been growing inside her for the past eight and a half months.

"Got the shoulders aaaaannnd here she comes. Got her!" the doctor said.

"It's a girl?" Holly said, looking up at Jack.

"It's a girl!" he said, glancing from the baby the doctor was cleaning up back to Holly. "We have a little girl, Holly."

"Another little girl," Holly said. "Why isn't she crying?"

"Just suctioning a little here," the doctor said.

"Is she all right?" Jack asked anxiously.

"Just give me—"

The baby let out a lusty cry, and then began to wail in earnest.

"That's our girl," Jack said with a grin. "Jasmine Tanner McKinley has arrived." He kissed Holly's lips, then looked deep into her eyes and said, "I love you, Holly. Thanks for giving me another daughter."

46

Kate was almost asleep when Jack returned to give her the news. "It's a girl!" he said, grinning from ear to ear.

"Congratulations! I'm so happy for you, Jack," Kate said.

"Is Wyatt out of surgery yet?" he asked.

"Not yet," she said. "Would you mind staying with the kids for a little while. I need to take a break."

"Sure," Jack said. "Holly and Jasmine are both sleeping."

"Jasmine. What a pretty name! I'll be back shortly, Jack. Thanks." Kate had decided that as long as she was in a hospital she might as well try to find out what was wrong with her. She headed down to the emergency room to see how busy it was. Maybe she could get seen by a doctor.

"You caught us in a lull," the admitting nurse said. "The doctor can see you right now."

Kate felt a little self-conscious describing her symptoms to a strange doctor, especially one so young.

"Sounds to me like you're pregnant," the doctor said.

"I took one of those home pregnancy tests and it came back negative," she said.

"You can get a false negative with those tests, you know."

"I didn't know that. Or maybe I did and forgot."

He did a pelvic exam and said, "I believe you're pregnant, Mrs. Pendleton. I'd say about three months along. Let's get a blood test and find out for sure."

Kate had blood drawn and was assured the results would be back the next morning. She headed back upstairs to the surgical waiting room in a daze. It wasn't cancer or the flu. It wasn't stress. Deep down, she'd known the truth. She was pregnant. Three months along. With Wyatt's baby.

She couldn't wait to tell him.

Then she realized the circumstances under which he'd told her he loved her. He'd thought he was dying. How would he feel in the bright light of day, when he knew he was going to live? How would he feel when he found out they already had another child on the way?

When she got back to the waiting room, Jack said, "We should take these kids home and put them to bed."

"My dad's coming to get the twins and take them to his house. I'm going to stay until Wyatt's out of surgery. I want to be here when he wakes up."

"I'm taking Ryan home to Twin Magnolias. My mom and dad have missed seeing him. They can keep an eye on him till Holly and Jasmine are ready to come home."

"I suppose we won't be seeing as much of each other from now on," Kate said.

"I don't know about that," Jack replied. "Our sons are Best Buds. Holly and I owe Wyatt our son's life. And you and I have been friends for a long time. I suspect we may be seeing a lot more of each other than you think."

"So long, friend," Kate said.

"So long, friend," Jack replied.

He picked Ryan up and the little boy whimpered as Jack gently laid him over his shoulder. "Come on, buddy. It's time to go see Mimaw and Pap Pap."

Kate feared all three of the boys would have nightmares for a while. They'd been through a terrible trauma and come out safe on the other side, thanks to the courage of their respective fathers. *And mothers,* a little voice said.

Kate smiled. Every time she thought of herself and Holly charging with a pitchfork and spade she wanted to laugh. Hysterically. What had they been thinking? Talk about crazy ideas. They were lucky they hadn't been shot.

"Hey, honey, wake up."

Kate heard her father's voice and forced her eyes open. "I must have fallen asleep."

"I think you probably needed it."

She stood and wrapped her arms around her father's waist and felt his arms close protectively around her. "Daddy, I've made such a mess of things."

"It'll all work out, honey. You have a good man this time. Jack told me what Wyatt did."

"You spoke to Jack?"

"I met him coming out as I was coming in."

"I love Wyatt, Daddy."

"That's always a good thing when you're living with a man," he said with a chuckle.

"I'm pregnant."

She felt her father's arms tighten in a hug before he said, "How does Wyatt feel about having another child?"

"He doesn't know yet."

"Then he has a nice surprise waiting for him when he comes out of surgery."

"Thank you, Daddy." She hugged him again. "Let me wake up the boys and tell them what's going on."

Kate put her hand on Lucky's shoulder and he jumped up with a frantic cry. She put her arms around him and said, "It's all right, sweetie. It's just me."

"I thought it was him. Dad, I mean. He was mean to us, Mom. And he was mean to Ryan. His face didn't look right and he didn't act right. Are you sure it was Dad?"

Kate knew her son didn't want to believe his father could act as badly as he had. Or that his father was really dead this time, murdered in front of his eyes.

Chance sat up and said anxiously, "Was it Dad?"

She glanced up at her father, then back at the boys, and said, "Your dad faked his death the first time. He did some bad things and some bad people were after him, so he ran away. They caught up to him and beat him up. That's why he didn't look like himself." She started to say, *He always loved you boys.* But she decided against it. They would have recognized the lie for what it was.

"Daddy saved us," Chance said.

"Yes, he did, along with Ryan's dad."

"He loves us," Lucky said.

"Yes, he does," Kate said, knowing they needed that reassurance. "As soon as he's well, we're all going back home to Houston. Meanwhile, you two are going to spend the night at Grandpa's house."

"Are you and Daddy gonna get married?" Lucky asked.

Kate met her father's gaze again and smiled. "We just might."

Kate fell asleep again within minutes after the boys left with her father. No one came to wake her, and it wasn't until the sunlight hit her eyes that she realized she'd slept the night through. She sat bolt upright. Surely Shaw must be out of surgery. He might even be awake.

She went to the bathroom and did the best she could to repair her makeup and fix her hair. Her clothes looked like she'd slept in them, but she didn't want to take the time to change. She needed to see Shaw.

She went to the nurses' station and inquired which room he was in.

"Are you a relative?" the nurse inquired.

Kate hadn't even considered the possibility that she wouldn't be allowed to see him. "I'm the mother of his children." That was the absolute truth.

"Down the hall," she said, giving Kate the room number. "He's already awake and clamoring for breakfast."

Kate hurried down the hall looking for the right room. The door to Wyatt's room was closed. She tentatively pushed it open.

"I hope that's breakfast," she heard from inside.

"It's just me," she said, pushing the door all the way open.

His eyes focused on her in that way he had of making her feel like she was the most desirable woman he'd ever seen. Even though she knew her mascara was clumped and she had a wrinkle in her cheek where she'd slept on the arm of the couch.

"Good morning, Kate. Have you been here all night?"

"I slept in the waiting room. My dad picked up the twins. How are you?"

"A little sore. Glad to be alive. What about Ryan and Jack and Holly? Are they all right?"

"Jack took Ryan to stay with his parents at Twin Magnolias. Holly went into labor."

"Is she okay?" Wyatt asked.

"She's fine. She had a little girl," Kate said. "They named her Jasmine." Kate had worked her way over to Shaw's bedside and stood beside him.

He reached for her hand and twined his fingers with hers. "Wow. Big night," he said.

"You were very brave."

"So were you."

"And foolish," she said, feeling the blush rise on her cheeks as she thought of herself with that pitchfork.

"And foolish," he agreed with a smile that took the sting from the words.

She met his gaze and watched the smile disappear.

"I was so afraid you'd be killed before I could say I love you, Kate. I want to spend my life with you. I want to marry you and have more children with you."

Kate felt the tension ease out of her shoulders. "That's really wonderful to hear, Wyatt."

He kept looking into her eyes and waiting. She suddenly realized that he was as uncertain as she had been. That he needed the same reassurance he had given her.

"I love you, too, Wyatt. I want to spend my life with you. And I'll gladly marry you." She hesitated and said, "About having more children—"

He put a hand to her lips. "I understand you may want us to spend more time getting to know each other and letting the boys get to know me, before we take that step. But—"

"I'm pregnant," she blurted.

Shaw's jaw dropped.

"How did that happen?"

"You should know," she said. "You were there."

"We haven't made love since the first night you spent with me," Wyatt protested.

"Then I guess your record is perfect."

Wyatt grinned. "Will you marry me, Kate?"

"As soon as you can get out of this bed."

He sat up and winced. "Just give me a couple of days—"

She put a hand on his arm and said, "Stay where you are. I'll join you." She hitched herself up onto the bed and lay down beside him, spooned with her back to his front.

He put his hand over her belly and said, "It's hard to believe you already have our baby growing inside you. I'm glad, Kate."

"Me, too."

"This must be what it's like at the end of those romances you read," Wyatt murmured.

"Hmm?" she said, pushing her rump against Wyatt's hips.

Wyatt laughed. "This definitely feels like happily ever after."

Epilogue

It was a small wedding. The bride wore white and carried a bouquet of lilies. The groom wore a tux and a broad, happy smile. The best man wore a navy-blue suit and kept trying to loosen the unfamiliar Windsor knot around his neck.

"Doesn't Jack look handsome up there beside the groom?" Holly said to Kate.

"I don't think I've ever seen Jack in a suit and tie," Kate said with a grin. "I didn't know he owned one."

Wyatt leaned past the twins and Ryan, who were sitting between him and Kate and said, "Shh. The minister's about to start the vows."

"Do you Grace Elizabeth Caldwell take Breed Grayhawk to be your lawfully wedded husband…"

Kate played with the beautiful sapphire and diamond ring on her left hand as she listened to Grace and Breed exchange their wedding vows. She and Wyatt had gotten married in a small church ceremony in Austin the day he left the hospital. She was halfway through her pregnancy and knew that she was carrying a little girl. She hadn't told Wyatt. He wanted to be surprised.

Breed's father, King Grayhawk, had walked Grace

down the aisle. His leukemia was in remission and he was doing well, much better than Ryan, who was still fighting the disease.

The Grayhawk clan—born to three different mothers—weren't close, but King had summoned them to Breed's wedding. And they'd all come: North, his wife, Joss, and their son and four daughters; Kate's mother, Libby, and father, Clay, and their children, Houston, Dallas and baby Austin; and King's Brats, Taylor, Gray and Victoria. From Matthew, there had been no word.

"You may kiss the bride," the minister said at last.

Kate met Wyatt's intent, gray-eyed gaze over the children's heads and smiled. She leaned toward him, he leaned toward her, and their lips met. It hadn't been easy finding each other, but Kate had become a firm believer in fairy tale endings.

They didn't need the words, but they said them anyway.

"I love you, Kate."

"And I love you, Wyatt."

And they lived happily ever after...

* * * * *

ACKNOWLEDGMENTS

Some books seem to write themselves. Others fight back. This novel was a mixture of the two, a joy and a trial. I want to thank my editor, Linda McFall, for her patient support and guidance as I figured out how to write this very different story.

As always, I want to thank my writer friends—you know who you are—for lending a sympathetic, educated ear and offering helpful suggestions. I also want to thank my publicist, Sally Schoeneweiss, of Talk Ink, Inc. for helping me get the word out when a book hits the shelves.

Finally, I want to thank you, the reader, for always coming back for the next book. It was your demand for Kate and Jack's story that led me to write Kate's story and Jack's story. If you want to read more about the Blackthornes and Grayhawks, look for *The Cowboy, The Texan* and *The Loner,* in stores now.

Watch for *Invincible,* the next book in my Benedict Brothers/Taggart men series, coming in September 2010.

I appreciate hearing your comments and suggestions. You can reach me at *www.joanjohnston.com.* Be sure to sign up on the mailing list at my Web site if you'd like to receive an e-mail or postcard when the next book is in stores.

Joan Johnston